HOUSEWIFE IN LOVE

Alison Penton Harper lives in rural
Northamptonshire with her husband
and two daughters.

Also by Alison Penton Harper

HOUSEWIFE DOWN
HOUSEWIFE UP
HOUSEWIFE ON TOP

ALISON PENTON HARPER

HOUSEWIFE IN LOVE

PAN BOOKS

First published 2009 by Pan Books
an imprint of Pan Macmillan Ltd
Pan Macmillan, 20 New Wharf Road, London N1 9RR
Basingstoke and Oxford
Associated companies throughout the world
www.panmacmillan.com

ISBN 978-0-330-46155-9

1 3 5 7 9 8 6 4 2

A CIP catalogue record for this book is available from
the British Library.

Typeset by SetSystems Ltd, Saffron Walden, Essex
Printed and bound in the UK by CPI Mackays, Chatham ME5 8TD

Visit **www.panmacmillan.com** to read more about all our books
and to buy them. You will also find features, author interviews and
news of author events, and you can sign up for e-newsletters
so that you're always first to hear about our new releases.

EPISODE FOUR

Previously in the life of this slightly desperate housewife . . .

My sister Julia, unexpectedly found herself up the duff at forty-three.

My best friend, Leoni, had a stab at poisoning her mother-in-law.

Julia's über PA, Sara, realized that marriage ain't all it's cracked up to be.

My upstairs neighbours, Paul and Sally, redefined the meaning of gay.

Now, what was the other thing?

Oh yes . . . I accidentally slept with my boss.

Oops.

speed-dating version of which goes something like this: early teenage years entirely uneventful save the odd inept fumble at the annual school disco with a spotty youth; despite my best efforts, remained unsullied until I was pushing twenty, by which time I had come to view my virginity as a burden rather than a virtue; gladly threw it away in unspectacular fashion to a twenty-six-year-old photocopier salesman who showed an inexplicable level of interest in me at an office party, whisked me away to a flea-pit hotel, and promptly disappeared off the face of the earth while I was blissfully doodling his name on the Travelodge message pad. Oh, well. He had crispy eyes and smelled of beans anyway. There then followed several abortive missions with a succession of no-marks boyfriends and fifteen years of deep-space nothingness until my husband died, which was nice. Since then, I have had one brief but memorable encounter with a lissom Indian chef who ignited my chillis and knocked up one hell of a snack afterwards, and two nano-boyfriends, neither of whom lasted for longer than, oh, five minutes I guess.

Unsurprisingly, I was predictably relieved to give up on the whole love thang and decided to dedicate the rest of my life to pleasing myself instead. Seemed like a perfect resolution all round, with some excellent fringe benefits thrown in, like not having to worry about my thighs looking like the surface of the moon. Once I'd chucked in the towel, I rapidly discovered that there was much to recommend the single life. There is no such thing as the Perfect Man anyway, although I have yet to interview George Clooney personally on this matter and reserve the right to change my mind.

The general equation I work to (because I like to reduce complex issues to a simple matter of basic arithmetic) is that a man can – if you're lucky – meet maybe fifty per cent of your basic human needs. The rest you will have to get elsewhere, and will usually include (among an endless list of other things): finding someone to give you emotional support, feign interest in your daily tribulations, offer to help once in a blue moon, notice when you've had your hair done, remember your birthday, and talk about anything other than sport/breasts/how much cleverer than you they are. It had got to the point where I had forgotten what sex was entirely, which, frankly, was no biggie.

If there is one thing that I should have learned by now, it's that you just can't plan ahead for anything. The moment you start making assumptions and taking life for granted, you can virtually guarantee that a shining quarter-inch spanner will come wanging in from out of nowhere and lodge itself firmly in your works. The spanner in this case is that the man in question happens to be my boss. It was his fault entirely. He caught me unawares and, despite my never having thought of him in That Way, stuck an unexpected kiss on my lips that made my socks sizzle. He then had the audacity to announce that he was crazy about me, and had been for quite some time. Well. Talk about women's intuition. I hadn't had the faintest idea.

There is something really weird about getting into a relationship with a man you already know rather well. It's like being catapulted at lightning speed through steps 1 to 18 of the Haynes boyfriend-formation manual. You can't pretend to be someone you're not because they already know who you are, and you're completely stymied if you want to introduce a little mystery into your honeymoon period because all your cats are already well and truly out of the bag and mewling their heads off. So there you have it. Romance is not generally well suited to a retro-fit situation.

I KNEW THAT RICK was about to wake up because the snoring had stopped. He stirred and lifted the corner of his Top Cat eye mask.

'Urrgh,' he said. 'Where are we?'

'Mid-Atlantic,' I guessed. 'Do you want a coffee or something?'

A smile crept over his face. 'The *something* sounds good.' He nodded towards the lavatory vacant light at the front of the cabin and gave me a salacious nudge. 'I'm up for it if you are.'

Had I been twenty years younger, or even ten for that matter, I might have considered it for a millisecond. But the prospect of trying to do it in the loo of a jumbo jet somehow doesn't electrify me these days. I can still (just about) manage to look relatively attractive provided I have low- (or better still no) level lighting and plenty of bed space upon which to arrange myself well in advance with at least one well-positioned sheet to cover my unmentionables, but I'd be pushing my luck to expect a similar result while playing sardines. And the thought of Rick trying to, well, you know, wedged up against the sink. Let's just leave it there, shall we?

'Don't you think we're both a bit past it for that sort of thing?'

'Speak for yourself,' he said, reaching up to press the overhead trolley-dolly button. Roger the Cabin Boy with the pungent tax-free aftershave positively dashed to Rick's seat, breathless with excitement.

'Yes, sir?'

'Bring us a coffee, would ya, mate?' Then turning to me, 'Want one, gorgeous?'

'No thanks,' I said, pointing at my glass.

'And a refill for The Mrs.'

'I'd better not,' I said. 'That's my second.'

'In that case, twinkle,' (talking to the steward, not me) 'sod the coffee and rack 'em up, eh? As far as I'm concerned, we're still on holiday until we hit the tarmac.' He put his hand on my knee. 'And I haven't finished with you yet. Not by a long chalk.' The cabin boy left with a flourish and Rick reached over to touch my hand.

'You really shouldn't call me that.' I found being referred to as *The Mrs* more than a little anxiety-inducing. It's not exactly a tag that I have fond memories of.

'Ah, go on, Hell! You love it really.'

'No, Rick, as a matter of fact I don't.'

I hadn't meant to sound snippy, but it came out all wrong and Rick quickly let go of my hand. In the few hours since taking off from JFK, I had become aware that the closer we got to Heathrow, the more agitated I was feeling.

'You all right, Hell?' he said.

I didn't answer.

Roger the Cabin Boy arrived with his glistening bottle and went to some trouble to display his expert one-handed Champagne pouring technique with a wide smile. Neither Rick nor I said thank you, delivering a brief flash of awkwardness, and I suddenly found my insides ping-ponging in one of those hideous reality-check moments. (Oh my God, I've just spent the last week shagging my boss: discuss.) Rick leaned forward and peered into my face, clearly expecting an answer.

'Rick?' I fiddled with my glass.

'Uh-oh,' he said, leaning back in his seat. 'I don't like the sound of this.'

'But I haven't said anything yet!' My hands went clammy.

'You don't have to. I know that kind of *Rick* only too well.'

'What's that supposed to mean?'

'Nothing. Except that whenever you say Rick like that, it's usually followed by something really complicated.'

'No it's not!'

'Oh, yes it is.' He picked up his drink.

'You see?' I let out a huge sigh of exasperation.

'What?'

'This whole thing is a monumentally bad idea. What on earth were we thinking of? You already believe that you can anticipate everything I'm about to say, and I already know that you're the most annoying person in the world.'

'Eh?' He seemed genuinely baffled. 'What on earth are you rattling on about now?' His eyes suddenly widened. 'Oh! Shit. Sorry. Are you, erm, well you know.' He went red, bracing himself in a politically correct non-misogynistic manner. 'If you're feeling a bit grumpy, that's OK. I expect you're – ' he grimaced and tried to look as though he wasn't embarrassed at all – 'a bit hormonal or something.'

'I beg your pardon?' I don't know which of us blushed harder. If he meant what I thought he meant, then I wasn't sure whether I should laugh out loud or punch him in the veneers.

'Well . . .' He patted my hand proudly. 'I'm not a complete philistine, you know.'

'No, Rick. But carry on like that and I can safely say that you will become a complete arsehole.'

Yes. I used the a-word. As averse as I am to foul language, by spending the last seven days with Rick I seemed to have accidentally found myself neck-deep in an immersion course in fluent Shitese. I could tell from his shoulders that he was trying not to laugh.

'Wanna watch a movie?' he asked. I shook my head and frowned. 'There's that new action flick with wass-name in it, Bruce Willies. And next time you think about calling me past it,' he mumbled under his breath, 'I'll have you know that he's a year older than me.' A brief vision of Rick running around in a string vest taking down a helicopter with a pea-shooter sent a shudder down my spine.

'Rick?' I tried to make it sound different this time. More positive. He tipped his head towards me with a submissive hang-dog expression.

'What's going to happen when we get back?'

'What now?'

8

'Waddya mean?' he shrugged, as though the question held no significance, studying the in-flight entertainment listings in the magazine.

'I mean, what's going to happen with *us*? Don't you think it might be a bit strange now that we've, well, you know.' I explained with a rapid circular motion of my hand, as I am prone to do whenever sex is mentioned. I'm working on that, and soon hope to be able to say penis without shrivelling with embarrassment.

'I haven't the faintest idea what you're going on about, woman.' He raised his empty glass towards Roger the Cabin Boy and waggled it around for a refill while I struggled with my conscience. I felt as though we had just done something terribly, terribly naughty and were about to be frogmarched to the headmistress's office to face the music. A swift, hideous vision of having to run the gauntlet with his rottweiler secretary, Angela, popped into my head. That woman hates me with a passion.

'In case it's escaped your notice, Rick, I've been your paid minion for over a year and we've gone and broken the absolute number one cardinal rule. I am now in that appalling category of Women Who Sleep with Their Boss. Oh my God . . .' The truth of it hit me like an oncoming Eurostar and I hid my face in my hands.

'So?'

'What do you mean, *so*? I can't very well come back to work for you now, can I? It just wouldn't seem right, would it?'

'Why not?'

'Oh, for heaven's sake.' I could see that we were going to have to do this the hard way. 'You can't just go around seducing the hired help then expect everything to go back to normal first thing Monday morning. That's just – ' I realized at that point that I wasn't entirely clear on what it was myself – 'I don't know. It's sexual discrimination or something.'

'Seduced?' He gave the magazine a flap and smiled to himself. 'I seem to recall that you threw yourself at me like a nymphomaniac on death row. And what about that time in—'

'Stop it!' I curled with shame, alive with the guilty pleasure of our first three days in New York, holed up in the hotel suite refusing to let the housekeepers in.

Roger the Cabin Boy kept his personality to himself this time as he refilled Rick's glass rather more soberly, trying to appear a little less fey.

'Look, Hell. You can call it whatever you like, doll, but I think you're making a mountain out of a mole-hill.'

'Typical!' I gave him a puff of womanly frustration. 'And how do you think I'm going to feel when you start ordering me about next week while you rush back to your life leaving me to pick up the dry cleaning? I know I'm not exactly board-level status here, but still . . .' I felt an immediate pang of possessiveness over my role as his professional housewife and couldn't bear the thought of anyone else muscling in on my patch should I find myself forced to resign. It may sound like a micro-job, but believe me, I am the Luke Skywalker of household management. There is nothing I don't know about running Rick's chaotic life. I know where everything is, how everything works, what brand of toothpaste he likes. I even know how to defuse Helga the Russian cleaning lady when she's been at the home-made slivovitz. Rick may well think of himself as Mr Bigshot when he's out there cutting one of his shady deals, but let me tell you something: it's me that makes sure he's got fresh flowers in every room and hole-free socks in his drawers, and nudges him about his kids' birthdays. Rick sipped at his drink, perfectly relaxed. 'So how's that going to work?' I pressed him. 'Do we act as though nothing's happened and carry on regardless? And another thing. How do you think it would feel to be paid a monthly salary by the man I'm sleeping with? Does that mean I'm now soliciting every time I turn up to work?'

'Are you serious?' He smiled into his glass.

'Yes I am!'

'Then you're even more unstable than I thought you were.'

I scowled at him. 'Are you doing this deliberately to annoy me?'

He started laughing.

'I'm sorry, Hell, but I just don't see what the problem is. You want to keep working for me, that's fine. If you don't, that's fine too. Either way, I'm nuts about you, so whatever makes you happy, babe.' My skin shrank under the *babe*. I closed my eyes against the offence rather than pull him up about it yet again. If we were to make a go of this shiny new relationship, I might as well start with the small compromises now, and Rick's navvy vocabulary had set like concrete years ago. 'Tell you what,' he said cheerfully. 'Why don't I find a replacement? Shouldn't be too difficult. I'll just get back on the blower to that agency who found you for me in the first place, eh? And let's face it, it's not as though you need the money.'

'What?' My cheeks went tight.

'Well, you're obviously not comfortable about working for me now that you're madly in love.' My mouth fell open. 'And being as you're always bleedin' right about everything, we might as well cut straight to the chase, yeah? So how about it?' He looked mighty pleased with himself. Done deal.

'You selfish, arrogant arse.' That was two arses in ten minutes, and if he carried on the way he was going, I might even be forced to escalate to a Level 2 expletive. 'You think I can be replaced just like that, do you?' I snapped my fingers. 'Have you any idea how much time and effort I put into running your home like a five-star hotel? You think everything happens as if by magic, don't you? And who the bloody hell mentioned anything about me being in love with you?'

'Er, that's not what I, erm . . .' Rick floundered, finding himself suddenly stranded in a field of unexploded mines.

'Oh yes.' I wobbled my head sarcastically. 'Just because I quietly go about your daily business without making a big song and dance about it and expecting a Mutley medal, you think that just anyone could manage your detritus the way I do. And tell me, Bigshot, do you really think that an agency – ' I did inverted commas with my fingers – 'could find someone else who's prepared to put up with your ridiculous demands? Well, you just try it, buster. I'll have you know that I have my job down to a fine art, and there's no one – ' I may at this point have been shaking my fist at him – 'I mean no one who could do my job better than I do.' I came up for air, but only for a second. 'In fact, I'll have you know that I'm the – ' go on, say it, Luke Skywalker, Luke Skywalker – 'I'm the—' I could feel myself getting upset.

'Hey!' Rick insisted on putting his arm around me.

'Don't get yourself all wound up about it, Hell! We've had a wonderful time, haven't we? What's all this about, eh?'

'Sorry,' I started snivelling. 'I think I'm just horribly nervous about going back to normality.' Noticing the sideways glances I had suddenly attracted from the cabin crew, I tried hopelessly to pull myself together. 'Nobody knows about any of this yet. I couldn't bring myself to tell anyone. For all they know I could be halfway to Panama in a canoe.'

'You don't have to do anything you're uncomfortable with, babe.' He let me go and patted my hand reassuringly. 'Whatever you want to do is fine. We'll work it out together, OK? Now why don't you just relax and try to grab forty winks?' He pulled the mask back over his face and stretched lazily into his first-class seat while I sat there, wide-eyed, worrying myself into an early grave.

Luke Skywalker indeed.

Feel the farce.

wine with a sensitive sediment, I must admit that I don't travel particularly well. It's that nauseous swaying sensation that hits me whenever I get off an aeroplane, a slight drunken giddiness that is anything but pleasant. I was still feeling discombobulated when the taxi dropped me off outside my flat as the moon began to rise over the leafy Kensington garden square, the driver deliberately ignoring my sighs and huffs as I manhandled my suitcase to the pavement while the relentless British weather lashed at my face.

'Thanks,' I said sarcastically, handing him the fare. He didn't even bother to look at me before flicking his orange light back on and speeding off. How utterly rude. People like that should be banned from working in any kind of public service. I'm sure they only do it to inflict their misery on innocent strangers. I should have taken a note of his number and reported him to the authorities. Slipping my key into the front door, I crept in quietly, returning it softly to the latch so as not to disturb the building's other occupants, and tiptoed up the stairs, lumping the dead weight of my luggage slowly up each step with the week's post wedged uncomfortably in my mouth. It felt strange to be home. Strange but good, as though I'd just returned from a brief spell stuck in a bizarre *Doctor Who* time warp. Being back reminded me gratefully that nothing here had changed. No matter what events had come to pass lately, nobody knew or cared. The buses were still running, the light switch in the hallway still reliably on the blink, and Waitrose would be open in the morning, no doubt.

Once safely inside, I felt immediately comforted by the sanctuary of my home, reassured by the knowledge that I could now do anything I pleased without worrying about whether or not it was normal (or indeed attractive) behaviour, like eating weird things straight from the fridge and gyrating enthusiastically to handbag disco hits on Radio 2. I dumped my suitcase by the door and shuffled off to the kitchen, filling the kettle and pulling up a stool while I waited for the water to boil, permitting myself to slump deliciously, blissfully unconcerned about letting my stomach out. Shrugging off my coat, I reached back to snap my bra undone, stretching with relief as the elastic gave way, allowing my body to return to its natural tribal configuration. God, that felt good. Kicking my shoes to the floor, I lifted my puffy legs and wondered how many cream buns I'd have to eat for my swollen British Airways ankles to get *that* fat all on their own. Lots, I decided. Perhaps best to stay off the doughnuts. I hit the flashing PLAY button on the answering machine.

Beep.

Helen? It's Leoni. All the labels have fallen off the dishes you made for my freezer and I don't know what anything is or what to do with it. Call me.

Beep.

Helen darling, come upstairs as soon as you get this message. Seriously. It's totally our fault, and we're really really sorry. In fact, you might already be on your way up here with a machete, in which case, we're out.

Beep.

Helen? It's me again. Listen. I really need to know what all this stuff is, OK? Marcus's mother is coming tomorrow and I may have to kill myself. Call me.

Beep.

Helen? It's your mother. Now you know I don't expect you to ring every day, dear, but I had expected you to pick up the telephone and wish us a Happy New Year (huge sigh). *Your father is in one of his moods again. Mrs Critchley's cat has been doing its business around his vegetables* (long pause). *I told him he can jolly well dig them up and throw the whole lot away. I'm not having those carrots anywhere near my table. It's disgusting.*

Beep.

Hey, neighbour. It's Paul. I sure hope you're picking these messages up wherever you are. I'm afraid it's worse than we thought. So, er, we need to talk. Fast.

Beep.

Helen? For God's sake! (Leoni again, drunk by the sounds of it.) *Marcus's mother is allergic to nuts and I've just fed her a piece of your almond cake. Marcus is on his way to the hospital with her now and I could really do with some moral support here.*

Beep.

Hel-en! Where the bloody hell are you?

And so the messages went on, indicating that things had been pretty much situation normal in my absence. Leoni in her usual blind panic; my upstairs neighbours getting excited over something that would turn out to be nothing; my mother trowelling on the guilt. Last time I'd heard Paul in such a tizz he'd been agonizing himself into a premature heart attack over a certain shade of taupe. Whatever it was, they'd all just have to wait until I'd got myself settled. First things first, a decent cup of tea then a nice soak while listening to *The Archers*. Things had been hotting up in Ambridge when I left, and there's nothing like a juicy nugget of fictional farmhouse scandal to make you feel glad to be back in Old Blighty. The travel tension began to seep from my bones as the kettle rumbled.

I leaned on the worktop, wondering how best to proceed.

I hadn't felt like this in a long, long time. Comfortable. As though everything was somehow in its logical place for the first time in years. There had been no thunderbolt, no host of angels giving it the old one-two on the celestial front, no head-rushing, roller-coasting thrill. It had all been far gentler than that. Far more, dare I say it, middle-aged. Yet there had been no mistaking the tenderness of his kiss, nor the thankful nature of my return. The thought of it still brought a flush of colour to my cheeks and lifted my mouth into an involuntary smile, the mismatch too ridiculous for words. Yet I couldn't help but feel an all-pervading sense of doom. I knew it couldn't last, the partnership destined to the same certain failure as each of my previous bungled attempts. I'm just crap at relationships. Double crap.

The *Mastermind* theme tune rose in my head in all its kettle drum glory, each pounding beat reminding me that I had better come up with some kind of strategy on the double-quick before the beeper went. I've started so I'll finish. My first instinct was to rush to the bedroom, lie under the duvet and hide, for several years if needs be, so that I wouldn't have to deal with it. Quite how I was going to explain to everyone that Rick was now my lover was way beyond my capabilities. Leoni would have a field day. The baiting would never end.

Getting a tenuous grip on my faculties, I reasoned that all I had to do was to formulate the Official Story, which may or may not include the part where Rick turned up on my doorstep just as I was thinking about drowning myself in Advocaat. I still can't believe I leapt into bed with him just like that. I don't even really know how it happened. From a respectability point of view, I like to think that he caught me at a vulnerable moment and that it was actually nothing to do with me at all. One minute I was leading him in through the door, and the next we were tangled up like a pair of cheap tights in the washing machine, heading for the bedroom. It can't have been a pretty sight after the lunch I'd eaten that day, but Rick didn't seem to mind and, I have to say, demonstrated himself as a highly competent mattress companion with some outrageously noteworthy equipment. After the initial shock, and believe me it was, I soon discovered that under all that weight he used to carry around before he discovered Dr Atkins, he had been harbouring a quite respectable physique. Probably not the kind of thing you'd want to see strutting around on a catwalk before you've had your cornflakes, I'll grant you, but still, not bad for someone who smokes like an Arbroath fish house, drinks like Boris Yeltsin and is incapable of saying no to a second slice of my legendary almond cake. To my mind, he looked like a man was supposed to look, the way they looked in the old movies before the Americans invented protein drinks and plastic pectorals. I had snuck a sneaky peek, pretending to be asleep while he went off to take a shower after our first close encounter, yet all I could think of was how I wasn't supposed to see my boss naked. It was a truly abnormal moment.

The kettle came to its rousing crescendo and I made my decision. No. I would keep that part of the story to myself. It then crossed my mind in a fleeting moment of Einstein clarity that it might actually be prudent for me not to tell a soul about any of this at all, at least not for now. I could say that I'd been to New York all on my own in a surge of spontaneity and pretend the whole episode never happened. Brilliant. That way I would be free to sit back and decide what to do about Rick in my own good time, and nobody would be any the wiser. Well, give that girl a round of applause. Sounded to me like a stroke of genius. Squeezing the teabag against the side of the mug while I thought this over, I realized that I had excelled myself once again by coming up with a solution of such dazzling ingenuity that it was almost frightening. Full-blown denial. The perfect fix every time. And to think that I'd got myself into such a state on the plane. Poor Rick. He'd been so sweet, trying to be helpful and telling me not to worry, and all I could do was brush him off like a gnat and moan about how insensitive he was. I looked at the kitchen clock, expecting he'd be home by now. Perhaps I should give him a little tinkle and apologize for being crotchety. I dismissed the idea immediately. He'd only accuse me of missing him already. Feeling distinctly better, I reached unthinkingly for the carton in the fridge. Before I could fully engage my brain, a huge lump of rancid milk plopped into my tea. Blurgh.

With the rain bucketing against the French doors like a bad Pinewood film effect, I abandoned the notion of popping out for a fresh pint and went for

the only consumable in the fridge tha
– wine – then set about decanting ever
a bin bag, wondering why on earth I had
stock up like that in the first place. Great b
stinky cheese, pots of chemically enhanced ....rt
that magically promised to speed up my sloth-like
metabolism (thus quickly ridding me of said cheese),
bags of salad that had turned to sludge. I suppose I
had been so excited when Rick turned up waving a
pair of tickets and told me I had one hour to pack that
I had overlooked the refrigerated death zone. The
whole lot went in the bin, riddling me with the guilt of
the wastage, my mother's voice shrieking that there
were people starving in this world. With the offending
contents tied up and consigned to the drenched balcony outside, I retired to the bathroom and slid neck-
deep into a steaming tub, my thoughts wandering to
Julia.

She's having a baby.

I repeated the words over and over again in my
head, knowing that it must be true, having heard it
from her own lips, but somehow unable to believe
it until I saw her for myself. Now, I realize that women
have babies all the time, but my sister is not one of
those women. She was told years ago that it would
never happen, on account of a silent disease that had
been visited upon her after a one-night stand with a
French pastry chef in the days when she was much

younger and freer with her affections. Such a cruel blow that had been, but she had learned to live with her ravaged tubes and chose to nurture her career instead with spectacular results. Then, at some point last year, it all suddenly seemed to unravel. To be honest, we had all thought she was having some kind of mid-life crisis. How David managed to put up with her testing behaviour was anyone's guess. As devoted to her as he is, from where I was standing it looked like curtains for their marriage. You know how these things can go. Of the three of us, I'm not sure who was the more shocked by her miracle fertilization, but I think it was probably her. Imagine that. The one thing you assumed would never happen, then wham. As I say, you just can't plan for anything.

I wished she were here so that I could put my arms around her and tell her how happy I was for her, but judging by the weather outside, she'd be well advised to stay put in Barbados for an extra week. I lay in the bath until my fingers began to pucker, dreaming of how it would feel to have a new life growing inside me. My hand wandered absently beneath the blanket of warm bubbles and slid down to my abdomen, swollen as it was by a week of five-star room service. I let the wine take the moment and pretended that the soft mound of patisserie flab was the beginnings of a beloved child, and found myself cooing to my expanded waistline, my eyes welling with slightly irrational tears.

Hauling myself out of the tub and reaching for a towel, I wasn't sure whether it was the air sickness, the heat of the bath or the Chablis, but I found myself feeling distinctly woozy. Probably a combination of all three. Best to go and have a nice little lie-down. Shuffling towards the boudoir and yearning for my bed, I reminded myself that I must remember to go to the window first and close the curtains before turning on the light. Once night falls, the view from the street into my first-floor flat is inescapable, as Paul and Sally had pointed out to me quite some time ago, having taken the trouble to ring me from their vantage point on the pavement outside and describe in minute detail everything I was doing, which I seem to recall involved eating guacamole-slathered nachos while plucking my eyebrows and trying to remove something from my nose.

The bedroom door stuck fast. That's odd, I thought, wrestling with the knob. There's no lock on the door and I could have sworn I left it wide open anyway. Living alone, I stopped bothering to close doors long ago, even when I was in the loo. Maybe I'd accidentally left one of the windows open and a rogue draft had slammed it shut. I tried the door again to no avail then leaned up against it and gave it a bit of shoulder.

Feeling it give a little, I let out a feeble roar of effort and shoved with all my might, the door crunching and splintering against the invisible obstruction behind. Then it hit me. The unmistakable, dank aroma of bad news. For a second it occurred to me that I had been burgled, and that the intruder had met their comeuppance with a timely heart attack just as they were helping themselves to my slippers, their dead body now composting behind my bedroom door. With one final mighty effort, I managed to push it open just enough to squeeze through the gap, adrenaline pumping, and snapped on the light.

'What the bloody hell?' My jaw dropped open, my eyes widening in disbelief.

To say that it looked like a bomb had gone off would be something of an understatement. It was unrecognizable. Unthinkable. My bedroom ceiling was now my bedroom floor. There was mess everywhere. I'm talking the kind of mess that you see on *DIY SOS* when some grinning halfwit lager lout has manfully taken a sledgehammer to the family home without the slightest clue about what he's doing, then left it all because he's incapable of tying his own shoelaces and won't get anyone in to fix it because that would involve admitting he's a moron. My poor, innocent bed was knee-deep in wet plaster, the once cream carpet now a mottled sewage brown, the mirror on the dressing table broken in half, and the smell, dear God, like a pack of wet dogs had been sleeping in there for a month of Sundays. I clutched the towel to my chest and tried to take in the scene of devastation, my eyes finally lifting to the sudden shaft of light that flooded down through the gaping hole in the ceiling. Sally's face appeared, peering over the abyss of what I presumed was once their floor.

'Hi, honey child!' He smiled down at me. 'Fancy a margarita?'

'So – ' PAUL PICKED UP a few nuts and flung them casually into his mouth – 'by the time we got back from the ballet, the whole place was awash! We knew the water had to have gone somewhere. After all, you don't leave a bath running for five hours without expecting some kind of drama.' I lay back on their sofa, trying not to moan under the erotic spell of Sally's expert foot massage. 'I think we thought we'd got away with it until we were woken up in the middle of the night by a God almighty crash.'

'Yeah,' Sally drawled, pausing to take a sip of his cocktail. 'He thought it was an earthquake and started screaming like a girl.'

'And I said to Sally, did you hear that?' Paul cupped his hand to his ear for effect. 'And Sally said to me, too much sex makes you blind, honey, not deaf!' His tinkling laughter finished with a wistful sigh and he shook his head with amusement.

'Well . . .' I dragged my carcass upright and fought against the jet lag now pulling relentlessly at my eyes. 'That'll teach me not to leave a key with you next time I go away.'

'We were going to break in,' Paul said bravely. 'But then we decided that it just wouldn't be polite.'

'That's his version.' Sally flashed his come-to-bed eyes at me. 'He took a run at your door in a blind panic, crumpled to the floor like a wet paper bag, then started rolling around wailing that he had broken his arm.'

'It really hurt!' Paul pulled gently at his dressing gown, exposing a slight bruise on his left shoulder and taking a sharp intake of breath as he touched it lovingly with his fingertips. 'I suggested we should call out the fire brigade, but Sally got all funny with me about it.'

'No firemen – ' Sally wagged his finger at him – 'not since that time you deliberately set fire to the dustbin.'

'It was an accident.' Paul feigned innocence. 'Could have happened to anyone.'

'So what are we going to do about the grand canyon in my bedroom?' I fell back on the sofa, resigned to the huge inconvenience of a team of surly builders tramping around my home for heaven knows how long.

'Don't worry,' Paul said. 'Our insurance have already said they'll cover everything.' He started fiddling with the belt of his robe and mumbled, 'Including your temporary accommodation.'

'My what?'

'Er, yes, well.' Paul squirmed uncomfortably. 'Sal?'

Sally refilled my glass from the icy jug, held my hand firmly and braced me for the big picture. 'There's the damage you can see,' he said slowly. 'But there's also the damage you can't see.'

'What do you mean?'

'Helen, honey. We ran enough water to irrigate the Sahara that evening, and most of it is still sitting above your ceilings. They're gonna have to come down.'

'What?' I felt myself blanch. 'All of them?'

'All of them,' he nodded. 'And trust me, you really don't want to be around when it happens.'

My heart sank into the floor. The shock of the devastation had been evil enough, but I'd thought I'd just have to sleep in the spare for a few weeks while Bob the Builder came along and did his thing. As this latest CNN newsflash washed over me, the wine and tequila began to hit home. I groaned and covered my head with my arms. 'Well that's just bloody brilliant,' I mumbled. 'Just throw a blanket over me here. I'll be fine.'

I don't remember terribly much after that.

Chapter Three

START SPREADING
THE NEWS

I FINALLY GOT around to returning my calls the next morning.

'Where the bloody hell have you been?' Leoni bellowed down the line.

'Noo Yawk,' I said in my best *Sex in the City* accent, waiting for her gasp of approval.

'Really?' She couldn't have sounded less interested if she had tried. 'Well never mind that – ' lowering her voice to a whisper – 'all hell's broken loose here. Granny Meatloaf has accused me of attempted murder.' I helped myself to another lemon puff from the biscuit tin and settled in for an update. 'Everything was going just fine until teatime, although God knows the woman had already eaten enough lunch to sink a Dutch barge. She gave me one of those looks, you know.' I did my best to imagine Leoni's fire-breathing mother-in-law. 'Then she said she didn't suppose I had made a cake to go with it.' I polished my nails on my sweater. 'So off I popped to the kitchen and came back with that one you baked for me,' (it's a long story), 'and the next thing you know, she's stuffing her face like a giant rodent again.'

'Didn't you know about her allergies?'

'Of course I did! All she ever bloody talks about is her sodding ailments. I've had the whole nine yards, morning, noon and night. It's all hip replacement this, osteoporosis that. Christ, you would have thought she'd have done the decent fucking thing and died by now.'

'Then why the hell did you give her almonds?'

'Well I didn't bloody know, did I? The kids peeled all the labels off, little bastards. All I saw was a home-made cake, ready and waiting to be passed off as my own work, and the next thing I know, she's wheezing and spluttering and blowing up like a balloon.'

'Oh God, Leoni. Why does this stuff always have to happen to you?' I licked the crumbs off my fingers.

'Yeah? Well you should have been here. I tell you.

Marcus thought she was choking and did the Heimlich manoeuvre on her. Then she started smacking him round the head and shouting something about nuts and demanding to know what I'd put in the cake.' She sighed tetchily. 'So what was I supposed to do? Admit that everything I'd fed her came out of your kitchen instead of mine? You can just imagine that, can't you? I'd never hear the end of it. She already thinks I'm the worst wife and mother in the entire universe. Give her ammunition like that and I might just as well kneel down in front of her and commit hara-kiri. Not that she'd appreciate it, the miserable old bag.'

'So what on earth did you tell her?'

'Well. I told her the truth, didn't I?' Here we go. 'I patiently explained that it was a secret family recipe and that my lips were sealed. You'd have been proud of me, Helen. I refused to utter another word, no matter how much they pleaded.'

'You didn't!' I slapped my hand across my eyes.

'What else could I say? I don't bloody know what goes in a cake, do I?'

'An almond cake, Leoni? The clue is in the question?'

'Anyway, it doesn't matter. By that time she'd started going a funny colour so Marcus bundled her in the car and shot off to A and E.'

'She could have died!' Dear heavens above. That

woman's just an accident waiting to happen. 'Nut allergies are very serious!'

'Good,' she sniffed. 'She's been making my life a misery for years. It's her fault that Marcus turned out the way he is. She's spent her whole life telling him the sun shines out of his arse, which is why he doesn't give a flying fuck about anyone except himself.'

'Is she OK now?'

'Mmm. Worse luck. On the upside, she did say that she was never going to set foot in this house again, so it's all worked out just fine if you ask me. Thanks for that. I owe you one, pal.'

'Don't mention it. How are the kids?'

'Alive.' She started eating something. 'Driving me insane. Whenever we move into a new year I find myself sagging under the prospect of yet another twelve-month motherhood sentence. It's like being one of those slaves in *Roots*.' She took a moment to clear her palate. 'Anyway. Enough of the spawn of Satan. It's boring, boring, boring. So what's all this about you and New York?'

'Didn't you get my message?' I said innocently.

'Are you kidding me? Every time Millie sees the light blinking on the answerphone she presses the DELETE button because she likes the noise it makes. Hang on a minute.' I heard the receiver clatter to the table then the unmistakable sound of Leoni hauling a cork out of a bottle. 'That's better,' she mumbled. 'Can't have cheese nibbles without a nice little glass of something, can you? And if I get started now, I might just have a fighting chance of sobering up in time for the school run. So, what made you go to New York?'

The impromptu lie flew out of my mouth before I could do anything about it.

'Nothing,' I said. 'I just fancied a bit of a change for a few days.'

'What, on your own?'

'Yes.' My face reddened.

'Aw, Helen! You should have told me! I would have come with you in a flash. Marcus wouldn't have minded. In fact, after the Christmas we had, he'd have been glad to see the back of me.' I heard her take a slurp. 'And before you say anything, don't ask. We had to take the bathroom door off its hinges.'

'Have you heard from Julia?'

I wondered if I had been the only person to receive a call from her, yet the moment I asked the question, I bit my lip and knew the answer.

'No, I thought she was still on holiday.'

'She is,' I said, trying to sound casual.

'So why would I have heard from her?'

'Oh, nothing. I was just wondering.'

'Sounds to me like your brain's going soft. So, when am I going to see you? I'm gagging to get out of this hellhole. You can tell me all about your amazing trip.

I still can't believe you didn't ask me to go with you. Come the revolution, you'll be first up against the wall.'

'Soon,' I said.

'Great. I was thinking about bunging a spare pair of knickers in my handbag and coming to stay with you tomorrow night. We could lie around watching Brad Pitt movies, hovering over the pause button, and get a massive takeaway. Fancy it?'

'Er, well, that could be a bit tricky actually.'

'Why? You got a hot date or something?' She laughed. A sudden pang of guilt gnawed at my insides. Many a true word.

'Nope,' I said quickly. 'Let's just say that my place is a bit of a mess right now.'

'Listen, Helen. Your definition of mess doesn't even come close, Grasshopper. My house has looked like a landfill site ever since the day we moved in. I can assure you, honey, however messy you might think your flat is, I can guarantee that to me it will be as clean as a verger's conscience.'

'All right then.' I reconsidered her suggestion with a sense of devilment, the destruction in my bedroom still fresh as a rotting dolphin washed up against the Thames barrier. 'Why not?'

I finished the call, then picked up the phone again and dialled Rick's number.

'Rick?' I made sure to put a positive slant on it.

'Hey, babe.' I could hear him smiling. 'Missing me already? Well, you're only flesh and blood. Play your cards right and I might just bunk off today and treat you to a little TLC. Waddya say?'

'No thanks.' I couldn't help but smile a little. 'Listen, Rick, I've been thinking.'

'Now why would you want to go and do a thing like that?'

'Don't be cheeky. Would you mind if I didn't come in today?'

'Course not. I told you. You do whatever you want, babe.' Urgh.

'It's just that I have a few things to sort out here. Something, er, unexpected came up.' I was glad of the genuine excuse. 'In fact, I think I'm probably going to need to take a couple of days if that's OK with you.'

'Everything all right, Hell?' His voice sobered. 'You're not starting to have second thoughts about all this are you?'

'No!' My voice became shrill. 'Of course not!'

'You know I'm nuts about you.'

'Uh-huh.' I pulled at the telephone wire.

'So how about dinner tonight?'

My stomach turned a somersault. Now that we were back in the land of the living, did I really want to have dinner with Rick this evening? And if I did, where would it lead to? Was I ready for a relationship?

Moreover, was I ready for a relationship with someone like Rick? Let's face it, his track record was hardly the kind of thing you'd want your parents to know about, with two ex-wives and five grown children (not all of whom were produced by the ex-Mrs Wiltons I might add). Don't get me wrong. He's been more than generous with all of them despite their general hostility towards him, such are his feelings of guilt and duty, but it's a messy set-up whichever way you look at it. Although I had given up on ever finding The One, that tiny little shred of hope that remained fruitlessly optimistic had somehow assumed that I might one day meet a nice, uncomplicated man with whom I could have a nice, uncomplicated relationship. I sighed forlornly, realizing there and then that my own history would make a worthy ticker-tape subtitle shocker for the *Jerry Springer Show*. I forgot the question he'd asked me in the first place and searched my addled brain.

'Hello?' he said.

'Yes, I'm here.' God, why do I have to over-analyse everything? Why can't I stop asking these endless, pointless questions and just enjoy the moment? Go on. I dare you.

'Pick you up around seven?'

'What?'

'Dinner, Hell. Remember?'

'Oh. Right. Yes, I suppose so.'

'You sure you're all right?'

No. I'm not sure at all. But a girl's still got to eat.

THERE ARE FEW PLEASURES in this world that come anywhere near to the joy of watching Salvatore Toledo Vargas stretching around a bedroom. The man's a puma. Gorgeous from his head right down to his French manicured toes. Why is it that gay men are so much more attractive than the straight ones? I've often wondered if it's because a woman will always want what she knows she cannot have, and that the phenomenon of fancying one's unattainable neighbour is therefore nothing more than basic psychology. Mind you, in Sally's case, there's always the off-chance that he'll make an exception. Believe me, worms can turn given the right soil conditions, and I have yet to meet the woman who fails to swoon in his presence. It's his voice as much as anything. That lazy South American drawl that makes your hairs stand on end. I watched him reach up to the high cupboards and bring the piles of bed linen down to the stack of packing boxes laid out expectantly.

'You really don't have to do this,' I said, wondering if I should get my video camera out.

'Yes I do.' He reached up again, his T-shirt lifting

with his lithe movements, exposing a generous eyeful of the ripped, tanned body beneath. His jeans slipped down, loose on the waist, and hung tantalizingly just below the rise of his jutting hip bones. 'We'll get everything packed away for you and put it in storage. All you have to do is keep out the stuff you need.'

'But haven't you got work to do?'

'Sure I do,' he said. 'But who cares? They'll hang on till I'm good and ready. They always do.'

'True.' I nodded proudly. Sally has a permanent list of eager customers waiting for his illustrations. They're utterly exquisite, a bit like him I suppose.

'I'll show you what I'm working on later if you like.' He threw a lazy smile over his shoulder. 'You'll love it. Do you want to keep any of these things up here?'

'Nah.' I waved it away. 'In fact I should probably have a good old life laundry while we're at it.' It's shocking how I manage to hoard so much junk. Every time I attempt to throw something away, no matter how useless or hideous it is, I find myself staring at it, convincing myself that it's bound to come in handy one day. The buzzer sounded in the hallway and I reluctantly tore my eyes from Sally's seductive form.

'Hello?' I picked up the intercom.

'Hey, babe! You ready? I've got a cab waiting down here.'

Buggeration! Is it that time already? A quick glance

at my watch confirmed that the afternoon had completely run away with me, transfixed as I had been by the moving masterpiece in the sinfully slack Levis.

'I'm running a bit late,' I excused myself. Damn. Of all the things I could have forgotten. Perhaps I had deliberately blotted it out. 'Come up.' I pressed the little red button and released the front door. The moment I heard it push open downstairs, I suddenly remembered with a rush of panic that Sally was in the bedroom and I had yet to admit to him the secret love tryst that had blossomed between me and the most unlikely man in the world. Right. You've got about ten seconds to come up with a plausible explanation, and it had better be good. I quickly stepped out onto the landing to head Rick off at the pass. He bounded up the stairs, armed with an enormous bunch of daffodils, smiling like a boy. The moment he saw me, his smile faded.

'Whassup?' He frowned at me, no doubt noticing that I was hardly dressed for dinner. I pressed my finger to my lips.

'It's Sally.' I pointed to the crack in the door.

'What? The poof?'

'Shhh!' I pushed his arm roughly.

'What's he doing in there?' Rick rumpled his eyebrows suspiciously.

'Ah,' I said. 'It's a long story. We'll get to that in a minute.' Sally started singing a risqué latin number inside the flat, sparing us none of the salacious lyrics. Rick craned his neck and tried to look past me.

'What the bloody hell's going on?'

'Listen, Rick – ' I tried to break it to him gently, pulling the door up quietly behind me – 'do you think we could not make this look like a date?'

'Eh?'

'Well, it's just that I kind of haven't told anyone about us yet.' He tried not to look injured. 'I know, I know,' I said. 'But it all still feels a little, well, weird.' I tipped my hand so-so. 'For all I know this could just be a flash in the pan.'

'You what?'

'You know. Boss gets off with minion. Minion shags boss. Boss wakes up one morning and thinks, oops, big mistake. Minion gets fired. Game over.'

'Well, that's bloody nice, isn't it?' His face drooped into a sulk. 'I can't believe some of the stuff that goes on in that insane head of yours. So what am I supposed to say to Tinkerbell in there?'

At that very instant, the door opened.

Rick whipped the flowers behind his back.

'Hi,' Sally said, flicking his eyes over us suspiciously.

'Wotcha, mate.' Rick offered him a firm heterosexual handshake. 'I was just passing. Saw the lights on and, erm, thought I'd stick my head around the door.'

'Are those for me?' Sally purred, pointing at the poorly concealed daffs.

'What? Oh these?' Rick seemed surprised to find the bouquet in his hand. 'Oh, er, sure!' He offered them to Sally. 'Fuck. Why not, eh? But I don't want you to read anything into it, right?'

Sally folded his arms at the flowers, raised a waxed eyebrow and gave me a nudge. 'I think somebody likes you,' he whispered loudly. I flushed scarlet. Rick cleared his throat, and the two of us stood there like a pair of incompetent shoplifters caught red-handed.

'Don't suppose you fancy grabbing something to eat, Hell?' Rick said, trying to sound as though he'd only just thought of it, although his fresh appearance and sprightly cologne somewhat gave the game away. 'There's a couple of things I need to talk to you about. Work stuff, of course,' he added quickly, adopting an unconvincing stern expression. 'So you'd better bring a notepad.' Genius.

'Oh, all right then. If I absolutely must.' I shrugged as though greatly inconvenienced, tutting and rolling my eyes at Sally. 'Although you really shouldn't be bothering me at home, Rick. It's not very professional.' Avoiding Sally's laser-beam gaze, I ducked back into the flat. 'Just give me a minute.'

'Great.' Sally stretched his hands over his tight stomach. 'I'm starving.' He winked at Rick. 'She's had me at it in the bedroom all afternoon. Wow, have I worked up an appetite.'

'Oh, really.' Rick narrowed his eyes. 'In the bedroom doing what, exactly?'

'Oooh, yeah. She really knows how to make a man sweat, doesn't she?' Rick's fists began to twitch. 'I reckon that's the hardest workout I've done in a long, long time.' Sally smacked his lips. 'Real good for firing up the hunger, if you know what I mean.'

'No, I don't actually, Tinkerbell. So why don't you enlighten me?'

'You're a man of the world.' Sally locked eyes with Rick. 'I'm just being neighbourly.'

By the time I got back to the door, Rick looked like thunder.

'Hell?' He brandished the flowers at me. 'Do you mind telling me what the fuck you've been doing in there all afternoon with old lover boy here?' Sally leaned languidly against the doorframe and unleashed his spectacular half-moon smile.

'Sally,' I growled. 'Have you been causing mischief again?'

'What?' Sally shrugged nonchalantly, inspecting his nails. 'I was just telling Rick what a good time we've been having this afternoon in your bedroom. And if I didn't know better, I'd say he's looking pretty upset about it.' He sucked his breath through perfect teeth. 'Can't think why. Can you?' He paused. 'It's not as though the pair of you are lovers, is it?'

'Listen, sunshine,' Rick squared up to him, baring his teeth right in Sally's face. Sally didn't flinch.

'Flowers? A little spritz of Mouchoir de Monsieur if I'm not mistaken?' Sally tapped his nose knowingly. 'Anyone might think that you've come here with more than dinner on your mind, man.' Whether Sally realized it or not, he was playing with fire, the telltale hard line at the corner of Rick's mouth a sure sign that he might be about to rip Sally's head off and impale it on the railings outside as a warning to others.

'No! Rick!' I threw myself in between them, flinging my arms out like a referee. 'It's not what you think!'

'It better fucking not be.' He scowled at Sally.

'Ah-ha.' Sally rested a hand on his snake hips and raised an accusing finger. 'I see I have stumbled across something very interesting. So – ' he slipped his arm seductively around my waist, raising the stakes as Rick's eyes burned with jealousy, and whispered in my ear – 'You wanna tell your Aunt Sally what's been going on, sugar? Or do I have to tease it out of you?' Oh, please do, you sexy beast. I couldn't stop the smile that crept across my face as Sally nuzzled my neck.

'OK, that's quite enough!' Rick shouted, pulling me from Sally's arms. 'I demand to know what you two have been up to, or I'm gonna smash your face in, sonny Jim.'

In a display of Victoria Cross bravery, Sally ignored

Rick's machismo, threw his head back and laughed triumphantly.

'I knew it!' He picked a tiny fleck of pollen from Rick's jacket. 'It's written all over your guilty little faces.'

'You mustn't tell anyone!' I clasped my hands at him.

Rick and Sally exchanged a glance and chorused, 'Why not?'

'Because I don't want everyone knowing my business!' Chicken. You just don't want to have to justify your sordid behaviour.

Sally frowned at Rick. Rick shrugged innocently. 'Don't look at me, mate. She's been like this ever since we got on the plane back from New York. Haven't had a word of sense out of her.'

'You liar!' Sally gasped and slapped my arm before returning to Rick. 'She told us she'd gone on her own!' I looked down at my shoes guiltily.

'Bloody tell me about it, mate,' Rick huffed. 'I don't even understand what she's on about half the time. Total fucking nightmare.' Rick reached into his jacket pocket for a cigar, stuck it in his mouth and struck a match. 'She's got it into her head that all I'm interested in is a bit of wham, bam, thank you ma'am. If I weren't such a nice bloke, I'd be bloody offended, mate. Want one of these?' Rick waved another cigar at Sally. 'It's all right. It's Cuban.'

'He's Colombian,' I mumbled.

'Oh, right. Whatever.' Rick put the refused cigar back in his pocket and concentrated on his own, biting off the end and spitting it to the floor.

'Paul's going to have kittens,' Sally said. 'You know, man, we've been trying to find her a decent boyfriend ever since she got here. But will she listen to us?' He rolled his eyes in defeat.

'Does that to you too, does she? You don't fucking surprise me, mate.' Rick nodded understandingly. 'Bloody in one ear, out the other, innit?'

Sally tutted and folded his arms.

'Oi!' I said, but no one appeared to be listening.

'Remember that Sebastian wanker?' Rick cupped the yellow flame in his hand and puffed away, filling the landing with a thick fog of expensive smoke.

'Oh, my God!' Sally flashed his eyes disapprovingly. 'Don't remind me! You don't even want to know what she went through there. We can hear everything through the floor if we're really quiet. It was better than *EastEnders*.'

'Excuse me.' I knocked on the wall. 'But would you mind not talking about me as though I'm not here?'

'Sorry, Hell.' Rick wasn't sorry at all. In fact, he seemed very pleased indeed that we'd been outed. 'But don't you think it's a bit daft, all this cloak and dagger stuff?' He nodded at Sally and received his instant blink of approval.

'I'm just not comfortable with broadcasting my private business.' I squirmed under the pressure of their camaraderie and wondered if I should make a quick dash for the bathroom and lock myself in. 'I know it's silly, but please just bear with me and let me have a little time to get used to the idea. OK?'

'Waddya reckon, Sal?' Rick sucked on his cigar and stuck his hands in his pockets.

'Well –' Sally rubbed his chin thoughtfully – 'I suppose I could keep it to myself for a little while, if the price were right.' He smiled mischievously. 'But it's not easy to keep things from Paul. You know what he's like. Too many detective novels. And once he finds out, you might just as well call the newspapers.'

'Pretty please!' I begged him. 'Just for me?'

'Too late!' Paul tore up the stairs and threw his arms around the instantly uncomfortable Rick. 'Isn't this great!' he squealed. 'I just knew something romantic was going to happen today. I could tell the moment I opened my eyes!'

'I DON'T MIND telling you, you really had me going there for a minute, babe.' Rick stabbed his fork into his man-sized steak, the plate running red instantly. 'That Sally's all right for a poof, isn't he? I'm not sure about the other one, mind you.'

'Who, Paul?'

'Yeah. Bit of a woolly wooftah, I reckon. We had a kid like that at school. All you had to do was say boo to him and he'd burst into tears. Do you think they're born like that? Gays, I mean.'

'Stop it,' I hissed at him. 'You can't go around saying things like that.'

The maître d' wafted to Rick's side. 'Everything all right, Mr Wilton?'

'Bloody great, Tone.'

'It's very nice to see the lovely lady with you again.' Tony smiled at me, refilling my water glass. 'We hope to be seeing a lot more of you, madam. You bring a certain charm to the place that is most welcome.'

'Thank you,' I blushed. In the few times that I had been here, Tony had been almost cloyingly attentive. His charm was undeniable, but I wondered what he might say behind his punters' backs each time he disappeared beyond the kitchen doors. Probably broke into fluent cock-er-knee and flicked fag ash in the soup.

'You can count on it.' Rick pressed a crisp pink note in his hand and sent him away.

'That's really very vulgar,' I said quietly, toying with my salad.

'What?'

'You know . . .' I nodded towards Tony's elegant fig-ure disappearing towards the bar. 'Throwing money at people every five minutes. Especially him. It's really not necessary.'

'Listen, babe – ' he pointed his fork at me – 'these people have been feeding me for years. I get the best table, the best service, the best food. You see those plebs over there?' He indicated towards a cramped table set within two feet of the constantly swinging kitchen doors, its occupants ridiculously overdressed, unable to hold a knife properly between them, peering around the room every two minutes, hoping to catch a glimpse of a famous face. 'They've probably waited six months for that table, and it's the worst in the whole joint. Nobody here will give a shit whether they come back or not, and if they don't like what they're served, Tony will have them thrown out before they can finish one more mouthful.'

'That's no reason to keep shoving notes into his hand.' I kept my voice down. 'It makes you look like you're trying to buy his friendship.' An awkward silence settled over the table, confirming my general premonition of this ill-fated coupling. This is exactly what I mean. Leave the pair of us together for long enough, and any idiot can see that we are several light years apart when it comes to our basic training and our wildly differing outlooks on life. As I said, doomed right from the start.

'He's got a handicapped kid.' Rick didn't look up

from his plate. 'Spends most of his life in a plaster cast from the waist up.'

'Oh!' Me and my big mouth.

'Tony and his Mrs are in and out of hospital with him all the time, and you wouldn't believe what they've had to spend on their house to make it right for him. Bloody NHS and social services – ' he shook his head a little – 'they've had to fight for every bit of help they've ever got, and believe me, it's not been nearly enough. The rest they have to pay for themselves. Let the man earn his living.' Rick gave me a rare glance. 'And let him have the dignity of putting an extra quid in his pocket without being on the receiving end of your judgement.'

My appetite deserted me, the expensive wine now bitter in my mouth. I felt like a complete and utter shit.

Chapter Four

DIET COKE TIME

THE BUZZER ANNOUNCED Leoni's arrival without me needing to check who it was. She had used her secret code. Two short buzzes, one long one, then another of indefinite duration as she jammed her finger on the button until I answered it. Hugely annoying, yes, but generally indicative of the way things usually went once I granted her access. My place had become a sort of home-from-home for her, a failsafe kid- and husband-free zone where she could moan to her heart's content without being called a chisel-faced harridan, and where she could be assured of a peaceful guilt-free hangover the morning after with nothing more taxing to deal with than a freshly baked croissant. I buzzed her in downstairs. My own door was ajar anyway, allowing for Sally's constant comings and goings while we continued to pack everything that wasn't nailed down. A van would be coming for the furniture in a day or two, although judging by the Neanderthal with the hairy knuckles who came to measure up my contents, I wasn't banking on seeing any of it ever again.

'Ta-raaaa!' she sang as she clanked up the stairs with her usual collection of bottle bags. 'I've got a whole roast chicken festering in here somewhere too. I expect Marcus was planning on feeding it to the kids for dinner tonight, but hey, why not make him suffer like I do? I wrapped one of the boys' trainers in tin foil and stuck it on the plate in the fridge instead. That'll teach him.' She reached the landing and planted a friendly kiss on my cheek. 'See?' she shouted as she marched past me, slinging her bag on the floor and making herself instantly at home. 'Perfectly tidy. What did I tell you?' She shook off her coat and threw it at the nearest chair, missing by a mile and not giving it a second glance as it landed on the floor. 'What's with all these boxes? You weren't thinking of moving home without telling anyone, were you?' She started pulling one of them open, tearing at the cardboard without a second thought. 'What's in here? Oooh! Shoes! You're not chucking these out are you?' Leoni pulled off her own and started trying to cram her feet into my favourite pink strappies.

'Not exactly.' I picked up her coat and hung it on the stand. 'But then again, you're not that far off.'

'Cos if you're getting rid of stuff, just bung it my way, honey.' I waited to see if she noticed anything odd about the apartment, like the fact that most of it was missing, but she seemed to be in her usual state of total oblivion as she trotted through to the kitchen in my shoes and started unloading her rations on the side. 'What do you want to hockey off with? Red or white?' She dangled a bottle in each hand, studiously weighing up the merits of each.

'Don't you think it's a bit early for that? I was just about to put the kettle on.'

'Early? Don't be daft. I've escaped. All bets are off.' She reached down a couple of glasses from the overhead cupboard and opened the white. 'Have you lost weight?' She frowned, handing me a glass.

'Er, not that I'm aware of.'

That wasn't entirely true. I had shamefully fallen into that auto-shrinkage habit so many women subject themselves to the moment they enter a new relationship. There was no way I was going to adhere to my usual eating habits in front of Rick, so I'd been on the pretend-healthy-lifestyle routine while everyone else in the land was soldiering through their fifteenth reincarnation of the Christmas turkey. Leoni circled me like a shark, looking me up and down critically.

'Are you sure? You definitely look slimmer to me.

How the bloody hell did you manage that? I'm sure I've stuck on ten pounds over the holidays.' She paused momentarily to open a big bag of crisps. 'Frankly, I don't care any more. I'm not even going to bother with a diet this time. It's just so bloody pointless. I'll only end up making myself miserable, then I'll have no choice other than to take it out on the kids.' She sighed, then stuffed in a fistful of Wotsits and spoke with her mouth full. 'Besides, my body keeps trying to go into hibernation. I hate winter. It puts me in a really bad mood.' You don't say.

'How's Marcus?' I put the kettle on, ignoring the glass she had poured for me, knowing that she'd polish it off herself if it hung around for longer than ten seconds.

'Same old tosser.' She filled her mouth again. 'Hoping for a promotion, I reckon. One of the bosses is about to retire, so the vultures are circling, Marcus included.' She took an enormous swig of wine, swishing it around her mouth like Listerine to loosen the Wotsits. 'It's all about dead men's shoes in that place. You should see the chairman. He looks like a walking corpse. Anyway, I've already told Marcus that he's wasting his time. If they were going to promote him, they would have done it years ago. He's never been anything more than a second-rate schmoozer. And he's too old now anyway. Young blood. That's what they want.' She did *Psycho* stabbing movements. 'Ruth-less little bastards.'

'Leoni! Don't be so horrible.'

'It's true,' she said matter-of-factly. 'I've seen more promising candidates working the checkouts at Netto. Let's face it, he's not exactly a stick of dynamite, is he?' She didn't wait for an answer. 'Now he's trying to look all with-it when he goes off to work in the morning, using that hair wax stuff and wearing snazzy ties. What he doesn't realize is that from behind it makes his bald patch twice the size, and the loud ties make him look like an ITV weatherman.' I laughed a little. 'So what's new, pussycat?' she demanded.

'Nothing,' I fibbed.

'Nothing?' Leoni squinted over her wine glass. 'Don't give me that. And don't pretend that your wardrobe isn't crammed with half the contents of Fifth Avenue.' Her eyebrows danced. 'Including something fabulous for little old me?' She twitched her nose and frowned. 'What's that funny smell?' Then checked her fingers and mumbled, 'Must be the Wotsits.'

'I didn't do any shopping.'

'Yeah, right,' she laughed. 'And Imelda Marcos wears brothel creepers.'

'Seriously!'

'You must think I was born yesterday.' She scowled at me childishly then skipped out of the kitchen. 'Let's have a look at what you got then!' I leaned up against the fridge, mug in hand, and smiled to myself. It took maybe ten seconds for Leoni to reach my room.

'Holy shit!' she yelled. 'Your bedroom looks like sodding Kabul!'

'It's my new open-plan look,' I shouted through to her, taking a sip of tea. 'What do you think?'

'The smell!' She came thundering back to the kitchen, her face a picture of shock. 'Have you been keeping dead bodies in there? What the bloody hell happened?'

The door swung open and in strolled Sally, lean, tanned, devastating.

'He did.' I pointed at Sally accusingly.

'Hi, sexy!' Leoni flew at him, shamelessly pressing herself against his audacious physique and firmly grasping hold of his buttocks. 'I'm so sorry.' She started chewing his neck. 'I just can't help myself. God knows I've even thought about getting a sex change so you can have your wicked way with me.' She flung her head back and stared into his eyes wantonly. 'What if I just offer you the tradesman's entrance?'

'I can do you at four o'clock.' Sally stretched to his full, dizzying height, towering over Leoni's quivering frame. 'But for now I have to move some more of this stuff.' He winked at me and shimmied out of the kitchen, leaving Leoni panting with frustration.

'Holy mother of Jesus.' She dabbed the perspiration from her brow.

'That good, huh?' I smiled.

'You're bloody telling me. I was about ten seconds away from a totally organic experience there. I swear, the only way I can face having sex with Marcus twice a year is to shut my eyes and think of Sal.' She clicked her tongue. 'Does it for me every time.'

'Glad to be of service,' Sally called through as he lugged more packing boxes out into the hallway.

'Looks like I'm going to have to move out to a doss house.' I wrinkled my nose at her and nodded up at the ceiling. 'Apparently there's a mini-tsunami sitting up there waiting to burst through my architraves any minute.'

'No! Really?' Leoni looked up nervously. 'Are we safe? I mean, it's not going to come smashing down on our heads and kill us all, is it?'

'Who knows?' I shrugged. 'Live dangerously, eh?'

'Well, in that case, I'd better have another drink.' As predicted, Leoni availed herself of the glass she had poured for me. 'You could always come and move in with me if you like.'

What? If I were completely out of my mind, you mean? Even a homeless economic migrant would think twice before shacking up in Leoni's ghetto. The twins-from-hell are currently specializing in gang warfare,

Joshua being one gang and William the other. Believe me, they only need one member each to wreak the kind of havoc you'd expect from any self-respecting Glaswegian sink estate. They've already set fire to the garden shed, hammered nails into the tyres of their father's car and shoved several pounds of Maris Pipers up the neighbours' exhaust pipes, and that was the fruit of just one weekend's labour. Occasionally the two gangs will come together and form a pact in order to turn their joint attentions on terrorizing their poor unsuspecting sister. Little Miss Millie has since taken to wearing a crash helmet while watching CBeebies. No. I think I'd rather give Leoni's place a wide berth.

'Thanks, Leoni.' I tried to sound deeply moved by her generosity. 'But I've got some hot needles around here somewhere which I would rather stick in my own eyeballs.'

'Wise move,' she conceded. 'And I'd rather stay here and lie on your floor until the roof caves in and puts me out of my misery.'

'Paul and Sally offered me their sofa for a while.' I hushed my voice to a whisper. 'Although, frankly, I'm not sure it's such a brilliant idea.'

'Why not?'

'Because Paul's the crumbliest, flakiest man in the world and – ' I checked behind her quickly to see that we wouldn't be overheard. Sally was casually picking up two boxes stacked on top of one another, the strength of his muscles straining gorgeously under his T-shirt. Leoni followed my candy-filled eyes. 'And I'm not certain that I can be trusted with you know who.'

'Oh, lordy,' she murmured, sucking in a long, yearning breath. 'Yeah, baby. I see what you mean.' She picked up her wine glass and casually slung its contents into her face.

Chapter Five

SURPRISE, SURPRISE!

LOITERING AT THE arrival gates, I scanned each new sea of faces as they emerged into Heathrow's frosty welcome hall, even though Julia's plane had not long landed and she was unlikely to make an appearance for a little while yet. In my heart, I was secretly hoping to witness one of those Cilla Black moments, perhaps a long-lost brother or sister who had been separated from their sibling at birth, finding them after thirty years and being greeted in this very hall by their estranged yet elated new-found family. Most of the passengers walked straight through, their faces bent to the floor with boredom, as though the miracle of air travel had become nothing more exciting than a bus trip. It saddened me that the glory of hopping over continents had been diminished to a necessary inconvenience in the living of international lives, unlike the old days when Liz Taylor and Richard Burton exchanged bourbon and diamonds across an airport lounge in movies like *The VIPs*. The Jet Set, they were called – those exhilarating, dangerous-to-know people who flew around the world and filled the newspapers with sensationally scandalous stories. Now it was mainly salesmen with laptop cases, checking their watches impatiently and trundling identical executive baggage.

I grabbed a cappuccino from the Costa stand and perched myself on an outfacing stool. Among the waiting greeters, some in ill-fitting suits holding up boards with absurdly misspelled names, a woman stood with two small children, anxiously checking the incoming faces just as I had been doing. Ah-ha. A perfect candidate. I sat back and waited for her loved one to arrive, warmed by the prospect of a running hug in the midst of all this modern-day dashing around. A couple of plane loads later, there he was, identifiable by the kid who broke free from her mother's grip and ran to him, shouting 'Daddy'. My spirits lifted as he reached down and scooped her up awkwardly, dropping his case to the floor. The wife, assuming that's who she was, made no move towards him. They came together without so much as a kiss hello, his demeanour instantly sunken at the sight of her scowling, lemon-sucking face.

And suddenly, there they were.

'Julia!' I shouted and waved, jumping down from the stool and surging forward. A momentary flash of confusion crossed her face, she said something to David and continued walking. 'Julia!' – much louder – 'Over here!'

Then she saw me.

They had no idea that I would be there to greet them, but I couldn't wait a moment longer to see her. Like a cat on a hot tin roof, I'd found myself pacing around fretting for her return until Sally suggested we find their flight on the tinterweb and insisted I go off to meet her. The surprise on her face was worth my hysterical dash across London that morning.

'Helen!' she shouted. We ran towards each other, our moment of impact almost violent as we threw ourselves into a tight embrace, the pair of us instantly reduced to tears as David looked on with a ridiculous smile.

And there it was, the Cilla Black moment, for the whole airport to see.

'I couldn't keep away,' I said, beaming at them both. David leaned down and kissed me. 'Congratulations!' I snivelled at him. He nodded emotionally and couldn't meet my watery eyes. I squeezed Julia's hand. 'How are you feeling?'

'Sick.' She smiled, a slightly crazed look in her eyes. 'All the time, except when I'm eating.'

I so wanted to stare at her, to reach out and feel for the swelling in her belly, but I couldn't do it. It felt like stealing. Like trying to take a slice of something that wasn't mine. Her face was aglow, tanned and brimming with health, her skin radiating vitality. Not that it ever did anything else, mind you. She had thrown out every cosmetic she owned on the eve of her fortieth birthday three years ago and since then had refused to give house or handbag room to anything that didn't include the words 'anti-ageing' on the bottle. It was not unheard of for her to blow three hundred quid on a pot of face cream, and she once shelled out a mind-boggling undisclosed sum for a tube of special edition serum that made a kilo of Beluga look positively cheap.

'Now I understand what they mean by the expression "glowing".' I insisted on taking her handbag to carry.

'You're not looking so bad yourself,' David said, eyeing me closely. I blushed instantly.

'I took the liberty of ordering you a nice car,' I admitted. 'Don't want you being jolted around by some nutter taxi driver, do we?'

Not that I like to fling it around willy-nilly, but there are times when the whole point of having a little extra money gathering momentum in one's piggy bank is so that you can splash out where splashing out is due, and I somehow thought that the big Mercedes circling the pick-up point would say more about my joy for them than a bunch of flowers ever could.

'Darling?' Julia pulled at David's arm, her attention caught by the refrigerated display beside the espresso bar. 'Do you think you could pop over there and pick me up a sandwich or something?'

'Sure,' he said, abandoning their luggage trolley. 'Tuna? Cheese? Ham?'

'Mmm, anything.' She nodded. 'And a lemon crois- sant if they've got one. Or a slice of fruit cake.' David was already making his way to the stand. 'And a smoothie!' she shouted after him. 'They hardly gave us anything to eat on the plane.' She stifled a yawn. 'I'm starving.' As she stretched the long-haul ache from her limbs, I noticed the startlingly sudden weight gain around her previously model-slender body. Instead of the gentle beginnings of a bump, she looked as though she might be preparing for an imminent famine.

'I've missed you.' I quickly brought my eyes to meet hers. 'Couldn't stop thinking about you since the phone call.'

'Me neither,' she said. 'My God, Helen, I can't tell you what a surprise the whole thing was. I suppose I just couldn't believe it. You should have seen David's face when I told him. The truth is,' she admitted with uncharacteristic shyness, 'I knew very well for some time before we left, but I wanted to wait until the right moment. Just couldn't get my head around it. It was our first night and we were having an early dinner as the sun went down.' I imagined the scene, the childless couple of unspoken disappointments, bathed in the golden glow of a tropical sunset. 'It seemed so perfect, but when it came to it, I could barely get the words out. He just fell to pieces.' She laughed slightly hysterically. 'Goodness only knows what we must have looked like.'

'I found your pregnancy test in my bathroom bin,' I told her.

'Sorry about that.' She blushed. 'I'd been doing them every day. Every time it went positive I got the same thrill! How stupid is that?' David returned with Julia's short-order picnic and she fell on it like a refugee, tearing the bag open and breaking off a huge piece of cake.

'What are you doing on Sunday?' David asked. I pictured myself wearing a gas mask, shovelling damp rubble out of the bedroom.

'Nothing. Why?'

'That's settled, then,' David said. 'Come over for lunch. I'll be cooking,' which, roughly translated, meant he'd be reheating half the Marks & Spencer food hall. 'We're going to get everyone over and make the big announcement. Think you can keep it under your hat until then?'

'No problem,' I said. 'You'd be amazed at how good I am at keeping secrets.'

'WELL, IT'S EASY, innit?' Rick lay back on the pillows, ashtray balanced on his stomach, and played with his cigar (in a non-Clintonian manner I hasten to add). I watched the smoke festoon upwards in the semi-lit room, rolling away in soft, blue clouds, the sheet tucked safely under my chin. In all my days, the one place I never imagined I'd end up was in this bed. Sure, I had shoved him into it once or twice and pulled his shoes off when he'd come home drunk. Brought him aspirins and the occasional steak sandwich when he'd been under the weather. Put a few must-read classic volumes on the bedside table whenever I've thought him in need of a little culture. But never did I ever expect to find myself lolling around in this bed wearing little more than a smile. I curled my arm beneath the pillows and congratulated myself for keeping him well stocked in only the bee's knees of Egyptian cotton and goose down. The duvet crackled softly with the reassuring rustle of his monumental housekeeping budget.

'What is?' I was miles away.

'That whacking great hole in your bedroom ceiling.'

'Oh, that,' I groaned. 'Don't remind me. I've got the builders turning up on Monday, which means I'll be living out of a suitcase for at least six weeks and sharing negligees with Paul and Sally. We'll probably be at each other's throats by the end of the first week. Maybe I should start on the Valium now. As they say, a friend in need is a bloody nuisance.' Rick smiled to himself. 'It's not funny! I just can't bear the thought of the mess it's going to make. What a complete nightmare.'

'Nah, Hell – ' he sucked hard on his cigar – 'it's bloody perfect, that's what it is. Fancy a glass of champers?' He flicked the covers aside before I could avert my eyes and got up without a hint of inhibition, flashing me a terrifying glimpse of his nethers as he bent to the floor for his robe. Good gracious. If men had any idea of how grotesque their vegetables look when dangled in rear-view like that, they'd never take their pants off again. It's enough to make you want to pluck your own eyeballs out. I reached for the remote control and switched on the flatscreen, hopping between channels, trying to wipe the vision of Rick's arse from my memory banks, and found myself caught up in the welcome (if momentary) distraction of a Channel Five trailer for a documentary about a man with no head, no arms and no legs. As they say, there's always someone worse off than you.

Rick bounced back into the bedroom, giving it a bit of Rod Stewart, bottle in hand and a glass in each pocket. He popped the lively cork with a single flick of his thumb, making no attempt to prevent the deliberate spillage. 'Wanna bit of rumpy pumpy with that, modom?' He spoke out of the side of his mouth and made farting noises with his hand tucked into his armpit.

'What's got into you?' I turned the TV off. 'You've been in a permanent state of excitement lately and it's extremely childish.' He leapt onto the bed, landing on his side, his face not more than two inches from mine.

'I think you're fucking amazing,' he said, then pulled a bunch of grapes out of his dressing-gown pocket and tried to caress me with them.

'Will you get off me.' I snatched them out of his hand.

'I love you.' He tried to nuzzle up to me.

'Don't say that. You know I don't like it. Now get off before I'm forced to do something you'll regret.'

'No,' he persisted, gripping the covers in mock horror, refusing to budge. 'Make me.'

For a moment, I thought I became vaguely aware of a noise. 'What was that?' I sat up.

'What was what?' He tried to look at my knockers.

'I thought I heard something.'

'Stop making excuses – now come here.' He lifted

his head and started growling, coming at me with curled fingers.

If there's one thing I can't stand, it's being tickled. Sadly, Rick now knows this and has taken to playing it like a trump card at every opportunity.

'No! Get off! Arrrggh!' My automatic reaction was to fight back, the kick landing dangerously close to the crown jewels.

Rick leapt from the bed, dramatically poured us each a flute of champagne then threw his robe off, flinging it away like a five-quid stripper. 'From the glass or from my rippling body?' He poured a great slug from the bottle down his torso. I took aim with the bunch of grapes, but before I could hurl them at his head, our afternoon's entertainment was shattered by a bloodcurdling scream. In the reflection of the dressing mirror, I caught sight of Helga the Russian Cleaning Lady, frozen in the doorway, the pile of clean laundry falling from her arms.

'Shit.' Rick reached for his robe, subjecting Helga to the same hideous sight I had recoiled from just moments earlier.

'Reek!' She covered her eyes with her hands, peeking through her fingers. 'Reek, you no make me look you like that! You make clothes now! Yes, now!' I saw her lower her hands. Quick as a flash, I flattened myself against the bed and threw the sheet over my head. Whatever else was sticking out would just have to fend for itself.

'Helg! What the fuck are you doing here?'

'Me work day! You stupid? Me work here!'

'Nah, Helg, not today. Remember? I told you. Come on Monday. Yeah? Mon-day?' She stared at him blankly. 'Muuuun-DAY!'

'*Nyet*. Not come Muuun-DAY. I come now. Make beds.'

To my horror, I felt her tugging at the sheets.

'No! Helg! Leave it!' Rick tried to head her off.

'*Nyet!* ME work my job. YOU lazy *zhopa*.'

I have no idea what those Russians eat, but even in her diminutive form, Helga had the strength of ten Ukrainian miners. I felt the sheet slide from my vice-like grip, the duvet being wrenched away with such force that it might as well have been tied to the back of a speeding pick-up truck. There was nothing I could do to prevent the whole lot flying into the air. I grabbed the pillow instead and held it over my face just in time to hear Helga's sharp intake of breath. What I must have looked like heaven only knows – and I'd really rather not think about it – sprawled flat out like a grilled Dover sole without so much as an Elasto-plast to hold anything in place.

'Yeep!' She squealed before lowering her voice to a growl of disapproval. '*Shlyuha vokzalnaya!*'

'Happy?' Rick said patiently. 'Now would you mind very much getting out?'

'You naughty Reek!' she scolded him.

'Yes, yes,' Rick said. 'Me very naughty Rick, now please, Helg, bugger off, eh?'

Helga snorted. 'Me bugging. Come back Muuuun-DAY, *da*?'

'*Da*.' Rick sighed.

I waited until I heard the click of the bedroom door, then peeled the pillow from my vermilion face and gawped at Rick in disbelief. Neither of us said a word, holding our breath until we heard the reassuring slam of the front door and the scampering of Helga's disappearing feet.

'Nice.' He winked, nodding at my enforced nakedness and taking a lazy sip of champagne. I could feel myself blushing from head to toe. Just to make things more interesting, my mobile then decided to start ringing from my handbag, offering me the added humiliation of having to shift my flab in broad daylight. There was no way I was going to leap up and bend to the floor to get it. I might not have vegetables, but still, I don't expect the view would be any better.

'Would you mind?' I waggled my hand towards my bag, doing my best to veil my ruined modesty with the one pillow. He picked it up and passed it to me, gallantly offering me the confiscated bedsheet at the same time. 'Thanks,' I mouthed gratefully, reaching my handset out of the bag. Upon seeing the name on the tiny screen, I smiled at Rick and shook my head. 'It's Helga!' I hissed. 'No doubt calling me to grass you up. I'll try to sound suitably shocked shall I?' I hit the green button and put the phone to my ear with a smile.

'Hell-yen!' Helga's voice boomed over the background traffic sounds, causing me to flinch away from the phone. She still seemed entirely unable to grasp the concept of modern technology, yelling like a fishwife in accordance with the distance of the call. You should hear her talking to her family back in Russia. Earplugs essential.

'Helga!' I winked at Rick conspiratorially. 'Everything all right? Where are you?'

'You naughty Hell-yen! You make sex with Reek!' She began cackling.

'I beg your pardon?' The hairs prickled on my arms.

'You leave coat on chair! I see shoes on floor! You make *trakhatsya*!'

A sudden, terrible screeching of tyres against tarmac followed by a hefty, dull thud brought my heart lurching into my mouth.

'Helga!' I screamed. 'Oh my God!' My eyes rushed to Rick's. Some scrabbling noises escaped through my handset, then came Helga's voice again, this time filled with fury and, judging by the distorted volume, some small distance away from her phone.

'*Pashyol ty, svoloch!*' she yelled.

'Oi, you stupid cow!' a man shouted back at her. 'You got a death wish or something?'

'*Zatknis na hui!*' The next muffled sound may or may not have been Helga hammering on the offending vehicle with her fists.

'You maniac!' A car door slammed hard, horns honking angrily through the open window from the street outside.

'Rick!' I pointed at the window. 'Quickly!'

He was there in an instant, pulling the curtain aside. 'What the bloody hell?' He turned on his heels and ran downstairs, wrenching the front door open and bawling into the street. 'Helga! Hell-GA! For fuck's sake, love, put him down!'

By the time the police arrived, Rick had managed to placate the man in the BT van while Helga hid in the kitchen and calmed her nerves with a shot of Stoli from the freezer. I sat at the table with her, murmuring platitudes and nodding understandingly while she re-enacted the moment when the telephone man tried to mow her down.

'Thank God you weren't hurt.' I took a little sip from my champagne glass, pulling Rick's oversized jumper across my knees. Well, no point in locking the stable door after the horse had bolted. She'd already seen everything I had to offer, which wasn't much, and my blushing mechanism seemed to be all worn out for now. Helga brushed off the last vestiges of the assault with a final huff, slamming her glass on the table with a shrug, then smiled at me slyly.

'You make sex with Reek!' She nudged her eyes at the ceiling. 'He have beeeeeg *moskovskaya*, *da*?' She winked at me and pointed to her lap.

'Helga!' I didn't know where to look.

'*Daaa!*' She went to the freezer and pulled the bottle out again. 'I see before,' she said. 'I see in bathroom. When I bring washing. *Da!* I see big *moskovskaya*.'

'Really, Helga! You shouldn't be spying on Rick. That's very bad of you.'

'Bad? *Nyet*. I Russian.' She pointed to herself proudly. 'Russian make good spy. Very good spy.' She poured herself another shot and threw it back without flinching. 'Now I go.' Picking up the crumpled Tesco bag-for-life she carries with her everywhere, she gave me a sharp salute. 'You tell Reek I go. Come back Muuuun-day.'

I guessed from the brief doorstep conversation that she passed Reek on the way out.

'Bloody Norah.' Rick ran his hands through his hair and dropped himself onto the kitchen chair beside me, picking up my glass and draining it in one huge swallow. 'That woman's a fucking danger to society.

And I'm bloody freezing.' He blew into his hands and rubbed them together.

'Police gone?'

'Thank God.' He scratched his head. 'They got a call about a punch-up at the coach station and lost interest. I had to bung the van driver a hundred quid and a pair of tickets to the next Chelski game to keep schtoom, greedy bastard. Bloody daylight robbery if you ask me. Mind you, better that than to have Helga hauled off by the fuzz again.'

I glanced at my watch and sighed. 'Talking of which, I suppose I really ought to think about putting some clothes on and dragging my sorry backside home. Paul's promised to cook something spectacular, which means he'll be in a constant state of heightened hysteria this evening. The guilt is eating him alive.'

'You know what, Hell?' He picked up my hand and kissed it. 'I've been thinking . . .'

Chapter Six

THE STIG

'HOW'S YOUR SECRET lover?' Paul flounced in front of me with the tray of dainty canapés he'd poured his culinary heart and soul into, the array of gleaming micro-utensils on the kitchen worktop more suited to an operating theatre.

'Fine,' I supposed, popping another stuffed prawn in my mouth, agonizing about whether or not I should say anything. I had left Rick's house in a blind panic two hours ago, and my heart rate had yet to return to normal.

'You should have asked him to come along!' Paul rearranged the remaining canapés, unable to stand the sight of their misalignment. Sally sauntered past and deliberately messed them up, flipping three into his mouth, bumping Paul hard with his hip.

I decided to just come out with it.

'He wants me to move in with him.'

Paul gasped, the tray falling from his hands. Sally stopped chewing. 'Now this – ' he nodded slowly – 'this is gonna be worth hearing.' He stepped over the mess and steered me to the sofa.

'How I didn't see it coming I really don't know.' It all came tumbling out. 'For one awful moment I thought he was going to propose, the way he'd leaned half off his chair, clutching my hand. Honestly – ' I shook my head – 'I thought I was going to have a bloody heart attack.'

'Sounds like you had a freak-out,' Sally diagnosed. 'You really need to work on that a little.'

'It gets worse,' I said. 'Much worse. He then tried to convince me that it was a sign, that my ceiling had caved in because of some kind of divine intervention, that it was destiny urging me in his direction.'

'That's feasible.' Paul nodded at Sally.

'Feasible?' I stared at them incredulously. 'Have you gone out of your mind? This is Rick we're talking about, remember? The man who always gets what he wants. Hang on a minute.' A paranoid thought flooded into my head for a split second. 'You didn't set this up deliberately, did you?'

'Now let's not start getting hysterical here,' Paul

reasoned. 'This could be a perfect opportunity for you to try and iron out some of those relationship issues you have.'

'What relationship issues?' Bloody cheek. So this is what happens when you spill all your darkest secrets to your gay friends in a moment of margarita madness. They take notes and test you later.

'That's like asking Robert Mugabe "what petrol crisis",' Paul clucked.

Sally stretched his feet out, pushing them deep into the sheepskin rug. I bet that's seen some action. 'So what did you say to him?'

'I said no, of course! The thought of living with another man?' I remembered my present company and excluded them from my decree. 'And we're talking straight men here, OK? There's a big difference.' They nodded their instant agreement. 'If you can think of a single good reason why I might want to do something so stupid, I'd really like to hear it.'

'Sex?' Sally suggested.

'Oh, for Christ's sake! Can't you men think about anything else?'

The protracted pause spoke for itself.

'How about the fact that your flat is going to be uninhabitable from tomorrow?' Paul said lightly. 'Just a small detail you might want to consider.'

'So?' I shrugged. 'I can stay here with you.'

'On the sofa?'

'Sure.' I sank into the deep leather possessively. 'I don't mind.'

'For six weeks?' Paul didn't even attempt to keep the horror from his voice.

'Ten, actually,' Sally said. 'At least.'

'*Ten?*' This couldn't be happening. 'Why is it that every time we speak it's gone up by a month? Am I the only one who can count around here?'

'Well, you know what builders are like,' Paul said sagely. 'Pathological liars, all of them. You'll probably be lucky to get back in before the summer.'

'But I thought you said I could stay here for as long as it took!'

'I know.' Paul sighed tetchily. 'But that was when I was feeling really guilty about it. Anyway, we didn't expect you to actually take us up on it, did we, Sal?' Sally raised one eyebrow but chose to stay out of it, putting his hands up in mute defence.

'What?' My bubble of denial dispersed with a tiny pop.

'Oh, do try to keep up, Helen.' Paul rose to attend to the dinner. 'You know very well that houseguests are like fish.' He disappeared into the kitchen, shouting over his shoulder. 'They go off in two days.' I turned my indignance on Sally.

'Thanks.' I raised my glass to him sarcastically. 'Thanks a bloody bunch, Brutus. And now what am I supposed to do?'

'Easy.' He winked slyly. 'Move in with your lover, baby.'

'RICK?' HE TOOK AGES to answer the telephone.

'Hell?' He coughed and spluttered for a moment, covering the mouthpiece ineffectually while he had a good old hack. I heard some fumbling and something crash from the bedside table. 'Jesus, Hell! It's four o'clock in the morning!'

'If I'm going to move in with you,' I barked at him, 'we need to set some ground rules now.'

'You what?'

'This is a temporary arrangement so I don't want you getting any funny ideas about it, OK? I'm used to my independence,' I asserted, 'so I will continue to do my own thing while we're under the same roof and I don't expect you to be asking me where I'm going, what I'm doing, and who I'm with. Is that clear?'

'Urgh,' he groaned. 'Can't we talk about this in the morning?'

'No, we can't,' I said, my insides churning. 'And before you start congratulating yourself on winning me over, I should let you know that this was not my idea.'

'I know,' he said patiently. 'It was mine, remember?'

'Whatever,' I said. 'And I don't want you making a big fuss about it either. It's just me coming to stay at your house for a while until the builders have done what they need to do, then I'll be moving straight back home. OK?'

'Sure.' I heard him strike a match, his words now muffled by the cigar he'd stuck in his mouth.

'And don't expect me to be in a good mood all the time either.'

'Fair enough.'

'Sometimes I like to be on my own.'

'OK.'

'And I hate all forms of sport on the telly, with the exception of Wimbledon.'

'Right.'

I ran out of things to say and sat there, nerves racing.

'Is that it?'

'Yes,' I conceded.

'Thank fuck for that. Maybe I can get some sleep now. When are you planning on coming over?'

'Erm.' I looked out of the taxi window as we rounded Rick's corner. 'That could be sooner than you think.'

WHEN I FINALLY woke up, the low winter sun was streaming through the windows, casting blinding white slats across the bed. Finding myself deliciously alone, I stretched out lazily, feeling the cool of the empty cotton sheets, moving away from the warm patch I had slept in. I pulled up an extra pillow, realizing with some surprise that I actually felt pretty relaxed, and gazed towards the bedroom windows, a typical pair of floor-to-ceiling Georgian affairs that looked out across the narrow street to a smart row of townhouses on the other side, all painted in the same chalk finish charcoal hue, just a shade away from black. Rick's bedroom was noisier than mine, his street a popular cut-through for those locals who knew their way around the back end of Victoria. Black cabs raced along the one-way street every couple of minutes, their distinctive diesel engines droning – a constant reminder that the outside world stopped for no man.

'Hey.' Rick spoke softly, appearing in the doorway with a tray. On it was a pot of fresh coffee as well as cups and napkins, a plate of monstrously calorific goodies from the local patisserie and the Sunday newspapers. 'I thought you'd never wake up.' He put the tray down on the bed.

'What's all this?' I smiled. 'I thought we agreed no fuss.'

'Who said any of this is for you?' He poured himself a coffee and stuck a Danish in his mouth. 'You can go and get your own.'

'Very funny,' I said, taking the cup from his hand. 'Sorry about last night.'

'Don't be,' he said. 'We're gonna have a nice lazy Sunday, just you an' me.'

It was music to my ears, although I couldn't help but feel a nagging sensation that I had forgotten something. I mentally ran through the luggage I had brought with me. Clothes: check. Toothbrush: check. Now what was the other thing?

'Shit!' I flung the covers aside. 'What time is it?'

Rick just managed to move the tray out of the way before my flying pillow knocked it off the bed. 'Dunno,' he offered. 'Half twelve? One? Something like that?'

'Oh my God!' I rushed to the bathroom. 'I'm supposed to be at Julia and David's! How could I have forgotten?' I rushed back out of the bathroom, realizing that I hadn't actually unpacked anything. 'Buggeration!'

'Can I help?' Rick tried to look useful.

'No!' I shouted, instantly changing my mind. 'Yes! Bags! I need to find something to wear. And a toothbrush. I need a toothbrush!'

'There's some new ones under the sink,' Rick said. Well, of course there are. I put the bloody things there myself. Stop panicking, woman. You're late and that's all there is to it.

'Why don't you give her a ring? I'm sure she won't mind.'

'Mind? Of course she'll mind! The roast beef is probably already tough as an old boot.'

'Sorry,' Rick muttered, heading for the door.

'Shit, shit, shit.' I reached for the phone and called Julia. 'Hello?'

'Helen?' David sounded a little frazzled. 'Where are you? Everybody's here and Julia's desperate to make the announcement.'

'I'm so sorry!' I wailed. 'I've overslept horribly! It's going to be an hour before I can get to you. Tell her to go ahead without me.'

'Are you kidding?' He hushed his voice. 'She's got this whole thing planned right down to the last detail. If you don't get here in—'

'Helen?' Julia's voice came on the line. 'Why aren't you here?'

'I—' suddenly the excuse of oversleeping just didn't cut it. 'I had an unavoidable emergency.' I widened my eyes at Rick in self-defence.

'What kind of emergency?' she asked suspiciously.

'Never mind,' I said. 'Just hold on. I'm on my way.'

Rick loitered in the doorway like a fart in a trance. 'Well, don't just stand there!' I ran back to the bathroom. 'Go and get the bloody car!' There was no way I was going to make it on public transport before sundown. I'd just have to think of a plausible reason on the way as to why Rick was with me. Oh, God. When did everything get so complicated? Once, just once in my life, I'd like to wake up and have a normal, uneventful day. I threw on a pale blue velour tracksuit with a white T-shirt in the hope that it would somehow transform my bed-head appearance to one of casual insouciance. I might have gotten away with it had it not been crushed to buggery in the suitcase.

If there is one command that most men will jump to without a murmur of complaint, it's 'step on it'. The dashboard of the Bentley lit up like a flight deck, flashing warnings about traction control and oncoming speed cameras, the sat nav system whining in confusion, unable to keep up with Rick's hurtling pace.

'Go right!' I shouted. 'It's quicker!'

'Where?'

'Here!' I yelled as he shot past the junction.

'Oh, for fuck's sake.' He stood on the brake, bringing the car to a screeching halt before shoving it in reverse.

'Then straight over at the lights and across the common.'

I went back to the vanity mirror in the back of the sun visor, trying hopelessly to shove my make-up on while Rick leaned into the corners. Abandoning the kohl pencil after nearly gouging my eye out, I attempted a lick of mascara instead. Bad move. Stabbing the wand on my cheek, by the time I had finished cleaning up the mess with a half-disintegrated tissue from the bottom of my handbag, I looked like I'd been punched in the face. Sod it. That would just have to do.

All praise to Rick, a journey that should have taken the best part of an hour turned into a forty-minute mad dash, the car speeding in through their gates and coming to a skidding halt, taking half the gravel drive with it.

'How do I look?' I turned to him, smoothing my hair with my hands.

'Er . . .' He tilted his head unsurely then issued the only right answer. 'Great,' he said. 'Although you might want to rethink the black stuff on your neck.'

'Helen!' David answered the door. 'Julia's been wearing holes in the carpet waiting for you.'

'You remember Rick.' I kissed David on the cheeks.

'Sure.' David extended his hand warmly and flashed me an inquisitive smile.

'You'd better hurry up and come in.' David stood aside. 'The peasants are revolting.' Judging by the volume of the chatter coming from the sitting room, I guessed that one aperitif had turned into three while they waited for the late arrival. The moment Rick and I walked in, all eyes turned to us, the conversation grinding to an awkward halt.

'Rick!' Leoni bounded to his side, spilling her wine. 'What a fantastic surprise! I haven't seen you for ages!' She linked her arm through his.

'Hello darlin'! What's all this in aid of then?' Rick, as always, was hugely flattered by Leoni's simpering attentions.

'Top secret.' Leoni wrinkled her nose. 'The suspense is killing me. Whatever it is, we're all desperate to hear the big announcement. Julia's been unusually coy this morning and refused to say a word until Helen got here.'

'Really? What kind of announcement?'

'Dunno,' Leoni shrugged. 'But it's bound to be a corker. David's pulled out a couple of bottles of Cristal from the cellar.'

'Sounds very intriguing.' Rick's brain started working overtime, putting two and two together. 'I wondered why Helen brought me along. She put on one hell of an act this morning to get me here.'

'Well, you won't have to wonder for much longer.' She batted her eyelids at him shamelessly.

I briefly did the rounds. A quick squeeze of Marcus's love handles, hello kisses for Sara and Dudley. Sara nudged me in the ribs and nodded in Rick's direction.

'Sunday afternoon with the boss?' She smiled.

'Something like that.' I looked over at Leoni, flirting outrageously with Rick, whispering sweet nothings in his ear, giggling coquettishly.

'Right!' David clapped his hands together. 'Julia will be down in a second, but before we have lunch, we'd like to share some very special news with you, so if you could all make sure you've got something in your glass—'

'Brilliant!' yelled Leoni, draining hers and reaching for the bottle on the mantelpiece. 'This is all so exciting, I just can't tell you,' she simpered at Rick.

'Blimey,' he whispered to her. 'The last thing I had expected was a big song and dance about it. Must have changed her mind. I had no idea everyone would go to so much trouble.'

'You already know?' Leoni frowned at him.

'Course I do.' Rick leaned down and whispered in her ear as Leoni's face twisted into a picture of shock.

'No!' she gasped. 'I don't believe it!'

David returned to the room, Julia on his arm.

'Shhh.' Rick patted Leoni's hand. 'Not a word, OK?'

Leoni nodded obediently.

'A-hem!' David said sheepishly. 'If we could have your attention for a few moments.' The room quietened instantly. 'Firstly, thanks for coming this afternoon. And a particularly big thank you to Marcus for not bringing the kids.'

'You're welcome.' Marcus tipped his glass towards him. 'I see you managed to get the paint off the car.'

'I think that's what you call a respray, Marcus. Moving swiftly on, I'd also like to take this opportunity to thank Sara.'

'About bloody time!' Sara shouted.

'Sara, I don't know what Julia would have done without you by her side all these years. She's ground herself into the dust, building that business. Making you a partner was the best move she ever made.' Julia nodded her silent approval. 'And, as her husband – ' David glanced at Julia adoringly – 'I have to thank you from the bottom of my heart for freeing my wife up to spend more time with me.'

'No sweat,' Sara said in her typical northern manner. 'I've been cooking the books for the last six months anyway, so either way, you'll be paying for it.' An appreciative ripple of laughter passed around the room.

'That's not funny at all,' Dudley said with a deadpan expression, missing the joke entirely. 'I'd get your accountant to check up on those numbers if I were you.'

'Oh, shut up, Dud.' Sara elbowed him in the ribs.

'And Helen,' David continued, 'what can I say?' Leoni was beginning to strain at her leash, unable to contain her excitement, hopping from one foot to the other. 'Julia and I lost you for many years,' he remembered sadly. 'But if ever there were a time when a woman needed a sister, I guess this is it. The next big step in life.' David cleared his throat lightly and picked up his glass. 'So, without further ado, please prepare yourselves for the biggest news since Fergie sucked that toe.' He put his arm around Julia. Drum roll . . .

'Helen's shacked up with Rick!' Leoni blurted before she could stop herself.

You *what*?

'Leoni!' I covered my face with my hands. 'Oh, I don't bloody believe it.'

A wave of confusion passed over David's face, Julia's smile evaporating, her face falling into a bemused frown. All eyes fell upon Leoni.

'I'm sorry!' she shrieked, turning to Rick. 'You shouldn't have told me! Everyone knows that I can't keep a secret! It's all his fault!' She pointed at him.

'You what?' David said.

'Helen's moved into Rick's house! They've been at it like rabbits since Christmas!' Leoni's gesticulations slowed as the dumbfounded audience failed to break into spontaneous applause. Rick clocked the stupefied expressions around him, reached out and squeezed Leoni's arm.

'Er,' he said, pulling a face. 'I think there's been a bit of a misunderstanding.'

'You're telling me.' David looked as though he didn't know whether to laugh or cry.

'I'm guessing that wasn't the big news, was it?'

'It bloody is now!' Marcus guffawed. 'You dark horse, Helen!' I didn't know where to put myself. 'I thought you were looking a bit sparky!'

'Oh, bollocks,' Rick apologized. 'I've gone and put my foot in it, haven't I?'

'Is this true?' David seemed more than a little shocked.

'Well, I, er,' I mumbled. 'It's not what it looks like.' Dear God, the way things are going I might just as well have that printed on a T-shirt.

'David!' Julia pulled at his arm. 'Say something!'

Too late. He'd well and truly lost the moment, everyone now nudging and giving each other knowing looks.

'You randy old bugger!' Sara bellowed.

'Less of the old.' Rick smarted. 'I'll have you know I'm a year younger than Bruce Willis.'

Chapter Seven

GREAT EXPECTATIONS

'THAT WAS ONE freaky afternoon last Sunday.' Leoni pored over the menu. I had a feeling that she might need glasses, squinting at the small print, moving the menu back and forth trying to bring it into comfortable focus. 'Anyone want to go halves on the rack of lamb?'

'How can you even think about food at a time like this?' I still felt terrible about stealing Julia's thunder.

'Speak for yourself.' She helped herself to another piece of bread from the basket and piled it with butter. 'But, amazingly, thinking about food is generally what I do when sitting in our favourite restaurant at lunchtime.'

'I still can't believe it.' Sara shook her head. 'She's said she has absolutely no intention of coming anywhere near the office for at least a year. Julia – the woman who never takes a day off. Bet you my last 50p she'll be climbing the walls in a month.'

'Talking of which, where the bloody hell is she?' Leoni's high-maintenance stomach grumbled impatiently.

'She told us not to wait for her.' Still the perfect assistant despite her promotion, Sara knew Julia's precise whereabouts, twenty-four hours a day, and guarded her like a publican's rottweiler. If push came to shove, she'd probably take a bullet for her. 'She went for her first antenatal thingy this morning. Said if she's not here by two she won't be here at all.'

I felt an immediate, selfish pang of hurt that Julia hadn't told me or indeed asked me to go with her. I suppose I'd just assumed that she would include me somehow. Maybe this was a taste of things to come, finding myself carelessly cast aside, redundant and unwanted, usurped by a manipulative embryo.

'Bloody hell. That takes me back.' Leoni shuddered. 'Jabba the fat midwife standing in front of a roomful of gum-chewing chavs, trying to teach them the difference between a carrot and a chip. "This is a carrot. Eat carrots. This is a chip. Don't eat chips." Most of them looked like they should have been at school, and some had a couple of snot-nosed kids with skinhead haircuts

already. That was a real bloody eye-opener. I stayed about five minutes then walked out.'

'No danger of that for our Julia,' Sara said proudly. 'I sent her off to the Portland. If it's good enough for Posh, it's good enough for her.'

'Yeah,' Leoni grumbled. 'I'll bet she didn't have to strain till her gizzards fell out. Bloody Marcus, yelling at me to push, like that was going to help. I told him, what the fuck do you think I'm doing? I vaguely remember grabbing his nuts and him sinking to the delivery room floor. That shut him up. And you should have seen the state of my noo-nah.' She stretched her hands into a circle the size of a basketball. 'By the time they got Joshua out it looked like a herd of wildebeest had migrated through it.' I crossed my legs and winced. 'And that's just the beginning. After a couple of days laid up in bed, sitting on a rubber ring, they confiscate your Weetabix and expect you to take the little bastards home and bring them up for the next twenty years.'

'If you're lucky,' I said without thinking. 'Kids are sticking to the parental nest until they're well into their thirties these days, especially boys, claiming that they can't afford to move out because of house prices. I saw an old couple selling everything they owned on *Cash in the Attic* the other day to give their forty-year-old son a deposit for a flat.'

'I saw that!' Sara laughed. 'He was a right dozy twat,

wasn't he? Ugly as sin too. Bloody hell. Imagine what he looked like as a baby. The midwife probably threw a towel over his face and gave the mum a tranquillizer.'

'Over my cold, dead body,' Leoni scowled. 'The minute those kids are in college I'm selling up and moving to a one-bedroom house in Croatia.'

'You don't mean that.' I reached out and pinched her arm.

'I bloody well do.' She sighed wearily. 'And as the only person at this table to have been stupid enough to breed, I can reliably inform both of you that you have no idea what you're talking about. Think of the worst thing that can possibly happen to you ever in the history of the universe, double it, and you're not even sodding close.'

'Well – ' I thought we needed a leveller to counter Leoni's mournful sermon of doom and gloom – 'I think Julia's going to make a brilliant mother. It's what she's always wanted her whole life, and I have never seen her so happy.'

'Weird, you mean.' Sara raised an eyebrow. I thought it disloyal to respond. Leoni perked up, piqued by the ripple of tension that crossed the table-cloth. 'You can't tell me you haven't noticed?' Sara lowered her voice. 'If I didn't know better I'd say she's had her brain dry-cleaned in Vanish Oxymoron.'

'Did you notice how much weight she's whacked on?' Leoni took a huge bite of her bread and spoke with her mouth full. 'She wants to watch that. I distinctly remember her telling us to shoot her if she ever put on more than three pounds. Annie? Get my gun.'

'I don't think she ever factored in a pregnancy,' I said. 'So let's just hold that thought for a little while, shall we?'

'I still say she has no idea what she's letting herself in for.' Leoni chewed noisily. 'Believe me, we'd be doing her a favour. The minute that baby arrives, she's not going to know what's hit her. When's it due again?'

'June the sixth,' I said.

'So when did she get pregnant then?'

'Dunno,' I said. 'September I suppose.'

'Spooky,' said Sara. 'Maybe it was something in the sausage rolls.'

'Wrong kind of sausage,' Leoni smirked.

'Did somebody say they want to see my sausage?' Mario abandoned the exasperated couple trying to order their lunch from a nearby table and broke into one of his glass-shattering arias. 'Just one sa-laaaaaami! Give it to mee-eeeeeee!' He clutched at his chest. 'It make your husband's look like a pee-eeeeeeeeee!' He winked at Sara.

'Wrong, Mario. My husband's salami is a bloody pea, make no mistake about that.'

'Is it?' Leoni sat to attention.

'Well, maybe that's a bit harsh.' Sara relented. 'Let's upgrade him to a Chantenay carrot.'

'No!' Mario cried, wringing his hands in operatic despair. 'Is tragedy for you! Why you marry husband with no salami?'

'Oh, don't ask,' Sara groaned. 'It seemed like a good idea at the time.'

'You decide what you want for lunch?'

'Excuse me.' The man from the couple at the next table tapped his menu. 'Weren't you supposed to be taking our order?'

'Hey!' Mario turned on him and scowled. 'You wanna sleep with the fishes, mister? I'm a-talking to my friends here, OK?' The other diner wisely bottled out of taking on Mario's famous Italian temper and buried his head back in his menu. We hurried the proceedings along and gave our orders, Leoni umming and ahhing until the last moment.

'I'll have the rack of lamb, please, Mario.'

'That's for two persons, daahling,' Mario said, pointing his pen at the note on the menu.

'Yep,' she said. 'Just drag it out here and I'll do my best with it.'

'*Bene!*'

Mario yelled our order through to the kitchen, then bared his teeth threateningly at the other table that had tried to demand his attention. How he's ended up with so many loyal regulars is something of a mystery. He gives new customers such a hard time that most of them never come back. You have to prove yourself by surviving a series of relentless trials over a two-year induction period – things like admiring his unfeasibly large salami (which hangs from the restaurant ceiling with the rest of the charcuterie), not screaming when he drops the fake cappuccino cup into your lap, laughing good-naturedly at the rubber snake in the salad bowl. His partner, Tommaso, has to break up the occasional fight, but apart from that, they've got a nice little business going and a head chef most Italian restaurateurs would willingly kill their mama for.

'Marcus's is shrinking.' Leoni topped up our wine.

'Is it?' Sara seemed rather alarmed.

'Yep. No doubt about it. It used to be about that big.' She gave us a hand-held demonstration of the width and girth department. 'And now it's like this.' She measured the minuscule distance with her fingers.

'You wicked woman!' Sara laughed. 'Marcus would be gutted if he knew the things you said about him.'

'Oh, he knows all right.' Leoni had a good old swig of wine. 'I've told him outright – hey granddad, your knob's getting smaller. Another few months and he won't be able to find it at all.'

The couple at the next table got up and left.

WHEN LUNCH BROKE up with no sign of Julia, I found myself wandering the streets, partially to aid my digestion along (seeing as Rick's fridge was free of gripe-inducing bifidus yogurts), but mainly to clear my head. It was one of those bright, crisp days when you really don't mind the cold at all, the air clear and dry, the bare trees stretching jagged sculptures against the blue sky. I've always found walking therapeutic, my own brand of low-impact pavement pounding no more taxing than a slow shuffle at window-shopping speed. It helps me to think things through, to make sense of the world when I'm unsure or unsettled. I took a leisurely stroll around the back streets of Knightsbridge, enjoying the bright winter sunshine, marvelling at the polar bear bravery of the smattering of red-nosed tourists choosing to perch at outside tables with their mid-afternoon coffees.

My autopilot had obviously engaged itself while I wasn't looking, because the next thing I knew, I found myself in Harrods, picking my way through the ghastly crowds, riding the escalator past the macabre flying statue of Dodi and Diana, wandering absent-mindedly into the baby department. In a matter of moments, it was as though I had crept through the back of the wardrobe and found myself in Newborn Narnia. Rows of tiny things on tiny hangers, powder blue and blossom pink. Cashmere sleepy suits. Bouquets fashioned from bibs and babygros. Pretty little displays of embroidered things called 'blankies' and 'burpies'. A gleaming row of prams, each costing about the same as a new car. I meandered through aisle after aisle, every one a revelation – designer collections bearing illustrious names like Christian Dior, tiny little polka-dot dresses swinging with prices that would feed a remote African village for a month or more. And suddenly I was crying, awash with grief for a thousand reasons I couldn't understand, filled with an over-whelming sense of emptiness.

'Are you all right, madam?' A young woman arrived at my side, touching my arm with concern.

'Yes.' I attempted a feeble smile. 'I'm so sorry. I don't know what came over me.'

'That's all right,' she said sympathetically. 'We get a lot of that in here. Can I bring you a glass of water?'

'No. No, thank you. I'll be fine.'

She was already leading me towards a chair – painted white, with soft pink cushions to match the utopian mood of the merchandise. 'Sit down,' she said, so I did. 'It can get awfully stuffy in here. We really ought to have more seating and a nice water cooler. I have suggested it once or twice,' she said pointedly, sniping at her superiors. 'Just take a couple of deep breaths.' She drew air in a protracted manner, dem-onstrating to me how it should be done. 'In . . . and out. There.'

'Thank you,' I said, starting to feel a little self-conscious.

'Any better?'

'Yes. Much.' I wished that she would stop staring at me and go away.

'I expect you had a funny turn,' she decided. 'It can get you like that sometimes, can't it?'

'Mmm,' I said, not wanting to commit either way.

'Is this your first?' She admired the paunch of undigested lunch beneath my sweater.

'No!' I leapt to my feet. 'I mean, I'm—'

'Of course it isn't.' The woman back-pedalled at lightning speed. 'It's just that we get a lot of older first-time mums in here.' She checked over her shoulder quickly then whispered confidentially. 'They're the only ones who can afford this stuff anyway.'

Pulling myself together in the ladies' room, I freshened up my puffy face with a slick of lipstick and ran a comb through my hair, taking my time amid the constant hum of the hand dryers and the regular clatter of the cubicle doors opening and closing as the orderly line of busting shoppers shuffled forwards, one after the other. I wondered how busy the men's room got and if they ever had to queue up to take a leak; or if they too had attendants who lined up old bottles of aftershave then demanded a hefty tip for a squirt. I couldn't imagine it somehow. If ever the gents did get a rush on, I expected it would be filled with grumpy boyfriends and husbands complaining about being dragged around the shops when they'd rather be home watching the football. Philistines. It's a good job so many women are dedicated to the art of extreme shopping. Were they to jack it in and find a less ruinous way to fill their free time, I reckon the British economy would go swirling down the nearest pan in a matter of hours. And seeing as it's mainly men who run this country anyway, they should be bloody grateful and throw in a few more bank holidays so we can spend even more time fighting at the tills. Perhaps I should drop the prime minister a note.

The stony-faced lavatory attendant unnecessarily wiped the sink a couple of inches away from me, accidentally on purpose nudging the tip dish in my direction. I noticed that she had picked out all the silver coinage, leaving only the pounds, clearly announcing that anyone thinking they could get away with spending a penny these days should steer well clear or feel the wrath of her mop. In a moment of loo etiquette rebellion, I sifted through my purse and deliberately dropped a big handful of copper shrapnel into the dish.

'RICK?' I CALLED OUT the moment I walked in through the door, still feeling like an infiltrator in his bachelor pad. To creep in silently would, I reasoned, be tantamount to espionage. 'Helloooooooo?'

There was no answer, despite the music seeping

down the stairs. Instead of the predictable mix of the Rolling Stones and other decrepit rock geriatrics, I felt my hips picking up the kind of Latin grooves I was used to hearing from Sally's place while he worked through the afternoon. Nice, I thought approvingly. Maybe Rick's decided to broaden his horizons and learn a little salsa.

I nipped to the kitchen and put my bags down, quickly hiding one in the cupboard with his unused saucepans. In it were the spontaneous presents I'd picked out for him after my mini in-store breakdown. To my surprise, the act of going into the trendy men's department and browsing the displays to buy something for My Boyfriend had been a major cheerer-upper. The sales assistant who scuttled to my side had been nothing short of a marvel and, with his expert guidance, I had managed to liberate not one but two totally fabulous shirts. Whether they'd look as good on Rick as they had in the semi-pornographic posters was yet to be seen, but either way, they'd make a nice change from his usual. Like most men, Rick is a creature of habit, sartorially speaking. Once he finds something he likes, he sticks to it like glue and orders it in every colour, as though that excuses him from ever having to shop creatively again. Trying something new is anathema to him, so he has developed a sort of permanent mufti-day uniform.

I heard footsteps on the stairs.

'Hell?' Suddenly, Rick was standing in the doorway of the kitchen, his face ruddy. Before I could say a word, a young woman appeared from his shadow and looked me up and down disdainfully. That she was half my age, and probably half my weight, could not have been more obvious. Beneath a minuscule slip of a top, her youthful breasts surged audaciously towards the ceiling, possibly assisted by a bag or two of silicone. It's hard to tell these days. Her skirt, which may actually have been a belt, didn't even attempt to cover her hot cross buns and sat precariously above a pair of lean, honey-coloured legs perched on vertiginous red patent heels. The whole scene moved to slow motion. I felt my insides turn to water.

'Oh,' was all I could say, silenced by the swaying shock. Oh. Oh. Oh.

I felt myself flush and, in that hideous moment, pictured a pink neon sign flashing over my head like a prize, lumbering chump. How could I have been so utterly stupid? Violent palpitations heaved beneath my chest, grasping at my lungs. I knew right from the very start that this was just a whole heap of trouble waiting to happen, and now, like a typical lily-livered chicken-shit male, Rick's chosen method for letting me know I was chucked was to unveil my adolescent replacement before I could unpack my Harrods black forest gateau. I yearned for the ground to open up and swallow me whole, but it just sat there coldly, shining its unforgiving polished surface beneath my feet, refusing to budge.

So this was it. Yet again. Out of a clear blue sky.

Well. You bloody, bloody bastard. Just you wait. Just you wait until I've decided what I'm going to do about this. Yes. It could be a long time, mister, but I swear, the moment I crawl out from under this rock and make a decision will be the moment you'll wish you had never been born.

I stood there like a fart in a trance, trying to get a grip on the surging waves of humiliation turning my stomach over and over. Knives. Yes. The knife block was right behind me. I could dip my hands behind my shoulders, bring them back fully loaded in one seamless manga movement and fling a matching pair of Sabatier carvers right between their eyes. I'd stand over them and watch them squirm, begging me to stop while I smiled down upon them malevolently, reaching for the corkscrew and a turkey baster as the blood spurted from their heads. Not even Quentin Tarantino could imagine the atrocities I would inflict. A huge rush of adrenaline flooded my veins. No. Not yet. Stay calm. Be cool. Be real cool. Keep your powder dry, then, ka-boom.

But no matter how I struggled, I couldn't think of a single thing to say.

'Hell?' Rick repeated.

'Yes,' I managed sourly. 'Although I'm surprised

you bothered to remember my name.' I couldn't bring myself to look at the creature standing beside him, oozing her outrageous confidence, flicking her ridiculously shiny waist-length black hair.

'Look,' he mumbled. 'I know this is going to be a bit of a surprise.'

The knives began calling to me in little voices. Kill him . . . go on . . . stab him in the grillocks.

'No, not really.' I picked up my bags, determined not to show a flicker of emotion, and wondered just how much of my ceiling had been pulled down by now. However big a mess awaited me, it couldn't be worse than the one standing in front of me right now. All I could think about was getting home and hiding in the broom cupboard where I could curl into a ball and cringe at my recurring stupidity. Mustering all my courage, I looked him straight in the eye.

'Surprise? Why should I be even mildly surprised when I've always known that you're a vain, selfish, lying, conniving snake in the grass.'

To my deep satisfaction, he looked genuinely shocked.

'Now, wait a minute.' He half-raised his hand as if to defend himself from my vitriol.

'No, Rick. I don't think I will.' I pulled my coat around myself and tried to look elegantly unconcerned, although my heart was pounding so hard I thought it would burst out of my chest like Alien. 'And as for you – ' I did up my buttons without giving him a second glance – 'I hope you die a slow and painful death, preferably from the syphilis you just contracted from her.' Not bad. Not bad at all. The varnished stick insect twitched at his side.

'Hey!' So the girl thing could speak. 'Who you think you are?'

Oh, foreign are we? Some kind of Latvian hooker, I suppose? Although she sounded more South American if I were to be mature about it, with a certain distinctive twang not a million miles away from Sally's accentual remnants. I chose not to acknowledge her at all and started heading for the door, willing my tremulous legs not to waver and let the side down.

'Done you let her speak like zat!' She thumped Rick angrily. 'You fire her! You fire her now!'

'Er, well.' Rick floundered.

'What?' I slowed and turned a spontaneous evil death stare on her, and in that moment the strangest of sensations came upon me. It was as though the very essence of Leoni's spirit somehow infiltrated and possessed my body. I felt her own personal brand of fury raising my hackles, deliciously prickling my skin. Right. That's it, lady. This is going to get ugly. And don't say I didn't warn you.

'*Fire* me?' I reached calmly into my carrier bag.

'Hell!' Rick paled. 'Don't!'

Chapter Eight

THE C-WORD

CRINGING IN THE CHAIR, bleeding all over Leoni's kitchen table, the whole, hideous chain of events went round and round in my head, playing itself over in slow motion.

'I couldn't stop myself. It was as though every injustice I had ever suffered in my whole, miserable life gathered momentum and made me smash that cake into her face.' Leoni made appropriate clucking noises, her sympathy aided by the half litre of cheap Chianti we'd seen off in the hour since she had managed to staple the children to their mattresses and banish Marcus to the sitting room with a begrudging sandwich for his supper. 'Why I didn't shove it in Rick's is anyone's guess.' I hid my shameful face in my thands. 'I suppose at that moment I hated her just that little bit more.'

'Yeah, well.' Leoni nodded, ignoring the dull, thumping noises coming from the twins' room directly above us. 'With tits like that, you can't say she didn't have it coming to her.'

'Why, oh why, oh why?' My head slumped to the table.

'Dunno,' said Leoni. 'Female spontaneity is one of life's great mysteries. Shall we move on to the hard stuff?' She was already on her way to the cupboard. 'Come on,' she said, shaking Marcus's prized stash of XO at me. 'Let's get slaughtered! I'll ring Mrs Gallagher round the corner and tell her I've got smallpox and can't get the kids to school in the morning. She'll give them a lift in. Always does. Thinks I'm the Antichrist anyway.' She poured a couple of big snifters. 'Her kid's a weird little fucker. Only eats white food, wears tin foil on his head to protect himself from microwaves and talks like a robot. You know, I asked him what he wants to be when he grows up. Guess what he said?'

'Dunno.' I squinted against the rise of alcohol from the brandy at my lips. 'Like I care anyway.'

'Oh, go on! Have a guess!'

I sighed accommodatingly. 'OK. A train driver? Drug baron? Astro-physicist? Whatever.'

'Nope!' She sat back and took a self-congratulatory swig. 'A roundabout.'

'You what?'

'Yep. The kid wants to be a roundabout when he grows up. What a freak, eh?'

'That's pretty weird,' I conceded.

'Yeah, well it just goes to show you. You never know what your kids are going to turn out like, and there's nothing you can do about it anyway. They're made like that. Josh and William came out a pair of little shits, and Millie was born to suffer them just like I have to. It's life's way of preparing her for having a husband.' I pretended not to have noticed the general wreckage on the way in, thinking it best not to mention the flowerbeds at the front of the house chewed up by BMX wheelies or the Spiderman stickers pasted all over the bay windows. I wouldn't like to hazard a guess at what had caused the hair-curling stains on the wallpaper up the stairs.

'They're a handful.' I smiled at her. 'But you're a fabulous mum and you've got great kids. They're a credit to you,' I added, trying to sound convincing.

'Thanks.' Leoni blushed with inner pride. 'You know, I never thought I'd hear myself saying this, but Josh is really getting into science. He's always hated it at school, but suddenly –' she snapped her fingers – 'it's all just clicked into place.'

'Really? That's great!' I lifted my head and attempted to appear interested.

'I know!' So relieved that Josh was at last showing

an interest in something other than torturing small animals, Leoni couldn't help but display her delight. 'He's done every bit of his homework for the last month, conducting all sorts of complicated experiments in his room and meticulously noting down the results in his best writing. I'm really impressed.'

'Wow,' I said. 'So they have to do experiments at home these days, do they? It wasn't like that when I was at school.'

'No!' Leoni beamed. 'That's the great part! He's taken on all sorts of extra projects and spends hours tinkering away like a nutty professor. Asked for a chemistry set for Christmas and seems to have taken to it like a duck to water. Look!' She went to the kitchen drawer and took out a list. 'He ran out of some of the stuff that came in the original test tubes and asked me to get him refills.' I looked at his very specific instructions and read them out loud.

'Potassium nitrate.' I made sure to look suitably impressed, trying to conjure a scrap of knowledge from my last science lesson twenty hundred years ago. 'I can't remember what that is. Sulphur. Oh yes. That's the stinky yellow powder isn't it?' Leoni smiled proudly as I admired the list. 'Are you sure none of this stuff's dangerous?'

'Of course not!' I raised an eyebrow of suspicion while she topped up her glass. 'It's a bloody miracle is what it is. And William is quite the budding artist these days. He's started working in charcoal.' She nodded proudly towards a couple of unintelligible, disturbed scrawls pinned to the fridge. 'Getting through boxes of the stuff.' Suddenly remembering herself, Leoni curbed her enthusiasm. 'Sorry.' She slapped her cheek gently. 'I don't know what came over me. There's nothing more boring than other people's children, is there? So, how many has Rick got again?'

'Five,' I said, followed by the standard, 'but not necessarily by his two ex-wives and most of them live abroad.'

'Rock'n'roll. That's a bloody lot of sprogs to have spawned.' Leoni grimaced. 'How old are they?'

'The youngest is sixteen. He doesn't see that one. The mother took out a restraining order years ago and changed their names apparently. The eldest two, Tom and Isabel, are from his first wife, must be in their late twenties I guess. They're all in Australia, happily living their own lives. Then there's the two in between, although I think there's still a question mark over the paternity of the one he had by the Italian waitress.' I could see from Leoni's rapidly glazing expression that I was losing my audience. 'It's all a bit complicated. Anyway, Lola's his daughter from his second wife, the Brazil Nut, as he calls her. She divorced Rick when he refused to move to Rio, and married her plastic surgeon instead.'

'Mr Buttocks?' A glimmer of recognition passed over Leoni's face.

'That's the one.'

'Crikey. My brain hurts just thinking about it.' Leoni dunked a chocolate HobNob in her brandy and nibbled at it daintily. I felt another wave of guilt wash over me and pushed the brandy away before I could slide uncontrollably into an alcohol-induced, full-blown panic attack.

'Do you think I should call him?'

'Definitely not,' Leoni declared. 'They're probably still stuck in Casualty anyway. Who'd have thought that a morello cherry could cause that much damage?'

'Don't.' My intestines twisted involuntarily. 'It doesn't bear thinking about.'

'Oh, come on!' Leoni stuffed the rest of the soused biscuit in her mouth and spoke as she munched. 'You have to admit it's pretty funny. Anyone would have thought she'd have had the sense to close her eyes when she saw it coming.'

'It must have really hurt.' I felt excruciatingly bad about the impromptu brawl that had broken out in Rick's kitchen. Reflecting on the red mist moment, it was almost like an out-of-body experience, as though someone else had been that banshee screaming towards Rick and his pert companion, armed with a patisserie mortar. 'The impact almost knocked her block off,' I groaned.

'I like the way you tried to shampoo it into her hair.'
A contagious smirk twitched at the corners of Leoni's
mouth while my face reddened with shame. 'I'll be
picturing that for months.' Had I known about the
girl's Raccoon extensions, I really might have thought
twice before massaging them with an entire Black
Forest gateau. There'd be no saving the ones that
didn't come out in my hands. By the time Rick managed to drag me off, she looked like Shaun of the
Dead.

'That screaming noise she made – ' I shuddered at
the recollection – 'my ears haven't stopped ringing
yet.'

Leoni sobered in a rare moment of lucidity. 'Do you
think she'll sue you for assault?'

'Now there's a thought.' My mood sank even lower.
'Although if she's anything like her father, she'll probably have me killed.' My handbag started ringing,
flipping my stomach.

'You gonna answer that?' Leoni stared at me levelly.
I shook my head at her and remained tight-lipped.
Before I could stop her, she snatched my bag from
the chair and answered it herself. 'Hello, handsome.'
Her eyes flashed at me. 'It's Leoni. Helen's just stuffing herself down the waste disposal unit.' Long pause.
'Uh-huh. Mmm. Yep. Yep. I see.' She got up from the
table and went to the fridge, pulling out a plate of
cheese. 'I know,' she sympathized into the receiver,

rolling her eyes at me as she hacked off a lump of Cheddar. 'Just hang on a minute.' She held the phone to her chest while she ate casually, winking at me with a finger at her lips, whispering, 'Let him sweat for a moment,' then put the phone back to her ear. 'You want to know what I think?' She didn't give Rick a chance to answer. 'I think it's you who should be apologizing, not Helen.' She squinted her eyes and gave me one of her highly dangerous don't-worry-just-leave-this-to-me looks. 'What would you think if you came over to Helen's place and found some gorgeous-looking guy wrapped around her? Oh. You have? Well, that's not the bloody point is it?' She tutted impatiently. 'Look. I'll get her to ring you back when she's a little less distressed. OK. Will do. Uh-huh. Bye.' She slung the phone back in my bag.

'What did he say?' I clutched on to the side of the table.

'Take a wild guess.'

WHOEVER COINED THE PHRASE 'It'll all seem better in the morning' had quite obviously never spent a night at Leoni's house. Her spare bedroom, which doubles as a municipal tip, resembles a small but perfectly formed slum. Running live with household wildlife, jack-booted spiders hunch menacingly in every crevice watching the hordes of woodlice merrily munching the corners of the unHoovered carpet while herds of escapee pets scurry around beyond the abandoned boxes of assorted junk shoehorned against the walls. I suppose none of this would matter so much were it not for the fact that the room wasn't much bigger than a biscuit tin. I had lain awake most of the night listening out for any sign of Gandalf the Neurotic Hamster, who had gone walkabout on Boxing Day. The twins had popped him in Granny Meatloaf's bed, no doubt hoping to scare her into an early inheritance, but Gandalf had promptly made a break for it, never to be seen again.

Waking up in the bosom of Leoni's dysfunctional family puts a whole new slant on the term 'good morning'. Marcus's alarm went off at stupid o'clock. There then followed a relentless stream of yelling and nagging before the children were hauled out of their pits to join the battlefield. By seven forty-five I was ready to ring the Samaritans and burrowed my pounding head beneath the pillows, plugging my ears with my fingers, hoping and praying that the noise would stop. It was like waking up onstage in the middle of the *Jeremy Kyle Show*, only much, much worse. Just at the point when I thought I would have no choice other than to sever my own head with the plastic gladiator sword sticking out of one of the boxes, the front door gave one loud, final slam, and everything went quiet. After the cacophony of the previous ninety minutes, the sudden silence was almost unsettling. I pressed myself against the wall and twitched the edge of the curtain, peering down into the street, where the children were piling happily into the back of a battered old people carrier, where another child sat motionless with his head clad in what appeared to be a Bacofoil balaclava.

'You can come out now.' Leoni shouldered my door open against the mess. 'They've gone.' I blinked at her emptily. 'Yeah,' she nodded, recognizing my dumbfounded expression. 'It's like this every morning. Coffee? Pain killers?'

'I think I'm in shock,' I mumbled as I peeled myself from the wall.

'Don't worry.' Leoni shuffled off towards the stairs. 'That's perfectly normal. It'll pass shortly, unless, of course, you decide to have children of your own.'

Upon reaching the bathroom, I made the mistake of looking in the mirror before I had made any effort to scrape my appearance together. Oh dear. I'd seen monitor lizards with better skin than that. Searching through the cabinet, there wasn't a single pot of anything that might have moisturized my way out of trouble, just a heap of half-squeezed Savlon tubes and a tin of sticking plasters mixed in with the dried-up toothpaste and ancient prescription clutter. I closed the cabinet door and bared my teeth at the grimy mirror before noticing that both the sink and the bar of soap were bone dry, thus proving Leoni's theory that her kids never wash unless she stands over them with a gun. After freshening up as best I could, I headed to the kitchen.

'Hi!' Leoni kicked the vacuum cleaner into action, pointing the upholstery attachment at the children's cereal bowls, instantly sucking their slushy contents into the whining Dyson. 'Won't be a minute!' The toast crusts went the same way, as did the orange juice spillage on the worktop and a couple of used teabags as she shouted, 'I've got this down to a fine art.' She gave the surfaces a cursory wipe with the tea towel and threw the bowls into the dishwasher. 'We're out of coffee,' she said, 'so I vote we go out for breakfast. I hate it here anyway.'

'I don't know.' I worried at my fuzzball hair. 'I think I should probably go home and have a rethink.' At that moment, my phone started to ring. Oh, for God's sake. Not now. At least give me half an hour to wake up and compose myself before ruining my day.

'Are you going to answer that?'

I handed Leoni my vibrating handbag without another word. It was too early to argue anyway.

'Helloooo?' She leaned coolly against the fridge. 'No, it's Leoni.' Her eyes rose to mine for a moment. 'Yes, she's stayed over at mine last night. Uh-huh. Mmm. Yep. Yep. Brilliant idea. What time? Uh-huh. Perfect. See you there. Bye!'

'Leoni!' I shuddered to think what she had agreed to. 'What have you gone and told him this time?'

'Who?' She dropped the phone back in my bag.

'Rick!' I sighed impatiently. 'You know what, Leoni? Sometimes I can really understand why Marcus gets exasperated with you.'

'Traitor.' She found a loose Coco Pop on the table and flicked it into her mouth. 'Anyway, that was Julia. She says you promised to go shopping with her today so we're meeting in Selfridges in T-minus sixty minutes and counting.'

JULIA HAS ALWAYS had the kind of figure that most women would kill for. At the grand old age of eighteen, she decided that she had no desire to grow any more (from a widthways point of view) and called an immediate halt to any further development of her perfectly trim waistline. One can only imagine the self-discipline this has demanded over the years, yet she has never faltered in her dedication. On those days when she allows herself a little indulgence for the sake of a special celebration or a premenstrual hormonal surge, she rigidly sets aside a two-day prison sentence afterwards to follow her unforgiving fruit-and-water regime in order to banish the extra poundage before it can land long enough to do any permanent damage. She describes anything with an elasticated waistband as an abomination, never goes more than a fortnight without visiting her celebrity hairdresser, and wouldn't dream of leaving the house with a chipped nail. High maintenance doesn't even come close.

As we entered the café on the second floor, Leoni and I barely recognized the shadowy figure hunched protectively over a decimated plate of pastries.

'Julia?' I tried not to look shocked.

'Hi!' Julia said, shoving the last of the cherry Danish into her face before wiping her lipstick-free mouth with her jam-stained napkin. 'Just grabbing a mid-morning snack to tide me over until lunchtime.' She rose from the table and gave me a kiss.

'Bloody hell.' Leoni looked her up and down. 'You having quads or something?' I administered a sharp elbow to her ribs.

'What?' Julia glanced down at her bulging jumper and rubbed her hands over her tummy protectively.

'Nothing.' I kissed her back. 'You look wonderful.'

'Mmm,' Julia purred. 'I know. David's just wild about my new cleavage, but I have to admit that my clothes seem a little snug.' She put her hands on her hips and jutted her chest out proudly.

'Good God!' Leoni reached out and grabbed a handful. 'They're bloody massive!'

'They're double F for Fabulous, aren't they?' Julia enthused. 'If they get much bigger I'll have to give up on the new bras every fortnight and call in a scaffold-ing company instead.'

'Yeah? Well you might as well enjoy them now.' Leoni pulled her shirt tightly across her own dimin-ished set of muffins. 'I used to have a right pair of gazongas before the kids were born, then they shriv-elled up overnight and left me with a pair of old man's slippers hanging from my ribs. They only look like this because I roll them up each morning and stuff them into a Wonderbra with a couple of chicken fillets.'

Julia let out a tinkling laugh and linked her arm through Leoni's. 'You're so hilarious! Anyone would think you were trying to put me off! Now come along and make yourself useful. I need a whole new ward-robe, and that includes . . .' – she took a deep, worship-ful breath before uttering the magic word that could transform even the most mundane of shopping trips into a pilgrimage – '. . . *shoes*.'

Like millions of women around the globe, Julia has long nurtured her illicit love affair with preposterously expensive footwear. Her appetite is insatiable, flitting from designer to designer, picking up whole collec-tions whether they had them in her size or not simply because she could not bear to live a single day without owning each and every one of them. It was like a sick-ness, a terrible addiction, and there was no way on earth that Julia would allow anything or anyone to come between her and her fix. Her shopping sprees have made her a legend in her own lunchtime and the favourite customer of every footwear salesman south of Eskimo territory. We made our way to the hallowed ground of the shoe department, listening to Leoni's appalling mental arithmetic while she feverishly tried to work out how much she could siphon off the housekeeping that month.

'Right,' Julia said, taking a seat and waving at the nearest assistant. Upon seeing her, the girl did a double take.

'Julia?' She slowed as she approached, fixing on her face a slightly uncomfortable smile. 'My goodness. I didn't recognize you. You look, erm, different somehow.'

'Yes, I know.' Julia flicked her hair over her shoulder. 'And I'm in the mood for new shoes.'

'Great!' The assistant shook off her wary countenance instantly. 'You just sit there and make yourself right at home – ' pound signs flashed across her eyes – 'I'll bring you all our new stock. You'll just die when you see them.' She scuttled away through an invisible door in the wall.

'Blimey.' Leoni plonked herself on the seat beside Julia. 'I usually have to start shouting the odds before I manage to get any service.'

'And when was the last time you bought a pair of

shoes in here?' Julia rummaged in her bag and pulled out a packet of Chewits.

'What's that got to do with it?'

'Julia could pay off the national debt with the wonga she's burned in this place.' I absently picked up a rather attractive dominatrix boot from the display and turned it over to check the price on the bottom before remembering with an enormous pang that Rick probably wouldn't be in the mood for dressing up for quite some time, if at all. 'I'm surprised they don't have a blue plaque on the wall with her name on it.'

'That's blatant discrimination against struggling housewives,' Leoni said.

'No it's not.' The tag on the boot said four hundred and fifty quid, so I put it back. 'It's a process of natural selection designed to weed out the commission runts.'

Julia slipped off her shoes and wiggled her toes in anticipation. 'Ooh, that's better.' She stretched her arches. 'I've been dying to get those off since the moment I put them on.' The assistant reappeared carrying a precarious pile of boxes, keenly followed by a junior with an even bigger stack.

'You're just going to love these!' she enthused, setting the boxes down on the floor and flipping off the lids. From beneath the reassuring rustle of expensive lining paper, she began to decant a heavenly array of shoes that any self-respecting woman would gladly do a pact with the devil for, handing them up for us to admire, each one with a migraine-inducing price tag. 'These ones are Dior. Look at the heel! Aren't they just divine?'

'Oh my God!' Leoni snatched the shoe and caressed it with her cheek. 'I love it! Please tell me they're thirty quid.'

'I don't think so,' the assistant said as pleasantly as she could. 'And Philippe put these aside for you, just in case you should pop in looking for them. They're sold out everywhere else.' She unveiled a delicious pair of red-soled Louboutins. 'The moment they appeared in Tatler, the phones went crazy! They have you written all over them, don't you think?'

'Holy moley!' Before Julia could respond, Leoni flung the Dior aside, her hands leaping to her face. 'This is it! The perfect shoe!' She pressed her knuckles to her teeth. 'All my life I've been waiting for this moment and now – ' she hushed her voice – 'we meet at last.'

Julia gave them the once-over then dropped them to the floor dismissively.

'How about these?' The assistant's smile was fading fast, her voice beginning to waver. She held up a perfectly formed summer slingback, set with shimmering jewels on the heel.

'I don't believe it!!' Leoni screamed. 'I saw those in *Vogue* yesterday! Have you got them in the electric pink?' She wrenched her shoes off, dropped to the seat and feverishly began to jam her feet in, her hands trembling over the delicate buckles.

Julia glanced at them quietly and frowned.

Whether or not the in-store air conditioning was on the blink I couldn't tell you, but at that moment, I am quite certain that I saw the tiniest bead of perspiration forming on the assistant's temple. She smiled up at us nervously from her squat position on the floor, seemingly unable to compute the complete lack of interest from their most passionate client. Leoni caught a hint of the chill that had settled over the sofa and stared at Julia, speechless.

'Hellooo?' she said. 'Julia? Have you slipped into a coma or something? Should we call you an ambulance?' Leoni shook her head at me, looking for some kind of support presumably. I was still thinking about the dominatrix boots, wondering if they would distract Rick long enough for him to forget that I'd attacked his daughter with a cake.

'Mmm.' Julia stifled a yawn and glanced around at the display shelves. 'It's just that these aren't really the kind of thing I'm looking for today.'

'What did you have in mind?' The assistant clutched gratefully at the straw she had been thrown. 'Was there a specific colour you wanted? A different style? Something with a more unusual heel, perhaps?'

'Oh, I don't know. Nothing in particular I suppose.' Julia wrinkled her nose. 'Take these back and see what else you can find me. I'm not fussed about style or colour, so long as they're . . . comfortable.'

The assistant's mouth dropped open, the Louboutin box falling from her hands. She stared at the junior in disbelief, but the girl just stood there in wide-eyed bemusement, totally unable to comprehend Julia's request as the shockwave of the c-word rippled around the stunned department.

my head. Cold and miserable, I had wandered the streets for a good hour after leaving Leoni and Julia still fighting it out in Selfridges among the kaftan rails, feeling suitably sorry for myself. Oh, do come on, Helen. It's really not that complicated. Just pull your socks up, get your act together, knock on his door and apologize. How bad could it be? Besides, you need a hot bath and a change of clothes pronto. Give it another couple of hours and you may well start drawing attention to yourself, not to mention flies. A woman passing me on the street gave me a funny look and I realized that I'd been muttering to myself.

By the time the cab dropped me off, I had whipped myself up into such a state that all I could feel was a sudden, overwhelming wave of fatigue. Having had quite enough trauma to deal with in the last twenty-four hours, I bottled out all together and went home. Quite what I expected to find when I got there I really don't know, but, frankly, it couldn't have been much worse. I didn't even need to go in to get the full, hideous picture – the view from the pavement painted the awful scene well enough. Noise and debris flew out from the open windows and balcony doors, send-ing intermittent clouds of masonry dust sailing across the street and over the garden square, leaving an un-neighbourly patina of grime over everything in its path. Tinny pop music blared from a radio, accom-panied by a tuneless, warbling whistle and the occasional glimpse of a builder's arse. A great big red plastic chute hung down from the balustrades, dangling dangerously from a series of worn ropes, and every now and then an enormous lump of my condemned flat came smashing down the pipe and joined the rest of the rubble heaped in the yellow skip below.

'Dear God,' I mumbled, staring up from the pavement. 'You really are a sucker for punishment.'

Sally answered my tentative knock wearing his usual enchanting smile and not much else, the soft white towel censoring his danger zone dangling precariously from one tantalizingly casual tuck at his waist. I wrenched my eyes back towards his face, although they ached to wander freely over every inch of his six-foot-two frame and linger shamelessly where they shouldn't. The delicious aroma of crushed citrus drifted towards me from his lush, shower-damp skin, leaving me feeling distinctly unfresh as I stood on the landing like a bag lady, desperately trying to quash the urge to wrestle him to the floor and demand he cover me in carpet burns.

'Hi,' I said with a pathetic attempt at a smile.

'Uh-oh.' He pulled me in through the door and kissed me on the cheek. 'We were wondering how long it would be before you turned up.'

'So you've heard.' My shoulders slumped a little lower. 'Why am I not surprised?'

'Yep.'

'I suppose he's been here looking for me.'

'Nope. He rang last night. Said you'd been on the missing persons list since four o'clock. He sounded worried.'

'Shit.' I shook my head. 'I can't believe what I did.'

'Hey.' He put his arm around me, bringing his nakedness so close that I started having thoughts I barely knew what to do with. I felt my temperature soar. 'Don't worry,' he drawled lazily. 'You worry, you make little lines here.' He traced my forehead gently with the tip of his finger, sending a shudder down my spine. 'Then you really have something to worry about.'

'Uh-huh.' I tried to clear the sudden tightness in my throat.

'You need to relax.' He pulled my coat away and slung it aside before moving behind me and bringing his broad, golden hands to my shoulders. Stroking my unwashed hair out the way, he began to squeeze out my tension. Softly at first, then firmer, harder, pressing his palms between my shoulder blades. Oh God. I closed my eyes and tried not to dribble.

'Mmm,' I attempted, although it came out more like a deep groan.

'Good?'

'Oooooh.' I felt my neck slacken, my head flopping forwards like a nodding dog.

'Is a little tight here?'

'Mmmmphh.' Bright, flashing colours danced in front of my eyes as my senses filled with his perfume, his strength, his soothing, mellifluous voice. 'Ohhh, yesssss, arrgh.' Everything went into slow motion, the room swimming around me as I felt my body sinking into the floor.

Then he stopped. Just like that. Leaving me hanging on a thread, panting softly and gagging for more. 'Better?'

I forced myself to snap out of it. 'Great. Thanks.'

'You shouldn't let yourself get so worked up.' I hardly heard a word, the blood still rushing around my head at a hundred miles an hour. He dovetailed his fingers and pressed them up towards the ceiling, snapping his knuckles, stretching his outrageous physique. 'It's bad for your mojo, baby.'

'No, Sal,' I corrected him. 'It's you who's bad for my mojo. I was going to ask you if I could abuse your hospitality and have a nice hot bath, but now, thanks to you, what I really need is an ice-cold shower. You should carry a health warning.' A huge, splintering crash rose through the floorboards from my flat below. I closed my eyes and winced. 'I foolishly thought I'd come home and regroup.' I shook my head at my own stupidity.

'Bad move, honey.' Sally made for the kitchen and I trailed behind him obediently. 'They only got started yesterday. All that bang bang banging – ' Sally shook his hands around his head – 'I can't be creative with noise like that. It makes me crazy every time I try to draw a line. Margarita time?' He bumped me on the hip. For some bizarre reason, I checked my watch, although between you and I, had it been eight-thirty in the morning I'd still have gone for the cocktail.

'Definitely,' I said. 'Then I have to get a grip. You may well need to give me a stern talking-to.'

'Just chill, honey, chill. Every man likes a woman with a little fire in her tank. You just hang out here for a while, then go get him and demand he makes mad, passionate love to you.'

'I wish I could be more like you.' I smiled. 'I think the world you live in must be a lovely place.'

'At least you know you made an impression.' Sally grinned mischievously as he filled the blender with ice and emptied the last of the tequila bottle over it. He tossed me a couple of limes. 'Squeeze those,' he said, casually stretching across me and flicking the PLAY tab on the kitchen iPod. 'Good for releasing tension. Pretend they're Rick's balls.'

In his inimitable style, Sally had once again lifted my mood, effortlessly injecting my weary bones with a healthy dose of his casual hedonism. We were soon shouting to be heard as the ice crashed around in the liquidizer and the hidden speakers blared a scantily clad rumba through the flat. The shock of my vandalized home quickly gave way as I squashed the life out of the limes while pulling stupid faces, smiling right back at Sally, soaking up his gorgeously relaxed demeanour. He flipped a couple of glasses off the drainer, dipped mine in the sugar and his in the salt, and high-poured a devilish slush puppy of his potent concoction into each.

'*Saluté*.' He winked. 'And if there's anything I can do to help, you have only to say the word.' Leaning against the sink as he lifted the glass to his lips, the careless tuck at his waist finally gave up the ghost and his towel fainted gracefully to the floor. Sally didn't flinch for a second as he stood there in all his glory, just as nature had intended, sipping his margarita with a wicked smile. I tried not to look. Really I did. But my, oh my, I'm only human.

THE TRICK WITH Sally's margaritas is to know your limit. One is never enough. Two is too many. Besides, I'd clean run out of excuses and, after giving myself a sharp telling-off in front of his bathroom mirror after snatching a shower and borrowing a vintage *Communards* T-shirt, it was time for me to take the bull by the horns. I rang Rick's doorbell, stood back and waited to be executed. After thirty agonizing seconds, the door opened.

'Hell-yen!' Helga flailed her mop. 'Where you bin?'

'Is Reek here?' I peered nervously past her, sniffing

the air for the distinctive aroma of Rick's trademark Cohiba.

'*Nyet.*' She shook her head crossly. 'He take the *bliad* shopping. She make beeg mess. Beeg mess all over. She blooding beech.'

'Do you know when they'll be back?' I followed her in and shut the door behind me, glad to have been given a short reprieve.

'Baaa-ck?' Helga frowned. 'Baaa-ck. *Nyet.*' She shrugged and gave up. '*Ya ne panimayu.*'

'What time?' I tapped my watch. 'Tiii-me, Helga.'

'There time!' She huffed and tutted, pointing at the wall. 'It clock! You stupid?'

The kitchen positively sparkled, all traces of yesterday's terrible mess magically eradicated. Although clinically insane, Helga is a charwoman to be reckoned with. Household grime gives her reason to live and she will happily spend several hours with her head jammed inside the oven, fishing the last flecks of charcoal out with a cotton bud. She's thrifty too, dismissing Cillit Bang as the work of the devil and preferring to stick to her tried-and-tested regime of meths and elbow grease, taking the occasional sneaky nip for herself.

'I'll make us a coffee, shall I?' The margarita was wearing off fast, the night in Leoni's critter-infested spare room catching up on my gritty eyes.

'*Da.*' Helga dumped her mop in the empty bucket

and slumped in one of the chairs. 'I no more work now,' she sighed. 'I blooding knacker. Reek make me put your things.'

'What?' I felt my skin prickle.

'He say, you get Hell-yen thing, you put them out.'

'*Out*?'

'*Da*, out!' She rolled her eyes as though dealing with an imbecile. 'I put on top. You find all on top.'

'On top,' I repeated, wondering what on earth she meant as I fed another coffee pod into the espresso machine. 'On top where exactly, Helga?'

'*Da*.' She nodded. 'Exact exact.'

'Just excuse me a minute, would you?'

Rushing up the stairs to Rick's bedroom, I found everything perfectly in order, the bed made, the carpet spotless, and not a single one of my belongings in sight. No bags, no shoes, no anything. His bathroom told the same story, nothing on the glass shelves save his shaving kit and cologne. Gone were my toothbrush, my tweezers vanished from the cabinet and, most worrying of all, my make-up bag was nowhere to be seen. It was as though I had never existed. I crept back down the stairs, heart pounding.

Helga had made herself useful, finishing the job that I had started and setting two steaming coffee mugs on the kitchen table. 'Is clean, *da*!' She beamed proudly.

'*Da*, Helg. Very clean.' I drifted in and sat next to

her, feeling horribly empty inside. Shit. This was bad. This was *really* bad. I'd realized he'd be cross with me, but to erase me just like that? I should have gone, right there and then, just picked myself up and got out of there, but I suddenly felt so tired, the wind knocked from my sails. It was over. Just as I had predicted. What a bummer.

'Hell-yen?' Helga shone a lamp in my face. 'You no happy?'

'Oh, I don't know,' I said miserably. 'I'm having a really, really horrible day. Everything was just fine forty-eight hours ago, and now – ' I sighed – 'now I don't know what to think. One moment he's all over me telling me I'm the best thing since sliced bread, and the next, well, let's just say it wasn't one of my finest moments. Did Rick tell you what happened?'

'Ah,' she looked perplexed, feigned a morsel of understanding and nodded sympathetically. 'Slice bread.'

'Right.' There was clearly no point in soldiering on. Some days, Helga's schminky-pinky English is almost passable, yet on others, trying to communicate with her is like trying to nail a jelly to the ceiling.

'You wait.' She patted my hand, got up and scurried to the corner of the kitchen where her ancient Tesco bag-for-life was hanging from a cupboard handle. From it she produced a foil bundle that she held up proudly and brought back to the table, humming a little Russian tune in a self-satisfied way. 'For you.' She started to unwrap it. 'Is no bread. Is better. You have. Me give you.' And from beneath the layers of crumpled foil, she loftily produced the mangled remnants of the cake she had scraped from the floor.

The pair of us started at the sound of the front door.

I leapt up from my seat and wished that my coffee cup would evaporate. By ejecting my belongings, Rick had already made it quite clear that I was no longer welcome. Yet somewhere in the back of my mind, I decided that I had done enough running away to last me a lifetime, and that this time it would be less psychologically damaging if I dusted off my pride and apologized before shaking his hand and walking away, head held high. Besides, I really needed my make-up bag back, as everything else I owned was locked in a storage unit in Hendon covered in five inches of dust. Straightening myself, I wished that I had pinched one of Paul's expensive linen shirts as my emergency outfit instead of a gaudy T-shirt featuring a has-been gay icon.

'Hell?' He did a double take as he saw me, his face registering perhaps a little more shock than he had intended. 'Where the fuck 'ave you been? I've been trying to get hold of you all day! Did you get my message?' A frisson of anxiety creased his rapidly reddening face. 'Please tell me that you got the message.'

Before I could say a word, Lola came stomping into the kitchen, talking over us in a whining barrage of sing-song Portuguese, on and on as she tempestuously ground her stilettos into the maple floor, oblivious to our gasps of disapproval. Rick looked at her forlornly as she cast her shopping bags to the ground then winced at the wrinkles they had left on her palms, yaddering on without taking a breath or bothering to look up. To my guilty relief, I noticed that new hair had been purchased and her mane restored to its former glory. Whatever damage had been done to her right eyeball was fashionably hidden behind an enormous pair of Chanel fly-man shades. She shook off her coat, slung it on the floor and kicked it aside.

Then she saw me, her intake of breath both sharp and immediate.

'You!' She wrenched the sunglasses from her face, revealing a bloodshot eye surrounded by a painful-looking purplish bloom. 'You look what you done to me!' She stamped her foot. 'You tell her!' She pushed Rick roughly on the arm.

'Now, now!' Rick attempted to put his arm around her, but she shoved him off and scowled at him petulantly. 'We talked about this, didn't we, Lola love?'

'Huh.' She bucked her head away, pouting at the

wall. 'You talk. I done want to hear. You make her go. I done like her.'

'Now listen,' he said, the slight firmness in his voice melting away before he could finish the sentence. 'Oh, Lola! Come on, love! Helen's all right really! And I'm sure she's come here to apologize and explain that it was all a big misunderstanding.' He flashed his eyes at me, his manner suddenly cooler. 'Isn't that right, Hell?'

'I no interested.' Lola remained unmoved, retaining her rigid stance, fluttering her false eyelashes at the ceiling.

'Look.' Rick tried to take her hand. She snatched it away. 'Helen's not going anywhere so you're just gonna have to make it up. She's my housekeeper and that's the way it's gonna stay. *Comprendo?*'

'Sure.' Lola turned on him, arms folded at her silicone chest. 'Me *compreendo*.' She mocked his rough cockney pronunciation of her mother tongue. 'Me *compreendo* that you selfish *bastardo*, like Mama call you. She selfish *bastarda* too. She say, I no want to live with her no more? Go live with the selfish *bastardo*. Now I here, you done care.' As her speech gathered momentum, so her body followed suit, her hips beating out every other word, her hands darting around and snapping fingers with each *bastardo* that left her pouting lips.

'Hell?' Rick's body language demanded my apology forthwith. Oh well. Here goes.

'Lola,' I said, wondering just how close I dare get to her temper. 'I can't begin to tell you how sorry I am about yesterday. It's just that I thought, well, erm – ' whatever you do, don't say prostitute – 'it's just that I thought you were someone else.'

'Hmph,' Lola tapped her Manolo in irritation.

'Excellent.' Rick clapped his hands together, no doubt hoping to bring the conversation to an immediate close. 'So that's all sorted then.'

'You see, I'm a little over-protective about your father,' I admitted shyly. 'I didn't realize quite how I felt until I saw him standing there with you.'

'Er, Hell?' Rick tried to interrupt me.

'It's all right, Rick.' I held up my hand in submission. 'I've done a lot of thinking since yesterday, and it's only right that I explain myself properly.'

'No.' He laughed uncomfortably. 'That's really not necessary.'

'You see, this was all still pretty new for me. He and I had only been seeing each other for—' Rick launched into a sudden, violent coughing fit, hacking away while his face turned puce. 'Rick?' I rushed to his side. 'Are you all right?'

'Get off heem!' Lola sprang in front of me. 'You make enough trouble already.'

'I'm OK.' Rick leaned an arm on Lola's shoulder while he recovered. 'Why don't I get Helga to take your shopping upstairs, love? Go on.' He tried to urge her out of the door. 'Try that lot on and come and show me what you got, eh?'

'OK.' Lola pouted at him then issued me with a withering stare before teetering off. Helga got up from the table and gathered up Lola's coat and bags, grumbling under her breath. Rick waited until the coast was clear.

'You and I need to talk.' He nodded his head towards his study.

'I know,' I said sadly.

Behind the closed door of the study, he leaned against the wall and covered his head with his hands, stifling an enormous roar of frustration. 'She's a fucking nightmare!' He let out a huge sigh, went to his desk and reached a fat one out of the humidor. 'I don't even know what the fuck she's doing here!' He struck a match and pulled hard on the cigar, filling the room with the rich, sweet aroma of Cuban tobacco. 'The Brazil Nut just laughed and told me to fuck off when I rang her to find out what's going on. Said that she's my problem now.'

'Rick?'

He fidgeted with his cigar and frowned at the carpet, his thoughts clearly elsewhere. 'What?'

'Helga already told me, so if you're worrying about how to break the news to me gently, you really don't need to—'

'Eh? What have I gone and done now?'

'My stuff.' I felt nauseous. 'She said that you got her to throw out all my stuff. But I kind of need it back. If that's OK.'

'What?' He wrenched the cigar from his mouth.

'Please.' I steeled myself and tried not to look gut-ted. 'It was great while it lasted, but I—'

'You didn't get my message, did you?' he interrupted.

'No,' I shrugged. 'Phone's dead and I'm presuming my charger is now in the bin with the rest of my things.'

'In the bin? Is that what she told you?' He stuck the cigar back in his mouth and chewed on it. 'If it ain't one thing, it's your bleedin' mother. Come here, you.' He opened an arm to me. 'Come on!' But I just stood there, looking at him suspiciously. 'Aw, Hell! Did you really think I'd do something like that?'

'Yes,' I snivelled. 'I went upstairs to your bedroom and everything was gone.'

'You daft woman.' He gave me a hug. 'How many times do I have to tell you? It's you an' me against the world, babe!'

'Really?'

'Yeah, really.'

I looked up into his rumply face then closed my eyes in preparation for the Hollywood kiss and make up. Just as his lips were about to make contact with mine, there was a rattle at the door handle. Rick sprang away from me as though I had just told him I had leprosy. I've never seen him move so fast. By the time Lola barged into the room, he was sitting at his desk, shuffling pieces of paper around, pretending to be engrossed while I stood there like a twit.

'You like?' Lola preened.

'Oh!' Rick tore himself away from the company report which, incidentally, he seemed to be reading upside down. 'Yeah! That's great, Lola, innit?'

'No.' She pursed her lips. 'It need new handbag. I done have colour to go with.'

'Ah. Right.' Rick's shoulders sank. 'Well, what say we go out and get you a bag to go with it tomorrow?'

'OK,' she said, her eyes wandering towards me. 'You can go.' She dismissed me. 'Go and do your work.'

'Pardon me?' I forced myself to smile politely.

Lola sashayed in and sat on the edge of Rick's desk, struck one of the extra-long matches and played with it as it burned down. 'Why she in here? I done like her,' she whined at him. 'You make her go.'

'Er, Hell.' Rick shifted uncomfortably. 'Would you mind?'

'What?'

He was out of his seat and heading towards me before I could utter another word, steering me out of the door, pulling it closed behind him.

'Listen, Hell.' He grimaced and scratched his head.

'I know this is gonna be a pain in the arse, babe – ' he hushed his voice – 'but Lola can be a bit difficult, if you know what I mean, so I've told her that—' Lola snatched the door open and glowered at me. 'Yeah,' Rick boomed, changing his stance instantly. 'So if you could get that sorted for me, Hell. That'd be great. That's it. You can go.'

I stared at him, totally perplexed. 'You what?'

'Brilliant.' Rick smiled nervously at Lola. 'If I need anything else, I'll ring for you.'

'I go upstairs and put other dress,' Lola announced, then flounced off. Rick leaned against the wall and closed his eyes.

'The message,' he said. 'It was all in the message. She doesn't know about us. It's strictly business, OK?'

'What?' I hissed at him. 'Well that's just bloody marvellous. First you sling all my stuff out, then you—'

'Nobody's slung anything anywhere. It's in . . .' He stalled for a moment. 'It's in your room.'

'My room?'

'Well, yeah.' Now he was starting to look really uncomfortable. 'How else was I going to explain it?'

'Which room?'

'Er . . .' He stared at the glowing end of his cigar. 'The top one.' My eyes narrowed.

'Which top one exactly?'

144

'The back one,' he mumbled.

'The *dungeon?*' I glared at him. 'You put me in the *dungeon?*'

There are five perfectly serviceable, gorgeously decorated bedrooms in Rick's house, each with their own bathroom, all of which are very generously proportioned. Then there's the dungeon. The sixth bedroom, clearly designated for the household slave, squirrelled away at the back of the top floor with a tiny en-suite shower cupboard which is good for nothing much except swinging a very small cat.

'What else was I supposed to do? It was hard enough trying to explain why your stuff was spread around the house.'

'I'll bet,' I said icily.

'I told her that you were really untidy and that I'd had to speak to you about it a few times before.'

'Great.' I threw my arms in the air in surrender. 'Now what?'

'Dunno, but I suggest we just play along and keep it all under wraps until she gets bored and leaves. I know what she's like. This whole thing will last five minutes then she'll be outta here.'

'So, you couldn't just say that I'm your girlfriend and make a proper introduction like a normal person?'

'Are you kidding me?' Rick's eyes widened. 'When I

say Lola's a bit difficult, that might be a major under-statement. She thinks the only people I should pay any attention to are her and her mother.'

'Attention or alimony?'

'Yeah, well, whatever.' He brushed my snipe aside. 'But when I dared to turn up in Rio with a girlfriend six years ago, she put rat poison in her *feijoada*. Bloody hell – ' he sucked his breath between his teeth – 'that was a night to remember. The poor cow spent three days in hospital. Needless to say, that was the first and last time I tried to introduce the concept of me with another woman. Trust me. This way, at least we have a reasonable chance of getting out alive.'

'I can't believe you've put me in the dungeon,' I muttered.

'I'm sorry,' he pleaded with me. 'I'll make it up to you, Hell. I promise.'

'Hey!' Lola shouted as she descended the stairs, having poured herself into a skin-tight silver lamé tube. 'I hungry,' she complained. 'When you make dinner?'

'Er,' Rick grimaced uncomfortably. 'Helen doesn't cook, love.'

'No cook?' She frowned at me incredulously. 'Of course she cook! She housekeeper!'

'Well, it's just that I don't usually ask her to—' Rick petered out, mortified.

'It's OK.' I nudged his arm briefly, seeing Lola

narcissistically distracted by her shining reflection in the hall mirror. 'I don't mind cooking. It's really no trouble.' Rick mouthed *sorry* at me through his pained expression, and I retreated dutifully to the kitchen.

Right, mister. You want me to cook? I'll cook. And don't say I didn't warn you. This is war.

Chapter Ten

PERFORMANCE ANXIETY

'THANKS FOR COMING.' Julia swept me into her sitting room, her voluminous new kaftan generously wafting behind her expanded beam. 'I know you've probably got a million other things to do . . .'

'Not really.'

'. . . but I can't keep talking to David about this stuff. I've come to the firm conclusion that it's strictly women's territory. He just glazes over and goes *mmm*, *mmm*, every few minutes like I'm some kind of idiot in possession of a fertilized egg.' She fluffed up the cushions on the biggest of the three sofas and lowered herself into position, reaching for the dish of salted nuts on the table. 'Whenever I ask his opinion about this he goes all defensive and says, "Whatever you want, darling," which is really, really annoying.' She threw a handful of honey-roasted cashews in her mouth.

'I can imagine.' I sat down beside her, arranging myself so as not to intrude on her extreme lounging.

'Oh, not there, Helen! Do you mind? I have to be able to stretch myself out properly. You know, make sure my pelvis isn't restricted in any way.' She moved in a slight but deliberate manner to make her point.

'Oh!' I got up immediately and moved to the next sofa. 'Sure. Sorry. I wasn't thinking.'

'That's better.' She took a couple of deep breaths. 'So I was thinking, the best thing for me to do is to have a little bit of everything. You know—'

'Uh-huh,' I said, not knowing at all.

'My consultant says one thing, my midwife says another, then there are all the books.' She waved at the piles of pregnancy-and-birth-related literature strewn around. 'And seeing as this might be my one and only chance to procreate, I want it to be the most amazing experience ever.'

'Naturally,' I agreed.

'Probably. But I haven't quite made up my mind about that either. It's a tricky one, isn't it?'

'What?'

'Whether or not to go the natural route, you know, trust my body to do its thing and let nature take over.'

'Oh.' I smiled and shook my head. 'That isn't what I meant. I meant that of course you'd want to have—'

'But then again, I don't want to be disappearing beneath a haze of drugs either. You know, some of those injections travel along the umbilical cord and affect the baby quite badly. They never tell you these things, the doctors. You have to do your homework and find out for yourself. Isn't that shocking?'

'Right,' I said. 'I expect you—'

'So I've started writing out my birth plan.' She reached to the table behind her, pulled down a big yellow boardroom pad and started flicking through page after page of notes. 'What to do in the weeks before the birth. How to prepare my body for the most amazing journey of its life – ' she flipped the page – 'dos and don'ts for the birthing mother.' She reached to the bowl in her lap for another handful of nuts. 'Because if I get it all worked out now, then nothing can go wrong. Think everything through properly, get Sara to do the research, and hey presto – we have an informed, reliable plan. It's the old scout motto *Be Prepared*, isn't it?' Her eyes flashed determinedly.

'Well, yes. I suppose it is.' Bloody hell. I don't think I'd ever seen a woman quite so manic.

'That way I'll have every base covered and there won't be any unexpected surprises.' She stretched to the coffee table, picked up the remote and flicked on the TV. 'Now have a look at this and tell me what you think.' The DVD burst into life. There on screen, a woman, roughly the size of a pilot whale, hung half in, half out of what looked like an enormous water butt, puffing and panting. I felt the blood drain from my face.

Way back, in the dark ages of the 1970s, some progressive-thinking teacher at my primary school decided it would be a really good idea to herd all the children into the school hall and show them a film of a woman giving birth. This gore-fest was to become the sum total of my sex education, without the word sex being mentioned at all of course, and with no one allowed to speak or ask any questions either before or after the event. So there we were, a little snot-nosed brigade sitting in neat rows of tiny wooden chairs while the teacher struggled to erect the ancient silver-screen sheet on a pair of metal poles. I remember having entered the hall, blissfully unaware of what was going to happen, then deducing for myself with great delight that we were about to be treated to some kind of Disney show, before sticking my thumb in my mouth and settling down for the main event that was to stay with me for the rest of my life. Without much in the way of preamble at all, the film quickly knuckled down to the nitty-gritty – a woman apparently being held down on a hospital table, yelling her lungs out as her nethers were ripped to shreds by an alien monster coming out of her noo-nah. Thank God it was in black and white. Needless to say, pandemonium broke out, the sound of screaming children running for the locked doors, the dull thuds as several of them fainted to the floor. I sat there wide-eyed, welded to my chair in terror. The girl sitting next to me, Madeleine Asher, never came back to school again. Anyway, that's about as far as my recollection goes, which isn't surprising considering I was only about six at the time. I sat on Julia's sofa, braced myself and stared at the television obediently, the sight of this groaning, delirious woman transporting me straight back to my terrified, thumb-sucking, six-year-old self.

'The water is very soothing, both for the mother and the baby,' Julia commented knowledgeably. The woman in the tub started swaying and moaning, closing her eyes while the water sloshed over the sides. 'I think it looks like the perfect way to give birth. Don't you? Sort of warm and comforting.'

'Mmm.' Unable to speak for the hand pressed firmly against my mouth, every bone in my body wanted to suggest that a general anaesthetic might be better.

'So I've concluded that I should probably go for a water birth.' A blood-curdling scream rose from the television set. Like the coward that I am, I diligently focused my offended eyes past the set, a couple of inches to the left, so that it would look like I was still watching when I was actually staring unblinkingly at the wallpaper. 'Although David's worried that the baby will drown, of course!' I tried to block out the blurred images in the corner of my eye and close my ears to the hideous, video-nasty soundtrack. 'Men have got some funny ideas about childbirth, haven't they?' Julia laughed, munching on yet another pound of nuts.

'Mmm.' Oh please, just turn it off before I pass out. The whale woman started hollering again and I accidentally caught a glimpse of the screen. It looked like that moment in *Jaws* when the kid on the lilo bought it, the sea running a murderous torrent of red. Instantly averting my gaze, I noticed Julia staring at the footage, completely transfixed. She seemed totally unaware that she was puffing and panting along, sucking her breath in short bursts, letting it out slowly as she flexed her legs on the sofa. Suddenly, there came the cry of a newborn baby.

'Wow!' Julia said. 'Did you see that?'

'Yes,' I lied. 'Amazing.'

'Isn't it?' She grabbed the remote control. 'A woman's natural ability to bring a child into this world is just incredible. There is no machine in the universe capable of doing what we do. Shall we put it on again?'

'No!' I stood up. 'I mean, no need! That was grrr-eat!'

'Wasn't it?' Julia stretched her pelvis in anticipation of her big, *Wildlife on One* moment. 'I thought you'd like it. I've got a few more that I want to show to you. You know – ' she started rummaging under the sofa –

'different approaches to birth. Squatting, kneeling on all-fours. The worst thing you can possibly do is lie on your back.' She started shuffling through the DVDs. 'They're really interesting.' Dear God, no.

'Fantastic,' I said, wringing my hands. 'And you've seen them all already, have you?'

'Oh yes. At least half a dozen times each. I've made notes about all of them to help me decide exactly what it is that I want. I thought we could run through them together, just to help me get this plan finalized.'

'There's no need for you to get them all out again just for my sake!' I tried to keep the hysteria from my voice.

'But I wanted your views.' She frowned at me. 'Otherwise how will I know I'm making the right choices?'

'Of course you are.' I managed to slip the remote from her hand and switched the evil tellybox off. 'And the last thing you want to do is to start inviting a load of opinions when yours is the only one that counts. It's your body, and your baby.'

'That's exactly what David said,' Julia marvelled. 'Isn't that incredible?'

'Incredible,' I agreed.

'Oh yes.' She went back to her notes. 'And I wanted to talk to you about the birth partner issue.'

'Birth partner?'

'Well, of course!' She laughed patiently. 'Everyone has to have a proper birth partner.'

'So that'll be David,' I ventured.

'No! He's the *father*,' she corrected me. 'That's different. Of course he'll be there. What I'm talking about is the person I choose to support me through my labour.'

'And – ' I tried to keep up – 'that's different, is it?'

'Oh yes,' she said, breezily finishing the last of the nuts and looking into the bottom of the bowl. 'It's traditional to have a woman in that role.'

'Really?' My face filled with heat. If I couldn't handle the sight of a spawning woman on the telly, then what possible hope would I have of being able to remain conscious when faced with the real thing?

'Well,' she said slightly uncomfortably, 'yes. Only, the thing is, er, and I don't want you to feel bad about this. The thing is, Helen – ' she rushed the words out – 'I wanted to have somebody who was experienced.'

'Oh . . .' I tried to hide my relief and sound disappointed. 'Yes. Of course you do.' Phew.

'So I've decided to hire a doula.'

'A what?'

'A doula! Surely you must know what that is?' I smiled in defeat and shrugged my ignorance, although why on earth I should have been in possession of that kind of information was quite beyond me. 'They act as companions for the birthing mother,' Julia explained eagerly. 'It's a sort of tribal tradition in some ancient cultures. They're spiritual rather than medical, you know, for the mother's emotional support.'

'I see.'

'It's a dying art,' she sighed sadly. 'And tracking one down round here is like trying to find a needle in a haystack. I was just about to give up hope when one of the nurses at the Portland put me on to a wizard of a woman. She's an absolute marvel, from what I've heard. How she managed to find a slot for me is a miracle! And I don't want you to worry. You'll still be there for a front seat at the birth,' she added. 'You're my sister and I wouldn't have it any other way.'

'Right!' My head began to fill with every plausible excuse I could think of. 'That's brilliant!' Run out of petrol. 'Can't wait.' Locked myself into the flat. 'It was really kind of you to think of me.' Got struck by lightning.

I turned to the window at the sound of the gravel crunching on the drive.

'It's David!' Thank God. Reinforcements. He got out of the car and mooched to the door looking like he barely had the energy to push it open.

'Hi, Helen.' His peck on my cheek was almost an afterthought.

'Darling!' Julia didn't bother to move her bulk from the sofa. He leaned down and kissed her.

'Rainforest Crunch, Chunky Monkey, two tubs of double cream and a box of custard tarts.'

'Did you remember the sausages?'

'In the other bag.' He held up the evidence. 'I'll get them on now. And here's something for you to be going on with in the meantime.' He pulled a grease-stained paper bag from the plastic carrier and handed it to her.

'Oh, goody!' She tore it open and fell on the out-sized Cornish pasty.

'Helen?' He nodded towards the kitchen. 'Want to give me a hand?'

'Sure!' I said.

'THANK GOD YOU'RE HERE.' David slumped down on one of the kitchen chairs, rubbing the bags under his eyes. 'She's like a woman possessed. I had to go out to the petrol station at three o'clock this morning to find her a Snickers ice-cream. The bloke on the night till window must think I'm some kind of lunatic. Last week it was Dime bars and Eccles cakes.'

'David, darling!' Julia called in from the sitting room. 'Can I have a glass of orange juice with a dash of milk, please?'

I pulled a face at David. '*Milk*?'

'I know,' he said, dragging himself up reluctantly and going to the fridge. The milk curdled the moment it hit the juice. 'And you don't want to know about the roadkill she's been eating for breakfast.' He delivered Julia's vile drink, came back to the kitchen and pulled the lid up on the Aga, then set a frying pan on the hotplate before reaching for a couple of onions and slicing them into thick rings. 'When she's not eating, she's either lying on the sofa snoring like an ox or watching horrific videos.'

'You don't say.' I raised an eyebrow at him.

'Oh God.' He put the knife down. 'Not you as well?'

'Afraid so.' I shuddered. 'I'll be having nightmares for months after this morning's special feature.'

'She wants me to deliver the baby and cut the cord.' He lowered his voice and grimaced. 'I'm supposed to get down the business end and deal with whatever it is that comes out of there.' The sausages hit the pan with a hiss. 'Whatever happened to the days when all the man had to do was pace around in the waiting room and wait for their cue to spark up a cigar?'

'You've had your chips there, mate.'

'It's like my wife has been kidnapped and replaced by a black hole. Everything revolves around her and gets sucked in and destroyed. I'm walking on eggshells here. She misunderstands everything I say, cries at the drop of a hat and is convinced that she's developed supernatural powers.'

'Oh, David.' I laughed softly and pulled at his jumper sleeve. 'It'll all be over before you know it.

She'll soon be back to her old self, and you'll have a beautiful baby to raise together, just like you always wanted.'

He stopped suddenly, rooted to the spot, his head drooping towards the floor.

'That's just it,' he said. 'I, oh.' He ran his hands through his hair. 'It doesn't matter.'

'What?' His stricken face fired an arrow straight into my heart. 'David? What on earth's the matter?'

He let out a weary sigh.

'Helen. I don't even know where to start.'

'Just take your time,' I said gently. 'And try.'

The clock on the wall ticked, each second clicking louder, slower. 'Whichever way I say this, it's going to come out badly.' I went silently to the door and pushed it softly closed. 'For years it seemed that it was the most important thing in the world, you know, to have a baby.' He looked at me urgently. 'We tried everything. No matter what the doctors said, we kept going. Kept trying. And yes – I went along with it. I went along with it because I thought that was what Julia wanted me to do.' He caught my hand, staring into my eyes as though desperately needing me to understand what he was saying. 'What else was I sup-posed to do? She was desperate. But all I ever wanted was for her to be happy, to get over it and learn to move on. I always knew it would never happen. It just wasn't meant to be. I didn't marry her because

I wanted to have children. I married her because I wanted her to be my wife. To have her for myself and for us to be together. Do you understand?'

'Yes,' I stammered, aware of the tightening grip on my hand. 'I think so.'

'We've been happy all these years, just the two of us. We can go wherever we want. Do whatever we please. For Christ's sake, we're hardly spring chickens any more, are we? And now everything's going to change, and I'm just not sure.' He stopped himself. Gathered himself for a moment. 'I'm just not sure that I ever wanted this. No matter what I said.' He let out a sigh of exasperation. 'It's easy to make the right noises and say the right thing when you know there's no chance. I never wanted children but it wasn't a big deal because I knew they weren't on the cards anyway.' Smoke started to rise from the frying pan but he seemed not to notice. I pulled my hand from his and reached over to give it a shake. 'And now I'm losing my wife. Every day I wake up and she's further away from me. Our life. This – ' he nodded at the kitchen – 'this charmed existence – it's over. It's not me she wants any more. It's this baby.' I didn't know what to say, so I remained quiet, wishing he would stop, hoping that he would give me one of those playful nudges and say he was just joking. 'She was the most beautiful woman I ever saw in my life,' he murmured. 'Tall. Elegant. *Slim.*'

'Oh, I see,' I said, allowing a little of my shock to

surface. 'So now she's pregnant and putting on a bit of weight—'

'A bit?' he whispered loudly. 'Have you seen the size of her?'

'Yes, but—'

'And it's not just that.' He looked over my shoulder, checking the door. 'You know very well that I'd love her even if she were the size of blimp, which she bloody well is.' He hesitated a moment, his face reddening just slightly. 'She wants me to do all kinds of things that I'm just not comfortable with.'

'Like what?'

'Well . . .' He hushed his voice even further, forcing me to strain my ears to hear him. 'Sex,' he mumbled.

'Sex?'

'Ssshhh!'

'What about it?' I whispered.

'I just can't!' He shivered involuntarily. 'It feels, well, *weird*.'

'Now you're being ridiculous.'

'No I'm not! There's, like, this little person in there.'

'Oh, for God's sake, David.'

'She keeps going on at me about it. Like she's turned into some kind of nymphomaniac.'

'I've read about that.' I remembered the article in the open magazine Julia had left on the bathroom floor. 'Some women can get a bit rampant. It's their hormones running wild.'

'Yeah? Well I'm going to have to start putting something in her tea.'

'Or get your head around it and stop behaving like a child. Honestly, David, you men do get some very funny ideas. If that's what she needs at the moment, then you should be rolling out the romance for her and taking full advantage of your extra rations.'

'It's not that bloody easy.' He shifted uncomfortably and turned his attentions back to the onions. 'You know, just because I'm a man, doesn't mean to say I'm some kind of machine a woman can just turn on and off whenever they fancy.' Well, well. Do I detect a boot very firmly on the other foot? 'She expects to be able to snap her fingers and, wham, there it is.'

'And you describe this as a problem?' I couldn't help but smile.

'Yes. Well.' He cleared his throat and mumbled under his breath so that his words were almost unintelligible. 'Mumble, mumble, performance anxiety.'

'You what?'

'I've got performance anxiety, all right?' he muttered. 'I can't do it. And the more I try to think of something else and come up with the goods, the worse it gets.'

'Oh!' My inner agony aunt came bubbling through, remembering its determination to be able to talk about sex and say penis without going beetroot. 'Do you want to talk about it?'

'Are you kidding me?' He tutted and slung the onions in the pan. 'Right now it's the last thing I want to talk about. In about five hours, when I'm completely done in and wanting to crash on the sofa in front of the Chelsea match, she's going to come over all Mata Hari and I'm going to have to plead yet another migraine. It's doing my noodle in.'

'Just close your eyes and think of England.' I turned the sausages over casually. 'It's what women have been doing for years.'

Chapter Elevenses

MUM'S THE WORD

THE STAIRCASE IN Rick's house acts as a natural conduit for sound. If you stand at the bottom and look up from the newel post, you can see all the way up to the top of the house, right up to the tiny round skylight window that peers back down from the roof. Similarly, from my vantage point on the landing outside the dungeon, I can see all the way down. That Lola had finally dragged herself out of bed was obvious. I could hear her size zero bones rattling around in the shower for a few minutes before she started screeching for Rick. I darted down the stairs in slippered feet, sticking closely to the walls, watching.

'Rick!' Again and again. 'I want to go out! Rick!

Rick!' Doors opening and slamming until she found him. You had to admire the girl's tenacity.

'Just hang on a minute.' Rick put his hand over the telephone. 'I'm on the phone, Lola, love.'

'I want to go out!' She ignored him. 'You said you buy me new handbag. I want to go to Fendi. I want go now!'

'I can't right at the minute.' Rick softened his voice, perhaps hoping that she would do the same. 'We'll go a bit later, OK?'

'No!' she shouted. 'Not OK! You say we go out so you take me now!'

I held my breath, pinned to the first half-landing, ready to spring into a normal paced stair descent if either of them spotted me.

'I have to work today, Lola, love.' Bloody hell. He was sounding more pathetic by the day. If only he were to give her a Foghorn Leghorn blast of his infamous temper, maybe he'd stand a better chance of getting it through her thick skull that she wasn't the only person on the planet. Oh well. It's really not for me to say. I inched forward, peering over the banister rail. Lola's surgically enhanced lips contorted into a doughnut-sized sulk. 'Just let me do what I need to do, and we'll see about going shopping later, OK?'

'When later?' she shouted. 'You say later but you big fat liar.' Her foot started up against the floor. A tiny movement caught my eye. My head jerked towards a skulking Helga, pressed up against the kitchen door. She winked and pointed gleefully towards the enemy spitting feathers at her father.

'I've got a meeting at my office in an hour,' Rick said, wasting his breath. 'Why don't you come along with me?'

'To office?' Lola snarled at him. 'Why I want to go office? I want to go Fendi. I want to go Fendi NOW!' She picked up the vase from the table and dropped it on the floor, the bulbous shape exploding with a loud pop, spilling its water everywhere. Helga's mouth opened in mute fury.

'Listen,' Rick barked into the phone. 'I'm gonna have to call you back.'

'You promise me yesterday.' She stuck her nose in the air.

'All right, all right.' He put his hands out to calm her as one might do a bucking horse. 'I'm ringing Angela now, OK?' He scrolled down his phone and put it to his ear, never taking his eyes off her. 'Angela? Listen, could you reschedule my meetings? Something's come up.' He glanced at Lola with a smile, hoping to secure her approval. She just sniffed at him and looked away. 'Yes, I know, Ange. Well, you'll just have to extend my apologies and tell them definitely next time. I know. I'm sorry. Yep. I'll give you a ring a bit later. No. I won't be in today at all.' He hung up. 'OK?' He tried to reason with her royal stroppiness.

'Hmph,' she said.

'I'll just get my coat, love.' The minute Rick's back was turned, Lola took the coffee cup he had left on the table and slowly, deliberately spilled it over the carpet. Helga bridled behind the door, jaw clenching and unclenching, the squeegee twitching in her hands. She glared up at me furiously and slid her finger silently across her throat.

'HELLO? IS THAT Harvey Nichols food market?' I'd already been put through to the knicker department once by accident. 'I've just faxed over a shopping list and I wanted to make sure that you could decipher my handwriting.'

I swung back presidentially in Rick's world-domination chair, bat phone tucked under my ear, and shoved his account details in the top drawer of the desk before running my eyes down my audacious list. Those dinners at Tony's gaff were going to seem like roadside trailer trash snacks by the time I'd finished. And if it bankrupted him in the process, so much the better.

'Yes. I'll hold.' I wondered if the thirty-quid bio-dynamic sausages might have been overdoing it a tad. Although my spaghetti carbonara is unarguably out of this world, Lola had turned her nose up at my fatigued effort yesterday. Admittedly, it was hardly the requisite four-and-twenty-blackbirds number required to win her instant applause, but what was I to do? There was bugger all in the fridge except the usual post-coital supply of bacon and eggs, bed champagne, cold beer and a few predictable standbys, and if he thought I was going to go schlepping to the shops after the day I'd had, he had another think coming. After condemning my carbohydrate-laden offering as disgusting and shoving the plate away, Lola had dramatically rung the number on the back of Rick's Centurion card and sent out for fresh sushi while I held my tongue and scraped her plate off in the bin.

'Hello?' At last, a voice of reason. 'Yes,' I said patiently. 'Of course I'm authorized to use the account. Yes, I know it's a big order.' I sighed irritably and inspected the end of my unlit cigar. 'For Mr Richard Wilton. Uh-huh. Yes, *that* Rick Wilton. And if you could get it all delivered here before two, he probably won't need to know about this little fiasco.' It never ceases to amaze me how Rick's name manages to light a fire under other people's pants.

The study door opened and in slunk Helga. 'You vanting coffee?'

'Good idea,' I said. She hovered by the door.

'Why you in top?' She pointed to the ceiling.

'Oh.' I guessed she meant the dungeon. 'Lola,' I explained.

'Tsk.' Helga shook her head and tutted. 'She no see

you, Rick, umm.' She searched for an appropriate word. Go on, Helg. Anything in English will do. 'She no, er . . .' Helga grasped the air in front of her and gyrated her hips violently.

'Exactly,' I said. 'Lola no like Rick with woman.'

'Ah.' Helga folded her arms across her chest protectively. 'She blooding beech. I blooding hate. She make you trouble, *da*?'

'*Da*.' I sighed. 'I think she's going to make plenty of trouble, all right.'

'*Nyet*.' Helga wagged her finger at me. 'She make trouble – ' she slapped her chest hard in a touching display of camaraderie – 'we make trouble, *da*?'

'*Nyet*, Helga. We don't make trouble. You make coffee, OK?' Besides, I had a much better idea. Helga snorted her disapproval and left the room. Five minutes later, back she came bearing a steaming mug and rested it in front of me, rubbing the coaster to a gleaming finish on her Billingsgate apron first. 'Thanks, Helga.' I gave her a thumbs-up and prepared myself for the onslaught. On a good day, her coffee tastes like stewed acorns laced with burnt dung. 'Just what the doctor ordered.'

She flicked her duster at me, shouting, '*Pazhalsta!*' which I think meant something along the lines of 'you're welcome', although I could be entirely wrong. Picking up the mug, I took a long swallow while she watched on appreciatively. Without warning, a searing fireball hit my throat like a pint of flaming paraffin, the slug of home-brewed vodka jerking my larynx into an uncontrollable spasm as I started to choke and splutter.

'*Na zdarovya!*' Helga cackled, punching the air and downing hers in one.

I HAD ARRANGED TO meet Julia later that morning at an address in Brunswick Gardens, not a million miles away. It was a glorious day, brisk if still a little bracing around the edges, the sky as blue as a child's picture book.

The moment the bus turned the corner and on to the road running along the side of the park, I felt an overwhelming urge to jump off and take to Shanks's pony, to stretch my dormant legs and to leave damp footprints in the grass. Only one can't hop on and off the buses any more these days thanks to the relentless slide of modern progress. Now we're all herded past a miserable driver shielded from all human contact by a bulletproof screen, wordlessly flashing our computer-chipped pre-paid transportation cards at a beeping box instead of handing a couple of groats to a nice bus conductor who whistles like a canary and knows which stop you want. The sad demise of the open-backed Routemaster sounded the death knell to a more innocent time. A time where it was OK to take a risk now and then and to hell with the consequences. So what if the occasional tourist fell off and got squashed under the wheels of an oncoming number 19? It's not our fault that they drive on the wrong side of the road. I pressed the bell and stood by the doors waiting impatiently to be deposited safely at the next stop, aching to stroll free.

The moment I turned off the pavement, passing through the wrought-iron gates into Kensington's manicured gardens, my skin began to prickle with that unmistakable sensation that comes over us but once a year. There was no doubt about it. Spring was finally in the air. The dark buds on the camellia bushes strained at their shiny husks, coquettishly exposing an exotic sliver of deepest pink, desperate to burst into bloom. I could feel my winter-weary body, greyed by the months of cold, grim weather, gagging to shed its knitted layers for the warmth of the rare spring sun. All around, the trees shimmered early pastel shadows of pale green, hinting at the clouds of new leaves to come. I filled my musty lungs; closed my eyes. Roll on summer.

Picking up the pace and heading towards the address scribbled on the slip of paper stuffed in my pocket with a couple of fluff-bound Werthers Originals, I couldn't help but notice the swank of the neighbourhood. Things must be pretty buoyant in the doula business. Wouldn't mind living here myself. Julia was already waiting on the doorstep.

'Hi!' I kissed her hello. 'Am I late?'

'No. I'm early. Ready?' she said, brimming with excitement. I nodded and she pressed the bell.

'Come in!' came a cheerfully tinny voice through the intercom. 'Right up to the top of the stairs, I'm afraid!'

Trudging up to the top floor, past the thick, gloss-painted anaglypta wallpaper that looked as if it had been hung a hundred years ago, I noticed the air held a certain fustiness about it. It reminded me of Mrs Critchley's house, next door but one to my parents. You could always tell what they'd had for lunch the previous day because the smell of it would stick to the walls. At the top of the stairs, the door to what must have once been the attic rooms had been left wide open. A tiny, round woman appeared from behind it, peering at us over the top of her Buggles spectacles.

'You must be Julia!' She thrust her hand towards me, bangles jangling beneath the long cheesecloth sleeve of her multicoloured tie-dye shirt.

'No.' I shook my head and pointed to the patently pregnant woman standing beside me.

'Of course!' She reached out and shook Julia's instead, nodding enthusiastically. 'Never let your mouth suggest the fat lady is the one having the baby!'

She laughed, oblivious to Julia's instant offence. 'I did that once or twice before I learned my lesson! Ghastly! Always accuse the thin one first and you can't go too far wrong! Come in! Come in!' She beckoned us in cheerily. As she turned, I noticed that she had an extraordinarily large bottom, quite out of proportion with the rest of her body, jutting out like a mantel-piece. 'The kettle's on and we have much to talk about.'

'This is my sister, Helen,' Julia explained.

'Make yourselves at home!' the woman shouted, pointing us towards her sitting room, a mismatch of junk-shop furniture set haphazardly within bright, psychedelic walls, each one painted a different, bilious colour with wonky pictures hung in no particular order. I recognized the faint aroma of patchouli, a couple of classic album covers from the free-love Six-ties propped lazily against the skirting, and came over all joss sticks. An enormous spider plant hung from the ceiling rose, dangling dozens of baby plants on sinewy tendrils that sprung from its heart, some of which had been poked into smaller nursery pots and urged to make a break for it on their own.

Everything in the room looked to be at least fifty years old. The brown, wood-effect television set with the V-shaped spiked aerial on top, the angular nest of ring-stained coffee tables, the display cabinet in the corner stuffed to the gunnels with all sorts of knickknacky oddments. And, I suddenly realized with a shudder, so did the seating. I ignored the beanbags, took my life in my hands and lowered myself onto one of the two sofas, certain as I was that I would not be its only living occupant. Julia seemed not to notice the tumbleweed dust balls in the corners of the motley room and arranged herself quite happily on the other one.

'Good!' The lady came back with a tray, carrying three old mugs and a plate of, well, brown things that looked a bit like Brillo pads after they've gone round your roasting pans a few times. 'I'm Eva,' she said in a new, whispery voice, slightly closing her eyes as she deposited the tray on the table. 'But here, in my role as your doula – ' she did inverted commas with her fingers, slid out the two smaller tables from the nest and put one next to Julia's sofa and the other beside mine – 'you may call me Crouching Raccoon.' She paused for effect. I wasn't sure if I'd heard her correctly. I dared not look at Julia and bit the side of my cheek. 'The native American Indians were totally at one with the natural world around them, and that is my constant inspiration.' You've got to be kidding me. Show us the nitrous oxide bottles or we're out of here. 'This, Julia, this is the way you will learn to be.' She handed out the tea. 'Camomile.' I noticed that she had a habit of raising her inflection at the end of everything she said, rather like you might expect from an in-store electric wok demonstrator. 'Although once you get a little further down the line, Julia – ' there it was again – 'you will move on to raspberry leaf.'

'Thank you.' Julia beamed at her, accepting the mug, lapping up every word.

'Now,' Eva said, settling herself on the sofa next to Julia and closing her eyes again. 'Whatever tea you're drinking at the moment, I want you to swap it for a nice, natural herbal infusion.' Her eyes remained flutteringly half shut while she spoke. 'Later I will give you raspberry leaf to tone the uterus nicely. You'll thank me for it.' She paused and breathed steadily, in through the nose, out through the mouth. Julia looked as if she were about to say something when Eva launched off again into another whispery singsong nugget of wisdom. 'I'll be bringing you my own special blend and making sure that you have regular sips throughout your very special time when your baby comes to meet you.' Julia and I waited, but then Eva opened her eyes and seemed to be finished.

'You come very highly recommended,' Julia said with uncharacteristic shyness.

'That's jolly nice to hear.'

'I'm so excited, I can't begin to tell you.'

'It's a very exciting time.' Eva folded her legs beneath her enormous rump on the sofa, bending them like rubber. I waited for the sound of snapping ankle bones.

'Thank you so much for fitting me in. I couldn't believe it when you said you had a free slot.' Free indeed. Judging by the local house prices, this little jaunt was going to set Julia back a pretty penny. I wondered when Julia was going to put her brain in gear and ask this woman about her qualifications. Certainly, from where I was sitting I could already see that she was (a) happy to live in a student swamp and (b) quite possibly a couple of sandwiches short of a picnic. 'My husband's still a bit freaked out about the whole thing.' Julia took on an apologetic tone. 'He thinks I should surrender myself to the nearest hospital and pre-book every anaesthetist within a two-mile radius.'

'Men find a woman's ability to give birth threatening. It's all to do with the penis,' Eva decreed, pressing her palms together and lowering her head. 'Losing control, losing power over your ownership of the miracle of life. His penis is a one-trick pony. But just look at you.' Julia gazed at her in awe.

'In fact, I should probably mention that this was quite a surprise for both of us. You see – ' Julia fiddled with her sleeve – 'I had a few problems when I was young which affected my fertility. Although we tried for a long time, we'd given up any hope of having a baby years ago.'

'Ah.' Eva sipped at her tea, taking tiny slurps and

smacking her lips approvingly. 'So he's subconsciously wondering where this baby could have come from?'

Julia froze, her face blanching. Her smile vanished. 'What exactly do you mean by that?'

'Your husband's brain, like those of all men, is still dwelling somewhere between a cave and a testicle.' Eva drew a protracted breath. 'If he knew about this when he married you, and I'm presuming that he did, then you can safely assume that he probably didn't want to have children at all. With no one to compete with him, he's still the child getting all the attention, which is precisely what men want. It's no wonder his nose has been put out of joint.'

'I beg your pardon?' Julia sat bolt upright, her body suddenly pervaded by her old, ball-breaking self. 'But that's—'

'That's men,' Eva interrupted matter-of-factly. 'They're scared shitless of the whole business of pregnancy and birth. In fact, if you want to get really technical about it, they're scared shitless of women, full stop. Mark my words. Your husband – what's his name?'

'David.'

'Well, your David thought that he was going to get away with it, and now you've gone and presented him with his worst fear.' I couldn't quite believe what I was hearing. Julia's eyes were like saucers. It seemed to me that old Crouching Raccoon here would be best advised to go crouch in the corner before Julia declared open season and skinned her alive. 'Now he'll have to knuckle down and show you just what kind of man he really is, won't he?'

'Worst fear?' Instead of going for the jugular, Julia seemed to deflate in her seat. 'But that's just not possible!' She shook her head in disbelief. 'What a terrible thing to say.'

'Not at all!' Eva brushed Julia's upset aside and reverted to her strangely calming, whispery voice. 'You have become an untouchable temple of miracles.' Her eyes began to close and flutter, then she started to hum softly. She reached out a hand and found Julia's. 'Woman! Know this. You have entered a new realm, where you, mother earth, feel the warm glow of a new life from within.' I watched Julia's eyes glazing, their lids seemingly heavy and following Eva's as they drooped. 'And now, I want you to close your eyes and imagine your body.' The humming changed to a soft whooping chant, like the kind of noises we used to make as kids when we were playing cowboys and injuns, having tied some poor unsuspecting toddler to a garden post with Mum's washing line. I sat there holding on to my tea, the hairs on the back of my neck prickling with embarrassment. Any moment now, I thought. Any moment now Julia's going to say, 'Excuse me, raccoon-lady. I think we've made a horrible mistake,' and we'll go out for a nice lunch at Mario's place instead. Without warning, Eva suddenly let out a couple of wolverine yelps. It gave me such a fright I accidentally jolted a big splosh of boiling camomile tea right into my lap, scalding my thighs. She then went all weird and started singing for a moment before lapsing back into the rhythmic chant.

Staring at Julia, willing her to open her eyes and tip me the wink to get up and run, it suddenly struck me that she had become putty in this woman's hands. Of all the crazy, psychic zone TV fakery I'd ever seen, this really was taking the Brillo pad biscuit. Eva began murmuring again.

'And inside your body, a tiny light shines, pure and white.' The tribal humming continued between her melodious words. 'And as you come closer to the light, so it glows more brightly. You can feel its warmth. Can you feel that, Julia?' A small smile crept across Julia's face. I watched on silently, my eyelids becoming irresistibly heavy, finding myself unable to fight the oddly hypnotic effect of Eva's voice. 'That's your baby,' she whispered. 'Glowing like a golden shrine, deep in your soul, growing stronger with every minute that passes, with every breath you take. Feel your baby.' Julia's hands rested on her tummy. 'Yes. Feel it. Love it. Believe in your body's ability to bring your baby into this world.' Her whispering voice trailed off, and she softly hummed until I drifted away on a cloud.

'And now . . .' It seemed as though an aeon had passed, her voice barely there. 'We hear the traffic outside, my voice in this room, and we feel happy, and cherished, and as free as the birds in the trees. Ready?' She paused. 'One . . . two . . . three.' She snapped her fingers softly.

I blinked my eyes open and stared at Julia.

Bloody hell. What just happened there? I had almost no recollection at all of how we had come to be sitting in this chakra-coloured room, or for how long, or what day of the week it was. It felt as though someone had emptied my brain, wrapped it in cotton wool and misted it with a fine spritz of fresh lavender water.

'Nice?' Eva sipped her tea with a smile. Julia burst out laughing.

'Brilliant!'

WHILE I HAD been out, Harvey Nichols had been in. There was no sign of Rick or the lolly-burning Lola, and Helga was long gone, having told me that morning she'd be firing up her broomstick at two o'clock sharp as she had an angry picket line to join outside one of the more obscure embassies. She likes to keep her hand in politically. I opened the fridge and found it groaning under the weight of organic, hand-reared groceries, then slit the tape on the white, polystyrene boxes that had been left on the side. Lifting the lids, a seething clutch of live lobsters the size of hobnail boots sat quietly, their claws taped into an undignified surrender, waiting miserably to be executed.

'Sorry, lads.' I picked a couple up and held them in front of my face. 'Life's a bitch, then you fry, with a knob of butter and a bit of garlic.' I put them all in the freezer where they could chill out together, say their goodbyes and blissfully lose consciousness. 'Right.' I clapped my hands and made a start on setting the scene for tonight's performance.

An hour and a half later, with my evil work done, I retreated upstairs with the bottle of wine I'd started on last night and a big plateful of the hand-crafted canapés I'd ordered in at a million pounds each. The dungeon was quite cosy actually, once you got over its initial humbleness in comparison with the rest of the house. Being so small, it had only taken me a few minutes to personalize the diminutive space after my enforced incarceration. A couple of pointless ornaments on top of the chest of drawers, the odd book here and there, and *voilà*. I pretended that I was banged up in Holloway and decided to do my time peacefully. Lighting a nice, soothing Jo Malone candle, I settled on the little single bed wedged under the eaves, pulled up a cold glass of wine and popped in a couple of munchy morsels. 'Mmm!' I frowned at the plate. Bloody yummy. I switched on the tiny television set I'd liberated from Rick's study and joined the lobsters for a major chill-out sesh while Lieutenant Columbo made a bumbling nuisance of himself with the guilty-as-hell millionaire playboy baddie of the day. Go on, old son. Get him.

God knows how long later, I woke up with a start, feeling like I'd been hit by a bus. The rest of the wine in the bottle had mysteriously evaporated, as had all the canapés, or at least so I thought until I tried to get up, hit my head on the sloping roof and found a mini choux bun stuffed with mousse de foie gras wedged down my cleavage. Fishing it out quickly, I couldn't think where to put it so popped it in my mouth to get rid of the evidence. The sound of voices downstairs filtered up to my ears. They were back. Excellent. I rushed to the en-suite sardine can, knocked back a gobful of Listerine and tried to talk some sense into my bed-ridden hair. Not to worry, I thought, scraping it back severely. There won't be a single one hanging out by the time I've finished anyway. Scrape, scrape. Spray, spray. Bob's your uncle. Bung on your outfit and chocks away. A quick Wonderwoman spin later, I stuck the last of the pins in my hair, ran a slick of pillar-box red lipstick across my mouth and made my way downstairs.

Rick paced the floor impatiently, picking his way over the piles of trophy shopping bags Lola had dumped by the front door, mobile pressed to his ear, barking furiously at the poor underling on the other end of the line.

'Waddya mean, Jacobs can't make it? Listen, sonny. You tell him that if he's not at that meeting tomorrow morning the deal's off. Right? I haven't spent the last three months putting this mother together to have arseholes like him messing me about.' He paused, listening intently. 'What? Well that couldn't be helped. I had an emergency to deal with.' He became vaguely aware of me standing at the bottom of the stairs behind him and half raised his hand over his shoulder, not wanting to break his stride, muttering, 'For Christ's sake. Have I got to do everything myself?' The organ grinder's monkey came back on the line. 'Yeah? Well I should fucking well think so too. See you there.' He hung up. 'Wanker.' Shoving the phone in his pocket, he finally honoured me with his company.

'Good evening, sir.' I dipped him a derisory curtsey.

'What the . . .' He gawped at me. '*Helen?*' Whatever he was about to say, and believe me, his face was doing the job for him, the clickety-click of Lola's killer heels as they dented their way along the polished floor brought him to a skidding halt.

'Good evening, miss.' I gave Lola a polite nod of deference. 'Dinner will be ready a little later.'

'What is it?' she demanded.

'Lobster followed by a tasting menu of European delicacies.' Rick hates the word delicacies. Says it

183

reminds him of sheep's testicles and makes him feel ill. 'If you'd like to make yourself comfortable.' I extended my hand suggestively towards the drawing room. 'I'll bring you both a little light refreshment.' She eyed me suspiciously and moved slowly in the right direction. 'You must be simply worn out after the busy day you've had.' I added a dry smile towards the bags on the floor before turning away and doubling back to campaign headquarters (the kitchen) and closing the door. This, in itself, should have been signal enough. In all the time I have been here, never once have I seen the kitchen door anything but wide open. To close it upsets the whole wah of the house. Less than a minute later the door opened a crack and Rick slid through.

'Hell?' He looked at me nervously, his smile definitely more than a little unsure. 'What the fuck are you doing?'

'Sitting room.' I pointed sharply, as though ordering a dog to its basket. 'And if you come in here one more time without a written invitation I'll have you shot.' I adjusted the pins in my hair and straightened my white apron in a no-nonsense way, its stark line a perfect foil against my black funeral dress. He loitered for a moment longer, then made the only smart choice he could have and ducked out. Good. I rubbed my hands and opened the fridge, taking out the first of the poisonous jugs I had mixed and left to chill. 'And here's one I made earlier,' I muttered to myself sadistically as I filled a couple of highballs with ice and topped them up with the innocuous-looking fluid dynamite.

'Allow me.' Removing the magazines from the low coffee table in the drawing room, I set down the silver tray Helga had polished to within an inch of its life. Handing out my deathly cocktails, I smiled sweetly at Rick.

'What's all this?' he said uneasily.

'Just a little pick-me-up with a twist of aniseed. Try it.' I wondered if he'd recognize the absinthe. 'It's delicious.' Lola sniffed at hers first then took a small sip and shrugged OK without a word of thanks. 'And do help yourself to a little something to keep you going while you're waiting.' I presented the canapés casually. 'Pepperdews stuffed with guacamole. Parmesan biscotti topped with black truffles. And as for the caviar and blinis – ' I smiled innocently – 'well, you know what to do with those, don't you?'

Lola dipped to the table, dug a spoon deep into the caviar pot and tried a mouthful. 'Mmm,' she admitted reluctantly. 'Is good.' At that price, I should bloody well coco.

'Nothing but the best for sir,' I clucked. 'Now if you'll excuse me.' I tugged my forelock at Rick. 'You guests will be arriving shortly so I must get back to work.'

'Guests?' Rick loosened his tie. 'What guests?'

'Your guests!' My confused reply sounded almost genuine. 'Surely you can't have forgotten?' I could see the alarm bells ringing behind the flashing whites of his eyes and turned gracefully to Lola. 'Your father is throwing a little party in your honour this evening. I can't believe it slipped his mind. Perhaps he wanted it to be a surprise. Silly me,' I demurred. 'I shouldn't have said anything.'

'Party?!' Lola squealed, her breasts jiggling excitedly. 'Oh! I loooove party!' She subdued herself immediately and pouted unhappily at Rick. 'You invite people for me? Young people? Not old like you.'

'Hey.' Rick bridled and sucked in his stomach. 'I'll have you know that I'm a year younger than Bruce—'

'Yes,' I said to Lola. 'He has invited the cream of London's eligible bachelors to come and meet you. In fact,' I reassured her, 'there won't be a single young lady here that could compete with you.' Lola preened. 'Because you will be the only one.' She emitted a high-pitched scream of delight. I left the room, throwing over my shoulder, 'And do be careful about calling your father old, miss. He's very sensitive about being past it.' I made myself scarce on the double, barely getting to the kitchen door before the fallout started.

'I no have time to change!' Lola flew into a rage, screaming at Rick. 'You do this on purpose! I no go to hairdresser. I no have right dress! You make me look stupid!' Storming from the sitting room, I heard her tear into the shopping bags and head for the stairs. The slam that followed sent a shudder thundering through the house.

Back in the kitchen, the lobsters were too dazed and confused to demand a crustacean rights lawyer and hit the pan of boiling water without a murmur of protest. Poor buggers. Still. They were about to be recycled into something much more interesting so at least they wouldn't be enduring death-by-simmering in vain. Loading up a couple of trays of neon-green cocktails, for a split second I was almost tempted to pour one for myself, then remembered that my brain was already lightly marinated from my afternoon wine-swilling fest and went for the reassuring hiss of a bottle of fizzy water instead. Phew. That was close. I'm generally very sensible about drinking, until I've had a couple of drinks, that is. Then I seem to forget which way is up and, well, anything can happen. Rick's head breached the kitchen door.

'Hell?'

'What?'

'I just wanted to say thanks,' he said penitently, excusing Lola's behaviour with an apologetic nod towards the ceiling. 'Don't worry about her. She's just a bit, well, you know.' Completely spoilt little madam by any chance?

'Really?' I continued arranging the canapés. 'You don't say.'

'It never crossed my mind to throw a party for her. You're a bloody genius, babe.' I ignored his attempted flattery. 'But you better let me know who you've invited otherwise I'm gonna look a bit of a plonker, aren't I?' He plucked up the courage to open the door a little further and looked as though he was about to step inside.

'That's far enough, buster.' I pointed a steel skewer at him. 'I'd like to say that I've never been so humiliated in my life, but sadly, Rick, that wouldn't be true now, would it? Seeing as humiliation seems to have become my middle name.' He hung his head in submission. 'So you just get back out there and salve your conscience, and I'll bow and scrape in all the right places, all right?'

'Yeah, but—'

'Yeah but no but yeah but,' I said with a snippy wobble of my head. The doorbell went. Great. Stand back and hold on to your eyelashes. 'Are you going to answer that or am I expected to be your sodding butler as well?'

'Right,' he said obediently. I hung back casually for a second then rushed to the door, peering through the gap, my knuckles white with mischief.

'Rick!' Paul screeched, flinging his arms around him and planting an enormous, lingering kiss on his face.

'Mmmmwah! You're such a sweetie to invite us all!' From behind him filed in a seemingly inexhaustible trail of immorally gorgeous men ... tall ones, short ones, brown ones, white ones, blond ones, dark ones, bald ones, and, last but not least, a matching pair of Argentinians, at least six foot tall, with rock-hard buttocks squeezed into skin-tight jodhpurs tucked into naughty riding boots, each of them carrying a twitching, leather crop. Whoa, Nelly. Before I could stop myself, my head filled with vivid flashes of sinfully carnal thoughts. Bless me father, for I have been a very *very* bad girl. So sue me. I mopped my pounding temples with the corner of the tea towel, shoving the rest of it in my mouth. Paul introduced his troupe of perfect physical specimens as they sauntered in while Rick stared on, dumbfounded.

'Now let's see.' Paul put his finger to his lips teasingly. 'That's Andy, and Spank, and Paolo, and Tobias ... naughty boy!' Paul leaned to Rick's ear and whispered something then pulled back giggling. The blood drained from Rick's face. I pressed my hand against my mouth, desperately trying to stifle my hysteria as the oozing pageant continued to swagger past Rick, filling the house with a heaving fug of testosterone. A high-pitched squeal announced Lola's imminent arrival as she bounded down the stairs, flicking her hair, bouncing up and down on her heels and clapping, accepting louche kisses and unashamedly suggestive introductions. The final sex-god line-up was no less than I had been promised. Had George Clooney put in an appearance, I suspect he would have been crushed in the stampede to get past. I quickly pressed the door closed and scurried back to the lobster pot. The kitchen door swung slowly open and there stood the ashen-faced Rick, dazed and confused until a sudden shockwave of thumping music exploded through the house.

'Is it just me?' he mumbled finally. 'Or has my house just been taken over by a load of—'

'There you are.' I put on my schoolmistress face and handed him a drinks tray before letting the door swing closed on him. 'Make yourself useful and hand these out. While you're at it, you might want to down a couple of those yourself then buckle up for the ride,' I shouted.

I had all the food laid out in less than an hour, stuck a notice on the front door saying 'Party in progress – come on in', hailed a passing cab and left them all to it.

Chapter Twelve

PLINK PLINK FIZZ

HAD THE RACKET from the builders downstairs not woken me up, I might well have slept in until noon. Stretched out on the sofa in my gone-at-the-knees baggy pyjamas, I yawned lazily, still mildly under the influence of the coma-inducing pill Sally had issued to me with my hot chocolate as we finished mopping our eyes to the final scenes of *Love Story* last night. Gets me every time.

While Paul was busy orchestrating Sodom and Gomorrah Evening at Rick's house, Sally and I had spent the perfect night in with a bowl of his secret recipe chilli and a couple of tubs of ice cream to put the fire out afterwards. By the time the credits rolled, my make-you-sleepy-pam had hit home like an elephant gun and the next thing I knew it was morning. My caffeine indicator beeped impatiently for coffee, so I dragged my carcass off the sofa and slouched to the bathroom, stopping for a quick peek in the bedroom where two bodies lay spark out. Paul must have crept in during the early hours while I had been unconscious. I pulled their door quietly closed and decided to stop off for a coffee somewhere on the way instead. Those two looked like they could probably do without the intrusion of a steaming Gaggia.

An hour later, double latte in hand, the overpowering gust of post-party fumes that hit me when I opened Rick's front door almost knocked me sideways. I stepped in tentatively, my feet searching for gaps in the sea of wreckage littering the floor as the bigger picture began to reveal itself. Holy mother of Jesus. It looked like hurricane Katrina had just passed through. Half-drunk cocktails lay abandoned where they had fallen, some swimming with cigarette ends that hadn't quite made it to the overflowing ashtrays. Empty bottles rolled drunkenly on the floor. I recognized a few of the canapés trampled into the carpet, but some I didn't. Creeping through the deathly silence and wondering if I should call the emergency services, I detected the faintest whiff of life and traced the low rumble of snoring to the sitting room. Oh, thank you, God. This just gets better and better. To my utter delight, there on the sofa lay Rick, in all his glory, peaceful as a babe in arms. And he was not alone.

I quickly slipped my shoes off, padded silently to the kitchen, then decanted my Starbucks livener into a cup and took it up to Lola's room. As fond as I am of my morning caffeine fix, this would be a sacrifice well worth making. Giving her door a perfunctory knock knock, I let myself in, marching past the tanned corpse lying comatose on top of the covers. From the state of her hair and dress, I assumed that some kind of food fight had featured along the way.

'Wakey-wakey!' I chirruped breezily, flinging the curtains open. A bright shaft of sunshine fell across the bed. No response. 'Good morning!' I gave her a little shake. 'Half past nine! Rise and shine!' Hang your knickers on the line. I dipped my finger in the pint glass of untouched water on the bedside table and flicked a few droplets in her face. Her eyelids twitched. 'GOOD MOOOOORNING!' I sang out. One of her fingers moved, just slightly, and a small, strangled gurgling noise escaped from her throat. 'Lovely!' I said. 'I've brought you up a nice cup of coffee.' I smacked the cup down beside her and hauled her up as she groaned in protest, stuffing a few pillows behind her head and throwing a dressing gown on the bed. 'So hurry up and come down for breakfast, miss. I'm sure your father is just gagging to get to Bond Street!' A glimmer of life passed across Lola's blotchy, make-up smeared face and she opened her eyes, just a slit. 'Come on!' I clapped my hands sharply. 'Letsby Avenue!'

Passing Rick's room, I heard clear evidence of occupation. Oh well. If they were burglars, they were obviously very particular about their personal hygiene because one of them was running the shower. Before I could get to the bottom of the stairs, there came the distinctive scampering of Helga's footsteps approaching the front door. I rushed to the latch and pulled the door open before she could engage her key, pressing my hand over her mouth to prevent her screaming her usual deafening greeting of, 'Goot monging. I here!' then slam.

'Shhh!' I rested my finger against my lips and pointed inside the house, urging her to follow me to the kitchen. She narrowed her eyes in immediate collusion and crept in like Inspector Clouseau, gasping under her breath at the terrible state of the house. 'Don't worry about it.' I closed the kitchen door behind us quietly and slid a couple of frying pans out of the cupboard and onto the hob. 'We'll call in the industrial death squad later. But for now, we must be very, very quiet,' I whispered. 'Just sit here and wait.'

'Wait?'

'*Da*,' I said.

'Why wait?' She frowned.

'Rick have big party last night. Big party for Lola.'

'Hmph,' she sniffed. 'I no like. She blooding beech.'

'You still want to make trouble?' I nudged her.

'*Da!*' She nodded. 'We make trouble today?'

'*Da*, Helga. We make plenty trouble.'

I fired up the burners, reached into the fridge for the thirty-quid sausages and waited for all hell to break loose.

RIGHT ON CUE, the action started, and I would gladly have given my right arm to be a fly on the sitting-room wall. I have no idea what Lola's face must have looked like when she wandered in and found her dad out for the count on the sofa, wearing somebody else's clothes, his head happily snuggled up against a bare-chested Argentinian polo player. The barrage of Portuguese gutter speak was up to her usual standard, if a little louder, and Helga and I played an amusing guessing game as we heard the familiar sounds of household objects being smashed against the walls.

'Vase?' I suggested.

'*Nyet.*' Helga shook her head knowledgeably. 'Wine bot.'

'Ah.' I stood corrected.

'*Bastardo!*' Crash. '*Eu te detesto!*' Smash.

'What the FUCK!' Rick bellowed, his voice creaking shakily before finding its full, booming stride. 'Holy SHIT! Lola!' Bam. 'Stop!'

Footsteps at twelve o'clock. Quick. Retreat. Retreat. Helga and I scurried to our positions. Me at the cooker worrying at the sausages. Her scrubbing the skirting boards with her fingernails. Helga casually broke into one of her Russian gulag songs just as the door flew open. A shape roughly resembling Rick swayed in the entrance, leaning against the doorframe for support, looking like an unmade bed.

'Good morning!' I said breezily. 'Gosh! What a lovely shirt!' His sequins twinkled and blushed in appreciation.

Before he could utter a word, Lola was on his tail.

'*Bastardo!*' she shouted. 'You say men for me, but no! Men here for YOU!'

'Now hang on just a minute!' He winced and staggered forward, his hand rising to his head. 'Jesus Christ,' he groaned. 'What the bloody hell happened last—' The Argentinian jodhpurs appeared behind him and administered a sneaky goose. Rick jerked bolt upright, wide-eyed, clutching at his behind. 'Oi!' he shouted. 'What the fuck do you think you're—'

'Hello, sailor. Feeling a little seasick?' So, the Argentinian had a smooth, Home Counties accent. Well, well. This morning was turning out to be just full of surprises. 'Oh dear.' He gave Lola's little performance in the corner a weary wave. 'What's the matter with princess pouty-face now?'

'You just watch where you're putting your hands,

sonny Jim.' Rick pressed his back up against the wall, although he was clearly in no fit state to defend himself. 'I'm warning you!'

'Fabulous party.' The jodhpurs blew him a kiss. 'Call me sometime, huh?' He placed his hands over his bulge suggestively. 'You've got my number.'

'*Bastardo!*' Lola shouted at both of them. 'Get out! You make me seek!'

'All right, sweetie.' The rock-hard buttocks rolled his eyes at her and swaggered towards the front door. 'Keep your fake hair on.' Lola screamed and threw a full cocktail, missing by a mile. I watched Helga's knuckles twitch as it exploded a bright green stain against the wall.

'Oh dear.' I turned the sausages casually and broke a few eggs into the neighbouring pan. 'Looks like somebody's not really a morning person.'

'*Paneleiro,*' Lola muttered. 'You wait. You wait I tell Mama you *fruta*. She never speak with you again.'

'Promise?' Rick closed his eyes and clung to the wall, moaning to himself softly while Lola continued to do her pieces, her tirade soon morphing into a droning, unintelligible white noise. If our troops continue to have trouble in Afghanistan, I suggest we drop Lola on the worst of the trouble spots with an inadequate wardrobe and wait for an early surrender. Lola threw herself dramatically on a chair, turning her back on Rick.

Signs of activity stirred on the stairs and the couple I suspected had spent the night in Rick's room turned out to be more of a *ménage à trois*.

'Hi,' said the bald one. 'That was some party, last night, huh? Can I smell breakfast?'

Rick stared at him blankly, as though every light-bulb in his brain had just blown.

'Yeah,' agreed his six-foot-four sidekick. I had to crane my neck to nod politely into his smiling, flawless face. How did anyone manage to look that good after a night like that? 'We just love your house.' He slung a casual arm over the bald man's shoulders. 'Is that Alexander McQueen wallpaper you've got on the stairs?'

'Yes,' I said on Rick's behalf. 'We're about to find out if it's washable.'

The third man, naked from the waist up, edged into the kitchen and seemed to sense the tension in the air, sexual or otherwise. 'Hi,' he said to Rick. 'Remember me?'

'Oh.' Rick replied vacantly, feeling around in his strange, skin-tight pockets for a cigar and finding nothing. 'Not really.'

'You and me?' The guy started swinging his hips and clicking his fingers trying to jog Rick's obliterated memory. 'No?' He bent into a low dip. 'You couldn't leave me alone? Demanding just one more tango before the sun came up?'

'Well.' Rick spied a crumpled dog end in one of the ashtrays and fished it out, blowing the ash off then sticking it in his mouth. 'Waddya know.'

'Really?' I pulled the eggs off the heat for a moment. 'I always knew he had a streak of flamenco running through his veins somewhere. Sunny side up?'

'No thanks,' the bald man spoke up for all of them. 'He's a vegan anyway.' He pointed at the tall one. 'And we really ought to get going. I'm late enough as it is.'

'Of course,' I said with a cheerful wave of my fish slice. 'I expect you've all had quite enough hot sausages to last you a lifetime anyway.'

'*Moskovskaya*,' Helga sniggered from the floor.

In between her increasingly unconvincing sobs, I caught Lola peeking out from her arms for a moment to check that she was being heaped with the attention she deserved. Upon seeing everyone else otherwise engaged, she reached angrily for a tissue and began blowing her nose, coughing and spluttering her presence loudly.

'Thanks for having us,' said the bald one. A small titter went up. 'And you make sure you get yourself down to the Choo Choo Club one of these Thursdays. It's an absolute scream!' Rick seemed not to be listening, concentrating instead on trying to get a drag out of the cigar butt. 'Well.' Baldie backed off. 'Maybe see you there.'

'Uh-huh,' Rick mumbled absently.

'Only, if you don't mind – ' topless tango-boy pointed his pinkie finger in Rick's direction, looking a little embarrassed – 'I could kind of do with my shirt back. If that's OK with you.'

'Eh?' Reluctantly, as if already knowing the hideous truth but unable to face it, Rick looked down at his shirt, then to his snakeskin-effect trousers, and seemed unable to comprehend how they had got there. His shaking fingers fumbled ineptly with the buttons. I stepped in to help.

'Oh, come on now, don't be shy!' It was off before he could protest. 'Trousers?' I snapped my fingers at his fly.

'Not mine!' the guy said quickly, shrugging his rippling shoulders back into his shirt.

'Of course not.' I apologized for my assumption. 'They're his own, no doubt. He's always been a bit of a Rod Stewart fan.' After a brief ripple of polite laughter, they made their excuses and left. Rick staggered to the table and sat, just in time for Lola to unleash another torrent, only this time it seemed to wash over him, his eyes staring ahead unblinkingly.

'How lovely.' I took the warmed plates out of the oven. 'It looks like everyone had a wonderful time. I do like a good party.' I chopped a bit of parsley unnecessarily, giving it plenty of vigour while Rick's head juddered every time my knife hit the board, then slipped Helga a prearranged nod. Abandoning her position, she scampered out of the room and fired up the Hoover right beside the open door, crashing it around on the maple floor, colliding with the skirting board. Rick groaned and dropped his head to his arms. The phone started to ring.

'Hello?' I chirped. 'Yes, just a minute.' I covered the mouthpiece and waved the receiver towards Rick. 'It's for you-hoo.'

'No!' Rick mouthed. He shook his head at me violently, then grasped it in his hands to stop it falling off.

'I'm sorry,' I explained politely into the telephone. 'But I'm afraid he seems to be temporarily indisposed. Yes. Mmm. I see. OK. I'll pass that on.' I hung up.

'Christ,' Rick managed. 'Make her turn that fucking thing off.'

'HELL-GAAAAA!' I yelled. 'Maybe do that a bit later?' She crashed the Hoover into the wall obediently.

'*DA!*' she screamed. 'ME DO LAAA-TER!'

'Here we go.' I slapped a pair of enormous greasy-spoon plates in front of Rick and Lola. 'The sausages are biodynamic,' I explained to Lola, her complexion turning green. 'So eat up, then you can let me know what you want for dinner. I've got a nice lump of liver in the fridge which I could fry up with a couple of onions if you like.' Her hand flew to her mouth and she ran from the room. Rick started swallowing hard, perspiration forming on his brow. 'Oh yes,' I said, as though it had slipped my mind. 'That was some chap called Jacobs on the phone, mentioning something about you being two hours late?'

'Shit!' Rick's head jerked up painfully. He tried to leap from his chair but stumbled the minute he got to his feet, steadying himself with a firm grip on the table. 'I don't fucking believe it.'

'Oh, don't worry.' I threw the frying pans in the dishwasher, slamming the door shut with an unholy crash. 'He said they've gone ahead and done the deal without you.'

Chapter Thirteen

LOVE IS A MANY-SPLINTERED THING

'I THINK I MIGHT have overcooked my biscuits,' I said guiltily, flapping out the boys' school shirts and folding them over the last few inches of free radiator space in Leoni's sitting room. 'Rick's hardly said two words to me so I thought it best to get out of his way.'

'Count yourself lucky.' Leoni untangled a bundle of wet socks. 'I've been trying to get Marcus to stop prattling on at me for years. From the moment he gets in from work, it's all Brian this and Colin that. I've got no idea who any of these people are, and, frankly, I don't bloody care either.' She took the empty basket back to the kitchen and sighed at the world laundry mountain stacked up by the washing machine. 'Look at this lot.' She stuck her hands on her hips. 'There's seven loads there at least, it's pissing down with rain outside and the tumble dryer's busted. I wish I could just get up in the morning and piss off to a nice quiet office while somebody else washed my pants and cleaned my house.'

'Any news on his promotion?' I helped myself to a biscuit.

'Nope.' She started stuffing the machine again. 'The big boss man is giving them plenty of time to grovel and lick his boots before he puts them out of their misery. I bet he's loving every minute of it.'

'I hope he gets it,' I said with genuine sentiment. I like Marcus. He could do with a break, not to mention a Purple Heart for putting up with his wife all these years.

'Yeah? Well I'm not holding my breath. I've told him, all he's got to do is tread water for another ten years or so and he'll be out of there with a cast-iron pension. And I swear, if he does anything to fuck that up I'll kill him, so help me.' She gave the washing machine door a mighty slam and switched it on. 'Right,' she said, glancing at the clock, 'better go and pick those little bastards up from school, I suppose.' That was usually my cue to leave. Only an idiot would hang about once the bell went off. 'Wanna come?' she asked hopefully, as she always does. With the atmosphere at Rick's house still thicker than Leoni's plutonium gravy, the thought of being packed into the car with Millie and the twins-from-hell suddenly seemed like the lesser of two evils.

'Sure,' I said. 'Why not?'

Housework has never been Leoni's strongest suit, but she struggles along with it the best way she can for the sake of appearances, having got the term *bare minimum* down to a fine art years ago. Yet there is one place where she refuses to keep up the pretence, where only a few are brave enough to tread. And, believe me, filthy just doesn't go far enough. When it comes to squalor, her car is the very axis of evil. Everything is caked in a waxy patina of ancient grime: the fabric, the carpets, the metalwork. Scraps of once-edible detritus hang like festering icicles, immovably welded to the doors. The only way to see out of the windows is to rub a little hole in the muck. And, my God, it stinks up to high heavens.

'Sorry about the mess,' Leoni said automatically. I brushed a half-mauled chicken nugget and a few loose chips off the passenger seat then got in, ignoring the horrible squelching noise of whatever it was that had been left underneath it. Probably Gandalf the Neurotic Hamster, now crushed to a pet-sized pancake. Winding down her window as we sped towards the school,

Leoni proceeded to throw all the reachable trash out into the street while we pelted along. Crisp packets, a couple of McDonald's happy meal boxes, a carrier bag full of sandwich crusts. I was particularly impressed by the way she leaned into the corners as though riding a motorbike, urging the clapped-out Fiat to make it round the bend without losing a wheel, then going hell for leather down the hill before coming to a screeching halt just before ploughing into the sea of noisy children spewing out of the school gates.

'I bloody hate the school run.' She wrenched on the handbrake. 'It's like having a permanent time bomb ticking away in my pocket. Wherever I am, whatever I'm doing, I have to put my life on hold and be standing at these gates by half past three come hell or high water. And it goes on for years.' Reaching to the glove compartment, she flipped it open and took out a packet of Rolos. 'I bet there's nothing about that in any of Julia's kiddie instruction manuals, is there?'

'I wouldn't know.' I accepted the Rolo and stuck it in my mouth, hoping my fillings would stay put as they wedged themselves into the rock hard, freezing toffee.

'Look out!' Leoni suddenly ducked down. 'It's bloody Mrs Gallagher!' She pretended to be searching for something on the floor. Bloody Mrs Gallagher tapped politely on Leoni's window.

'Mrs Franklin?' Leoni pretended not to have heard

and kept her head jammed in the footwell by my legs. I prodded her gently.

'You're not going to get away with it,' I whispered through gritted ventriloquist teeth. 'She's seen you.'

'Oh, bollocks,' Leoni muttered before pulling her head up and forcing a tight smile. 'Hello, Mrs Gallagher,' she said, winding down the window a fraction. 'Everything all right?'

'Yes, fine!' Mrs Gallagher recoiled from the ripe aromas seeping out of the car. 'And you?'

'Yep.' Leoni beeped on the horn, craning to see through the crowd of yelling reprobates, hoping to catch a glimpse of her brood. 'Nice to see you.' She snuck me a tiresome glance and crossed her eyes then turned her head away, as if to close the conversation with the other mother.

'I was wondering,' Mrs Gallagher persisted, leaning her hand against the partially open window as if to deter Leoni from closing her off completely. Not a particularly smart move as I doubted that Leoni would think twice before crushing her fingers if she felt like it. 'Now that the weather's cheering up a bit, perhaps Felix could come over and play with the twins some time?' Leoni raised an eyebrow at her. 'Or,' the woman back-pedalled quickly, 'they could come over to my house if that would be more convenient.'

'Mmm.' Leoni sucked her teeth. 'I dunno if that's such a good idea.'

'Oh.' Mrs Gallagher began to wring her hands. 'It's just that Felix doesn't really have that many friends, and seeing as your boys sometimes share a lift with him, well, I just thought that it might be nice for them to—' Felix appeared through the throng of other children, his head clad in silver foil, bent determinedly towards the ground, placing his feet awkwardly, moving like a robot.

'What's he doing?' Leoni asked.

'Pavement cracks.' Mrs Gallagher sighed. 'If he steps on any of them, or puts both feet down on the same slab, he'll cause an earthquake.'

'Oh. Right.' Leoni nodded. 'Of course.'

'Please!' Mrs Gallagher's hands gripped the edge of the window in desperation. 'Just let him come over and play after school one afternoon!'

'I don't think you understand,' Leoni said coolly. 'If you send Felix into my house, there's a very real possibility that he'll never make it out alive.'

'Right now –' Mrs Gallagher swallowed hard – 'that's a chance I'm prepared to take.'

'Hi.' Rick sounded tired. 'It's me.'

'Hi,' I said, closing my eyes and cringing behind the relative safety of Leoni's broom cupboard door. I'd tried answering the call in the kitchen, but there was no competing with the head-splitting racket the kids were kicking up while Leoni incinerated a packet of fish fingers and wrestled open a bag of oven chips. Admitting to Leoni that I had maybe overplayed my part was one thing, but fixing the damage I had done to my ailing relationship with Rick would be quite another.

'Are you planning on making an appearance later or what?' Oh God. Why doesn't he just fire me now and be done with it? This was all getting much too complicated by far.

'I wasn't sure if you wanted to see me,' I said remorsefully. His protracted silence wasn't exactly the pillar of reassurance I had been hoping for. 'Look,' I said, trying to salvage something, anything. 'We both know that it's been a total disaster since Lola turned up. Why don't I just move out?' Hearing nothing, I checked the screen on my mobile in case we had been cut off. His name just sat there, scowling at me. 'Then maybe we can pick up later where we left off?' Silence. 'Hello?'

'Yeah,' he sighed. 'I'm still here.'

'You sound awful.'

'I'm not fucking surprised.' I heard him light up a smoke. 'I've just lost a three million quid deal and my daughter thinks I'm a shirtlifter.'

'Sorry.' I didn't know whether to laugh or cry. 'But I have to ask, were those really your trousers?'

'No, they fucking weren't! Waddya take me for?' I

had a brief vision of one of Rick's colourful gatecrashers staggering out from the party *sans-culottes*. He quietened again, the fleeting glimpse of humour gone in a moment.

'I'm really sorry about the deal.' I hung my head in shame. 'I had no idea.'

'Nah.' He took a long drag. I could almost smell the sweet aroma of his Cohiba. 'It's my own fault. How were you supposed to know something I didn't tell you?' He sighed. 'I guess you're right, Hell.' Oh no. Where was the *babe*? I braced myself for the inevitable. 'Maybe I was a bit hasty, insisting you move in with me when you didn't want to. I shouldn't have done that. I guess I just got a bit carried away in the moment.'

'No!' I began to protest.

'And now I'm living in a house with a daughter who hates my guts and a madwoman who's hell-bent on revenge. It's all a bit of a mess really, innit?' There wasn't much I could say to that, so I said nothing. 'So, I guess I'll see you when I see you.'

'OK.' I bit my lip, tried to get a grip, and unhooked my coat from the back of the cupboard door.

'You all right?' Leoni ignored the smoke pouring from the frying pan.

'Not really,' I said. 'I think I'd better go.'

'No!' She clawed her fingers and adopted her well-practised witch's voice. 'Don't leave me on my own with the evil Little People.'

'That's no way to talk about your children.' I smiled at her.

'Maybe not,' she conceded. 'But they've bloody done me more psychological damage than I've done them. Even if I spent the rest of my life in therapy, I'd still be a basket case. Need a lift?'

'No thanks,' I said, pulling on my coat. 'I'll get the bus.'

I can't have been more than ten yards from the door when I heard the explosion, like an enormous, dull thunderclap, muffled by the bricks and mortar. A small plume of black smoke lifted from the rooftop. For a split second I froze, as though trying to compute an unimaginable equation: Leoni plus fish fingers plus gas cooker equals . . . I sprinted back to the house, screaming her name, pounding for a second on the front door before realizing that she was hardly likely to answer me if all her limbs had been blown off. I ran round the back instead, wrenching the door open and flying in like a banshee. 'Leoni!' I yelled at the top of my voice, before noticing that the kitchen was still intact with nothing more than a pan of peas boiling over on the hob. Then, from upstairs, came the unmistakable sound of Leoni's patience snapping.

'You little BASTARDS!' she screamed. I dropped

my bag to the floor and raced up the stairs, my nose instantly sensing the same acrid smell that hangs in the air the day after fireworks night.

'Leoni! What the hell was that?'

'Look!' she screeched at me, pointing towards the boys' room. 'Just look at what they've done!'

To say that it looked as though a bomb had gone off would have been spot on. They'd made one, put it in the chest of drawers, and blown it to smithereens.

Chapter Fourteen

NEVER IN A MILLION YEARS

I DAWDLED ALL the way back to Rick's house, dragging my feet, taking a quick shufti in a couple of estate agent's windows, hoping to spot a reasonably priced rentable stop-gap, but it all suddenly seemed so depressing. The thought of coming home to someone else's neutrally decorated, buy-to-let investment weighed heavily. I didn't want to feel like some rootless, floating nonentity. Not again. It would be like losing my sense of self all over and sliding inexorably back into the general melting pot of Sad People With No Life. I

caught sight of my reflection in a shop window, looking like a cross between a bag lady and a forty-year-
old frump, and felt very sorry for myself indeed.
Before I knew what I had done, I found myself a
couple of miles up the road where Kensington segues
into Fulham, standing on Sara's doorstep.

'Helen?' I have to say, I was more than a little taken
aback when Mr Suave answered the door in his bathrobe, unshaven at six-thirty in the evening, and quite
apparently not in the mood for visitors. 'What a pleasant surprise!' he lied seamlessly, stepping aside and
motioning me in. 'Darling!' he called. 'We have company!'

'What *now*?' she bellowed from upstairs. 'For
Christ's sake. I've only been home for two minutes
and you're already snivelling at me for attention like a
five-year-old.' Dudley, usually so calm and collected,
wilted with injury.

'Excuse me,' he snivelled, reaching a handkerchief
from his pocket. 'I don't think I can do this right now.'
And with that, he rushed tearfully upstairs, pushing
past Sara on the way. As usual, it seemed that my
timing had been impeccable.

'Helen!' Well, at least someone seemed pleased to
see me. 'What the bloody hell are you doing here?'
Sara, resplendent in a perfectly cut scarlet wrap dress
that clung to her youthful body, planted a friendly pair

of kisses on my cheeks, leaving an impression of her exotic perfume on my skin. In a brief moment of déjà vu, I was reminded of the fabulous vision that Julia had cut when she first broke away from her day job and took the world by storm twenty years ago. It seemed that Sara had shed some of her sharp edges and become one of the new generation of go-getters while no one was looking.

'I'm really sorry,' I whispered, tilting my head towards the stairs. 'Have I caught you two in the middle of a massive row? Crikey, he seems really upset.'

'Don't ask,' she said. 'Fancy a gin and tonic? I was just about to mix myself a real mother. Might as well go the whole hog and head for oblivion. It's either that or listen to Dudley whining all night.'

'That's the best offer I've had all day. Listen – ' I nudged her discreetly, still unsettled by Dudley's apparent hysteria – 'are you sure I'm not disturbing you? I mean, I was only popping in to say hello.'

'Course not! Try to leave and I'll bite your legs off. I've been so bloody stacked I haven't seen anyone.' Her brow furrowed for a moment, as though doing a quick tot-up in her head and wondering where on earth the time had flown to. Welcome to the club. 'Then I get home knackered and have to deal with that.' She flicked her eyes upstairs. 'How's the flat coming along?' she asked, pouring us both a large one from the drinks cabinet she keeps permanently stacked to the gunnels.

'Don't ask.' I shook my head.

'I heard you had a major disaster. Sorry I haven't been in touch. With Julia out of the picture, things have been dead busy at the office.'

'Have you heard much from her?'

'Sort of,' Sara said, handing me an icy glass. 'Although I'd rather she didn't bother. To be honest, she's been more of a hindrance than a help lately. She rings up daily with the excuse of asking how it's all going then starts rattling on about rusks and placentas.' She pulled a face. 'I told her to go make a bloody nest somewhere and sit on it instead of bothering me. I've got a bloody business to run.' I took a sip and shuddered pleasurably at the double measure of Bombay Sapphire.

'Mmm,' I mumbled. 'That's good.' Sara dropped herself in one of the big cream sofas and I followed suit.

'So, what brings you here?' she said, adding hastily, 'Not that you're not always welcome. You're bloody lucky to have caught me in, mind. This is the first time I've been back before eight in the last month. There just aren't enough hours in the day.' Déjà vu indeed. I wondered if I should point out the evils of workaholism then decided to keep my oars out of her pond.

'I don't want to talk about it.' I raised a weary eyebrow. 'Just keep my glass topped up and roll me out of the door when the bottle's empty.'

'Well, that's done it.' Sara put her drink down. 'You turn up out of the blue, collapse on my sofa and refuse to tell me why?' She folded her arms across her chest and gave me one of her no-nonsense Lancashire interrogation glares. 'So go on then. Out with it.'

'Oh, nothing,' I sighed and tutted. 'Men, eh? Can't live with them. Can't shoot them.'

'Uh-oh. Have you two gone and hit The Wall before getting out of the starting blocks?'

'Why is it that whenever the chips are down they turn into spineless, lily-livered cretins?' I chose to ignore the fact that I do a pretty good impression of a lily-livered cretin myself now and again. 'I'm talking about Rick,' I added, as though I needed reminding.

'You don't say.' Sara didn't even try to keep the sarcasm from her voice.

'Ever since his monstrous daughter turned up on the doorstep.'

'Daughter?'

'It's a long and not very interesting story.'

'Right.'

'Anyway. She turned up, just like that – ' I snapped my fingers – 'and Rick refused to introduce me to her as his girlfriend. Judas. Just brushed me under the carpet like I didn't exist. How cowardly is that?

What – ' I felt a good old rant coming on – 'like I'm not good enough to be introduced as his squeeze? I know I'm not exactly Angelina Jolie,' (understatement of the century), 'but I do have my pride, you know.' I took a big swallow of gin. 'He practically begged me to move in with him when my ceilings caved in,' (oh, go on, a little embellishment between girlfriends is de rigueur anyway), 'and there we were, having a perfectly nice time, then Lola comes bowling along and suddenly I'm history.'

'Lola?'

'The daughter with the sawn-off voice box.'

'Right.'

'You know what he did?' I realized I was pointing at her and lowered my finger.

'Go on – ' Sara inspected her nails – 'surprise me.'

'He told Lola I was nothing more than the house-keeper, had the cleaner move all my stuff into the crappy little box room at the top of the house, then demanded that I start cooking for the pair of them.' I let out a huge sigh of indignance. 'I've had to skivvy around like a servant, pretending to be the hired help—'

'But,' Sara frowned, 'you are the hired help, aren't you?'

'Whatever.' I flapped that inconvenient detail away with an impatient wave of my drink. 'And now I've got nowhere to live, a boyfriend who's not my boyfriend any more, and – ' I wondered how to put it, bearing in mind that I was speaking to a frost-hardened northerner – 'everything's gone tits-up and I feel like shit.' Perfect linguistics.

'Good.' Sara said. I beg your pardon? Well that's bloody nice, isn't it? 'I'm glad I'm not the only one who's suffering as a result of,' (she raised her voice, shouting at the ceiling), 'being forced to share a house with a completely DOZY TWAT.' So, it seemed that her marriage had finally settled down into the usual delightful melange of public fakery interspersed with the hurling of indiscriminate insults. She took a deep breath and calmed herself with a couple of sips before continuing to me in a less aggressive tone. 'I don't know what to do with him,' she shrugged. 'He'll stay upstairs sulking for a while, then he'll get bored and come down on the pretext of needing something from the kitchen, huffing and sighing in the hope that I'll start cooing at him and ask what the matter is. Then we'll have the same old revolving conversation until I'm forced to punch him in the udders.'

'Is he ill?' I whispered. 'I mean, I've never known Dudley not to shave. He's usually polished up like a new sixpence.'

'It's all Julia's fault.' She slurped at her drink, poking the ice down with her finger to get a better purchase on it.

'Julia? What's she done?'

'Durr!' Sara pointed at her head and scowled at me like I was dumber than the average village idiot. 'She's bloody gone and got herself up the duff, hasn't she?'

'So?' She'd lost me somewhere along the line.

'Well you know what Saint Fucking Dudley's like, don't you? His dad's a preacher, remember?' As if I could forget. 'It's like Julia's gone and opened his traditional family-friendly floodgates, and now all he wants is a bloody baby.'

'Aaaah.' The penny dropped. 'I see.'

'No, Helen. Believe me, you don't see the half of it. We've gone round the houses about it a thousand times. I'm not ready. I'm not interested. And I'm not some kind of battery hen. But will he listen? Will he fuck. Then he started mooning around like a wet weekend, and everything snowballed from there.'

His footsteps on the stairs spurred an immediate change of subject.

'So I went to the garden centre and bought an organic compost mix instead,' I said loudly.

'Oh really?' Sara replied, straining her ears towards the door. 'That's very interesting.' We listened intently while Dudley moved around the kitchen, exchanging the odd decoy phrase while he huffed and sighed, and waited until he had gone back upstairs, dragging his feet miserably. Sara slumped back in her seat. 'See what I mean? So what are you going to do about Rick?'

'Dunno.' I shrugged uselessly. 'Sit here with you until the gin's run out then chalk another crap relationship on the great graffiti wall of life I suppose.'

'Well, it could be a lot worse.' Sara cleared her throat and prepared to raise her voice at the ceiling again. 'You could have gone and MARRIED THE ARSEHOLE.' A shudder ran down my spine as my dead husband walked over my grave.

'No chance.' I shook my head. 'Never in a million years.'

'You can stay here with us for a while if you like,' Sara said. 'There's plenty of space.' True. Dudley's house had always been a big plus in the attraction stakes, as had his bulging wad. It didn't take a rocket scientist to work out how come Sara had chosen to marry the world's most boring man, even if she hadn't realized just how deep the rabbit hole went. If being boring were a sport, nobody else would even bother to take it up because Dudley's unbeatable. I can feel my shutters coming down just thinking about it. Still, she'd made her bed and now she was just going to have to lie in it, and if I had to lie in the one in the next room for a while, it was definitely a more attractive prospect than moving into a faceless bedsit.

'Thanks,' I said, giving it some serious thought. 'I might just take you up on that.'

'Please do. Maybe it'll jolt some sense into Dud By Name and snap him out of it. You can keep him company when he comes home from work early, yet again, complaining of backache or indigestion or chronic fatigue.'

'Don't you think you should get him to see the doctor? Sounds to me like he could be suffering from a bit of depression,' I suggested. 'It can get you like that. Strange little aches and pains. You know how men tend to put things off until they get really bad. Then whatever it was in the first place is ten times worse. Perhaps you should get him checked out.'

'You must be joking,' she scoffed. 'He was just fine until a couple of weeks ago. I didn't notice at first. God, I was so rushed off my feet at work, what did he bloody well expect? Moping around trying to get me to notice his inner pain. Southern softie. I knew I should have married a coalminer. At least then we could have had a decent fist fight instead of all this poncing around.'

'Sara,' I cajoled her gently. 'You've been married less than two years and, while I fully appreciate that you've decided to go the Big Career route, surely you must understand that your husband needs a little attention too?' It seemed to me that she didn't know which side her bread was buttered. I'd have killed for a husband like that when I was her age. Kind, generous, good-looking in an unmemorable way. Yes, I might well have been bored rigid, but I could always have taken a string of lovers or booked myself in for a quick lobotomy.

'Stuff that.' Sara finished her drink and gave out an almighty burp. 'I reckon he's having a phantom pregnancy.'

'HI,' I SAID, waving Rick a small, white-flag smile. 'I've come to pick up my things.' He stepped back and held the door open for me, the pair of us loitering awkwardly in the hallway while I tried to look like it didn't matter.

'I don't suppose there's anything I can say to make you change your mind?'

'No, Rick, I don't think so.'

'Sure about that?' He searched my face.

'And I ought to give you this.' I held out my key.

'Oh.' He pursed his lips thoughtfully. 'So it's a double whammy?'

'I think it's the only way,' I said bravely. He made no move to take the key from me, so I put it down on the table.

'Fancy a drink?'

'And run the risk of Lola catching you fraternizing with the staff? I think not. Anyway, I just had a stiff one with Sara.'

'Dutch courage, eh?'

'Something like that.'

'She's not here.'

'Oh?' Thank God for that. I felt my shoulders relax a little.

'Helped herself to half the cards in my wallet this afternoon and fucked off to some fancy clinic in Paris to buy herself a new nose.'

'You're kidding.'

'Nope. Dunno when she'll be back either, that's if she bothers to come back at all.'

'Still not speaking to you?' I continued to loiter. Oh, for God's sake Helen. Stop pissing around. Just go upstairs and get your stuff.

'That depends if you count calling me every name under the sun speaking.' He scratched his head and laughed ruefully. 'Mind you, I suppose it's no less than I deserve. I've not exactly excelled myself in the parenting department.'

'Don't beat yourself up about it. Maybe if you'd brought her up yourself things might have been different.'

'You mean she might actually have turned into a half-decent human being? I doubt it.'

'Perhaps it's a cultural thing,' I shrugged. 'You never know.'

'Yeah, well, it's just another supersize cock-up if you ask me.' He reached into his pocket for a cigar and stuck it between his teeth. 'And I'm about done with all that. Time to make a few changes, I reckon.' A yellow flame burst violently from the match in his hand. I watched him lift it to the end of his Cohiba, drawing on it hard until the end glowed brightly. 'How about a little glass of bubbly to toast my epiphany?' For a moment, he had that twinkle in his eye. 'Better late than never, eh? Go on. Be a devil.'

'Really. I'm fine.'

'Sure?'

'Yep.'

'Because you don't look fine to me.'

'I'll just pop upstairs then,' I said, edging away. 'Won't be long.'

Up in the dungeon, sitting on the little bed, gathering up my smalls and stowing them neatly in my suitcase, I got the distinct feeling that I had been here before, then found the exact point of reference – it was the day I went off with the Girl Guides for a week at that rat-infested campsite just outside Portsmouth. The night before I had diligently folded and packed my vests and pants, all of them sewn with the obligatory nametags, feeling like I was being thrown to the lions. I had detested every long minute of Girl Guiding. All those pointless evenings in the freezing church hall down the road, being forced to take part in a variety of utterly fruitless tasks. Having to go and visit crazy old people who lived on their own in musty houses, offered you soggy biscuits and could never find their teeth. When I told my mother how much I hated it, she insisted that it was character building and signed me up for the camping trip. Yep. That night had been a major low point, and I felt as though I had zapped back in time and ended up right back at square one. Well, that's just brilliant. Thank you, God. When I die, which knowing my luck could be any time soon, I'm going to have some pretty stern words once I've done my three million years in purgatory. And don't worry about me forgetting about it either, mate. I can hold a grudge indefinitely. My phone rang. I fished it out of my bag and checked the screen. No name. No number. Hmm. An anonymous caller just as I was about to slit my wrists? Could be a good omen. Could be a misdirected call leading me straight into the arms of Mister Right.

'Hello?'

'Are you sure you're sure?'

'Rick.'

'Afraid so. Listen. I've been thinking.' I thought I could smell something burning. 'What if I admitted that I've been a complete prat and offered to stand on the corner naked with a big sign around my neck saying, well, you know, I'm A Prat.'

'Where are you?'

'On the bat phone.'

'Oh,' I said. 'Look, Rick.' I screwed up my face and

stuck to my guns, despite my crumbling resolve. 'You're not making this very easy.'

'Maybe I don't want to. Wanna go out for dinner and talk about it?'

'Not really.' At the mention of food, my stomach gurgled loudly, reminding me that I hadn't sat down and had an uneventfully square meal in days.

'How about dinner and not talking about it? I won't say a word. Promise.'

'You're relentless.' I sighed.

'I know,' he said. 'That's what makes me so adorable.'

'I'm hanging up now,' I said, and hung up.

A few minutes later, I snapped the hinges shut on my latest failed romance and dragged it to the stairs where Rick stood, waiting.

'Here,' he said, pulling the case from my straining hands. 'Give that to me.' He lifted it with ease and headed down. 'I might be an arsehole, but I still know how to carry a woman's bags and see her safely home.'

Outside on the street, Rick stuck his fingers in his mouth and let out one of his eyeball-shattering whistles. 'Where to?' he asked as the cab pulled up.

'Gilston Road,' I said. Then, as if needing to explain myself, 'Sara and Dudley have offered me kennels.'

'Oh, right!' he said, crushing the burning end of his cigar between his fingers to put it out and stuffing it in his pocket. 'Jump in.' Rick put my suitcase in the front, exchanged a few words with the driver, then, to my dismay, piled into the back with me and shut the door.

'What are you doing?'

'Dinner,' he said, staring straight ahead non-negotiably at the traffic. 'And I'm not taking no for an answer. You and I have unfinished business, young lady.' I felt my stomach lurch, knowing there would be absolutely no point in arguing with him.

TRUE TO HIS WORD, we ate peaceably under Tony's watchful eye, the conversation between us a carefully constructed Switzerland of neutral topics. On those few occasions I had seen Rick in contemplative mood, he had demonstrated himself to be a creature of surprisingly fine sensibilities. Yet such glimpses had been rare. I suppose we're all multifaceted in one way or another: the fun side; the serious side; the side that's more comfortable when we're pretending to be something we're not.

'What are you thinking right now?' he asked out of the blue. I blinked back at him, realizing that I had been miles away. Moments passed. 'Too late,' he said. I smiled.

'Our timing's been pretty rotten, hasn't it?'

'Well, you see, Hell –' he raised a hand at Tony,

presumably to ask for the bill – 'I dunno about that. Do you want anything else?'

'No thanks.' I shook my head while the table was cleared of the remnants of our last supper. 'That was lovely.'

'Are you sure?'

'Quite sure.' I nodded.

'Good.' Rick straightened himself and winked at me. 'That's what I like to see. A woman who's capable of making a decision.' He sat back in his chair.

I'm not sure at what point I became mildly aware of the four waiters hovering beside our table, none of whom I recognized. Perhaps it was something to do with the whispering frisson that ran through the restaurant as they lined up right beside me, the tallest of them producing a small harmonica from beneath his long apron and blowing a single, apologetic note. A sweeping hush descended. The smiling waiters put their arms about each other's shoulders and took a sharp intake of breath, then, swaying like a summer breeze, they began to sing in perfect barbershop harmony. 'Blue moon . . . You saw me standing alone . . .' Soft and gentle like a lullaby.

Well. I just didn't know where to put myself. My hands leapt to my face, my hair crimping with embarrassment, but the spontaneous smile on my face must have been wider than a mile. Rick watched me closely and seemed satisfied with what he saw. I caught his gaze briefly then looked away, unsure of what I was supposed to do in response to his outrageously ostentatious gesture. Without warning, amid the honeydewed voices, Rick rose from his chair. In perfectly rehearsed modulation, the quartet lowered their voices, humming a melodious backdrop.

'Ladies and gentlemen,' Rick announced loudly enough to be heard right through to the back of the kitchen. 'If I could have your attention for a moment, I have a very public apology to make to the woman I love.'

Then he turned to me. I cringed in my seat. This is that moment that I have in nightmares sometimes, when everyone's staring at me and I look down and realize that I haven't got any clothes on and I'm in the middle of Tesco's searching for my shoes. Rick cleared his throat, demanding my attention.

'I know I'm not exactly a bargain,' he said. A small, appreciative ripple of amusement passed across the tables, heads craning. 'But I am smart enough to know that you're the best thing that ever happened to me. And I'm sorry for being an arse.' A few diners stood up at the back to get a better view. 'I've made quite enough mistakes in my life and I'm not about to make another one.' Then, in front of everyone, Rick dropped to his knee. The barbershop waiters stopped humming. The cutlery on the tables stopped clattering. Heads appeared from around the now silent kitchen door. Every hair on my body stood up and started screaming.

'Helen Robbins.' Rick reached out and took my hand. 'Will you marry me?'

The whole room held its breath.

I sat there, dumbfounded, staring at him wide-eyed. It was inconceivable, incomprehensible. I'd once made myself a solemn promise. Never, never again. Never in a million years. The moment stretched and ached with the pain of a thousand unwanted memories as the agony of my first marriage clawed at my insides. My heart clenched, my mouth opened, but nothing came out. Suddenly, from the pin-drop silence in the room, a woman's voice piped up.

'Where's the ring, you idiot?' A smattering of tense laughter rose from a few tables. To my astonishment, Rick casually reached into his inside pocket, brought out a small, dark blue box, and slid it onto the table.

'Open it,' he said quietly. 'It's yours anyway, whatever you decide.'

Lifting the lid to a brilliant flash, mine wasn't the only gasp that went up, and I found myself staring open-mouthed at the jewel that sat there, snug in its little box, revelling in my gawping admiration. The main event, which I think the Tiffany flunky might have described as 'substantial', was an Edwardian cushion-cut stone, clear as a droplet of water, surrounded by a sparkling diamond setting that extended prettily around the shank. Even though it must have been the size of a Smartie, there was something deliciously understated about its attraction, its cut more elegant than showy, like a naturally pretty woman who knew she didn't have to try. The lady at the next table dropped her spectacles from her face dramatically and gave me one of those if-you-don't-say-yes-I-bloody-well-will looks. At that moment, I really don't know what was going through my head, only that each brief, terrifying thought hurtled past at a hundred miles an hour, leaving me unable to grasp hold of any of them.

'I don't know what to say,' I said, feeling sick to the pit of my stomach.

'Say yes.' Rick clasped my hand and kissed it. 'And I promise you'll never regret it. Never in a million years.'

Looking into his face, his darkened, anxious eyes, I felt the sand shift beneath my feet, and, as if by magic, my battered heart let go of all those years of anguish that had held me bound. Unable to say yes, I just sat there and nodded before bursting into tears as the whole room erupted.

Chapter Fifteen

RULES OF
ENGAGEMENT

'HOLY SHIT!' LEONI almost wrenched my arm off. 'It's the Rock of Gibraltar!'

'Do you think it's a bit much?' I asked unnecessarily.

'Are you kidding me? Oi, Fatso!' She shouted at Marcus over the music, ignoring the disapproving clucks from a few of the better house-trained guests. 'Now that's what you call an engagement ring.' She shook her left fist at him. 'Not this crappy microscopic crumb you fobbed me off with, you tight git.'

I found Rick at my side, smiling proudly. 'Come

on,' he said. 'There's a few people I want to introduce you to.' Leoni released her vice-like grip on my wrist and I slipped away, allowing Rick to lead me through the multitude that had descended upon the house for this supposedly intimate soirée.

'Gosh,' I whispered. 'I never expected so many people.'

'Tossers, most of 'em.' He gave me a sly wink. 'But everybody wanted to come and take a good look at the woman who stole my heart.' Yeah, I'll bet. Had I not been hiding behind a fabulous new frock and a proper shop-bought hairdo, I would have felt positively naked under the glare. I recognized a face in the group of tuxedos we slowed towards. 'You remember Mike Rowles?' Rick said.

'Yes, of course!' I reached out my hand and smiled, trying to obliterate the big neon pre-nup sign flashing away in my head. 'Mike, how are you?'

'Miserable and twisted,' he said. 'That's what makes me such a good lawyer. I'd like to offer you my congratulations, but I'm afraid my wife managed to beat all sense of joy out of me years ago.' It was hard to tell whether or not he was joking.

'And this is Julian – ' Rick indicated the bespectacled man to Mike's left – 'my accountant. Knows far too much about me so I couldn't fire him even if I wanted to.'

'Hello.' I shook his hand, trying to burn his name into my overstretched memory banks.

'True, although he could always have me killed I suppose.' Julian smiled disarmingly. 'Not that I'd recommend it. There's no taper relief on assassination fees.'

'Very funny.' Rick patted him amiably on the back. 'Just keep counting the beans and robbing me blind.'

And so we moved on, Rick easing me gently past one face, then another, pausing only long enough to make the obligatory introductions and to exchange a sentence or two. For him, it seemed the most natural thing in the world, mingling with consummate ease. For me, it was instant information overload with the added danger of a floor-length hemline that had already caught around my heel once, almost sending me head first down the stairs. After a couple of minutes, my concentration went. All names flew in one ear and straight out the other, facial features blurring into a homogenized mass. Oh yes. Of course. How do you do. Yes. Very happy. Thank you. Have we set the date? No, not yet. (Palpitations. I'd cross that bridge too far when I came to it.) My face began to ache with the constant effort of maintaining an interested smile.

'Just one more,' Rick nudged me. 'Then we'll kick this lot out and keep the interesting ones for the after-party, OK?' I nodded as we approached the chisel-faced woman I had noticed snarling in the corner earlier.

'Angela?' Rick said to her. My interest piqued instantly. Ah-ha. At long last I get to meet the secretary who's never made any secret of hating my guts and has rarely missed an opportunity to make me feel like a complete twit whenever we've spoken. Now this was an introduction that I was really looking forward to. I did my best to appear highly sophisticated and wished that I were just that little bit taller. 'This is the lovely Helen,' Rick said. Angela visibly prickled and forced a grimace of a smile. I could see exactly what she was thinking. Words like *housekeeper*, *Jezebel* and *how-could-he-do-this-to-me*, went ching ching behind her cold, unforgiving eyes.

'How do you do?' She kept her hands firmly by her sides, conceding the merest hint of a nod instead.

'At long last.' I smiled at her innocently. 'A chance to put a face to that charming voice on the telephone.' You old bag. 'Rick tells me that you're an absolute gem.' I slunk my arm through his, flashing my cahoona of a ring, just to rub it in.

'Well,' she replied tightly. 'One does one's best.'

'Excellent.' I reached out and touched her arm condescendingly. 'Keep up the good work.' Back of the net. Yessssss. I excused myself graciously and went in search of a friendlier face.

'Yoo-hoo!' Paul raised his hand in a high wave,

pushing through the room with no thought to the drinks he upset in the process. 'Sorry we're late! I just couldn't decide what to wear!' He grabbed hold of me, kissing the air around my face, hissing, 'Is that an Oscar de la Renta dress?'

'Yes.' I held my head high and did my best to fend off the guilt that had eaten me alive ever since I set fire to my Barclaycard. This was no time to be thrifty. Might as well be hanged for a sheep as a lamb.

'It's *sensational*,' he gushed, grasping my arm to affirm his point.

'You took the words right out of my mouth.' Sally loped in a pace behind, slid his arm around my waist and went straight for the jugular, placing a brief but deadly kiss on my neck. 'Where's the big man?' Sally scanned the sea of heads easily from his height advantage, ignoring the furtive glances from every red-blooded woman in the room. 'We've brought a present for him.' He dipped his face down to my ear and whispered discreetly. 'It's a little peace offering from Paul.'

'Over there somewhere.' I waved my glass towards the place where I had last seen him. 'But for God's sake don't let Paul kiss him. I'm not sure he's recovered from his accidental homoerotic experience yet.'

'Champagne, sir?' The almost dumb waiter who slid silently to our side appeared instantly concussed by Sally's presence.

'Thanks,' Sally drawled, expertly lifting three glasses in one hand from the boy's quivering tray before disappearing in search of Paul's high-pitched *coo-eee!* of recognition in a far corner of the room.

'You're looking very pleased with yourself.' Julia had secured prime position near the drawing-room door, where she could oversee the incoming canapés and skim off the top anything that took her fancy. David stood by her protectively, offering his upturned hands as makeshift plates.

'Let's just say that I've scored a minor victory,' I said smugly.

'I'll bloody say!' Marcus stuck a thumb in his belt and rocked back on his heels, taking a quick look around to check Rick was out of earshot. 'What do you reckon he's worth, then?'

'I really wouldn't know.' I blushed.

'Go on.' He nudged me. 'Have a guess. Just for fun.'

'Honestly, Marcus.' Oh, do shut up you silly old sod. I looked to David for support, but he seemed more than happy to allow Marcus to keep digging an embarrassing hole for himself.

'Couple of mill? Five? Maybe more? I wonder if he's got proper insurance? He's exactly the kind of client that could swing things in my favour, if you know what I mean. The others wouldn't stand a chance if I dragged an account like that back to the boardroom table.' Marcus took a big noisy swig from his champagne glass, looking up and around the ornate cornic-ing. 'I mean, this place must be worth a mint, even in today's market, don't you reckon?' There was no stopping him, his lips moist with excitement. 'What's a house like this go for these days?'

'Three-ish,' Rick said casually over Marcus's shoulder. 'Maybe a bit more with a fair wind.'

'Oh!' Marcus span around, blustering. 'Rick! Didn't see you there!' He laughed nervously then feigned having just remembered something. 'Is that the time? Bloody hell! Where's my wife got to?'

'That way.' I pointed across the hallway, giving him a clear path on which to beat a hasty retreat.

'So, Mr Wilton.' Julia folded her hands and placed them on top of her fabulously conspicuous bump. 'I should give you fair warning that if you ever do anything to hurt my sister, I'll track you down and shoot you like a dog.' I winced. Nice one, Julia. Keep the conversation breezy. She took a cool sip of her mineral water and looked him straight in the eye. If she had been a formidable opponent pre-pregnancy, now that she was toting an extra couple of hundred-weight and devoid of all rational thought, I wouldn't have fancied any man's chances against her in a ruck.

'Too fucking right.' Rick bit down on his smoulder-ing stogy and grinned at her.

'There you are!' Paul stopped to catch his breath. 'I've been chasing you around for the last fifteen minutes. Didn't you hear me calling?' Rick narrowed his eyes at him, chewing on his cigar.

'Kiss me and you're dead.'

'Oh, come on now!' Paul tinkled. 'We're practically related already! Tobias sends his love, by the way.'

'Great.' Rick let out a long plume of blue smoke. 'At last, I'll be able to sleep at night.'

'And I've brought you a little something to kiss and make up.' He produced a parcel from behind his back. 'Although I'll quite understand if you'd rather not do the kissy bit.'

'What's all this, then?' A small smile crept over Rick's stern features. He loves presents.

'Go on!' Paul thrust it at him. 'Open it!'

'Oh, all right then.' Resting his cigar in the nearest ashtray, Rick accepted Paul's peace offering and tore off the pink, flocked paper.

'Isn't it gorgeous!' Paul gushed. Rick held up the shirt, its sparkling sequins flashing bright dapples across the walls.

Chapter Sixteen

MEET THE F***ERS

'ANOTHER SLICE OF CAKE, Richard?' Mum drove her knife hard into the concrete slab on the cake stand, struggling with both hands, her mouth twisting with effort. To add an extra stressful dimension to the afternoon's proceedings, she had dusted off her prize Minton china, hand-painted with daisies, and she twitched nervously each time a teacup rattled against its saucer. The service had belonged to my eccentric old grandmother, who had held a penchant for delightfully frivolous things and always took tea wearing a hat, even if she was home alone in her dressing gown. Mum used to call her 'an impossible woman', which I never really understood because she seemed just fine to me, if a little bonkers. She knew lots of stories about interesting people and had learned to ride a motorcycle in the war, which she kept up on the quiet for many years afterwards until she came a cropper one summer afternoon, having driven straight into the village duck pond after a few too many sherries. Now there was a woman who really knew how to bake a cake. To this day, I wouldn't dream of deviating from her idiot-proof recipe. 'Weigh your eggs, missy,' she'd say with a wonky smile as I stood on a chair to reach the bowl, making a merry mess of her kitchen. 'Then put in the same amount of all the other ingredients and give it a bit of gumption.' Despite the clouds of flour, egg spillages and piles of sugar all over the floor, her method never failed and we would tuck into the results together, spread with home-made bramble jam before it had cooled, not stopping until we both felt thoroughly ill.

'Er.' Rick had done well to get through the first slice. 'I don't think I could manage—'

'Go on! Force yourself!' she gushed, pressing the second slice on him.

'You don't have to eat that,' my father said from behind his newspaper. 'Even the dog thinks twice about going in for seconds.'

'Frank! Really!' Mum puckered her lips in annoyance. 'Will you please put that paper down and mind your manners? What on earth do you want Richard to think of us?' Which, of course, was the most important thing in the world.

'Thirty-two down.' Dad flapped the paper aside momentarily and peered at Rick. 'Collared in an old-fashioned way, eight letters, ends in L and I think there might be a C in there somewhere.'

'Sorry, Frank,' Rick said. 'I don't even understand the question, mate. Now, if it had been a clue like, say, type of monkey, three letters, begins with A and ends with E with a P somewhere in the middle, I might be able to help you.'

'Oh!' Dad seemed pleasantly surprised. 'Not a cross-word man?' I suspected he'd be glad to remain unchallenged as the self-appointed family intellectual.

'Afraid not.' Rick picked up the cake and smiled bravely. 'Left school at fifteen without a single O level to my name and went straight into the motor trade. The only crosswords I got involved with after that were the sort you sling around when you're having a bit of an argy-bargy.' He girded himself and bit into the cake. 'Mmm. Lovely, Mrs Robbins.'

'Please! Joyce,' she corrected him. Rick nodded, his jaws temporarily locked together, unable to cope with anything more than the mammoth task of chewing his way through a second slice of Mum's coffee and walnut breeze block.

'Cars, eh?' Dad put the paper down. 'Must have done very well for you judging by that little number outside.'

When we'd pulled up in the Bentley, Mum had quite taken leave of her senses, fawning over it and asking if she could sit inside while Dad stood there, puffing on his pipe, trying not to feel totally inadequate. Rick insisted on taking her for a short spin, leaving Dad and I alone together for a few brief but welcome minutes.

'I'll go in and put the kettle on, shall I?'

'I wouldn't,' he'd warned me with a smile. 'If either one of us puts one foot in that kitchen there'll be trouble. She's planned this afternoon with military precision.' Putting the pipe back in his mouth, he'd slung his free arm around my shoulder and watched the car disappear up the hill.

'I know this might all seem a bit sudden, Dad. But it isn't really.' For some reason, I felt that I should explain myself. Perhaps it was because I knew he wouldn't ask. 'We've known each other for quite a long time.'

There had then followed a long pause, not uncomfortable you understand, because that was the way it always was with the old man.

'There's only one thing I'm interested in,' he'd said finally. 'Are you happy?'

'Yes.'

'Then there's nothing else I need to know.' And that was pretty much that.

Sadly, Mum wasn't singing off the same hymn sheet.

After a few minutes of gargantuan effort, Rick somehow managed to swallow. 'Yes,' he said, breaking his habitual *yeah*, just for the afternoon as I had asked. 'I did quite well out of the old motors game. Mind you, that was back in the seventies when you could pick up some real good dodgy bargains and everything was done cash, no questions asked.' He touched his nose. Mum flustered with the teapot, instantly uncomfortable at the mere mention of money.

'More tea, anyone?'

'Dodgy deals, eh?' Dad smiled with interest. 'I'd like to hear more about that.'

'Frank.' Mum's voice tightened, its pitch rising uncomfortably. 'Let's not go asking Richard personal questions that really are none of our business.' She smiled at Rick obsequiously. 'You must excuse my husband. He doesn't get out much these days, I'm afraid.' I rolled my eyes at Dad.

'I'm sure he doesn't mind – ' Dad crossed his legs and sat back – 'seeing as he's about to marry my daughter.'

'Course not,' Rick said. 'You can ask me anything you like, Frank. I don't mind. I've got nothing to hide. Yeah, I got involved with a few shady customers when I was a kid. It's kinda what you did in those days if you wanted to make something of yourself. You either had to be born with a silver spoon in your mouth or pull yourself up by the bootstraps and grab whatever opportunity came your way.'

'Just how shady are we talking here?' Dad wasn't interrogating him as such. He was just interested, that's all. I could tell by the way he had relaxed into his seat and his pipe had gone out.

'Really shady,' Rick said with a small, devilish smile. 'Mind if I smoke?'

'Help yourself.' Dad motioned towards an ashtray.

'Want one'a these?' Rick offered him a cigar, which, to my surprise, Dad took.

'Mmm.' The old man passed it under his nose. 'Smells expensive.' The pair of them lit up.

'Well.' Rick took a couple of big puffs. I noticed Mum trying not to choke, her polite smile gurning into an uncomfortable spasm as she did her best to suppress a series of inconvenient coughs. 'There was this one bloke, right? Bunce was his name. Don Bunce. Used to knock his missus about a bit, but that's another story. Anyway . . .' Rick leaned towards Dad conspiratorially. 'This geezer could get you anything. Anything you asked for – Lotus, Roller, a new set of caps for a Merc. I dunno where he got this stuff from. Then one night, he asked me if I was interested in doing a job.' Rick paused for a slurp of tea to sweep away the last few grains of shrapnel. 'So I says to him, yeah all right, cos at that age, you don't think to stop and ask what kind of a job it is, do ya?' Dad chewed on his cigar a bit and nodded knowingly. 'So off we goes, right, down some place in the middle of nowhere. Out in the countryside it was. Somewhere a bit like this but there was much less traffic in them days.' He inspected the glowing end of his cigar. 'So it's pitch black, he's pulled up, and we've got out the car, opened the boot, and bugger me—' Tea flew out of my mother's mouth. 'Oh sorry!' Rick said as she jumped up. 'I'm such an arse.'

'No!' Mum shrilled like a canary. 'Really! It's quite all right, Richard. Oh, clumsy me,' she said, brushing the tea from her lap. 'Look what I've gone and done.' She rushed off to the kitchen to mop the mess from her royal garden party dress. I stole a sneaky glance at Dad. He caught my eye, just for a second, and seemed thoroughly amused.

'Go on,' Dad said.

'Where was I? Oh yeah. Right. Anyway. So we gets these crowbars out of the boot, jemmy open this barn and – and I swear this is true, right? There's all these cars in there. I mean, the kind of stuff that you dream about. Ferraris, Caddies, Mercs. There was even a bloody Bugatti in there under a big cloth.' Rick shook his head incredulously. 'I mean, who in their right mind would keep a collection like that right out in the middle of nowhere? I thought there'd be dogs or something, but it was all just sitting there for the taking.'

'Beats me,' Dad said, puffing away, hunching his shoulders forward like a gangster.

'Well exactly, Frank. So we 'elped ourselves. Just like that. The bloke took out this list of stuff and we just grabbed whatever we could carry and left.'

'So you didn't steal any of the actual cars?' Dad frowned, apparently disappointed.

'Nah!' Rick waved the accusation away. 'I didn't. But he did. And the other bloke an' all. I drove the Jag back to the lock-up round the back of the arches in Mile End. It was just like that one off *Morse*, only it had a split windscreen.' He thought about it for a moment. 'Probably nicked come to think of it. Yeah. We were a right bunch of monkeys. I didn't even have a driving licence at the time.' He laughed and shrugged apologetically. 'Those were the days, eh? Seems like a million years ago now. I jacked that in pretty sharpish. Learned a lot, mind you.'

'So no more cars after that?' The old man's eyes twinkled.

'Hell, yeah! There was a lot of dosh to be made on the really swanky imports back then. So I got in with the right kind of people, made a few contacts, you know, and it was all kosher. Except customs of course. They were bent as coppers, the lot of 'em. You just brought the cars in round the back door and gave 'em a big bung, so everyone was happy. And once I'd sussed out how to make money, well . . .' Rick decided to leave it there. 'Let's just say I've had more than my fair share of luck.' He looked at me, his face more content than I had ever seen.

'There!' Mum came back to the sitting room, having changed from her royal garden party dress into a lilac polyester number more suitable for a christening. 'What did I miss?'

'Nothing much,' said the old man, tipping Rick a little nod. 'It seems our future son-in-law is a salt-of-the-earth type who's not afraid of hard work.'

'See?' Mum said with a sigh of relief. 'And there we were last night, worrying that you might be some kind of dreadful womanizer with a string of ex-wives and half a dozen children scattered around the country!'

MUM AND I DID the washing-up while Dad took Rick up the garden to see his leeks. 'He seems nice enough,' Mum said, handling each teacup as though it were a pint of nitro-glycerine.

'He is,' I said.

'A little rough around the edges here and there, which is all right if you don't mind that sort of thing I suppose.' I sighed inwardly. 'It was all quite different in my day. Now it's all swear word this, swear word that on the television no matter what time of day it is. Do you know, I heard the S-word on Radio 4 in the middle of the afternoon last week?' She tutted. 'I don't know what the world's coming to. What if there were a mother at home, listening to the afternoon play with her children?' Yes, Mum. That sounds highly likely. 'It's hardly the kind of place you'd expect to find foul language. Hmph. I switched it off right there and then. Should have rung the BBC and told them I was withholding my licence fee until they clean up their act.' She held the cup to her mouth and huffed on it, giving it a final churlish polish before putting it back in the box with the others. 'He does have a very nice car though. I've always approved of a man having a good car. It says a lot about him. Now, if you had turned up here with a man driving a big red flashy sports car, then we'd have been worried. I said to your father – he'd better not be one of those boy racer types. You know the sort.'

'I think I'm a bit long in the tooth for a boy racer, Mum.'

'That's not the point,' she said sharply. 'They prey on women like you. Alone. Not getting any younger. Vulnerable. Desperate for a husband.'

'Excuse me?' I tipped the washing-up water into the sink and pulled off her fur-trimmed Marigolds.

'Oh, it's quite all right, dear. There's no need to be embarrassed. It looks like you've done very well for yourself, and your father and I are very pleased for you.'

'Thanks,' I said wearily, wondering if Rick and I could get away with leaving yet.

'Of course, we'll have to sit down and go through the guest list. I doubt if anyone will have been expecting another wedding in the family. Not at your age anyway. Auntie Jean had been wondering if you weren't . . . well . . .' She curled her lip distastefully. 'It doesn't matter. We don't want to talk about unpleasant things now, do we?'

'Ah,' I said.

'Now, I know you'll have friends of your own that you'll want to invite.' She wiped her hands unnecessarily on the tea towel and went to the drawer where she kept her dog-eared address book. 'But your father and I made a start on going through the relations and family friends.' I very much doubted that Dad would have had any say in the matter.

'Mum.'

'Although we probably wouldn't want to ask Peter and Caroline Scott. They got divorced last year you know. Very nasty business. I wouldn't have thought she'd be the sort either, carrying on like that in broad daylight. It's quite unseemly. Heaven only knows what would have happened had that old shotgun been loaded. It was his grandfather's, apparently. Riddled with dementia and kept pointing it at the postman.'

'Mum.'

'I've made a note of the vicar's telephone number for you, Father Maurice. He's very nice, although I do wish he would do something about that dreadful mole. It's impossible not to stare at it, waggling around like that on the end of his nose. His wife is on the WI committee but her jam really is a disgrace. I thought you ought to call him before you go, see if he's—'

'MUM!'

'Yes, dear?' She sighed, put out at having been interrupted mid-flow.

'We haven't decided about the wedding yet.' I chose not to mention that my feet had been getting colder by the day.

'Not decided!' she scoffed. 'What a ridiculous notion! Of course you've decided. You're getting married, dear.' She tutted. 'It's another chance for you to have the big day you always wanted.' Her tone sharpened. 'After that dreadful first wedding of yours.' Oh, here we go again. 'A pretty fine mess that all was, wasn't it?' I knew it had been a mistake to come here. When will I learn? She picked up the teapot and began drying it aggressively, her mouth pinched into a bunch of sour grapes. 'But we all put on a brave face and soldiered on with it. I knew it would be a complete disaster, right from the very beginning.' Then why didn't you say something? I seem to recall that her only interest had been that ridiculous dress

252

she insisted on wearing with the hideous sailor collar and the hat that didn't quite go. 'But what else were we supposed to do? You'd made up your mind and we had no choice other than to go along with it. Even Auntie Jean said you looked miserable. What kind of a start is that? Well, it's not going to be like that this time around, let me tell you.'

'Quite,' I said, making up my mind on the spot. 'Because we're not inviting anyone.'

'What?' The teapot froze in her hands. 'Don't be so ridiculous.'

'It's not ridiculous. It's the way I want it. A quick in-and-out-job at the local registry office with no fuss, and that's that.'

'You're just being silly now.'

'No I'm not,' I snapped back at her. 'I have no interest in having a big wedding. Just the thought of it is enough to put me off the whole idea.'

'You can't do that,' she decided. 'It's not proper. People will expect to be invited.'

'What people?' I threw my hands up in the air. 'I've not seen hide nor hair of anyone for fifteen years and now I'm expected to roll out the red carpet just because I'm getting married?'

'I see.' She rearranged the teacups, rustling the shredded paper crossly. 'I suppose we're not good enough for you now that you're mixing in fancy company.'

They say if you want to know what a woman is going to be like in thirty years time, look at the mother. My heart sank. Two and a half hours. That must be some kind of record. How she had managed to bite her lip for this long heaven only knows.

'Don't start.'

'I'm not starting anything. I couldn't give two hoots about it myself.' She refused to look at me, her slight sniff of distaste all that she was prepared to share. 'But your father will be bitterly disappointed.'

'Rubbish,' I said.

'It's his duty to give you away.' She pushed the flaps closed on the box. 'Not that you've given any consideration to his feelings or anyone else's. Selfish. That's what you are.'

'Now, just you hang on a minute. You always do this, trying to make me feel bad, but I'm not having it, not this time, do you hear me?'

'If you insist, dear.' The disapproval in her voice matched the line of her mouth. There's just no pleasing some people, and why I should even bother to still try is beyond me. It's as though she can't help herself. I'd seen her wrestling with her vitriol when she came back from her ride in the car – something to do with what I was wearing, I expect, or my untended hair. She'd looked me up and down, settled on something to criticize, but then sighed and said nothing, which in a way was even worse. Why she couldn't keep a lid on it for just one day I really don't know. 'Then I suppose your father and I shall have no choice in the matter.'

'No, you won't,' I said sharply.

The kitchen door opened and in wandered Dad and Rick, chattering away, Dad with a pair of muddy leeks in his hand.

'Say, Hell! You never told me your dad was into growing prize veg! Have you seen the bloody size of that marrow out there?'

'No.' Mum and I stood rooted to the spot, the atmosphere thick with tension. I found myself unable to smile. 'I guess it must have slipped my mind.'

Dad weighed up the scene in an instant and pushed gently past me, dropping the leeks in the sink before giving my hand a brief squeeze. 'I'll give these a quick rinse then you can take them home.'

'Thanks, Dad.' I felt like crying.

'Not in there!' Mum shouted at him. 'Go and wash them under the outside tap! I've got to get supper started and you're right in my way, spreading muck all over my worktops. Just look at the mess you've made!'

'We should think about going before the traffic starts building up.' I threw in the tea towel.

'But you've only just got here!' Mum put her apron on and went to the fridge, yanking out a plate of flaccid value pork chops and a big Pyrex dish of soggy cabbage that she'd par-boiled for six hours previously.

'You won't be going anywhere until you've had a proper dinner.'

WE SAID OUR GOODBYES on the doorstep, Mum and I exchanging a terse embrace, Dad and I keeping our counsel with a fond kiss and his stock-in-trade, 'Try to stay out of trouble.' Rick started up the engine and let the windows down, reaching out a hand.

'I'll take good care of her, Frank. Don't you worry.'

'No,' Dad smiled. 'I don't think I will.'

'Oh, by the way – ' Rick pulled the cigar stump from his mouth – 'you might wanna try "piccadil" in that crossword of yours. It's one of them old-fashioned stiff collars. My mum used to make the old man wear one whenever he was up in front of the beak.'

the contents and wondered if I was hungry. Perhaps not. To come back to bed with chilly feet was one thing, but to turn up stinking of garlic sausage and gherkins was probably pushing it a bit. I settled for a glass of milk and parked myself at the table, gazing out at the warm glow of the orange street lamp on the raised pavement opposite.

So this was it. This house. This kitchen. This chair. I felt as though I was sitting in the middle of a dress rehearsal, trying it on for size, seeing if the part suited me. I didn't want to become my mother, tied up in a pointless life of minutiae with a husband who preferred to spend his time hiding up the vegetable patch. I wanted to feel alive, to be free to discover everything the world had to offer should I feel so inclined. Did that preclude getting married? There was only one way to find out, and by that time it would be too late. It's not as if I've pushed the boat out and turned into a regular Chris Bonington since becoming single anyway. Come to think of it, it's all been horribly predictable (if you discount the embezzling incident). I took a few sips of milk and realized I didn't really want it after all. It was a matter of pros and cons, I supposed. Would I gain more on the roundabouts than I would lose on the swings? Who knows. As far as Mum was concerned, a woman without a husband was conspicuously incomplete. Or a lesbian. Either way, it was an unnatural state of affairs and she was noticeably relieved that I was about to restore the natural equilibrium so that she could once again hold her head up high on pension day in the Post Office. Dad had asked if I was happy, and I'd said yes, just like that. But the more I thought about it, the less relevant the question seemed under the glare of the lamp-bright moon. Happy today does not necessarily equate to happy tomorrow. And happy has a nasty habit of masking symptoms, allowing silent lesions to fester undiagnosed elsewhere. Happy was an easy question to answer. It was the unasked question that had kept me awake, gnawing at my bones. I wondered what I might have said had the question not been 'Are you happy?' but 'Are you doing the right thing?' I hadn't the faintest idea. Quietly I made my way back upstairs.

'Are you asleep?' I whispered.

'No,' Rick said without moving a muscle. 'I'm inspecting the insides of my eyelids.'

'Can I ask you a question?'

'Would it make any difference if I said no?'

'Why are we doing this?'

At last, he stirred.

'Doing what?'

'Getting married?' I sat up, pulling a pillow into my arms and hugging it. 'I mean, it's not as though either of us *needs* to get married.' In my experience, which doesn't count really because it was just a whole heap of crap from beginning to end, getting hitched was rather like inviting another person into the relationship. Suddenly you had this other entity to deal with. The Marriage. It then starts demanding all sorts of privileges, imposing its personality upon you, exerting its unreasonable powers, and however much you try to feed it, it's never enough. The farmer wants a wife. The wife wants a child. The child wants a dog. The dog wants a bone. The bone is glad it's dead. 'What if it changes things between us?' I said.

'It won't,' he said sleepily, reaching out and squeezing my hand to stop me talking.

SMOKE POURED OUT OF Leoni's exhaust, leaving a pungent trail of gas clouds billowing down the street behind us. The sun tried to stream in through the filthy windscreen, sending splintering flashes of brilliant, white light scattering from the ring on Leoni's finger. She kept looking at it, taking her eyes off the road for hair-raisingly long periods while I held on to the edge of my seat and tried to keep myself from screaming 'Look out!' every ten seconds.

'I've said to Marcus, he can forget replacing his car next year.' She held up her hand and admired it again, narrowly missing a row of parked cars. 'It's about time I put my foot down and demanded an upgrade. I've told him that his wife's jewellery is a direct reflection of the kind of man he is, and that if

I'm seen to be wearing a Ratner's crapola special by his colleagues, they'll all know that he's as tight as a gnat's chuff, and they won't want a man like that in the boardroom, will they?'

'Just try not to drop it down a drain when we get out of the car, OK?' I don't know why I was wasting my breath really. Leoni had taken to tearing it off my finger and sporting it herself whenever we were together, saying that she needed the practice. We came to a skidding halt in Sainsbury's car park. 'Are you coming in or waiting here?' I said, this being no more than a quick pit stop to pick up some flowers on our way to Julia's.

'I might as well come in with you and grab something for later I suppose.' She wrenched on the hand-brake. 'Although, God knows, I am so sick to death of trying to think of something to cook for dinner. Once you've gone through *A Hundred and One Ways with Mince* five bazillion times, everything starts to get a bit samey.' Clambering out of the car, I kept thinking I could hear another voice, distinctive but small, as though coming from a biscuit tin. I dismissed it as nothing more than a mild bout of schizophrenia.

'I said, "Excuse me!"' The woman parked next to us leapt out of her shiny silver Kompressor. 'Did you just bang your door on my car?'

'No,' Leoni said.

'Yes, you did!' She marched around to the passenger

side, heels click-clacking, and began examining her paintwork, running a perfectly manicured hand along the bodywork. 'I heard it!' She tossed her well-dressed hair in irritation. Suddenly, I had a dying urge to know what this woman had bought, to rummage through her Sainsbury's bags and try to piece together who she was, what kind of life she had, and why it was necessary for her to go to the supermarket looking like that. Her make-up was spookily flawless, as though she had just been done up by one of those gargoyles at the cosmetics counter, and she wore an as-seen-in-*Grazia* outfit, everything nauseatingly co-ordinated, right down to the gimcrack necklace. 'You'd better not have caused any damage,' she said.

'I didn't touch your sodding car,' Leoni sniffed, pulling her handbag over her shoulder.

'Are you calling me a liar?' The woman stood, hands on hips, and glared at us with no idea of what she was getting herself into. I held my breath and took a couple of steps backwards, as is wise to do when a grenade is about to go off.

'Listen, lady.' Leoni spoke calmly. 'I said I didn't hit your car, OK?' The woman started on again about how she had heard it, seemingly unaware that Leoni was calmly removing her bag from her shoulder and handing it to me for safekeeping. 'Now, if I had done *this*.' Leoni took hold of her door and smashed it as hard as she could into the side of the Mercedes. It landed with a sickening, metallic thud. The woman's jaw dropped. She stared in gobsmacked silence at the shiny new dent planted right in the middle of the silver panel. Leoni closed her door and locked it, cool as a cucumber. 'Now *that* would have been bumping your car with my door, capiche?'

'You . . . You!' The lipstick-perfect mouth opened and closed.

'Come on.' Leoni linked her arm through mine, steering us neatly away.

'Look what you've done to my car! How dare you!' the woman screamed. 'Come back here this minute!'

'Prove it.' Leoni flicked the bird over her shoulder, flashing her victim a spangling glimpse of my ring. 'And before you think about calling the old Bill,' she shouted, pointing at the disclaimer on the sign above our heads. 'We're on private property. You parked here at your own risk, love. Suck it up.'

We arrived to find Julia's door propped open on the latch. Picking up the post from the mat, a few bills and a whole bunch of pointless mailers, we called hello and trooped through to the kitchen. There was no answer.

'Mmm,' I said. 'I wonder where she's got to?'

'Probably upstairs taking an overdose if she's got any sense.' Leoni went straight to the biscuit jar and

helped herself to a couple of those old-fashioned chocolate teacakes you used to get at children's birthday
parties.

'Listen, Leoni. Far be it for me to tell you what to
do, but you've really got to can it with the grim reaper
parenthood stuff.' I filled a couple of vases in the sink
and started arranging. Julia loves to get flowers, but
hates dealing with them. I've known her to leave gift
bouquets in the sink for days before slinging them in
the bin because she couldn't be arsed. 'Just because
you detest having kids, doesn't mean to say that everyone else will.'

'Trust me.' She peeled the foil off and started licking
the chocolate off the marshmallow. 'Not only is she
not going to know what hit her when that baby stakes
its claim, she's going to be pushing sixty before she
even comes up for air.'

It took a moment or two for the penny to drop.
Julia. Sixty. And me, romping home a close second.
'No!' I gasped. 'Don't say that! It's hideous!'

'Oh, yes.' Leoni raised an eyebrow and sucked noisily at the marshmallow, trying to draw it through the
hole she had made in the shell. 'At least I won't be
staring down that particular barrel by the time I've got
rid of mine. I'll be having a facelift and a fanny tuck,
then I intend to shag my way through all the men I
missed out on first time around. And believe me – '

she stuffed the rest of the mauled snack in her mouth
– 'Marcus won't be one of them.'

'Sixty,' I whispered, lowering myself into the chair
next to her. 'I'm sorry. That just doesn't compute.'

'That's because you haven't had any kids,' she said.
'It's a deliberate fault in the female psyche, designed
to trick you into thinking you want to breed, then,
bam! You're stuffed. First it's nappies, then school
runs, then exams, then college, or in my case borstal
or jail.' She set about the next wrapper. 'At the beginning of each year, I get a piece of paper from the
school telling me where I've got to be and on what
days, when I can and cannot take a holiday, and a
million other things that are of no interest to me at all.
I haven't got a life of my own any more. I'm just here
to facilitate other people's.'

So that was it as far as Leoni was concerned. Julia
now had the next twenty-odd years of her life mapped
out, almost to the minute, whether she liked it or not.
There would be no more spontaneity, no more surprise
weekends away with her husband, no more lengthy
lunches that recklessly ran way beyond the school bell.
The last vestiges of broodiness fled from my body.

'That's *pensioner* age.' I tucked the purple lisianthus
in the vase with the stargazer lilies, my brain well and
truly stuck with the picture of being an ancient, wiz-
ened old bag.

'Yep. She'll be nothing but a dried-up husk, shuffling around her local Co-op with a tartan wheelie shopper, squinting at the aisles searching for Fixodent and special offers on Sanatogen. What's this?' She picked up an empty CD case from the table and read the front. 'Amazonian Legend; authentic sounds from the heart of the ancient rainforest to soothe and relax body and soul. Blimey. Chilling out to a bunch of screaming monkeys. That's a new one.'

'I thought I could hear somebody!' Julia sailed in, a pair of odd socks shoved on her feet, wearing David's bath robe, and dropped a couple of empty ice-cream tubs in the bin. 'Oh!' She admired the flowers. 'Are those for me?'

'Yes.' I plumped up the blooms, wondering how long it would be before their fleeting beauty shrivelled and died. I caught a glimpse of Julia standing there with grey hair, her middle expanded through age rather than pregnancy, deep lines etched around her eyes and mouth. Being the more attractive of the pair of us by several million miles, I expected she'd still be able to cut some kind of dash, albeit on a free bus pass photo, but as for me – well, I couldn't bear the thought of it. I'd degenerate into one of those shapeless, invisible women without a single memorable or redeeming feature. The prospect of allowing Rick to pin me down for keeps suddenly took on a whole new meaning. We all had a shelf life, being the perishable goods that we are. Sure, there might be some life left in the old dog yet, but how much longer before I started to look like an old dog? Give it a few more years and my only choice would be either to go for the embalmed look, courtesy of a few needles in the face every three months, or to let nature run its course and hope for the best. It's a shaky strategy. Perhaps I should call Rick now and demand we flee to Gretna immediately.

'Come and see my fabulous new toy.' Julia broke into my stark hallucination of a long, lonely old age. 'It came yesterday morning and I think I'm addicted!' She led us to the sitting room and pushed open the door. 'Ta-raaaaaa!'

'What the—' Leoni shoved past me to get a closer look at the blue roundabout that appeared to have taken up residence in the middle of the room. 'I don't bloody believe it. Tell me you're joking.' It was vast, and made low, rumbling noises like a small power station. Julia switched on the stereo by the fireplace, pulled off her socks and flicked through a small pile of CDs before dropping one into the slot. Strange sounds began to seep from the concealed speakers, a sort of semi-melodic wailing punctuated by tinkling glass and a bit of voodoo drumming in the background.

'What the bloody hell's this?' Leoni squinted at the air around her.

'Shaman Moods from the Mystic Mountain.' Julia breathed deeply. 'Just empty your mind and go with it. Lie on the floor if you want to! It helps to align your energy fields with the natural flow of the universe. Try it. I swear it's completely calmed my tendency towards control issues.' Leoni and I looked at each other.

'Well done, Julia,' Leoni said incredulously. 'For once, I'm bloody speechless.'

'I know! Isn't it amazing?' She undid her bathrobe and flung it aside, unveiling a hideous maternity costume beneath it, her breasts positively surging with excitement as she pulled herself into a couple of awkward stretches before clambering over the side. 'My very own birthing pool!' She slid neck-deep into the water. 'Right here in the comfort of my own home!'

'Julia?' I said tentatively. 'You're not actually thinking of having your baby in this thing, are you?'

'Of course I am!' She smiled. 'It's perfect for my aqua-based antenatal exercise regime, and I've come to the firm conclusion that water is the most natural environment in which to give birth.'

'Assuming you fill the pool with morphine,' Leoni muttered. 'How the bloody hell did they get it in here?'

'I don't know! David supervised the whole operation.' Julia laughed. 'I suppose it comes apart. A truck turned up yesterday, and four hours later, hey presto!'

'Where does the water come from?' Leoni investigated the back of the pool.

'A tap, you idiot.'

'How long did it take to fill up? There's enough water in there to float a sodding battleship.'

'About six hours.' Julia hooked her elbows over the ledge. 'Want to hop in and give it a bash? There's more than enough room for all of us. It's designed to accommodate the mother and at least two birthing partners with plenty of space to move about and try different positions.'

'No thanks,' Leoni grimaced. 'I feel a bit moby just looking at it.'

'This wouldn't have anything to do with Crouching Raccoon, would it?' I asked.

'Absolutely,' Julia said. 'That's why it's been set up where I can see out into the garden. And once in this pool –' she closed her eyes and leaned back seductively – 'I become Sacred Otter, in touch with my femininity, playful in the water, at one with my surroundings. She suggested I should get some big indoor plants too. Palms and things, and place them around the edge to make it feel even more authentic.'

'That's it.' Leoni flapped her arms at her sides in defeat. 'Your sister's gone out of her mind.'

Chapter Eighteen

THERAPY

SOMETIMES, WHEN IT feels like the whole world's gone mad, there's nothing else for it but to call in re-inforcements. It was as though I just couldn't quite get a handle on anything, the nature of everything around me changing so fast that I might as well have been grappling a bucket of live eels. I didn't like feeling like this. It left me stranded, uneasy, unsure of my own mind. For a short time, I had managed, but then began those tiny telltale signs. The faint niggles that would begin quietly in the back of my mind, burrowing away, making their little holes, leaving a honeycomb of dis-content. After that would come the wakefulness, then the hollow feeling deep inside, and finally, the one-way trip to the pharmacy. It would be better if I could avoid that this time. Better to nip it in the bud.

The decision in itself was something of a break-through moment, given my propensity to overcomplicate just about everything, rarely able to see what's staring me straight in the face until someone points it out and lets off an air horn. It had been three years since I had last sat in this room with its polished, panelled walls and the dark oak floor that had seen its comings and goings for the best part of two centuries. How times had changed. I tried not to fiddle with my hands.

'I wondered if you would remember me.' Feeling self-conscious, those small words stuck to my tongue like toffee.

'Of course,' Tim replied in his steady, therapeutic way. The clock ticked sedately from the black marble mantelpiece, pacing each moment, doing its job methodically like the meter in a taxicab. 'How have you been?'

'Fine! Just fine,' I gushed before I could stop myself. And in that tiny moment, we both knew that I'd started the lying game less than ten seconds into my session.

'No more panic attacks?'

'No.' I smiled brightly. 'Not really.' My hands betrayed me, fists clenching, palms clammy. 'Except, maybe, for the occasional little one,' I admitted. 'But we're talking really, really tiny.' I measured an inch with my fingers.

'Oh? Do you want to tell me about that?'

And say what? Same old, same old.

'They're nothing. Really.' I brushed the minor issue of my permanent anxiety under the Persian rug that lay there listening intently, warming the dark, silent floorboards. Tim smiled at me, a small, professional smile designed to encourage me in a non-threatening way. In the olden days, I expect I'd have been diagnosed as suffering from female hysteria and prescribed an earth-shattering orgasm to be taken twice daily with the help of a steam-driven vibrator. Prozac has a lot to answer for. 'It's just me being silly.' I glanced at the thick file with my name on it. 'You know how I can get.'

'Mmm.' He made a note. 'I see that you've moved since we last met. How's that worked out for you?'

'Great!' At last, an answer that didn't add an inch to my nose. 'It's been brilliant. Really. Once I'd plucked up the courage to throw off the old and bring in the new, there was no stopping me. God knows what would have happened to me had I stayed in that suburban rut. I might well have topped myself by now.' Too much information. Pull back. Pull back. 'Not that I'd ever consider doing something like that,' I added quickly, keen to show my sensible side.

'Not far from me I see? Fancy that.' He tapped the address. 'We're practically neighbours.'

'Yes.' I felt myself relax a little. 'I expect the seed was sown the first time I came to see you. Gosh. What a lovely morning that was. The blossoms in full bloom. The sun shining. It would never have occurred to me to move back to London had I not been reminded how lovely it is around here. So I have you to thank for accidentally pointing me in the right direction. It was as though that flat had been just sitting there waiting for me.'

'Nearly three years.' He flicked over the top page. 'With you just around the corner. Imagine that.'

'Yes.'

'And in all that time, you've never once knocked on the door for so much as a coffee.'

'Er.' I felt my smile twitching uncomfortably. 'No.' I shrugged, feeling suddenly sheepish. 'But you're so busy. I couldn't possibly have just—'

'Now, Helen.' He removed his spectacles. 'I think you and I both know that I'm never too busy to brew a fresh pot and say hello.'

'Sorry.' I felt myself blush. 'I suppose I should have—'

'Should?' He wagged his index finger at me. 'What did I tell you about using that word?'

'Could,' I corrected myself. 'I suppose I could have come to see you.'

'Good,' he said. 'That's better.' I sat there like a maroon, taking my medicine, aware that my carefully constructed façade was hanging in tatters already. 'So, let's have a little recap, shall we?'

What? But we haven't even started yet! I got the distinct feeling that I had nowhere to hide and wished that I'd put on a more confident shade of lipstick. Tim pulled his spectacles from his face and began to polish the lenses on his jumper.

'The panic attacks are quite clearly no longer a problem,' he said. 'Your life is – and these are your words, not mine – great, fine and brilliant.'

'Yes.' My response rang hollow.

'And you're obviously quite fit and healthy.' His smile paid me a quiet compliment.

'Thank you. Yes, I am.'

'Right.' Tim sat back and discarded the file, slinging it casually down on the desk, leaning back in his chair and pressing his fingertips together. 'Well, Helen. I have to take my hat off to you. I wish I could say the same. My daughter, Emily, has just dropped out of uni in order to run away with her ne'er-do-well boyfriend, and my wife's vowed to kill them both the moment she tracks them down. We suspect she may be pregnant.' Tim smiled pleasantly and picked up his coffee cup. 'My wife insisted on getting on the first train up to Sheffield yesterday morning. I told her she's wasting her time. You can't stop people making their own mistakes, can you?'

'No.' I hid behind my cup. 'I guess not.'

'So, I'm jolly glad to hear that you've got everything in your life so marvellously under control and that it's all great, brilliant and fine.' He paused for a sip of his trademark strong, dark Arabica. 'We'll have to have you stuffed and put in a museum.' Although the joke was at my expense, it was funny enough to be worth it. I started laughing. 'That's better,' he smiled and put his cup down. 'Now, why don't you tell me what really made you pick up the telephone after all this time, or would you rather we play cat and mouse a little longer?' I took a deep breath.

'I'm getting married.'

'Ah.' He put his glasses back on. 'And, let me take a wild guess here, you're not sure if you're doing the right thing?'

'Exactly!' I accidentally shouted, almost lurching from my seat before quickly trying to regain my composure. 'I mean, yes.' I smoothed my skirt. 'Sorry.'

'I see.' He pursed his lips for a moment and looked out of the window, his eyes settling on the magnolia tree, its creamy blossoms offering their fragrant cups to the early bees. 'So you thought that I might be able to help you decide what you should do?'

'Well, yes.' When he put it like that, it sounded a bit stupid actually.

'Of course you did.' He reached for a fresh notepad.

'Otherwise you wouldn't be sitting here spending two hundred pounds an hour, would you? So. Where do you suggest we start?'

'Erm,' I struggled. 'I was hoping that you'd be able to tell me.'

'Oh!' He knotted his eyebrows. 'Right, then. So . . .' He started scribbling, concentrating deeply on the pad. 'You want to get married –' scribble, scribble – 'but you had such a bad experience the first time around that you've decided this can't possibly be as good as it looks,' full stop. I opened my mouth to say something, but he held his finger in the air, entertaining a lofty thought, put the end of the pencil in his mouth for a moment, then started scribbling again. 'If you don't get married, you haven't lost anything. If you do –' he frowned and bounced the eraser tip on the pad for a few seconds – 'you might finally find the happiness that you feel has always eluded you. Mmm.' He cocked his head at the page. 'Tricky. Do feel free to throw a few ideas in here yourself, Helen. We're just working the problem, as they say in the City.'

'Oh,' I said, suddenly devoid of a single, useful thought.

'Note to self,' he mumbled, putting pencil to paper once again. 'Text Emily and warn her that her mother is on the warpath. Remember to take chicken out of the freezer. Feed cat. Spray next door's Virginia creeper with Weedol.' He looked up momentarily. 'Anything coming through yet?'

'Afraid not,' I said uneasily. 'At least, nothing useful.'

'Never mind.' He waved the session on without hesitation. 'It is a bit of a stinker, isn't it? I'll just sit here quietly and wait for you to have a flash of inspiration.'

'But . . .' I didn't like to be rude. 'Aren't you supposed to be inspiring me?'

'About love and marriage?' He picked up his cup again and made some show of enjoying the remainder of his coffee. 'I'm as happy to take your money as the next shrink.' He dabbed his mouth with a handkerchief then took a sip of water. 'But I seem to remember that we covered most of these rudimentaries quite some time ago.' I frowned unhappily, feeling like a twit. 'Oh, come, come, Helen.' He perked up, offering me some childish encouragement. 'You know the drill! You go talk, talk, talk. I say, ah yes, very interesting, come back next week. Then you eventually tire of paying my crippling bill and come to a sensible decision all on your own.' He relaxed into his chair. 'So we can do this the long way, or take the short cut. What do you think? My diary's pretty flexible right now. God knows I might have to drop everything and jump on a train to Sheffield to identify two bodies at any moment. Isn't life exciting when you accept a little frisson of unpredictability?'

My mouth sank into a petulant sulk. 'I'm an idiot, aren't I?' Tim noted my words on the dreaded pad.

'Anything else?'

'His name's Rick.'

'Good.' Tim continued writing, 'Does he do drugs? Wear your clothes while you're out? Beat up old ladies?'

'No.'

'No?' Tim frowned a little. 'Oh dear. You do disappoint me. It looks like this is going to be harder work than I thought.' I allowed him some time to think. 'What about the sex?'

'I'm sorry?'

'I presume the two of you have sex?' A-ha! Here we go. The frustrated, hysterical woman in need of some earth-moving equipment. I knew it. I broke the news to him as gently as I could.

'The sex is fine.'

'Fine? What does that mean? Fine OK, fine good, or fine I don't want to talk about it.'

'Fine, great.' I said.

'And do you manage to—'

'Yes!' I cut him off.

'Good.' He drew a line across the pad. 'Not that I'm a Freudian you understand. Frankly, I think the man

278

was sick in the head, but people do expect you to ask these questions, just to get them out of the way.'

'I understand.'

'Excellent. I'm jolly glad that one of us does. More coffee?'

'Please.'

'And, just to be clear here –' Tim filled our cups carefully, taking his time – 'you want to marry him.'

'Yes.' Did I? 'I mean, no.' I shook my head, awash with confusion. 'I don't know!'

'Yes, you do, Helen. Now come on. This is Rick we're talking about.' He poured a little milk in each cup.

'He's great.'

'Good. And?'

'And he's the complete opposite of everything I ever expected.'

'Expected from what?' He handed me my cup.

'I don't know!'

'Husband, Helen.' He tutted at me patiently, passing the sugar. 'The answer is husband.'

'OK. Husband,' I conceded.

'Because your expectations of a husband are pretty low, aren't they?' This time he looked me straight in the eye, no smile, no encouragement, just the bare-faced facts. I wanted to look away, to pretend to be fully occupied with my cup, but he wasn't giving an inch. I'd been rumbled. To my shame, I felt my bottom lip going, my nostrils flaring. Tim passed me the box of tissues he keeps strategically placed on top of the stack of books beside his chair. 'Because we're all just a bunch of selfish, lying bastards pretending to be nice until we can stick a ring on your finger before reverting to type and making the rest of your life a complete and utter misery.' He smiled. I began to wail. 'Now, now. Come along, my dear. No need to upset yourself. You just sit there and have a good old wallow for a couple of minutes then we'll pull everything out of your closet and have a look at what's really going on, shall we?'

'No,' I sobbed. I didn't want to have my onion skin wrestled off again, layer by painful layer. Sitting there in the same chair I had unravelled in many times before, I suddenly remembered how it had been – like a home-pack sulphuric acid peel. And beneath it all, after those long, gruesome hours of therapy, the only thing I found was myself, small like a seed pod, lost in the grand scale of the intensive farm of modern humanity. All Tim had done was to wrap it up in a tissue and hand it back to me, with the suggestion that I take better care of it in the future. I could save myself the humiliation this time if I wanted to. Ask for a quick session of primal-scream therapy instead then release myself back onto the street, fresh-faced, ready to mingle with the unsuspecting crowds once more.

'You've had a tough time of it, Helen. No doubt about that.' Tim spoke earnestly, nodding a gentle reminder of the work we had done together, month in, month out, until I had felt better able to cope with the world I found myself in. 'But that's all over now. He's dead. You're free. It's a beautiful spring day out- side and, if I'm not very much mistaken, that's possibly the prettiest engagement ring I've ever seen. May I?' He reached forward and took my hand to admire it. 'Golly. You'd better not let my wife see that,' he said wryly. 'It's our silver anniversary next month and I suspect that's exactly the kind of thing she has in mind.' I dried my tears and attempted a weak smile.

'Thanks,' I mumbled. 'I knew you'd talk some sense into me.'

'Sense? God forbid. Highly over-rated. In any case, it was my pleasure entirely.' He gave my hand a friendly squeeze before letting it go. 'I'm very glad you came by today. It's been lovely to see you again, Helen, and I'm really not just saying that.' He became thoughtful for a moment. 'But of one thing I'm sure. After what you've been through, I don't believe for a single moment that you would have said yes to that man if your heart hadn't meant it. Am I right?'

'Yes,' I nodded. 'I think so.'

'Don't think,' he said with a smile. 'That's half your trouble.'

'I can't help it sometimes.'

'Then maybe we should book in a few sessions. Nothing heavy. Just a little cognitive work to undo some of those crossed wires of yours, hmm?'

'Perhaps you're right.'

Tim stood up, lecture over. I picked up my handbag and took his lead as he walked me to the door. 'Today's on me.' He smiled, placing a reassuring hand on my shoulder.

'No! Really,' I protested. 'I'd feel obligated, and that would never do.'

'Good.' He said. 'Then perhaps you'll pop in once in a while rather than waiting until you have a crisis. Think of it like bringing your car in for a service every now and then.'

'I will,' I said, gratefully shaking his hand.

'Oh, and one last thing.' He paused at the door briefly. 'There's an exercise I want you to do which I think might help, but you have to promise me you will give it your full attention and not cut any corners.' We'd once spent a whole session doing really bizarre things like trying to push each other over and standing on one leg with our eyes shut. Whatever the point of it was, I felt no compunction to question him.

'Of course,' I said obediently. He leaned down and whispered in my ear.

'Go and buy your dress.'

*

282

'RICK!' I BURST IN through the door. I couldn't wait
to see him, to tell him that everything really was
brilliant and fine and great. Tossing my keys on the
table in the hall, I wrenched off my coat and threw
it rebelliously to the floor. 'Rick?' Oh, don't tell me
he's not in. That's really boring. There were a million
things that I wanted to say. Things that I should have
said a long time ago. That I was the luckiest woman
alive. That I didn't care about all the What Ifs. That I
wanted to get married right now this very second and
have the most completely brilliant time, every day, and
bollocks to everything else. I may even throw caution
to the wind and say 'fuck' every now and again. I was
going to be Mrs Richard Wilton, and nothing was
going to stop me. Now all I had to do was try not to
explode with excitement before he got home from
wherever he was.

Nipping to the study, I threw myself into his chair,
stuck a cigar in my mouth and picked up the bat
phone. Zero one, speed dial. Here we go.

'Hi, Angela? It's Helen.' An icy chill ran down the
line. 'Where's Rick? Uh-huh, I see.' I sat up a little
and lowered my voice. 'Well let me tell you something.
It bloody well is my business, because I'd like to know
when to expect him home. And if you ever speak to
me like that again, I'll see that you're fired so fast,
your arse won't touch the ground. Am I making myself
nice and clear?' I cheerfully mangled a paperclip.

'Good. Now, where were we? Six o'clock? Yes. Why
don't you do that, and remember to put lots of kisses
on the bottom.' I dropped the receiver back on the
cradle and flicked the Vs at it.

One of my very favourite things in Rick's house just
has to be the little television screen set into the wall at
the end of his monolithic bathtub. If you've never
experienced one, I cannot begin to describe how sinfully fabulous it is to lie back and luxuriate neck-deep
in hot bubbles while channel-hopping daytime TV.
Trust me. You absolutely have to get one. Armed with
a nice cold glass of wine in one hand and the remote
in the other, my one hour do-it-yourself beautifying
session would have been perfect had it not been for
the house phone ringing persistently. I'd left it on the
bed and there was no way I was going to tear myself
away from Poirot and drip through to get it just when
he was about to gather everyone in the library and do
the big reveal. Whoever it was would just have to ring
back or leave a message. And if it was Rick, what I had
to say to him needed to be done in person anyway.
Nudge nudge, wink wink.

I shaved everything to within an inch of its life, even
paying a little attention to the undercarriage. Nothing
too outlandish, you understand, but enough to raise
an eyebrow should I be run over by a bus and end up
in Casualty later. What the hell. Jerry Hall once said
that in order to have a successful marriage, a woman

had to be a chef in the kitchen, a maid in the parlour and a whore in the bedroom. Of course, having a husband who didn't go around shagging waitresses might have helped, but there we are. You can't have everything I suppose, and I was going to make a rip-roaring success of this one if it was the last thing I did. Wrapped up in a couple of warm, fluffy towels, I sat on the edge of the bath while all my body hair went down the plughole, drying my toes one by one, still glued to the telly. Ah-ha, mon ami. It was the valet's trollop of a girlfriend, for she was the love child of Lord Henkinson, and her half-sister had foolishly left the murder weapon in the conservatory. Of course. How elementary my dear Whatnot. I flipped the telly off and padded to the bedroom.

No one had bothered to leave a message on the house phone, so that was one more thing I didn't have to worry about. Right. Let's get this show on the road.

Despite my mother's strongly voiced disapproval, there was a very good reason why I had stayed away from the hairdressers for so long. It's called Trying to Grow My Hair. Now I know that I'll never have a tumbling cascade of glossy, raven locks like Julia, mine being a much mousier affair, but when I'd mentioned to her that I wished mine was a bit longer, she'd just looked at me like I was some kind of idiot and said, 'Well stop having it cut then, stupido.' I don't know why I didn't think of it myself. The big, secret weapon in Julia's armoury is a good old-fashioned set of heated rollers. Whack them on, bung them in, and bingo – Hollywood hair. At least, that's what she says. I read the instructions on the box, threw all the packaging aside, and went in for my first ever attempt.

Ow. Ouch. Bugger. Burnt thumbs. Pins gouged in my scalp. Hair caught up in a roller that won't come out. Whatever you do – don't panic. That's what she'd said on the phone. Relax. Take your time. Do not, under any circumstances, use scissors. OK. I went down to the kitchen with the one maverick roller still hanging from the back of my head and fetched another glass of wine. True to her word, once I'd calmed down a bit and stopped tearing at it, it soon worked itself loose and dropped harmlessly to the floor. I ran my fingers through the finished result with a squirt of mousse. Oooh, yes. That's rather nice. A subtle hint of just-fell-out-of-bed in a tousled, come-hither way. Not bad at all, and a bloody good job I'd gone for the warmer shade rather than letting the girl at the salon talk me into going blonde. I checked the clock again. Ten to six. Perfect timing. And now . . . (drum roll) . . . for my *pièce de résistance*. I tipped the contents of the glossy carrier bag out on the bed, pulled the layers of pink tissue paper aside and succumbed to an immediate surge of self-doubt. Regardless of what the woman in the shop had said, I just wasn't sure if I was ready to pull something like this off.

'Just put it on!' she'd urged me a few hours before, shoving me in the changing room.

I poked my head through the curtains a couple of minutes later. 'I think it's too small.'

'Let's have a look.' She barged in without being asked and started wrenching at the straps. 'Nope. It's bloody sensational. You've got to just stuff your zongers in like this – ' squash squash – 'and pull the knickers a little lower, like a fifties bikini – ' shove shove, hands on my buttocks – 'and do the ribbon in a big bow like a Christmas present.' My goodness, this girl had no shame. 'There you go!' When she turned me around to face the mirror, I saw what she meant. Everything had gone a bit Marilyn Monroe. Slightly plumpish, sure, but going in and out in all the right places. 'Here, put these on.' A pair of maribou-trimmed high-heeled satin mules appeared through the curtain. 'And you absolutely have to wear the little cotton wrap with it. Don't want to give the whole game away.' Her smiling face popped through, framed by the velvet drapes. 'They like a couple of layers to get through.' She winked. 'Makes them go nuts. Trust me. I'm a sexologist.'

I swear, if my mother could see me now, she'd have a coronary. For a split second, it occurred to me that I might have the same effect on Rick. Oh well, I could always go back to the shop later for the nurse's outfit. I couldn't help but smile at my scandalous reflection. I switched on a couple of lamps to lend a bit of extra warmth to the proceedings, left the ceiling light off and arranged myself invitingly on the bed with a couple of frivolous magazines, bursting with excitement.

The minutes ticked past. One. Two. Ten. Oh come on. Fifteen. I couldn't concentrate, the magazines being unreadable props just to add a certain *je ne sais quois* to the Slightly Sluttish Stepford Housewife look. I wasn't sure how much longer I could hold my flab in either.

Then, there it was. The door. Oh yes. I heard it swing closed. Keys hitting the table. Now come on, Rick. Feel my telepathy. Come upstairs. Don't bother with the study. Notice my handbag in the kitchen, coat on the floor, wonder where I am then come looking for me, big boy. You know it makes sense. I froze into position, the suspense almost killing me, trying not to grin like an idiot. I had to look nonchalant, like I did this kind of thing all the time. The woman in the shop called it 'getting into character'.

'You can do it,' she'd said to me as she handed over the shiny pink carrier bag. 'Just throw all your inhibitions out of the window and shag his brains out. Works every time. Are you sure you won't change your mind about the handcuffs?'

I toyed with the ribbon around my neck, checking the key was still there. At last, footsteps on the stairs. Unable to bear the anticipation a moment longer, I threw him a little clue, coughing daintily to announce my presence. The bedroom door opened. I barely had time to glimpse the *Silence of the Lambs* mask before a blood-curdling scream flew from my throat.

'You!' she screamed back.

'Lola?' I gawped at her in disbelief. 'What on earth?' I mean, who in their right mind wears a plaster cast on their face? Her teeth bared, eyes narrowed, but that's about all I could see.

'You *whore*!' she screeched, her serrated voice rattling the windows. Well yes, that was the general idea. I saw absolutely no point in trying to make a dash for a bathrobe, so I stayed put, right there on the bed. Besides, this was about the best I'd looked in ages.

'What the bloody hell's going on?' Rick's voice boomed as the front door opened and slammed shut again. 'Lola?' I heard his heavy gait pounding up the stairs. 'What are you doing here? And what the fuck is that thing on your face?'

'*Whore*!' she screamed again, pointing at me. 'He no want you! He like man!' She tossed her head aside, folding her arms tightly across her chest.

'Whatever it is this time, Lola –' Rick barged past her – 'I'm just not in the fucking mood. OK?' Reaching the bedroom door, still in his overcoat, he stopped dead in his tracks before doing a massive double take. His mouth dropped open, burning cigar falling to the carpet.

'That's a pity,' I shrugged lamely, drumming my scarlet fingernails on the magazine. 'Although had I realized Lola was coming back today, I'd probably have worn something else.'

Chapter N-N-N-Nineteen

GOOOOOAAAAAAL!

'WELL, I HAVE to say.' Leoni lay back in the jacuzzi, poking her newly pedicured feet out of the bubbles to admire her chintzy coral-pink polish. 'I'm very, *very* impressed.'

'It's pretty darn good,' Sara was forced to admit. 'Packing you off for an overnight lux-o-rama break with us lot.'

'With as many treatments as we like!' Leoni squealed. 'You know he even offered to send me a babysitter?'

'Really?'

'Yeah.' Leoni clicked her tongue. 'But I turned him down. Let Marcus bloody look after the little shits, that's what I say, although he'll probably be speeding down the motorway to dump them on Granny Meatloaf as we speak. Bloody lazy bastard.'

'What I'd really like to know – ' Julia took a sip of water and watched on from the side, dangling her legs in – 'is what your fiancé's feeling so guilty about.'

'Guilty? What do you mean?'

'All this! The fabulous interconnecting suites, the endless massages, the flowers and champagne waiting for us when we arrived. A man doesn't go to that kind of trouble unless he's hiding something. It's a smokescreen if ever I saw one. You'd better watch yourself, Helen. He might be up to no good.' All eyes turned to me suspiciously.

'Nonsense,' I insisted. 'He's just a kind and generous man who thought we all deserved a nice girly weekend together.'

'And why not?' Leoni chirped. 'He can bloody afford it. Unlike my own, defective ready-sliced breadwinner. I'm lucky if I've got enough housekeeping left over at the end of the week to buy a sachet of Boots face pack. But little does he know – ' she breathed deeply for dramatic effect – 'I've got a cunning plan.'

'Oh, do tell,' Julia purred.

'Nope.' Leoni pulled a zip across her lips then spoke through the side of her mouth. 'Secret Squirrel. But let's just say it might well be me picking up the tab next time.'

'Don't tell me.' I raised an eyebrow. 'You're planning to hold up the old codger at your local post office.'

'No chance,' she said. 'This is much bigger than that. But I'm not saying another word. Just watch this space.' She clammed up, leaving us all hanging. We waited for her to buckle, but she just closed her eyes and smiled smugly. Blimey. This was a turn-up for the books. I'd never known Leoni to be able to keep her mouth shut about anything for longer than ten seconds tops.

'There is another possible explanation of course.' Sara filled her mouth with water and squirted it in a high arc through the obliging gap in her front teeth.

'And what might that be?' asked Julia.

'Well,' she winked. 'We're all women of the world, aren't we? Why else would a grateful man start showering his woman with treats?'

'Oh!' Leoni lit up like a runway. 'You mean a bit of French polish on the old banister rail, eh?'

'Sara!' I didn't know where to put myself. 'Really!'

'Ah-ha!' she shouted, pointing an accusing finger right in my face. 'She's gone red!'

'No, I haven't! It's the jacuzzi. They always make me look a little flushed.' I felt my cheeks burning.

'Yeah, right.' Sara nodded at me sarcastically then turned to the rest of the coven, tapping the side of her nose before letting out a vulgar cackle. A whining howl of approval went up from my grotesque little group of friends, shattering once again the supposed tranquillity of our surroundings.

'Look out.' Leoni slid down in the water. 'It's the fuzz.'

We quietened and pretended not to notice the silent approach of the rubber-soled spa slave in her white coat. 'Ladies, I really must ask you to keep the noise down.' She was having trouble maintaining her polite smile, this being the fourth time we had been taken to task. 'We have other clients here who expect to be able to relax and enjoy themselves in peace.'

'Yes, of course,' I apologized immediately. 'So sorry.'

Sara let out an enormous, echoing belch.

'Pardon.' She thumped her fist on her chest. 'Must have been that fry-up we had on the way.' Leoni started sniggering. The spa slave bit her lip and walked away.

'I'm starving,' Julia groaned. 'Have we eaten all the contraband we snuck in already?'

'Yep,' Leoni said. 'I accidentally absorbed the last packet of Jaffa Cakes while I was waiting for my nails to dry.'

At the merest hint of Julia's need for nutrients, Sara jumped to attention. Old habits die hard. 'Want me to see what I can rustle up for you, boss?'

'Would you, darling?'

'I'm on to it.' Sara leapt out of the hot tub, pulled on her robe and disappeared.

'Bloody hell,' Leoni said. 'If I could have one thing in this world, I'd have a Sara. Is there nothing that girl can't magic out of thin air?'

'Hmm.' Julia gave it some serious thought. 'I don't think so.'

'God,' Leoni kicked back. 'This is the bloody life, eh? I think all women should live in spa communes just like this and banish men from their lives completely. After all, they're the ones who cause all the trouble, driving like maniacs in their gas-guzzling penis extensions and starting wars everywhere. We could keep a couple for breeding purposes. Say, that naughty boy off the Aero adverts and Benicio del Toro.' A small murmur of approval passed around. 'Then send the rest to work camps.'

'They'd never survive.' Julia slid her legs out and wrapped them in a towel. 'I mean, can you imagine that lot looking after themselves?' She shuddered.

'Urgh.' Leoni shuffled along a bit to sit directly on top of a stronger water jet. 'Last time I left my lot to their own devices for a couple of days I could barely get back in the house for the stench. Men stink. Even the small ones. I have to follow them around with a can of Oust. You know, the boys' bedroom is like a giant hamster cage that hasn't been cleaned out for a month. And in the mornings! Yeeuch!'

'I wonder what they're all doing?' I sighed, when what I really meant was that I wondered what Rick was doing. That evening in the bedroom, having seen the best offer he'd had in years go up in smoke as I took myself off the menu, he'd feverishly pledged to take Lola in hand and made me solemnly promise him a rematch. The spa weekend was his way of clearing the decks so that he could tackle Lola's temper with me placed at a relatively safe distance from her lashing talons.

'David's invited everyone over to watch the football tomorrow afternoon.' Julia got up and stretched lazily.

'I hate bloody football,' Leoni groaned. 'Whenever it's on the telly, all I can hear is that constant low Neanderthal roar of hooliganism. It does my head in. And if someone scores a goal – ' she shook her head – 'you know I dropped a whole pan of roast potatoes once? I thought a fucking plane had landed on the house.' Julia and I murmured sympathetically. 'Still, I got my own back. Scraped them up off the floor and took them through as a celebratory snack.' My stomach turned. Leoni's kitchen floor harbours more single-cell organisms than the average tramp's under-pants. 'As I say . . .' She nodded her approval. 'Revenge is a dish best served with ketchup.'

Sara reappeared.

'Hey, chicks.' She tipped us a wink. 'We're on. Meet you in the room in ten minutes.'

Leoni and I were charged with creating a small

diversion while Sara did the deal with the pusher outside.

'So what about the colonic?' Leoni practically yelled at the two receptionists, leaning across the desk, filling as much space as she could to obscure their view of the main doors.

'We can arrange that for you, madam.'

'Yeah, but what's it like?'

'It's very cleansing, madam.'

'What do you reckon?' She waved the brochure at me. I wasn't sure what I was supposed to say, seeing as we hadn't rehearsed any of this.

'If you like,' I said breezily, hoping to God she wasn't actually serious. You never know with Leoni.

'How much is it?'

'It's eighty pounds, madam.'

'What?' Leoni blared. 'Eighty quid for an enema? That's a bit steep isn't it? I could bloody do it myself with a bit of garden hose and a lively tap.'

The two receptionists consulted briefly, one of them checking her computer.

'Your account is taken care of, madam,' said the skinny one with the tangerine spray tan. 'So you might as well have any treatment you fancy.'

Leoni looked at me, flicking her eyebrows around, urging me to pick up the ball and run with it. Just as I was trying to conjure a plausible ad-lib, I caught a glimpse of Sara's reflection in the mirror behind the desk, her dressing gown bulked up with whatever it was she had hidden beneath it, sneaking up the stairs.

'Tell you what,' I smiled confidently. 'I'll give it a miss, but why don't I leave you here to book yourself in?' I turned on my heels and scarpered.

Sara answered my gentle tap on the door with a full mouth and a beer bottle in hand. 'Wotcha!' She pulled me inside. 'Where's the nutter?'

'I abandoned her,' I said, the aroma of something sinfully delicious wafting to my nose. 'What's that I can smell?'

'Pizza!' an appreciative arm appeared from behind the sofa, waving a big slice in the air. 'Sara! You're a genius. Give yourself an obscene pay rise immediately.'

'You better believe it.' Sara threw herself on the bed, wrenching open another box. 'I reckon the local Dominos must be raking it in. That bloke on the scooter said they ought to set up a mobile unit right outside the gates. He's probably running a Porsche on the tips and bribes he gets. Says they get loads of calls in the middle of the night from women almost weeping with hunger.'

'Oh, food!' I planted myself on the floor near Julia and helped myself, sinking my teeth into the heavenly stodge. 'Mmm.' My God, that was good. I was so hungry I didn't even bother to check it for green peppers (which have a habit of coming back to haunt me for the next six hours). Since arriving, we'd barely been given enough calories to keep a flea going. Julia had received special treatment, of course, seeing as she was expecting an elephant, but even so, the chef's healthy option plan for expectant mothers had left her yearning for a mountain of carbs. The three of us fell into a contented silence, nursing our illicit feast amid intermittent groans of satisfaction.

Leoni slammed into the room. 'Thanks a bloody bunch you turncoat.'

'Don't mention it,' I mumbled, picking an anchovy off. Julia took it from my fingers delicately and dropped it into her mouth.

'Holy mother of Jesus! Is that pizza?' Leoni rushed at the bed. 'Oh, thank God!' She took Sara's head in her hands and kissed it hard before stuffing the sharp end of a huge, cheesy wedge between her teeth.

'Wanna beer to go with that?' Sara conjured a bottle of Bud from her dressing gown and smacked the cap off against the bedside table, leaving a big chip in the varnish. 'Oh, yeah,' Sara said as if suddenly remembering something. She reached in her Mary Poppins pocket again, pulled out a massive bar of chocolate and threw it at Julia's sofa. 'In case you should get the munchies later.'

'Now that's what I call service.' Leoni could barely move her crammed mouth. 'So what we gonna do later?'

'I've got another massage at six,' I said. 'Then I'm done for the day.'

'I'm staying put until dinner.' Julia sank possessively into the sofa. 'Just leave me here with the chocolate and stick the telly on. I expect I'll be asleep in half an hour anyway.'

'I might have my toenails done again.' Leoni squinted at her feet. 'I'm not sure I like this colour after all. It's a bit boring, isn't it?'

'Well I'm gonna spend the afternoon in the gym,' Sara announced. 'I saw one of the trainers in there earlier. Phwoar.' She got up from the bed and went to the window, shoved it wide open and hung herself out. A couple of sparks later, cigarette smoke wafted back in the room.

'Sara!' I said. 'You saw the signs! You're not allowed to smoke anywhere on the premises.'

'Oh yeah?' She pulled the curtain back. 'Then come here and take a look at this.' From our high vantage point with uninterrupted views of the manicured, organic grounds, we could see puffs of smoke rising suspiciously from several far-flung bushes. Sara took another long drag and pointed her cigarette out of the window. 'I think that's what you call Scotch mist.'

THE LAST THING I was expecting when I turned up for my six o'clock appointment was to be placed in the hands of a barely legal surf dude. To make matters worse, he was better looking than anyone has a right to be, with perfect teeth, shoulder-length sandy hair and the kind of peachy skin you only find on someone who has yet to see their twenty-first birthday. I realized that this must have been the therapist Leoni had mentioned earlier. The one she had stopped in the corridor to ask if he did extras.

'Hi!' he said in a thick *Home and Away* accent. 'I'm Luke and I'll be doing your treatment today.'

'But you're a man.' When put on the spot, I find it a good ice-breaker to state the blindingly obvious.

'Er, I reckon so,' he said. 'Is that OK with you?'

I didn't have a thing on under my dressing gown except a pair of gruesomely comfortable pants. Bloody typical.

'Of course!' I shrilled automatically, reluctantly accepting my penance for insisting on hanging on to my underwear for several years after its amuse-by date.

'Right,' he said. 'I'll just pop outside the door while you get changed. Please make yourself comfortable. If you could lie down face first, that would be great.'

Oh well. When in Rome. I flung off my robe, scrambled onto the massage table and hid under the towel, pressing my face into the hole, concentrating on the floor, grateful that I wouldn't have to witness the horror on the lad's face when he peeled back the cover and got an eyeful of my globular cellulite. I heard the door open.

'Comfy?' he said. I mumbled a vague acknowledgement. 'OK. I'm going to use the relaxing oil blend this evening. Get you nice and loosened up so you'll get a great night's sleep tonight. I won't chat to you too much either.' Thank God for that. 'I just want you to focus on where I'm putting my hands and let your mind lift up and float away.' Oh well, if you absolutely insist. I felt like I was in a freaky episode of *Neighbours*.

The next thing I knew, the towel was down to my nethers and, oh boy, those hands were doing the work of ten men.

'Blllrrrghhhh,' I said.

'Good, huh?'

'Mmmmmph.'

Whatever it was he was doing, I was soon seeing stars, my head spinning, bright colours kaleidoscoping behind my eyes. This kid knocked my morning therapist into a cocked hat – some young girl who hadn't the strength to massage a bowl of soggy noodles with any real degree of oomph. I felt myself melting into the table, drifting off under the influence of a wildly erotic hallucination about being stuck on a desert island with nothing but a dozen muscle-bound champion Aussie surfers for company, all of them with that lustful look in their eyes. My bikini became inexplicably tangled on a mango bush. I stumbled gracefully to the sand, my ankle twisting, requiring immediate first aid from all of them.

'Would you mind turning over?'

Eh? I hauled myself out of a deep coma. It can't have been twenty minutes already. That's just soooooo unfair. Reluctantly, I hauled myself over and onto my back while he held the towel up and, thank God, averted his eyes. I lay back and settled myself once more. He lifted the towel aside and started on my front.

'I'm just gonna do a little work on your abdomen.'

'Uh-huh,' I mumbled, closing my eyes and willing my subconscious back to the point where I was being rescued and given the kiss of life by Rampant Surfboy, my wrists now mysteriously bound by the ankle bandage. As I began to relax again, a warm sensation started up just where I didn't want it to.

My eyes sprang open in alarm, and in that awful moment, I realized just how ill-advised I had been to charge head first into that pizza without checking it first. It was a pepper. No doubt about it. And it had decided to join me for my evening massage. Oh please. Not now. I clenched my buttocks and grimaced.

'Good?' he asked.

'Mmmmph.' Come on, Helen. Concentrate woman. This is no time to send up the Hindenburg. Think Jane Fonda. Work those muscles. You can do it.

'Hang on a mo,' he said, frowning up at the ceiling

as he kneaded away with his fingers. 'I can feel a little knot of tension here. Just bear with me. I think I can get that out for you.' Arrrrgh! I felt beads of perspiration running down my brow. 'Just take a deep breath for me.'

'Wait!' I strangled through gritted teeth as the groaning pocket of pepper gas worked its way home.

'And . . . relax.' Too late. He pressed down hard with both palms, forcing the issue out of my hands while I died a thousand deaths.

THERE IS NO FEELING to compare with the squeaky-clean sensation of having been spa-bound for two days. It was like I'd been soaked in Milton Fluid, my skin glowing a healthy, exfoliated pink, its only perfume a faint whiff of chlorine. Before leaving, we'd pushed Rick's boat out and gone the whole hog in the finishing department, having our hair flounced and make-up done. Leoni went a little bit mad and got herself a set of semi-permanent eyelashes which she batted at us invitingly all the way home.

'You look lovely, miss,' said our driver as he dropped us off. 'You all do.'

'Thank you, Terry.' I pressed a note in his hand in accordance with Rick's strict instructions. Terry's been one of his regular drivers for years, even though he's a bit past it and creeps along like a snail. It's the only thing in his life since his wife dropped dead one Saturday morning during Wimbledon week. Rick wouldn't dream of letting him go.

'Looks like you've got a full house.' Sara thumbed Julia towards the line of cars on the drive. My heart leapt at the sight of the Bentley, sitting there solid and reliable.

'Let's sneak in and surprise them!' I said childishly. Well, why not? Give it a few years and I might be groaning at the thought of being reunited with my husband after a 24-hour mini-break. We stayed low, keeping to the grass verge to avoid the telltale crunch of gravel underfoot. Sara gave Julia a hand, guiding her zeppelin figure along the soft bank seeing as she was no longer able to see her feet anyway. Sliding the key in the latch, we pushed the door open and crept into the hall, our small sounds drowned out by the constant low Neanderthal roar of hooliganism blaring out from the television.

'Ssshhh!' I put my finger in front of my lips, edging towards the sitting room. 'On the count of three,' I whispered. 'Then we all burst in and go Surpriiiiiiise! OK?' They humoured me politely. I began to mouth at them, one . . . two . . .

'GOOOOOOOAAAAAAAAL!!!!!!' The shockwave of the deafening roar that thundered through the house shook the pictures on the walls, temporarily blurring my vision. 'YEEEEEEE-HA! WOO!' Our perfectly groomed hair stood on end as we pushed the door open to find six grown men cavorting wildly in Julia's Sacred Otter pond, spraying beer at each other while a wall of water sloshed over the sides. It was a good ten seconds before any of them noticed they were no longer safely in the *Loaded* land of men. Suddenly, Paul stood up and froze guiltily, a pair of peeled-off beer bottle labels obscuring his nipples.

'Guys,' he said, tapping Dudley softly on the shoulder.

'IN-GER-LAAAAAAND!' David sang, sloshing water around the room as he swung a sopping football scarf around his head and tried to pull Paul back down into the splashing frenzy.

'GUYS!' Paul shouted. 'A-HEM!' He pointed a tentative finger at the scowling group of women tapping their feet by the door. Rick turned around, hair fashioned into punky spikes, the soggy cigar in his mouth dripping a pale yellow stream of nicotine-stained water down his chest. We tried not to stare at the wet T-shirt clinging to Sally's pecs.

'My pool!' Julia screamed. 'How could you!' She burst into tears and fled from the room.

'Julia!' David hauled himself out. 'Shit! Shit! Shit!' he muttered, tearing after her.

'Oops.' Sally drawled with a mischievous smile, before closing his eyes and sliding under the waves.

'Hi, darling!' Marcus tried to make light of the

situation. 'Did you girls have a nice time?' He stood up and clambered his flaccid, middle-management body out of the pool.

'Dear God.' Leoni looked him up and down disparagingly. 'It's alien autopsy.'

Chapter Twenty

HOLD THE FRONT PAGE

Skulking at the back of the coffee shop in a dimly lit corner where I felt relatively confident of remaining anonymous, I checked one more time to see that no one was watching before reaching discreetly for the plain paper bag containing the magazines I had guiltily liberated from the newsagent stand in the tube station. Sliding them out onto the table, blood rushed to my face as I read the dayglo subheads advertising the articles within. 'Up or Down? Every Bride's Hair Dilemma'; 'Confused? Follow Our 12-Month Checklist for Perfect Planning'; 'My Honeymoon Hell: one woman's fairytale turns to disaster'; How to Look Like Liz Hurley on Her Wedding Day' (have surgery and land yourself a squillionnaire, I presume).

I flicked through the pages, subliminally noting the utopian photographs of fresh-faced college girls in fairytale dresses, wearing perfect smiles, simpering at their impossibly good-looking grooms. They're models, I kept reminding myself. No one really looks like that. 'Sensational Wedding Lingerie!' screamed another headline slashing through a picture of a blue garter clinging prettily to a cellulite-free peach-skinned thigh that couldn't have been more than seventeen. I tore open a sugar sachet, poured it through the cappuccino froth and flipped the page. 'I Lost a Stone in a Month!' announced the grinning portrait, as though she had finally achieved her life's ambition. I stared at the picture with morbid fascin-ation and, despite my earlier promise to keep a level head, soon found myself being pulled helplessly along, caught in a World of Weddings riptide.

One toasted ham and cheese panini and two more coffees later, having read all three magazines cover to cover and thoroughly overwhelmed by the sheer pointlessness of it all, I was forced to admit that I wasn't really making any progress, unless of course my task for the day had been to make myself feel fool-ish, fat and forty. Did women really put themselves through the mincer like that and plunge themselves into Third World debt just because a magazine told them to? It's no bloody wonder it's a global industry. Mind you, I seemed to recall having walked that sugar-coated line once before, powerless to resist the temptation at the culpable age of twenty-three before I knew my arse from my elbow. Naturally, a couple of months after the event, once I realized just what I had gotten myself into and the cake had gone mouldy, I felt like a prize twit. Dad had spent a fortune without a murmur of complaint to deliver a wedding far beyond their means, knowing all along that it was doomed. As my mother had said, any idiot could have seen that. Any idiot, that is, except me. Doh.

I got up from the table to relieve myself of at least one of the three medium cappuccinos sloshing around in my bladder. If only I had read that article an hour ago about not eating anything and drinking only water before trying on dresses. Oh well. I doubted the wedding police would be waiting outside Costa with a high-powered rifle.

'YOU REALLY OUGHT TO start with your foundation wear.' The assistant raised an eyebrow at my bra and pants, all new(ish), matching, and, so I'd thought, perfectly adequate for today's sortie. I'd chickened out yesterday after reading (then binning) the magazines, retreating home to digest the panini instead, before regrouping this morning with a more positive outlook, reciting my mental mantra: 'You ain't no spring chicken – do not get suckered by the hype.' I stood there and refused to feel inadequate.

'I'm just trying to get an idea of what kind of dress would suit me best,' I retaliated confidently. 'Then I'll decide about my underwear.'

'Oh,' she said, her air of condescension quite deliberate. 'That's rather unusual. It's just that our customers normally bring their underwear with them and arrive with their hair and make-up done so that they can get the proper effect.' Thwack. Right between the eyes.

'I don't want to look like mutton dressed as lamb.' I ignored the sliver of sympathy in her eyes. 'Perhaps I could try on a few different styles and take it from there?' The only decision I'd managed to make since Monday was that whatever I went for, it would have to be off the peg.

'Of course.' This already felt like a disaster. 'Whatever you want.'

Before we go any further, if you're thinking of getting married and you're, well, let's just say you're in the target audience group for pentapeptides, let me give you one piece of advice: do not, under any circumstances, put yourself in the hands of a big-store bridal department. For a start, your plea to 'keep it simple' will fall on deaf ears. Before I knew what was happening, like a lamb led to slaughter, I found myself swamped by the varying assistants' wildly differing ideas of the perfect bridal ensemble. First came the highly flammable meringues, then the celebrity-inspired *Hello!* magazine disasters and, finally, the dregs of the stockroom when they finally realized that they were flogging a dead horse and lost interest. Even I know that you can't make a silk purse out of a sow's ear. Believe me. I've tried. I pulled on my boring old day clothes and slunk away.

Perhaps I wouldn't have felt quite so defeated had this not been my fifth pathetic attempt to find the kind of dress that I'd seen so clearly in my mind's eye when I'd left Tim's house. I didn't want anyone interfering either. Tim was right. I should hunt alone, know my own mind, fulfil my own dreams. I knew exactly what I wanted. Something elegant yet flowing, poised yet pretty, with a hint of let's-make-a-fresh-start-and-pretend-we're-young sewn into the seams. Simple enough, you would have thought, but oh, no. I'd initially tried my luck at a couple of the smaller bridal boutiques that looked quite promising on the surface, only to find myself caught up in the maelstrom of trying to commission a one-off wedding dress. Anyone would have thought that I had asked them to design a replacement for the Eiffel Tower. Sitting through each appointment with sagging spirits, I looked on ineptly while they scribbled ridiculously unsuitable suggestions on sheets of paper and threw bolts of mind-bendingly expensive fabrics before me, expecting me to understand what the hell they were talking about. It had been a grim week all right.

I hit the abort button and admitted defeat.

HELGA LAY MOTIONLESS, most of her upper half still wedged in the cupboard under the sink, her thick brown tights gathered in saggy wrinkles around her ankles.

'Are you sure we wouldn't be better to call a plumber?' I said.

'*Nyet*.' Another deafening whack with the spanner. 'It come. I make bang. It come soon.' Whack, whack, then an almighty clang. '*Da!*' Her legs twitched. 'We try now!' I turned on the tap and gave the waste disposal unit another go. It buzzed viciously into life.

'Perfect!' I shouted. 'It works!' That woman's a bloody marvel.

'*Da!*' Helga dragged herself out of the cupboard and stood up, wiping the sweat from her brow. 'It work good, *da!*'

'*Da*, Helga. It work very good. Thanks. I'll make you a coffee,' I said. 'With a nice big piece of cake.'

'Russian coffee?'

'Sure.' I went to the freezer and pulled out a bottle of vodka. 'Big or small?'

'Beeg.' Helga puffed up her chest. Of course. How silly of me. Just as she was about to sit down, Helga caught sight of something over my shoulder and scowled. I followed her gaze to where Lola stood, coat on.

'I go now.' Lola threw her key at the table. It bounced off with a metallic clatter and landed on the kitchen floor.

'Lola! Won't you sit and have a coffee?' This was the first time she had spoken to me at all since Rick came clean and broke the news. I suspect it all went tits-up when he used the word 'stepmother'. Oh well. He can't say I didn't warn him. The atmosphere had been awful ever since, so I had chosen to stay well out of her way.

'No,' she sneered. 'I want car for airport. My bags upstairs.' She flicked her eyes over Helga. 'You go get them.'

'*Nyet*.' Helga stuck two fingers up. 'You blooding beech. I hate.'

'Does your father know?' I asked gently. The petulant smile that she threw me said no. 'Oh, Lola!' So help me, one of these days I'll run out of patience and box her ears again. 'You can't just run off like that without speaking to him. He'll be mortified. Here.' I reached for my mobile. 'Why don't you let me get him on the phone now?' I was already dialling. 'I'm sure we can sort this out.' By the time I looked up from my handset she had turned her back on me and marched off anyway.

'Good.' Helga poured four fingers in her coffee mug. 'She go. We happy.'

'Hello? Rick? Yes, I know. Look. I'm sorry to disturb you, but it's Lola.' I held the sudden blare away from my ear. 'No! Nothing like that. She's packed her bags and is determined to leave.' Helga did a big thumbs-up. 'What? But don't you want me to stop her?' Helga shook her head bitterly and took a swig straight from the bottle. 'No? Are you sure? Oh.' I listened a while. 'All right then. If you say so.' I hung up and redialled. 'Hello, Angela? I don't suppose you could call Terry and ask him to come to the house? We need him to run Lola to the airport. Yes. Thanks.'

'*Na zdarovya.*' Helga raised her mug and clanked it against mine.

I felt terrible. This couldn't be right. That Lola was a complete and utter shit was unquestionable, but surely it's a parent's job to try and show them the error of their ways? Then again, what do I know? Nothing much, it would seem. I didn't even know how to fix the waste-disposal unit when it got clogged up with cigar butts.

'Oh, Helga.' I ran my hands through my hair. 'I do wish she'd come round.'

'Pah,' she said. 'Make trouble? Get trouble.'

'Mmm. I suppose you're right.' I thought about it for a while. 'Maybe I should go up and speak to her. It's not easy being young, you know. She's probably still angry about all sorts of things.' Helga's eyes glazed over. 'Wait here,' I said confidently. 'I won't be long.'

I found Lola in Rick's study, helping herself to cheques from the top drawer, store cards and anything else that took her fancy. I pushed the door quietly closed. 'Lola?' She ignored me. 'Lola? Do you think we could have a little talk? I really don't think you should leave like this.' Still nothing. 'It's not fair on anyone.'

'No fair?' She gave out a nasty little laugh. 'You think he want to marry you? You think he want to be all his life with *you*? No. I don't think. Look at you.' She let her eyes wander cruelly up and down. 'You servant. You nothing. My mother beeeeeautiful! You look like old dishwasher lady.' Me and my big mouth. Rick was right. Let her go, and good effing riddance. 'You clothes! You hair!' All right, all right. I get the picture. 'Huh!' She slammed the drawer shut, stuffing the loot in her Fendi handbag. 'You in weeding dress?' The splintering laugh that dripped from her collagen mouth finished the sentence for her. I loped back to the kitchen, licking my wounds.

'Bad, *da*?' Helga slouched back on her stool, entirely unsurprised by my forlorn expression.

'*Da*, Helga. You right. She blooding beech.'

'*Bliad*,' she snorted, and poured another four fingers of vodka, this time into my mug. They say that the truth is always the hardest thing to hear. Me in a wedding dress? Lola was right. I hadn't a hope in hell.

'HI.' PAUL FLOUNCED his man-bag confidently on the glass-topped counter, demanding the girl's immediate attention. 'We're here to buy a dress.'

Sally slid his arm around my waist and bent down to nuzzle my neck.

'Yeah.' He unleashed a deadly dose of Class A pheromones directly at the gawping assistant. 'And we mean a *dress*, honey. Know what I'm saying?'

'Of course, sir.' She flustered, unable to get a handle on how on earth a woman like me could come to be standing in a couture shop with a man like that. It was written all over her face, her bemused expression a symphony of blind confusion. I smiled demurely. Sally unpeeled himself from my tingling body and led me to the chaise longue, a sumptuous deep-buttoned affair swathed in black silk damask, and dropped himself gorgeously onto it, pulling me to his lap. The girl fought to tear her eyes from him, mesmerized like a python's next supper. 'I'll just go and get Madame Arienne,' she stammered.

A stiff breeze of tight whispering drifted indiscreetly from the room at the back before three faces peered slowly round the door. I pretended not to notice while Sally toyed with my hair. The heads disappeared as quickly as they had come.

'Chop, chop!' Paul sang out, clapping his hands sharply. 'I'd like to say that we haven't got all day.' He emitted a fey sigh and flopped down beside us. 'But I'm afraid we have! Isn't this just too romantic for words! So help me, I could burst with excitement! Why didn't you come to us sooner?' He slapped me playfully on the leg. 'This is like my biggest fantasy. You know, the one where I appear at the top of a big sweeping staircase with all the cabaret dancers?' In the Ginger Rogers dress which later falls off all on its own? How could I forget?

'How you doing?' Sally nudged me gently.

'OK,' I swallowed hard – 'I think.'

'Don't panic. You did absolutely the right thing.' It was as though he could sense the swarm of frantic butterflies migrating through my chest. 'We're not going to let you out of that door until we've got this cracked, OK? I promise. Cross my heart.'

I nodded, unconvinced, my throat too tight to do anything else.

'Can I 'elp you?' A bird-like woman, well into her sixties, with a clipped cordon bleu accent, had been fetched from the sewing room to deal with us, presumably with the notion that her breeding hormones had dried sufficiently for her to be impervious to

Sally's charms, and that she would thus be able to string a sentence together without becoming hopelessly tongue-tied.

'Oh, my stars!' Paul leapt up. 'What a sensational suit! Is that vintage Balenciaga?'

'Mais oui!' The woman preened.

'From the sixty-four collection?'

'Why, yes!' She appraised him with renewed interest. 'My goodness, you certainly know your, 'ow you say, onions?'

'What did I tell you?' Paul turned to Sally and I, opening his arms like a minstrel. 'If you can't get to Paris for a dress, this is the next best place!'

'Is it for an occasion particular?' the woman enquired.

'I'll say!' Paul squealed excitedly. 'It is to be worn as a wedding dress!' He pulled a polka-dot handkerchief from his pocket. 'Oh, sugar puffs! Here I go again!' He blew his nose and dabbed delicately at his eyes.

'You wish to wear one of my gowns as a wedding dress?' She took a step back dramatically. 'How enchanting!' She clasped her hands together in professional pose, feet daintily arranged in first ballet position open, smiling warm-heartedly, eyes dropping momentarily to clock the ring. 'And you must be ze blooshing bride?'

'Correct,' I said coyly.

'And zis is?' She eyed Sally.

Before I could answer, he slid me off his lap and unfurled himself, standing up and placing a kiss on the back of the woman's hand.

'Salvatore Toledo Vargas.' He offered her a small, respectful bow. 'At your service, madame.'

'Oh, mon dieu!' Her hand rushed to her pearls. 'What a charming man! Well!' She flashed me an altogether more intimate smile. 'Aren't you ze lucky one!'

'It's me who's the lucky one,' Sally purred. 'Although how you are going to make her even more beautiful than she already is – ' he reached down and touched my cheek affectionately – 'it is an impossible task for you, I know.'

'Helping your bride pick out her dress? My goodness. How *très moderne*.'

'We don't want to see anything that's going to wear her.' Paul took out his list and began to check it off. 'Nothing strapless. That's a no-no once you're over thirty-five, I don't care what anyone says.' The woman tipped her head in accord. 'No white, although we've agreed that white-moving-slightly-towards-pearl might be quite nice. No sparkles.' He looked at Sally.

'Definitely, no sparkles,' Sally agreed.

'And nothing too – ' Paul screwed up his face disapprovingly – 'well, you know what I mean.'

'We say *de trop.*' She nodded her agreement, quietly assessing me all the time.

'*Naturellement.*' Paul folded the piece of paper in his fingertips and slipped it back in his handbag. 'I think we're all speaking the same language here.'

'Leave it to me.' She snapped her fingers behind her head. 'Lucy! Come out 'ere and see if our clients are in need of *un petit* refreshment.' She nodded at us briefly. 'Some champagne perhaps! And bring me ze sketches and calico models for ze London couture collections.'

The girl called Lucy stepped out briefly, confusion rumpling her brow. 'What? The new ones?'

'Of course, ze new ones!' madame shrilled.

'But they're not—'

'Just get zem!' she barked aggressively, before returning her gaze to us, softening like butter. 'Pardon my Lucy. She is imbecile, but 'er mother is a very good client. I wish to show you something very special, just because it is you. Strictly confidential until ze autumn, you understand,' she whispered. 'But I am guessing you two will not wish to waït zat long. *N'est-ce pas?* You see something you like? We make it up for you in the pale silks. I 'ave some so gorgeous, zey make you want to weep.'

In the two heady hours that followed, I was whisked away to the land where lollipops grow on lemon trees and seamstresses rush around with pin cushions on wrists and smiles on lips. Each time they stepped back and implored Sally with a nervous, 'Yes?', he would run his smouldering eyes up and down my figure, stroking his chin thoughtfully, nodding slightly or shaking his head before the flurry of fussing began again. Paul just sat there on the chaise, transfixed, trying to keep his ravaged emotions in order. The Balenciaga suit pointed and assessed, cajoled and conceded, before finally handing Sally the scissors in exasperation and allowing him to hack at the prized calico model I had been permitted to try on, to demonstrate exactly what he meant. With no mirror in front of me, I could only assume that he had dealt it a fatal blow when he tore away yet another great swathe of cotton, throwing it to the carpet as everyone went horribly quiet. Lucy let out a small gasp, staring in wide-eyed alarm at the speechless madame.

'See?' Sally stood back and raised one eyebrow.

Madame Arienne remained quiet for a while then calmly took the scissors from Sally's hand. 'Do you have any idea what you 'ave just done to the best gown in my new collection?' Sally shrugged nonchalantly.

'You like it?'

Madame Arienne stood before me critically, her eyes following the clean, pared-back lines Sally had left in the wake of his flashing blades. She nodded slowly, circling me like a shark. 'It is masterpiece,' she whispered. 'You must be an artist, *non*?'

'*Bien sur*.' Sally broke into his beaming half moon and blew me a kiss. 'Honey? I think we're done.'

Paul's face contorted, doe-eyed, and he reached for his hanky again and began to sob uncontrollably. 'It's beautiful!' he wailed. 'I don't know how you do it! Everything you touch becomes fabulous! Even me! Waaaaaaaah!' He blew his nose and tried to wrestle his shredded voice to order. 'This . . .' He waved his hanky in the air and spluttered. 'This is the happiest day of my life!'

'Hey, baby!' Sally quickly went to his side and pulled him in for a long, tender hug. 'Don't cry!'

'I can't help myself.' Paul succumbed to another involuntary howl. 'I've been sitting here watching you and wishing—' His shoulders convulsed again, and he pressed his face into his hanky.

'Wishing what?' Sally sought to console him, while the rest of us stood around, beginning to feel just a little uncomfortable. Paul wrenched his tear-stained face from his hands.

'Wishing I was a giiiirl!' He buried his face again. 'Waaaaaah!'

Sally smiled at us and shook his head, then patted Paul softly on the back. 'Come on now,' he said. 'Stand up.' Paul reluctantly allowed himself to be dragged to his feet, still sobbing hysterically. 'Pull yourself together before you spoil your make-up.' Paul nodded hopelessly while Sally held his hands and urged him to calm down.

'Fetch a glass of water!' Madame Arienne barked. Lucy scurried off and came back moments later with a small bottle of Evian and a champagne flute.

'Here,' Sally said. 'Drink this and dry your eyes.'

'Thank you.' Paul snivelled, forcing himself to take a few sips.

'Better?'

'Yes. I'm so sorry.' He pulled in a few short, laboured breaths and tried to compose himself, his forehead mottled pink like an overwrought child. 'I think it all just became too much for me.'

Sally took the water bottle from his hand and put it down on the floor before taking a firm hold of Paul by the shoulders.

'Paul,' he said, his tone soft and sweet. 'Don't you know that it is only because of you that I see beauty in all things? It is because of you that I was able to free my spirit and become exactly what I always wanted to be.'

Paul managed a small, boyish smile. 'Really?'

'Yes. Really. And no matter what happens – ' Sally took Paul's soggy face in his hands – 'you'll always be my girl.' A tiny gasp escaped from the sewing room. I snuck a glance at Lucy, her face puckered into a vexed muddle of discomfiture.

'I couldn't live without you,' Paul said meekly, wringing his sodden handkerchief.

'Then don't try.' Sally gave him a piece of the torn calico and put his arm around his shoulders. 'Marry me.'

I heard a dull thud as Lucy slid to the carpet.

Chapter Twenty-One

THE WAY TO A MAN'S HEART

I THOUGHT IT would make a nice change from the space-age kitchen. Passionate ox-blood walls. Tasteful art. Gilded mirrors here and there to throw the soft light from the chandelier back into the room. I'm not sure if I'd have gone for the London Dungeon black curtains myself, mind you. No. They'd definitely have to go.

'Bloody hell.' Rick picked up his side plate and had a good look at it. 'I dunno if I've ever eaten in here before. Is this china mine?'

'Of course it is.' That he'd never got around to using his dining room, I could sort of understand, but how could he have two full dinner services and not even know it? Men, eh?

'Blimey.' He put it down. 'I'm just full of surprises, aren't I?'

'You can say that again.' I came back from the kitchen and set down the big dish I'd spent most of the afternoon constructing, knowing very well that it was Rick's favourite thing in the whole world to eat, except when he was pissed, in which case nothing but a doner kebab with extra hot chilli sauce would do. His eyes widened.

'Oh, you doll!' He flapped his napkin enthusiastically and tucked the corner in his open collar. 'I bloody knew I could smell a shepherd's pie the minute I walked in!' I took one of the virgin plates, loaded it high and slapped it in front of him with a bottle of Lea & Perrins on the side. 'Don't suppose you've done any peas?' he said hopefully.

'Of course I have.' I swished away the lid on one of the gilded servers. 'And none of your frozen rubbish either. I shelled these for you myself with my own fair hands.'

'I don't deserve you.' He filled my wine glass before his own.

'I know. And if you're very good – ' I picked mine up and took a sip – 'I might even spoil you with a little dessert later.'

327

'Spotted dick?'

'I jolly well hope not.' I arranged my napkin seductively. 'As that would rather put the mockers on what I had in mind.'

'Steady on, tiger,' Rick growled. 'If I didn't know better, I'd say you were trying to butter me up.'

'Maybe I am.' I tried to sound intriguing without giving the game away. So far, so good. Don't rush it. Keep shtoom and wait for the right moment. A few mouthfuls of that shepherd's pie and he'd be eating out of my hand anyway.

'Oh, my good godfathers,' he mumbled through an obscenely full mouth, closing his eyes and swaying his head ecstatically, pointing his knife at his plate. 'Unbelievable – ' chomp, chomp – 'that – ' he took a huge gulp of wine – 'is the best fucking shepherd's pie I've ever tasted.'

'Of course it is,' I said immodestly. 'And there's a lot more where that came from, mister. I haven't even begun to scrape the tip of my culinary iceberg yet. By the time I've finished with you, you're going to be the size of a house.'

'Uh-uh.' He shook his head. 'My fat bastard days are over. You wouldn't even look at me when I was packing all that timber.' True, although I chose not to enlighten him. No woman wants to admit to fancying a weeble.

'That's because I didn't know what I was looking at.' Why tell the truth when a fib will do just as nicely?

'Sweet.' He gave me a sideways glance. 'But number one, I know you're lying through your teeth and number two, I'd rather not drop dead of a heart attack just as I've found happiness. If that's OK with you, babe.' I chased my peas around the plate.

'Rick?'

'Uh-oh.'

'What?'

'You've said Rick in that way of yours.'

I really must try to do something about that. It's like trying to play poker when everyone else can see my cards.

'I've been thinking about the wedding.'

'Oh, yeah?' He forked his pie a little too casually.

'And, well, I was kind of wondering how you felt about it.'

'Waddya mean?'

'You know.' I shrugged. 'Keeping it all so simple. Just us and our closest friends.'

'And your parents.' His slate-blue eyes found mine and issued a brief reprimand.

'I know, I know.' I sighed. 'Although Mum's bound to cause a scene and start up with her usual parsimonious comments about people who are forced to get married in registry offices. I swear they must have picked up the wrong babies when Julia and I came along. How can I be related to that?'

'It's a non-negotiable, Hell. If you don't invite them you'll be paying the price for years, and I'm not going to get into the whole spiel about them not being around forever and you feeling guilty about it for the rest of your life. Correction – ' he filled his mouth again and waved his fork at me – 'for the rest of *our* lives. No thanks, doll. I'm not listening to that for the next twenty years 'til I finally go deaf. You just make sure they're there and we'll avoid a whole lotta trouble.'

'I said I'd invite them, OK?'

'OK.' He winked at me. 'It's for your own good.'

'On one condition.' I kept my eyes on my plate. 'You have to ask Lola.'

'Eh?'

'You heard me.'

'No fucking way.' His manner clouded. 'You saw what she's like.'

'I'm sorry, Rick, but from where I'm sitting it's the same thing. I have no intention of embarking on a marriage blighted by family feuds. This is a fresh start for all of us, and if you can't be bothered to put in the effort then I'm not sure that you're the kind of man that I want to marry.'

'You what?' He stopped chewing. I gave my napkin a cursory flap.

'If that girl had had the benefit of some proper joined-up parenting instead of being spoilt senseless, she might have stood half a chance of turning into a nicer person. You should speak to her mother and see about getting her into college or something. What young people need is guidance, not credit cards. It's obscene.'

'Hmph.' He played with his food. 'She doesn't seem to think so.'

'Well, it's high time you did something about that. So here's the deal. I have to endure my mother? You have to endure your daughter.'

'I'll think about it,' he said stiffly.

'Good.' I resolved to steer the conversation back on course. 'You know, Rick, I was thinking maybe we could do something extra special to make our day really memorable.'

'It's already pretty special, innit?' He brightened a little, coming out from his Lola thunder cloud. 'I mean, we're getting married for fuck's sake. What's more special than that?'

'I know, I know. I mean . . .' I felt myself dithering. 'Do something a bit spontaneous and crazy.' How was I sounding? OK. Don't ask. Maybe I should just come right out with it and tell him. What's the worst that could happen? I started imagining all sorts of dire consequences and bottled out immediately.

'Like what?'

'Oh, I don't know,' I lied. 'Something a little unexpected perhaps.'

'Whatever you want, babe. Tony said you're to call him if there's anything spesh you want him to do for the reception. He's closing the place down for us so it's yours to do with whatever you will.'

'That's kind of him,' I said. The one thing I knew I didn't have to worry about was the reception. Tony had promised to oversee every detail personally and said that I was not to waste one moment fretting needlessly. I had gladly left the whole thing to his own impeccable discretion – choice of food, music, everything. Frankly, after the sausage-roll-and-Kajagoogoo-hell that had followed my first wedding, anything would be an improvement.

'He'd have killed me if we'd tried to hold it anywhere else.' Rick shovelled another forkful of peas into his gaping mouth. 'The pastry chef started working on the cake the minute that ring went on your finger.'

'Now that really was a wonderful night, wasn't it?' I sighed.

'You bet. I'll never forget that look on your face. Talk about rabbit caught in the headlights.' Rick paused his cutlery and became thoughtful for a moment. 'You know what, Hell? This is your big day and what the fuck do I know? I'm just the git in a new suit who does what he's told. You're the bride, babe.

You just go right ahead and arrange anything you bloody well want. And I mean anything. You can turn up riding an elephant and have me dress up like a clown if you want. I don't care how we get married. All I want is you.'

'Are you absolutely sure?' Maybe I should have been a little more specific.

'Deffo.' He scraped his plate clean then slumped back in his seat, stuffed.

'In that case . . .' I took his plate and stacked it neatly beneath my own untouched supper. The dress might well be gorgeous, but Sally had left little room for school dinners. 'I won't bother you with any more of the details.'

The phone began to ring.

'We had better get that.' I broke my rigid rule about telephones interrupting dinner. 'It might be Lola responding to the invitation I sent to her and her mother.'

'You WHAT?' Rick balked.

'And before you ask, you've offered to pay for their flights and accommodation, OK?' I got up from the table and went to get the phone. 'Hello?' I spoke into the receiver.

'Hello, is that Helen?' The man's striding voice was strangely familiar, but I couldn't quite place it.

'Yes?'

'It's Chris Tarrant from *Who Wants to Be a Million-aire*? I've got Leoni here and she's doing rather well . . .'

'SURPRIIIIIIIIISE!' WE ALL CHANTED in unison the moment Sara led Julia through the door.

'What's all this?!' She knocked her way past a huge bunch of pink and blue balloons. 'Oh, my God!' She pointed at us and laughed like a drain. Leoni and I stood by the fireplace rubbing our backs, each of us wearing a hideous tent dress with a pillow stuffed up the front.

'Baby shower!' Leoni blew a party squealer and let off a couple of poppers.

'You!' Julia pushed Sara playfully. 'I thought you said this was a meeting!'

'Well, it is! Sort of!' Sara said. 'Besides, when have I ever held a meeting in my sitting room? If your brain weren't so addled you'd have guessed an hour ago.'

Julia gladly allowed us to make a big fuss of her while we cooed over her presents and picked at trays of fancy cakes washed down with colourful mocktails.

'Oooh! It's a rabbit!' Julia pulled the soft-as-soap toy from its ribboned wrapping.

'No, it isn't,' Leoni corrected her. 'It's a bunny-wunny.'

'Aaaaaahhhhhh!'

'And these – ' Leoni picked up a pack of newborn Pampers – 'are nappy-wappys. Get it?'

'I think so.'

'All you have to do is make everything, yourself included, sound as stupid as possible.' Leoni threw back the dregs of her mocktail and screwed up her face. 'Oi, Sara!' she shouted towards the kitchen. 'Do you think some of us could have a proper drink?' Sara was already on to it and returned moments later with a magnum of rather excellent champagne, beaded with condensation.

'I've been saving this for a special occasion.' She opened it with a practised hand, the cork coming free with the soft sigh of a contented woman. 'One of Dudley's clients sent it for our wedding, but I thought, I'm having that, and stuck it at the back of my wardrobe. Who wants straight and who wants it with a bit of fruit juice?'

'Straight,' Leoni said, as if she needed to. 'I keep cheese and crackers in mine and a load of those ready-made gin and tonic cans. Then I pretend to have a really bad headache and wedge a chair behind the bedroom door so that no one can get in.' She accepted a glass.

'God, that's proper champagne, that is.' I smacked my lips deliciously.

'I should bloody well think so too.' Leoni puffed herself up. 'I dunno about you lot, but I've got a twenty grand windfall to celebrate.'

'You should have made her agree to give you half the money before you told her the answer.' Sara threw a cupcake at me.

'She's welcome to it!' I laughed. 'Anyway, money doesn't make you happy.'

'Bollocks, it doesn't! I've never been so chuffed in my life. Marcus is so jealous he can barely speak. It's perfect. Cheers!'

'What about me?' Julia held out her hand for a glass.

'I thought you weren't drinking, boss?'

'Sure, when the baby was little, but now? I'm sure it's OK for me to have a glass, isn't it?'

'Rack 'em up!' Leoni shouted. 'I got completely arseholed when I was seven months gone with the twins and fell over a garden fence!'

I waddled over to Julia and lowered myself to the sofa beside her, arching my back and huffing like a pantomime dame while I adjusted my pregnant pillow. 'How does that feel?' she asked.

'Funny,' I said.

'I wish you were having one with me. We could bring them up together.'

'I know.' Like that hadn't occurred to me before. There had been some days when I had thought of little else, but I viewed motherhood as a boat that had long since sailed.

'Do you think you and Rick will have any?'

There it was. The million-dollar question. I didn't like to say that this really wasn't the time.

'Thank God!' Leoni drained her glass and waggled it at Sara for a top-up. 'The topic that has been burning on everyone's lips that we haven't dared to ask.' She looked at me. 'Well?'

'I don't think so,' I said in a small voice. 'Maybe if we'd met ten years ago things would have been different.' I picked up the bunny-wunny and squeezed it gently. It gave out a tiny squeak. Oh, don't start howling now! This is meant to be a party! My eyes went all hot. I tried to think of anything other than what my life would have been like had I had children.

'Too bleeding right,' Leoni said. 'You've got the best of both worlds anyway. You can borrow Julia's whenever you feel broody, then hand it back when you come to your senses a few hours later.' I smiled bravely.

'I'm never having kids,' Sara declared. 'It's of no interest to me whatsoever.'

'You're still young,' I told her sadly. 'You'll probably change your mind once that clock of yours starts ticking.'

'Clock?' Leoni helped herself to another cake. 'Let me tell you, that sodding thing is more like a time bomb. If you don't want to have kids, which I have to say is a thoroughly excellent decision, I suggest you have all your eggs removed then douse them with napalm.' She sunk her teeth into the pink icing. 'Better safe than sorry, eh?'

'What about this?' Julia held up a cute-as-buttons babygro embroidered with little yellow ducks. 'Doesn't that make you feel just a little, well, you know!'

'Nope.' Sara snarled at it. 'It makes me feel a little bit, well, NO FUCKING WAY.'

'So it's all bloody happening this year, isn't it?' Leoni paused to burp. 'Weddings. Babies. Are you going to show us the dress?'

'No chance,' I said. 'Anyway, it won't be ready until next week. Then I'm hiding it.'

'Have you asked him the questions?' Julia said.

'Questions?' I must have missed something here. 'What questions?'

'You know!' Sara clicked her fingers. 'The list of questions you're supposed to ask a man before you decide whether or not you want to marry him?'

Hello? This was all news to me. How come I'm always the last person to find out this kind of essential information?

'Like "Have you ever slept with a prostitute?"' Leoni began to rattle off her own list. 'And "Do you have any criminal convictions?"'

'Have you ever had sex with a man?' Sara added. 'Or an animal?'

'Are there any mad people in your family?'

'Does your mother still use your pet name?'

'How often do you call her?' Julia nodded.

'Well that one's easy,' I tried to join in. 'She's dead.'

'You haven't asked him any of this, have you?' Sara glanced at me, unsurprised.

'No,' I admitted, feeling a bit stupid. 'It never occurred to me.'

'Well, don't you think these are things that you ought to know?'

'I suppose so.' Excuse me while I throw myself off the window ledge. 'How come nobody's mentioned this to me before?'

'Durrrr!' Leoni made a spaz face. 'You're supposed to have your list done and dusted by the age of fourteen, stupid!' Julia banged her fist on the table.

'OK, people. Let's move on, shall we? Next item on the agenda, Sara?'

Sara consulted her list. 'What sex is the baby?'

'Oooooh!' Leoni and I nodded. 'That's a good one.'

'Don't know.' Julia balanced her champagne glass on her bump. 'Don't want to know either.'

'Are you sure about that?' Leoni took the floor. 'Because, I tell you, if I had my time over, I'd definitely want to know, especially if it's a boy. Then you can at least make some pathetic attempt to build a nuclear fallout shelter in the garden and prepare yourself for the havoc they will wreak on your life.'

'What if it's a girl?'

'Girls don't shanghai you into buying all the ingredients they need to make gunpowder then try to blow up the house.' I bloody knew there had been something seriously suspicious about that shopping list. Extra homework indeed. What a mug. The house still stank like a bonfire.

'I don't mind if it's a boy or a girl.' Julia rubbed her tummy affectionately. 'Although I know David would prefer a boy.'

'It's the football thing again,' Leoni explained sympathetically. 'Although by the time the kid is old enough to have a kick-around, the husband is usually too fat and past it to shift his arse and join in.'

'Are you still going for the water birth?' I pulled Julia's shoes off and began rubbing her feet.

'Of course!' She looked at me as though I were mad. 'I made David clean it out and give it a good scrubdown after they'd used it as a sports bar, but apart from that, it's as good as new. I can't wait. It's going to be the most amazing experience of my life. Oooh!' She took a sharp intake of breath and leaned forwards.

'Julia!' I leapt to my feet. 'Are you all right?'

She held on to the back of the sofa for a moment, puffing softly. 'Yes –' puff puff – 'yes, I think so. It was just one of those little Braxton Hicks.' Whoosh, straight over my head.

'Was that the front door?' Leoni's ears pricked up. We all quietened, straining to listen.

'Sara?!'

'Shit.' Sara scrambled to her feet. 'What the bloody hell is he doing home at this time of day! Quick.' She started flinging everything behind the sofa. 'Help me get rid of this stuff!'

'What on earth are you doing?' Julia snatched a pair of matching teddies from Sara's hands. The door opened.

'It's Dudley-wudley!' Leoni chirped, waving the wabbit at him before lifting its ear and speaking into it. 'Bunny-wunny? Meet uncle Wudley.'

Dudley's eyes filled with tears.

NOBODY EXPECTS THE SPANISH INQUISITION

'MY GOODNESS,' I WHISPERED, wandering slowly through each room. It was as though nothing had happened, the clock turned back to another time and place when everything was different. When I was different. I stepped into the bedroom, the freshly plastered ceiling now mirror-smooth, the replacement rose in the centre a perfect replica of the original, the carpet with its brand-new smell spotless.

'If you could just sign here.' The man waved a blue clipboard at me. 'To confirm that all the works have been completed to your satisfaction, then I can get going and leave you to settle in.'

'Certainly,' I said, taking the pen from his chubby hand and sticking my moniker on the form. Helen Robbins. Suddenly, it took me aback. I stared at it for a moment and wondered how many more times I would put that name to paper before it ceased to be. One of the first things I had done as a merry widow was to change my name back to Robbins. It had seemed so important, like some part of a grand plan to reclaim my identity, to discover whatever was left amid the pile of rubble that had become my miserable life. I promised to keep digging until I found her. Helen Robbins, the schoolgirl who was rubbish at maths and could never run into a moving skipping rope without getting tangled up. Helen Robbins, the bright young thing who shared a cramped flat near Gloucester Road with three other girls and watched *Dallas* on a Thursday night while drinking cheap plonk and eating pâté because she didn't know how to cook. I handed the clipboard back, giving away the name that had once meant so much to so few. Goodbye, Helen Robbins. Thank you. And farewell. A lightness came over me.

'THIS IS AN unexpected pleasure.' Rick raised a languid hand to summon Tony. 'A cryptic little text message demanding I drop everything and meet you for lunch?' I smiled enigmatically, feeling strangely empowered, as though everything was finally falling into place. 'Did you have something special in mind for dessert again?' he winked.

'Maybe,' I said. 'I just thought that you and I could take a little time out. It seems that we've both had a thousand distractions to deal with. You know, the wedding, Lola, Julia. We've hardly had a moment to catch up together properly.'

'Lola.' He rolled his eyes. 'You can say that again.'

'Have you heard from her?'

'Nope.' He reached inside his jacket pocket for his plastic nicotine inhalator, a sure sign that I had hit a nerve. A tiny shred of guilt loitered in my conscience. Perhaps he'd been right about leaving that particular wasp's nest undisturbed. He'd go bananas if he knew what I'd put in the letter, which was basically a full confession of his parental ineptitude and a promise to try harder in future, signed on his behalf. I'd thought that I'd be doing everyone a huge favour by playing mediator and peacemaker, but in the absence of any response, I'd been forced to reconsider my position. They'd probably burned the note ceremoniously alongside a couple of flaming effigies of me and Rick. 'I don't expect either of us will hear from her again until she wants something, although I've had plenny of calls from the card companies. She's been stripping cash machines all over Rio.' I chose not to remind him for the hundredth time that he really ought to cancel them. God knows he pays both her and her mother quite enough anyway. I've seen the bank statements. You could run a small country on the dosh they've leeched from him.

Tony appeared at our table.

'Mr and Mrs Wilton!'

'Not yet, Tone.' Rick shook his hand, leaving behind a crisp, pink note.

'Can I bring you something to drink?'

'Champagne, please, Tony,' I answered before Rick could.

'You heard the lady.' Rick smiled. Tony nodded and vanished. 'Are we celebrating again?'

'I suppose you could say that,' I said. 'Let's just call this a special lunch that you probably won't forget in a hurry.'

'Oh yeah?' he said. 'That sounds intriguing.'

I waited until we had polished off our first course before plunging in. This was no time to go into battle on an empty stomach. Rick's steak arrived. Good. He was gonna need it.

'Rick?'

'Mmm?' He slathered a dollop of French mootard on his forkful and shoved it in.

'Have you ever slept with a prostitute?'

The mustardy lump of fillet shot out of his mouth and landed on the neighbouring table.

'Sorry!' Rick leapt up. 'Really sorry!' Tony rushed to the commotion. 'That table's on me, Tone!' Rick raised his hand in a final apology to the startled grey-haired couple then sat back down.

'What fucking kind of question is that?' he hissed at me. 'Jesus Christ, Hell! I could have choked to death!'

'Well?' I nibbled at my salad. 'Have you?'

'No, I bloody haven't.' He frowned. Then, just for a second, I thought I saw something flicker across his face. 'At least – ' he looked to his side absently – 'Nah. Can't have been.'

'You're sure about that?'

'Yes,' he decided. 'I'm sure. Now can I please eat my lunch?'

'Of course.' He got stuck in. 'Have you ever had sex with a man, or with an animal?'

'*What?*' He paused his fork.

'You heard me.'

'No! What the bloody hell's got into you today?'

'How about criminal convictions? Got any of those in the closet that you haven't mentioned?' He threw down his cutlery.

'Now, you know very well that I'm no saint.'

'I want specifics,' I said.

'OK,' He looked me directly in the eye. 'I did three

346

months after someone stitched me up over a duff batch of motors back in '81. I've been done for drink-driving twice – ' he started counting on his fingers – 'got a twelve-month suspension for assault, although fuck knows the bloke deserved it. Wanker. What else can I impress you with? Had a couple of cautions when things got a bit boisterous, but no more than anyone else. I've been acquitted more times than I've been sent down, and I haven't been anywhere near the nick in twenty years.' He cut into his steak aggressively, shoved a big lump in his mouth and chewed. 'You wanna know all about it? Speak to my lawyer.'

'Oh, don't you worry. I will.' Prison? He bloody never mentioned that before. I let him calm down and eat for a little while before hitting him with the next one. 'Is there any history of schizophrenia or psychosis in your family?'

'You have got to be kidding me.' He stabbed his steak hard.

'It's a perfectly reasonable question,' I said. 'I have no intention of marrying a man who might wake up one morning thinking he's Adolf Hitler.'

'I don't believe this,' he muttered. 'And what about you?' Uh-oh. I hadn't banked on the tables being turned. My grandfather on my mother's side had gone stark raving before he was thirty and spent the rest of his life in a loony bin eating insects.

'I'm asking the questions today, mister.' I decided

to brazen it out. 'I don't want any nasty surprises once we become man and wife, is that understood?'

'Fuck me.' He picked up his glass and drained it. 'It's the Spanish Inquisition. Tony!' He lifted the empty bottle. Tony gave him a nod of understanding and went to fetch another. 'Excuse me if I get pissed.' Rick shoved his plate away. 'It seems that I've accidentally got engaged to Attila the Hun.'

'So?'

'So what?'

'Are there any mad people in your family?'

'Not at the moment,' he said. 'But quite clearly, that's all about to change. Do you mind telling me what's brought this on?'

'Nothing!'

'Bollocks,' he said. 'You bloody women have been off whispering in corners and making mischief, haven't you?' I went red. He reached into his pocket for his phone and scrolled down the numbers. 'Mike? Yeah. Rick. Listen mate. I want you to set up a meeting. You and Julian and the new Mrs, OK? She's gonna ask you a bunch of stuff and I want you to tell her exactly how it is, right?' His eyes wandered to mine temporarily. 'Yes, of course I'm fucking sure! You just tell her whatever she wants to know. Is that clear? Good. Right. Well just set it up. Cheers.' He stuck it back in his pocket and shook his head. 'Now it's him who thinks I'm mad.'

Tony arrived with the replacement bottle and smiled at us romantically as he soothed out the cork and set down a fresh pair of glasses. 'Everything all right with you love birds?'

'Fucking marvellous,' Rick said, deadpan.

'You two are so wonderful together,' Tony ventured, pouring the bubbles. 'I can see you from my corner, talking so deeply, being so – ' he waved his hand, looking for a suitable adjective – 'impassioned.'

'Thank you, Tony.' I smiled sweetly.

'You are most welcome.' He clicked his heels together and nodded a small bow. 'We are looking forward to your wedding party very much. Everything will be perfect. Just you wait and see.'

Rick raised his glass to toast me. 'Well, babe. You certainly know how to inject an unexpected twist into a perfectly ordinary day.' He took a long sip. 'Now, before we move on to dessert, are there any other bombshells you're planning to drop on me today?'

'Absolutely.' I picked up my glass and clinked it against his. 'I'm moving out.'

I'D ALMOST FORGOTTEN the joy of having my own space. I put my feet up on my sofa and soaked up the fading remnants of my life lived here. My lovely home, invisible for so long under its cloak of familiarity, seemed to blossom around me. Its perfect proportions.

The bright light that streamed in so tirelessly through the south-facing windows. The French doors that opened out onto the pretty balcony running the length of the stucco-fronted house. Even though I probably hadn't been thinking straight at the time, buying this place was the best thing I ever did. It had been my sanctuary. My best friend whenever I needed quiet time to think, to grow. How I would miss it here. Sure, Rick's place was a pretty serious piece of kit, but this? This was different, for a million reasons, and I'd never be able to thank it enough. There came a gentle knock on the door. I took a breath to enjoy the moment, then went to the spy hole. Paul peered back at me through the jungle of lilies in his arms.

'Not disturbing you, am I?' He walked straight past me. 'Wow factor!' he gasped. 'My God! Everything looks brand new!' Yes Paul. I feel pretty brand new too. 'Is it here yet?'

'It is.' I nodded. 'Would you like to see it?'

We stood in the bedroom together, admiring the heavenly dress that had arrived in a cab three hours earlier. It hung quietly from the wardrobe door, softly reflecting folds of sunlight from the gentle waves of trailing silk.

'Have you tried it on?' he whispered.

'No.' An involuntary shudder crept up my spine. 'If it doesn't fit now, then it's not going to fit on Friday, is it?' Not only that. I couldn't. Part of me didn't even want to touch it. I might put a jinx on the wedding.' Paul raised an eyebrow.

'That's brave,' he said unsurely. 'I'd have to put it on three times a day, just to make sure.'

'How about you?'

'Oh!' He became all a-fluster. 'I can't tell you how excited we both are. We've got our outfits ready, right down to the matching shoelaces. It's going to be the best day ever.' We smiled at each other conspiratorially. I had a feeling he was right.

Chapter Twenty-Three

DEARLY BELOVED

'Aren't you supposed to have bridesmaids to do this sort of thing for you?' Dad fiddled in the small of my back, his fingers delicately finding their way with the zipper, as though pinching out the tops of his fledgling tomato plants in early spring.

'I didn't want anyone here except you. They'd only get me into a panic.'

'There,' he said, stepping back.

The pair of us stood quietly for a while, watching my reflection in the mirror, father and daughter. Had he been anyone else, he might have said something like, 'You look beautiful', as they do in all the films. Instead he held his counsel, smiling a little, unable or unwilling to rely on a handful of words to send me on my way.

'What's the time?' I asked. He seemed grateful for the excuse to look away.

'Two.'

'Shall we have a stiff gin and tonic? I think I need one.'

'I'll get it. Don't want you spilling anything on that dress, do we?'

'Thanks, Dad. You'll find everything in the fridge. Ice in the freezer.'

I sat at the dressing table, watching him pull at his jacket, uncomfortable in the new suit forced upon him.

'Hello,' I whispered to the woman in the mirror. She smiled back at me, calm, collected, with the reassurance of all the people she had ever been. I knew we would meet one day, that she would finally surface and make herself known to me. Where have you been? Right here. What took you so long? You weren't ready. Did you really have to put me through all that first? Yes.

'Here we go.' Dad returned with a drink in each hand. 'Get your laughing gear round that.'

'Thanks.'

'You're sure about this?' He perched on the end of my bed.

'Yes, Dad.'

'Because if you're not, that's OK, love. We can get

out of here right now. I'll take you anywhere you want to go. Just say the word.'

'I know.'

'It's not easy – ' he looked in his glass – 'marriage.'

'I know that too.' A rueful smile settled on my lips.

'Your mother and I have had our ups and downs, of course. She worries too much about what other people think. I've always told her that it doesn't matter. So long as everyone's healthy and happy, what more is there?'

'Not a lot.'

A silence stretched between us.

'You know,' he finally said. 'We had a May wedding too.'

'Eh?' No he didn't. What was he talking about? Don't tell me the old man's decided to go senile today of all days. 'I thought your wedding anniversary was in December.' I reminded him. 'That's why we've always done the double thing at Christmas.'

'No, love. It was May. May 23rd 1964. On a clear blue day, bright and sunny, just like this.'

'1964?' I frowned at him. 'Don't you mean 1963?'

'Nope. It was '64 all right. Liz Taylor had just married Richard Burton. It was all over the papers.'

'But I thought that—' The rest of the sentence stuck on my tongue. Rubbish at maths as I might be, the calculation clattered through my internal abacus in about a millisecond. 'Julia was born that October.' He gave me one of his special looks. 'Oh, my God! You mean Mum was—'

'Ssshhh.' He lifted a finger to his lips. 'I just thought it might make today a little easier for you when she gets on her high horse and starts up with her non-sense. Although this is to remain strictly between you and I, is that understood?'

'Well I never.'

'She was a bit of a goer, your mum.'

'I don't believe it.'

'Oh, it's true,' he sighed. 'Mind you, it was a short-lived thing. I think the guilt of it ate her alive. She never forgave herself for ending up saddled with me. Had all sorts of big ideas about marrying her way out of Dullsville, I suppose.' He trailed off. I shook my head in disbelief. 'I think we just about got away with it, although I'm pretty sure her mother suspected something was up.'

'What about Granny Spongecake?'

'Oh!' He laughed. 'It was her that helped us throw the wedding together once we knew we were in trouble. You know what my old mum was like. I'm sure she wouldn't have given a flying monkeys herself, but your mother's family, well. That's a different story. We just told everyone that we couldn't wait to get married and that was that.'

'I'm stunned,' I said, struggling to put these shiny new pieces together. No wonder she'd spent the rest of her life looking over her shoulder. 'You know what, Dad? That little ember is going to keep me warm for years.'

'Here's to you.' He raised his glass. 'May your new husband live long enough to deserve you.' We took silent sips, waiting for the clock to move. I so wanted to think of something worthy to say, but my head just filled with well-worn platitudes and empty, meaningless words. How could I even begin? The buzzer went, both of us glad of the intrusion, yet feigning rude interruption.

'Expecting someone?'

'No,' I frowned. 'Do you mind getting that for me, Dad? Just pick up the white telephone thing on the wall and press the red button if you want to open the front door.'

'Sure.' He jumped up, man on a mission.

I examined my reflection again, tempted for a moment to make the smallest of adjustments here and there, just to keep my hands busy, though knowing that there would be no improving the first-class effort Paul had already poured into my hair and make-up. He always maintained I was his own personal *Girl's World* styling head, and there was no doubting that I would sorely miss those cosy nights in with the pair of them, watching old Humphrey Bogart movies while giving each other a make-over and joining in with the dialogue, acting our hearts out. His earrings twinkled in my lobes, something borrowed.

'Delivery for you.' Dad handed me a small package. 'Who from?'

'Search me.' He shrugged. 'I didn't ask.'

'Hmm.' I turned it over. No sender.

'Well, aren't you going to open it?' Once you reach pensioner age, a major highlight like an unexpected delivery is about as exciting as life gets. I tore off the paper, then through a thin layer of protective bubble wrap, leaving me with a flat, red leather case in my hands, gilded at the edges. My pulse quickened. 'What is it?' Dad hovered.

'I don't know.' But I could sure take an educated guess. 'Here.' I passed it to the old man. 'You open it.'

He did so without hesitation, flicking up the clasp and lifting the lid. 'Wow,' he said slowly, staring for a while. He picked up a small, plain card and adjusted it in front of his bifocals. 'Until three. Rick. Kiss.' He turned the case around to show me.

'Oh, my God,' I whispered, leaning from my chair to pick out the delicate golden daisy chain, each life-size flower agonizingly fashioned from pink-white pearls set around a tiny cluster of shimmering yellow stones. 'Isn't that beautiful?' I ran it over my hands, the sunlight through the window playing on the tiny enamel leaves.

'Here.' Dad stood up. 'Let me.' I felt the roughness of his green fingers at the nape of my neck, his face in the mirror set hard with concentration. 'They're just like real daisies,' he remarked. 'I expect your mother would have liked something like this on her wedding day. I didn't even know you were supposed to give the bride a present. I thought the ring was kind of it, not that I had two pennies to rub together anyway.'

'Gosh.' I gazed at the necklace, the thought that someone had sat down and made something so exquisite, only to let it go, almost unfathomable.

'Let's have a look at you.' Dad took me gently by the shoulders, stood back and appraised me. Nodding gently, he dropped his head a little, his mouth tightening. 'You'll do, love.' He patted me and let go, turning away. A car horn sounded from the street below. Dad straightened himself, the back of his hand lifting momentarily to his face, and went to the bedroom window.

'Is Rick picking us up?'

'No.' I smiled. 'That'll be Terry in the Bentley.' Dad stood and watched the street below. 'Crikey. He's a bit of an old duffer isn't he?' I took a deep breath, reached for my silk shawl and the tiny bag Madame Arienne had made for my essentials. Lipstick. Tissues. Get-away car. Dad sniffed hard, sighed and returned from the window.

'Ready to face the firing squad?'

'Ready as I'll ever be.'

'Shall we?' He offered me his suited and booted arm. I linked mine through his and felt him lean down to kiss my hair. 'Although I feel duty-bound to warn you, your mother's not going to like this one little bit.'

'I'LL GO AROUND the block, miss.' Terry touched the peak of his cap. 'Looks like we're a couple of minutes early.' He put his foot down, accelerating to a break-neck twenty miles per hour, streaking geriatrically past the jostling crowd of guests shuffling their way up the wide, grey steps of the town hall. I turned and stared out of the back window, trying to pick out the faces.

'Is that what you call a handful of people?' Dad pressed his nose up against the window.

'Well, you know how these things snowball,' I said. 'What's Mum wearing?'

'A pink sofa cover.' His hand clutched mine still, the good earth scraped from his nails. 'With a bloody awful hat that makes her look like Mr Pastry.'

'I said no hats,' I clucked.

'Oh, I shouldn't take too much notice, love. It's just her way of making her mark. You know. Mother of the bride and all that. She wants to stand out from the crowd. That ruddy thing on her head ought to do the trick.'

By the time Terry crawled back round, the crowd

had dispersed. We drew up at the kerb and sat patiently while Terry waited a couple of years for a safe gap to open in the oncoming traffic before releasing our doors. 'Good luck, miss.' He helped me out onto the pavement then handed me to my father. To my astonishment, Dad reached into his pocket and pressed a twenty into Terry's palm with a nod of thanks. A warm breeze caught my dress, sending it swirling in a billowing pearl cloud that drew smiles from passing strangers. We took the stairs at a careful pace, neither one of us in a rush to see away this brief moment too quickly. I squeezed Dad's arm, grateful for all that it had extended me with open heart and silent affection for so many years. If Rick turned out to be half the man my father was, then I would be blessed indeed.

'Darlings!' Paul rushed at us, blocking our path before we could get through the door, wrinkling his nose and whispering, 'You might want to give it five minutes.'

'What's all that noise?' Dad craned his head in pursuit of the raised voices inside.

'Oh, nothing.' Paul smiled diplomatically. 'A couple of unexpected guests have turned up. Listen – ' he pulled me to one side – 'are you sure you told everyone this was a wedding?'

The scuffle inside broke through the doors, spilling messily onto the outside steps. '*BASTARDO!*' screamed the woman with impossibly pneumatic lips, scorching red with rage, dressed in floor-length black with a diaphanous funereal veil. She bent forward to lift the hem of her dress, tearing off her shoes, throwing them viciously behind her, their spike heels spinning deadly daggers through the air. 'I curse you! I curse your marriage!'

'Ow! Fuck!' Rick's voice bellowed.

'Quick!' Paul shrilled, hauling off his jacket and urging Dad to do the same. 'He's coming! Hide the bride!' I caught the briefest glimpse of Rick frog-marching Lola's stick-thin bones towards the screeching virago at the door before being plunged into sudden darkness as Dad's tailcoat flew about my head.

'You pig!' The woman's deep voice carried the same inflection as Lola's. 'You no marry him! You make me big insult!'

'For Christ's sake! How many times do I have to tell you that I'm not marrying a man!'

'Then why Lola say you *fruta*? Why you have man in there with you?'

'What the bloody hell's going on?' I mumbled through the sleeve lining, feeling myself being bundled out of the way.

'Sshhh!' Paul said. 'Don't let him see you!'

'Listen, Maria, I really haven't got time for this right now, OK? You wanna come in and enjoy the wedding? Fine. You wanna cause trouble? Then piss off and we'll call it quits, OK?' I heard a match strike. 'And another thing. If that daughter of ours isn't in college by the time I get back from my honeymoon, there'll be no more money from me. *Compreendo?*' The inside of Dad's jacket reeked of mothballs.

'Excuse me?' Another voice joined the general cacophony, this one less hysterical. 'We've got a strict schedule to keep to here and it's gone five past. The registrar wants to know if you're coming in or not. There's another party booked for three-thirty and he's about to move you on.'

'I'm already there,' Rick said. I heard his heavy footsteps turn and pound away.

'Thank God!' Paul whisked the jacket from my head and set about tidying my hair. As if sensing my presence, Lola span on her heels and locked eyes with me.

'Hello, Lola,' I said softly, taking my dad's hand for moral support. 'This is my father, Frank.' The old man automatically proffered his hand, his bemused 'How do you do' still trying to get a handle on what the hell was going on. 'Dad, this is Rick's lovely daughter, Lola, and her mother,' I presumed. With a temper like that, it couldn't have been anyone else. Lola stared at him for a moment, a portly old man with gentle manner and grey hair. All at once, she seemed disarmed and muttered something to her mother before attempting a reluctant smile in return. 'They've come all the way from Brazil,' I explained, bracing myself against any further sudden explosions. 'I'm so glad you could come. It means a lot to your father.' Her eyes dropped to her Manolos. If I didn't know better, I might even say that she looked a little shamefaced.

'A-hem!' Paul pulled his sleeve back and wielded his watch at us. 'Can we please get inside now?'

'Excuse us.' Dad doffed his cap at Lola and her wide-eyed mother who nodded at him blankly, barely able to move a muscle in her face for the twenty litres of botox pumped under her skin. 'I've only got one job to do today.' He steered us through the door. 'And this is it.'

'They're all in there waiting for you.' The smiling official, whose voice I recognized as the one-woman peacekeeping force who'd been sent out to chivvy Rick along, motioned us towards the main room. 'Another two minutes and you'd have had your chips. Mr Gooding's a right stickler for his timetable. Everyone fit?' she asked.

My father kissed my hand.

'You look beautiful, love,' he said.

The official nodded her head into the room and a string quartet struck up the wedding march.

'I know it's corny – ' Paul blushed bashfully – 'but what else does a girl want to hear on her wedding day!'

'It's perfect,' I reassured him with a wide smile.

'Ready?' Dad offered me one arm, Paul the other,

and in we walked, heads held high. At the end of the guest-flanked aisle, two men waited. Rick, beaming from ear to ear in a silver shot-silk suit; Sally, resplendent in a sleek, black tuxedo with a scarlet sash slicing a flash of colour at his waist. I caught Rick's slate-blue gaze and held it guardedly. He raised a slow finger and tapped his temple, a small laugh shaking his shoulders, then blew me a kiss.

'Good afternoon, ladies and gentlemen,' the registrar addressed his colourful audience. 'My name is John Gooding, Superintendent Registrar, and I would like to welcome you all here today to celebrate the weddings of Rick and Helen, and Salvatore and Paul.' I heard the distinctive sound of my mother choking and snuck a sideways glance. She was sitting bolt upright, body set with rigor mortis, her mouth puckered into a pink, frosted cat's arse. Dad raised his eyes to the ceiling and slipped me a tiny thumbs-up. From the door behind him, Lola and her mother slid in quietly and took seats at the back, black veils removed to expose a matching pair of painted faces.

The four of us stood side by side, Paul gazing adoringly at Sally, his eyes misty with tears. I felt Rick watching me intently, his breath close by. The registrar's voice faded from the room, seeming to leave just Rick and I, perched at the edge of the precipice, wings still wet, ready to hold hands and leap off into the wild blue yonder together. I felt the whole world stand still.

'I do solemnly declare that I know not of any lawful impediment why I, Helen, may not be joined in matrimony to Richard.' I realized he was talking to me. My mouth moved and some noises came out that sounded like mwah, mwah, mwah. More words were said, smiling faces, occasional smatterings of laughter, all swirling around me without making contact, as though I were separated from it all by an invisible glass dome, suspended way up above. Some small disturbance from the seated congregation. A short pause. Are we all right to continue? Yes? Yes, fine. I called upon these persons here present to witness that I, Helen, take you, Richard, to be my lawful wedded—

'Aaaaaagh!' We ground to a halt again, turning to the commotion, much louder this time. Julia was on her feet, her face a tense grimace, eyes flashing wide.

'Julia?' I rushed to her, forgetting everything else. 'What's wrong? Tell me!'

'Aaaaaagh!' She bent double and sank back in her chair, clutching the back of the seat in front, panting hard.

'Oh, my God!' I threw my arms around her. She grasped at my hand.

'Shit,' she puffed. 'I'm sorry!'

'It's OK!' I took my shawl off and wrapped it around her. 'Braxton Hicks?'

'No way.' She seemed to calm for a moment. 'Oh, God. I think this is the real McCoy.'

'What?' I looked up at David, now on his feet, frozen to the spot, staring down at his convulsing wife with terror in his eyes. 'But she's not due for another four weeks!' Julia leaned back and pressed a hand against her spine.

'Oh, God,' she groaned, closing her eyes. 'Here comes another one.'

'How long?' I demanded. David didn't move. 'David! How long has she been getting the pains?'

'I don't know,' he mumbled uselessly. 'She's been a bit funny all day and started rocking in her seat about an hour ago.'

'What?'

'Aaaaarrrrgh!' Julia roared.

Paul started babbling at the registrar, yaddering at a hundred miles an hour. 'And I call upon these persons here present to witness that I Paul take you Sally to be my wife/husband/whatever.' The registrar wrenched his attention from the mob in the room. 'Come on!' Paul shouted at him, glancing nervously over his shoulder.

'Hell?' Rick pushed through. 'What's going on?'

'Get the car!' I bawled at him. He took just one look at Julia's reddened face.

'Got it!' he shouted back.

'Excuse me!' The registrar craned his head to see over the affray.

'Never mind them!' Paul snapped. 'Just get on with it!'

The registrar flustered with his page. 'Erm. OK, here we go. A-hem.' He stood up straight. 'Paul and Salvatore, you have both made the declarations pre-scribed by—'

'Never mind all that!' Paul shouted. 'Cut to the chase! NOW! You know – blah blah, man and wife? GO!'

'Yes, yes.' He mopped his brow, flipped a few pages on. 'Where are we?' Then back again, in a complete fluster. 'Oh, whatever!' he said, slamming the book shut in his hands. 'I now pronounce you man and man together!'

'Aaaaaaagh!'

'Hurry!' I shouted towards the door.

The kind lady official who had seen us in so regally now cleared a path like King Canute, tearing through the room, waving her arms like a banshee. 'Mind your backs! Mind your backs! Pregnant woman coming through!'

'Don't just stand there, you cretin!' I yelled at David. 'Help her!'

He stepped forward mutely and tried to uphold some of Julia's impossible weight. I took her other arm and draped it over my shoulder, propping her up as best I could.

Outside, Rick was already revving the engine, Terry standing befuddled on the pavement, spinning in a daze.

'In the back!' I urged Julia. 'David! You get in the front.'

'Make way!' Leoni started stuffing herself in behind us. 'Marcus!' she bellowed. 'Get the other car!' Quicker than a streak of lightning, Sara sprinted past like a mythical Grecian warrior, her flaming Gucci dress flying behind her taut, athletic legs.

'Leave it to me!' she yelled over her shoulder. 'You just get going! Go! Go! Go!' She leapt out into the traffic, bringing the Number 22 to a sliding halt as the driver stood on the horn, eyes popping from his head in the first throes of a heart attack.

'Aaaaaaagh!' Julia kneeled on the back seat, clinging to the headrest for dear life.

'Breathe!' Leoni started panting. Huff, huff, huff.

'I caaaaaan't!' Julia howled.

'Yes you can. Now come on!' She took Julia's hand and stared into her face. 'Just go with it. With me, in . . . out. In . . . out. Watch me.' She pointed two fingers in her own eyes then at Julia's. Julia nodded at her, blanching with pain, and tried to keep up a steady rhythm. 'That's better. Good girl.' She turned and stared at Rick and David, the pair of them rigid. 'Well?' she blasted at them. 'What are you waiting for?

Fucking step on it, you prat!' The car screeched away from the kerb.

'Where to?'

'A hospital you moron! Good God.' She shook her head at me incredulously. 'See what I mean?'

'Which one!'

'Chelsea and Westminster!' I shouted. 'It's nearest!'

'Oh my GOD!' Julia started up again. 'Aaaaaaarrrrgh! FUCK!' She turned around and slapped the back of David's head really hard. 'You BASTARD! I HATE YOU! How could you have left me like that all day? Arrrrrrgggggh!'

'You hit me!' His face pale with shock.

'Just shut up and get me to the hospital NOW!' A sudden deluge of water drenched the Bentley's calf-skin seats.

Rick skidded around the corner into the Fulham Road, the car barely keeping four wheels on the tarmac, the G-force throwing us around like marbles in a jam jar while Julia screamed blue murder and Leoni talked her off the ceiling. My heart flooded with admiration for the friend I had known for so long, seeing her in a new light, her calmness an oasis in the face of this violent eruption, her kind, soothing voice never wavering, encouraging Julia, whispering softly to her, stroking her hair as she bellowed and roared.

'Maternity!' Rick yelled out of the window, mounting the pavement and bringing the car to a juddering stop just before we hit a brick wall.

'Upstairs,' someone shouted back. 'Third floor.'

'Get a wheelchair!' Leoni commanded. Rick raced through the entrance, then ran back out again, searching frantically while we eased a panting Julia from the back seat, me buckling under her weight.

'Hurry!' we all shouted.

A young man in an Arsenal shirt with a fresh plaster cast on his arm sat outside the entrance, smoking a cigarette and hating the world, watching us with disdain. He had a spider's web tattooed across his sullen face.

'Excuse me, mate.' Rick took hold of the back of his wheelchair and tipped him out.

'Oi!' he yelled. 'What the fuck do you think you're—'

'Can it, arsehole!' Rick shook his fist at him. 'Unless you want a pair of busted legs as well!'

'Take her!' I gave David an ungracious shove. 'You're the one who should be rushing her in, not us!' He vacantly grabbed hold of the wheelchair and began to steer her blindly towards the lifts, her howls of pain fading as the polished steel doors rolled closed and carried them away.

Marcus ran in. 'What's happening?'

'What do you think, you brainless, single-celled organism?' Leoni glowered at him. 'Where's Sara?'

'Outside punching a traffic warden. Said she won't be a minute. Dudley's in a bit of a state, too. I dunno what's the matter with the man.'

'Come on.' I pulled at Leoni. 'Third floor!'

The very fabric of the labour ward seemed to strain and groan with the effort of keeping the burgeoning human race on track.

'He-len!'

'I'm coming!' I shouted to the air, rushing towards the voice disappearing down the end of a corridor, snatching up my oyster silk puddle train, now horribly mangled and marked with grubby black streaks, having sped all the way from the registry office unceremoniously jammed in the car door. I barged into the delivery room and took her outstretched hand.

'Drugs,' Julia groaned, her eyes bulging with pain. 'I want drugs.' Her hair lay in damp strands across her forehead, my knuckles cracking as she squeezed the life out of my fingers. She lifted her head. 'Aaaaaarrrrgh!'

'She needs pain relief!' I pleaded with the unflustered midwife, who hummed herself a pleasant little tune while she had a good rummage beneath Julia's gown.

'Epidural,' Julia gasped at me. 'Get me a fucking epidural! Oh Christ! Uuuuurrrrgh! Somebody just kill me!'

'Mmm,' the midwife said, snapping off her gloves. 'I

think we might be a little late for that. Looks like this baby's in a hurry!'

'Aaaaaaaarrrrgh!' Julia lurched forward suddenly, sweat springing from her brow.

'Give that to me!' I snatched the Entonox mask from David's face. He slumped in the chair. 'Here!' I jammed it over Julia's mouth, her hand reaching up instantly to clutch it tightly. 'Breathe deeply!' She nodded and pulled her breath in hard, laboured gulps, until her body slackened. David stared at her, wide-eyed, unable to move.

'Oooh!' The midwife admired my frock. 'Aren't we all dressed up today! Were you all on your way some- where nice or is this all part of the plan?' Whatever this woman was on, she should be passing it around the room. Julia began moaning again, head thrashing. In a rare moment of lucidity, she suddenly noticed David sagging in the chair next to her.

'You selfish bastard!' She landed a fist on his leg. He stifled a yelp. 'How can you just sit there like that?!' Her breath came in short, sharp bursts. 'You've been nothing but a spineless chicken shit since day one. Well, have I got news for you.' She grasped a handful of his hair.

'Arrrgh!' He tried to wrench her fingers from his scalp, looking up at me in desperation. 'I don't know what to do!'

'What the hell are you asking me for?' I told him.

'For Christ's sake. Just how bloody useless are you planning to be?'

'Aaaaaarrrrrgh!' Julia slumped back on the bed. 'FUCK!'

'Can't you give her something stronger?' I begged the midwife.

'Not really.' She shrugged apologetically. 'Now, if you'd got here an hour or two ago—'

'NOT helpful!' I shot daggers at her. 'Understand what I'm saying?'

'Aaaaaaarrrrghhhh!'

'Julia?' She came to the head of the bed and tried to secure Julia's attention. 'My name's Tess. I'm your midwife. I'm not going to be able to give you anything other than the gas and air I'm afraid. There isn't time. Do you want to try the birthing pool? Some people find it eases the contractions.' Julia ripped the mask from her face and grabbed the scruff of Tess the Midwife's uniform, pulling her close, snarling into the whites of her eyes.

'Do I look like I want to go for a fucking swim?' she spat. 'I want DRUGS! Get me an epidural! NOW!'

'Bloody hurts, doesn't it! I've got four!' She unpeeled Julia's fingers from her collar and smiled. 'Next time you'll know to come in earlier and nab the nearest anaesthetist! Never mind, eh?'

'There won't fucking be a next time. Arrrrgggh!'

'That's it!' The midwife pressed the mask to Julia's

face again. 'Take a few nice deep breaths! It'll all be over before you know it.'

'Aaaaarrrrrgggh!' Julia rammed her face back into the gas just as David began to slide from his seat, slumping towards the bed. Julia snatched the water jug from the side table and crashed it over his head. 'Get him out of here!' she screamed. 'Before I kill him!'

'Come on.' I dragged his deadweight body from the chair. 'If you're going to faint you can bloody well do it somewhere else.' He staggered to his feet, bewildered, and I shoved him out of the door. 'Wait there. And don't you dare move.' He leaned up against the wall, his pupils dilating. 'Oh, for heaven's sake.' I rushed up the corridor, shouting, 'Rick!'

'Yeah, babe!' he called back, heavy footsteps stampeding towards me seconds later.

'Hold that, will you?' I pointed at David swaying precariously, head in his hands, then ran back to my post.

Julia seemed to have quietened a little, mask in hand, her head lolling back on the pillows, eyes half-closed as she moaned to herself gently. The midwife held her hand, mopping her brow with a damp flannel.

'Don't worry. She'll be all right,' she reassured me with a sunny smile. 'Everything's pretty normal. Let her rest for a while now, eh? Believe me, it'll start up again soon enough, then I expect she'll be wanting to push this baby out. Why don't you take a break? I'll come and fetch you the minute anything happens.' I nodded reluctantly, my heart racing, and slipped quietly from the room.

Out in the corridor, Rick had David firmly pinned against the wall. 'Listen!' He slapped his face. 'You just pull your fucking socks up and start acting like a man, OK?'

'Uuurggh.' David wrenched in deep breaths, his eyes rolling in his head.

'Now, you just listen to me, right? You think your wife wants some flaky ponce in there with her while she brings your kid into this world? Hell? Get me a glass of water or something would ya, babe?' I quickly fetched a cupful from the cooler and gave it to him. 'Here!' He slung it in David's face, threw the cup aside and gave him a good shake. 'You'd better get your shit together right now or you're gonna be paying for this for the rest of your life. Believe me. I know.'

'Urgh.' David spluttered and started coming round.

'Don't make me hit you again, mate,' Rick implored him. 'You're a nice bloke and all that, but it's show time. Unnerstand?' David nodded unsteadily.

'Yeah. Sorry.' He wiped the water from his face with his hands. 'Thanks. Just give me a minute, will you? I'll be fine.'

'Good man.' Rick punched him gently on the arm. 'Everyone's counting on you. Don't fuck it up, right?'

'Psssst! Helen!' Leoni beckoned wildly from the end of the corridor, hopping from one foot to the other, flinching briefly as an agonized scream sailed out from one of the nearby delivery rooms.

'What is it?' I hissed at her.

'Your bloody mother's here!'

'Oh, God.' I felt my heart sink. 'Whatever you're about to tell me, I really can't deal with it right now. Just keep her out there in the waiting room and don't, under any circumstances, let her burst in on Julia.'

'Not here! Downstairs! She's doing her pieces in the emergency room, demanding that she be treated at once for shock, ranting that her daughter's just forced her to attend a gay wedding.'

'Yeah,' I mumbled, my head spinning. 'Well she can bloody talk.'

'Excuse me!' the midwife called, nodding me back towards the delivery room.

'Look, Leoni, I've got to go. Why don't you get down there and suggest the doctors try driving a wooden stake through her heart?' I turned on my heels, muttering, 'I'd do the bloody honours myself, but I'm afraid I've got my hands full.'

Rick stopped me outside the door. 'David's already in there.'

'OK, thanks.' I began to push it open.

'No.' Rick caught my arm gently. 'What I mean is, her husband's with her. Let them be, eh?'

'But, he's—'

'Leave it, babe.' He smiled at me gently. 'This ain't nobody's business but theirs. They'll be fine. Trust me.'

Julia's low, rumbling roar carried through the closed door, her intermittent gasps, David's voice as he comforted her, the midwife calling words of encouragement. Rick steered me away.

'How's she doing?' Marcus leapt up from his seat the moment he saw us.

'Fine,' Rick said. 'Just waiting for nature to take its course.'

'Me too.' Leoni nodded menacingly at her husband. 'I'm killing him slowly on a high cholesterol diet.'

Chapter Thankaverymush

HELEN ROBBINS HAS LEFT THE BUILDING

BY THE TIME we scraped ourselves off the hospital walls and piled over to Tony's, stinking of spent adrenaline and cheap disinfectant, the after-party was in full swing. Unsurprisingly, our limp-wristed arrival amid the general hullabaloo went largely unnoticed, me feeling like rent-a-ghost, wilting against the door, sapped of every last shred of energy. Rick loitered with intent for a few moments, weighing up the chances of his being heard over the din, before reaching behind the bar and picking up an ice bucket, emptying its contents to the floor in one swift flash. He held it high above his head and clanged it mercilessly with a serving spoon. Beneath the din, the room quietened. The music stopped. All heads turned.

'Listen up, you lot!' Rick boomed. 'It's a boy!'

The news detonated a deafening thunderclap of drunken cheering, the roar so loud that my fillings rattled. Rick pulled me close, another river of tears springing from my knackered eyes, dripping what was left of my mascara down my car crash of a dress. Tony rushed to greet us, showering me with kisses, pumping Rick's hand.

'Ladies and gentlemen!' he yelled to the braying mob. 'Pray welcome . . . Mr and Mrs Rick Wilton!'

Ta-raaaaa! went the band.

'Er . . .' Rick pulled on Tony's sleeve. 'Not quite, Tone.'

'What?'

'I'm afraid we didn't actually get around to that,' Rick whispered in his ear before addressing the rabble. 'As you were, everybody!' He flicked his hand inconsequentially. 'Move along now! There ain't nothing to see here!' Tony gesticulated wildly at the Mexican mariachi band, their bobble-trimmed sombreros wobbling back into action as the fat one gave it some welly with his maracas.

'You're not married?' Confusion clouded Tony's face. 'What happened?'

'Don't say nobody's told you.' Rick pulled a cigar from his pocket. 'And before you tell me I can't light this thing in here.' Tony had a flaming lighter under the end of it before Rick could reach for his matches. 'Thanks.' He puffed away.

'I thought it was maybe some kind of joke,' Tony said, trying not to look at the state of me.

'Reek!' The mighty slap that landed on his back sent the end of his cigar scorching into my dress. Not that it mattered. I might as well have got it out of a skip anyway. 'I make you beeg congratulate!' Helga waved her vodka bottle at us. 'Now you make me kiss!' She puckered up. Rick took a deep breath and planted a fat one on her face.

'Thanks, Helg. You havin' a good time?'

'*Da!*' She beamed, opening her Tesco bag-for-life and showing him the piles of food she had liberated. 'I get lompster, breed, chiz – ' she started rattling off her booty – 'and vodka! Three bots!'

'Good for you.' Rick patted her affectionately.

'Hel-yen.' She nudged me in warning. 'She in here.'

'Who?'

'Lola *bliad*! Blooding beech. She with her mudda.' Helga stretched her facial skin back with her hands and ballooned her lips. 'You want me make rid?' She slid her finger across her throat.

'No thanks, Helg.' Rick squeezed her hand. 'But

you might want to go and keep an eye on them in case they try to burn the place down.'

'*Da!*' Helga snapped a curt salute and scurried away.

'Rick?' I pulled on his sleeve. 'Don't you think we should go over and say hello?'

'What for?' He shrugged.

'You know, pour some oil over troubled waters.'

'You're never satisfied are you?' He let out a plume of blue smoke. 'They're here, aren't they? Nobody's pulled a gun. Ain't that enough for you?'

'But don't you think—'

'Listen, Hell. Rome wasn't built in a day. It just looks like it.' He put his arm around me. 'One step at a time, OK?' I nodded in a small way. 'Although if it's any consolation, you were right, as always. I'm glad she's here really, and I promise to sort things out with the Brazil Nut.' Our eyes wandered unanimously towards Lola's table, where she sat with her mother, the two of them admiring each other's handbags while Helga loitered in the shadows, eating from her bag, ready to pounce should things get ugly.

'Yoo-hoo!' Paul attempted to cha-cha his way through the messy dance floor of tangled feet, dragging Sally behind him, his red sash now tied in a sassy bow around Paul's head. 'Hi,' he hiccuped, failing miserably to open his bloodshot eyes more than a quarter inch, his hands wandering unsteadily to Rick's lapels and hanging there. 'Wasss a sssschhame.' His head dangled, unable to draw a breath as his diaphragm gave out another huge spasm. A small belch escaped. 'Essssccuushe me.' By the looks of things, it was only just starting to dawn on him that he was having trouble remaining upright. His head slumped against Rick's shoulder.

'We're drunk.' Sally swept a low, gracious bow before us, swaying like a palm tree caught in a tropical storm. 'Very, *very* drunk.'

'I can see that, mate.' Rick helped him to his feet and slapped him on the back. 'I'm glad that at least one of us managed to come out hitched. Congratulations. You make one hell of a colourful couple.'

Paul slithered to the floor.

'Here.' Rick picked up a couple of charged glasses from the passing flunky and handed one to me before draining his in a flash.

'That's the best idea you've had all year.' Well why not? I followed suit, not a single bubble touching the sides, and nodded enthusiastically when he loaded us up with another, feeling my body succumb almost immediately to the sudden headrush of the first. Rick clanked his glass against mine with a wry smile.

'Another day in the life of Helen Robbins, eh?'

'I did warn you,' I said. 'Tornado alley, every time.'

'Just two more minutes and we would've been spliced. I should've talked a bit fucking faster.'

'I'm sorry.' Not to mention absolutely done in. My jaw yearned to stretch into a monstrous, tonsil-wielding yawn.

'I have to say – ' he raised a rueful eyebrow – 'it did occur to me that maybe Julia's timely interruption was just the excuse you'd been looking for.'

'No!' I protested too much. 'How could you say that!'

'Sorry,' he conceded. 'But I know how much all this has been on your mind lately. I can tell from that look in your eyes.'

'What look?'

'*That* look. You know – ' he poked my tummy gently – 'the one that says *everything's fine* when really you're about to have a Chernobyl meltdown. It's the way your eyes flick away whenever I try to get a straight answer out of you. You do it a lot, you know.'

'Do I?' Fog-horn alarm. Why don't I know these things?

'Uh-huh.'

'I'll have to work on that.' I found my eyes flicking away and forced them to behave.

'Don't,' he said. 'I kinda like it.'

'I'm truly sorry about today, Rick. Honestly I am.'

'Some other time, maybe.' His laugh was tender. Disappointed.

'Not maybe,' I said firmly. 'Definitely.'

'You sure about that? Because you're spot on with

all that stuff you've said. Neither of us needs to get married, and, as you've already identified, I am the most annoying person in the world. You could put today down as a near miss and count yourself lucky, if you like.'

'And would you count yourself lucky too?' I asked.

'Yeah,' he said after a short pause. 'Cos I got to see your face this evening when that baby was put in your arms.'

Oh, what a moment that had been. So, so small. So breath-holdingly vulnerable. Tiny fingers, with perfect fingernails, a whole human being in miraculous, fragile miniature, just a few breaths into his brave new world. I had gazed into his wide, searching eyes, feeling awestruck as I stole a glimpse of those deep-blue rock pools that seemed to know the purity of everything, wondering what his life would be in this terrifying, marvellous world. He squeezed my finger, and my heart simply upped and flew away.

'I really did want to marry you today,' I said quietly, realizing that I meant every word.

'You sure about that?'

I looked him square in the eye.

'I've never been so sure about anything in my life.'

'Wanna get outta here?' he whispered.

'Sure.'

He picked up his phone and scrolled down, then pressed it to his ear, plugging the other with a free finger. 'Ange? You in here somewhere?' A hand went up in the seething mass of bodies and Angela fought her way towards us. Rick stuck his phone back in his pocket, slung down the remainder of his drink and dumped the glass.

'Yes, sir.' Angela, stone cold sober, stood to attention, document wallet tucked under her arm.

'Did you manage to get that stuff I asked you for?'

'Yes.' She rustled through her file and pulled out a large, brown envelope. 'It's all in there.' Rick didn't bother to check it.

'You're a fucking gem.' He grabbed her and kissed her hard, full on the lips.

Angela stumbled backwards, hand rushing to her mouth, red-faced and wide-eyed with shock.

'Come on.' He took me by the hand and we fled into the darkness of the night.

I MUST HAVE fallen asleep, the steady, soporific drone of the taxi's diesel engine having lulled my eyes to close almost the moment Rick pulled me to his chest.

'Where are we?' I came round to bright lights flooding through the windows of the cab, feeling as though I had slumbered for hours.

'Hurry,' Rick urged me, worrying at his watch. 'We're gonna have to make a run for it.'

'What?' I tried to shake the sleep from my eyes as

he wrenched me out of the taxi, flinging a handful of cash at the driver.

'Oh, for fuck's sake.' He made a snap decision in the face of my semi-conscious state, took a deep breath and looked as if he were about to come at me for a rugby tackle. The next thing I knew, my feet were swept off the ground as he threw me over his shoulder. Everything went blurred, colours rushing past. A shining floor, a montage of different feet, all hurtling past upside down, Rick puffing and panting as I held on to the bottom of his shining silver jacket for dear life, the air pressed from my folded body. He slowed to a near collapse, bending forward and depositing me on my unsteady legs, my head swimming through lack of blood.

'Here!' he shouted at the uniform behind the counter, hurling the envelope at her. 'Just us! Nothing else!'

'Yes, sir!' She saluted him, clearly unable to hide her delighted amusement at the dishevelled appearance of our trashed yet fabulously glamorous clothes. Hurriedly clacking away at her computer, she quickly slapped the envelope back on the high desk. 'You'll have to run, sir,' she said, finishing up. 'Gate 14. They'll be closing any minute.'

Rick stuffed everything back in his pockets and girded himself.

'It's OK.' I backed off quickly. 'I can run.'

We sprinted for all we were worth, me with my dress gathered in my hands, no doubt flashing a good eyeful of my sky-blue knickers judging by the gasps as we streaked along, skidding to a momentary untidy halt in front of the passport control Gestapo man. He eyed us suspiciously without a word, determined to take his time trying to match the panting couple in front of him with the dour photographs in our passports. Picking up his little rubber stamp, he blew on the end of it then landed it, bang, bang, before handing the passports back to Rick disapprovingly.

'Come on, babe!' He grabbed my hand again and we ran for all we were worth, hurtling through the X-ray machine, ignoring the beeps.

'I realize this might not be the best time to ask.' I snatched at my breath as we pounded along the walkway. 'But where the bloody hell are we going?' Holy mackerel, my sneaking suspicion that I'd become a bit unfit lately had rapidly turned into the understatement of the century. I felt like my heart was about to explode. Rick ground to a halt and bent double, holding up a hand to wait a minute, fighting for air. Finally pulling himself up, still clutching his chest, he gave me the cheekiest smile.

'Vegas!' He pulled a shining wedding band from his jacket pocket. 'I'm gonna get this fucking thing on your finger if it's the last thing I do.'

Not Really a Chapter at All

SARDINES

'Sssshhh!'

'Urgh!'

'Arrgh!'

Whisper whisper.

'Hang on, babe. I've got a tap in my arse.'

'Swap places?'

Muffle, muffle, shove.

'Better?'

'Yeah!'

Zzzzzzp.

'Oooh!'

Snigger, snigger. Flump, flump.

'Aaaaah!'

Flump, flump, flump, flumpflumpflumpflumpflump.
'Uuuururrrrrrgrggh!'
Rustle, muffle, zzzzzzp, snigger, snigger.
'Ssshhh!'
Pounding on the door. Shouting.
'You two come out of there at once or I'm going to call for the captain!'

Visit **www.panmacmillan.com** to read more about all our books and to buy them. You will also find features, author interviews and news of any author events, and you can sign up for e-newsletters so that you're always first to hear about our new releases.